The Brotherhood

Book Three

Templar Blood

By

K. M. Ashman

More books by K M Ashman

The India Summers Mysteries
The Vestal Conspiracy
The Treasures of Suleiman
The Mummies of the Reich
The Tomb Builders

The Roman Chronicles
The Fall of Britannia
The Rise of Caratacus
The Wrath of Boudicca

The Medieval Sagas
Blood of the Cross
In Shadows of Kings
Sword of Liberty
Ring of Steel

The Blood of Kings
A Land Divided
A Wounded Realm
Rebellion's Forge
Warrior Princess
The Blade Bearer

The Brotherhood
Templar Steel – The Battle of Montgisard
Templar Stone – The Siege of Jacob's Ford
Templar Blood – The Battle of Hattin

(Coming Soon)
Templar Fury – The Siege of Acre
Templar Glory – The Road to Jerusalem

Standalone Novels
Savage Eden
The Last Citadel
Vampire
The Legacy Protocol

Audio Books
Blood of the Cross
The Last Citadel
A Land Divided
A Wounded Realm
Rebellion's Forge
The Warrior Princess
The Vestal Conspiracies
The Tomb Builders
The Mummies of the Reich

More being published soon

Map of the Holy-land
(Circa AD 1187)

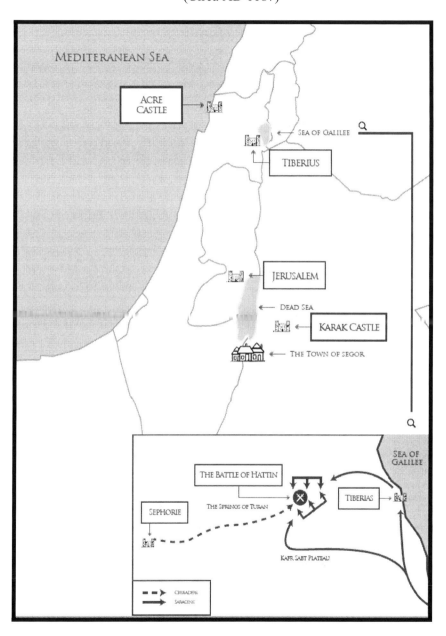

CHARACTER LIST

Main Christian Characters

Baldwin IV – King of Jerusalem until 1185
Baldwin V – King of Jerusalem until 1186
Guy of Lusignan - King of Jerusalem from 1186
Sibylla of Jerusalem – Queen of Jerusalem from 1186
Raymond III – Count of Tripoli
Raynald of Chatillon – Lord of the Oultrejordain
Reginald of Sidon – Lord of Sidon
Balian of Ibelin – Lord of Nablus
Roger De-Moulins - Grandmaster of the Knights Hospitaller
Gerard of Ridefort - Grandmaster of the Knights Templar from
1185 onwards
Jakelin De Mailly - French Templar Knight
William of Tyre – Catholic Prelate – King Baldwin's advisor
Thomas Cronin - Sergeant at Arms
James Hunter - Scout
Hassan Malouf - Bedouin Tribesman
Arturas – Mercenary Leader
Sumeira – Healer
John Loxley - Physician

Main Muslim Characters

Salah ad-Din (Saladin) – Sultan of Egypt and Syria
Muzaffar ad-Din Gökböri – Emir of Edessa
Al-Afdal ibn Salah ad-Din – Saladin's son
Fakhiri – Egyptian Cart-master

Prologue

In AD 1177, King Baldwin of Jerusalem led the Christian army into battle against a vastly superior Saracen force in the battle of Montgisard.

Led by a group of eighty or so Templar knights, the Christians devastated the Saracen army, sending their leader, Salah ad-Din racing back to Egypt with few survivors.

The victory for Baldwin was total, and he took advantage of the Saracen collapse to build a new fortress on the river Jordan north of the sea of Galilee at a place called Jacob's Ford. Up until that date the crossing had been unclaimed by either Christian or Muslim forces and everyone used it uncontested. However, knowing that Damascus was always a threat in the north, and desperate to protect the Christian lands to the west of the Jordan, the king, encouraged by the Templar grandmaster, seized the opportunity to control the crossing and commissioned a new castle high on a ridge overlooking the river.

Over the next two years, the formidable castle walls grew, and though it was still unfinished, in AD 1179, Salah ad-Din realised he could not sit back and let its creation go unchallenged. At first, he offered the king sixty thousand bezants to abandon the construction, followed up by an improved offer of one hundred thousand when Baldwin refused. When the second amount was also turned down, the sultan knew he had no other option than to attack the castle.

In August of that year, after a five-day siege, Salah ad-Din's sappers succeeded in bringing down one of the walls by tunnelling underneath and undermining the foundations. The Saracen army poured through the breach and totally destroyed the garrison, killing hundreds of men and enslaving hundreds more.

The castle had fallen, and after his victory, the sultan had it dismantled stone by stone, spreading the building materials far and wide so they could no longer be used in any attempt at reconstruction.

The consequences were dire for the Christians, and Salah ad-Din went on to unite the eastern tribes and grow his power base. For the first time in years, the Saracens posed a serious threat to the Christians, and though there were many more fortresses scattered throughout the Outremer, the tables had finally been turned, and the very future of the Holy-land was at stake.

Chapter One

The Negev Desert

February - AD 1185

The sun blazed down on the rocky landscape, scorching the arid earth and forcing most living creatures into the life-giving shade. Lizards crept under boulders; spiders closed the silken trapdoors at the entrance of their lairs and even snakes vibrated their bodies deeper into the sand to find the cooler levels beneath. The desert was barren and silent, seemingly devoid of life, yet even in the most desolate of places; you could find what you were looking for; if you knew where to look.

Abdal-Wahhab lay silently between two rocks, protected from the worst of the sun's rays by the overhang of another rock above. Behind him, his two Saluki, the lithe and powerful hunting dogs that were the pride of all Bedouin tribes, lay silently on the ground, patiently waiting for the chance to run free. Abdal's waterskin was getting low, and he knew that if things didn't change soon, he would have to break cover and head down into the rocky valley below, seeking the tiny pool of water hidden amongst the rocks that had filled many Bedouin tribesmen's waterskins for generations. Such pools were well known to those who made the desert their home, and though they were often well-kept secrets, their location was also known to other creatures of the Negev; wolves, desert cats, but most importantly, the skittish deer that had occupied Abdal's mind for many days.

The deer rarely drank, getting most of the moisture they needed from the morning dew that lingered for the briefest of moments on the leaves of the resilient plants struggling to exist in the unforgiving landscape, but when the sun was at its hottest, even the hardiest of deer had to run the risk of predators to find water. This was what the Bedouin hunter was waiting for, the rare chance to take down a young deer and fill his food bags with enough dried meat for another month. He had killed many in his day and despite his thirst and frustration, knew that patience was the only way to guarantee success.

For the third day running, he settled down to stare into the wadi. If the deer were to come, they would be there before nightfall as the dark held many dangers. The deep canyon stretched away into the distance, filled with many rocks and side canyons, ideal escape routes for the nimble-footed gazelle, but he knew that when they came, as he knew they would, he could not allow them to head back the way they had come.

Slowly he closed his eyes, a light doze perfected over many years of hunting, deep enough to conserve energy, yet light enough to hear even the tiniest of lizards scuttling over a rock in search of a meal. The day dragged on, and the hunter was about to give up when one of the Saluki raised its head to let out the tiniest of whimpers.

Abdal was instantly awake yet kept as still as the stones at his back. His dogs were well-trained, and the fact that they had broken their silence could mean only one thing, something was coming. He peered into the wadi and within a few moments, saw the slightest of movements amongst the rocks - a buck deer. Years of experience took over, and despite his yearning to start moving further down amongst the rocks, Abdal stayed where he was. He knew that the deer had exceptional senses and would be away as fast as one of the countless dust-devils that wandered the Negev desert, should he be detected.

Slowly it came closer, stopping every few steps to sniff the air. This was one of the most dangerous times for any deer for the wadi held countless places from which a predator could launch an attack. Its only defences were its excellent senses and its speed over broken ground, but they would be worth nothing if one of the bigger meat eaters had chosen its ambush well. Again, it crept forward, occasionally stopping to pick at the pieces of undergrowth that had managed to retain some moisture, and it chewed nervously as its large eyes continuously scanned for danger. Onward it came, knowing that at the lowest part of the wadi, the tiniest trickle of water oozed from a crack in the rocks. Not a lot, but enough to fill its belly with water for another few days.

Abdal Wahab waited as still as death itself. Behind him, his dogs trembled but made not a sound. This scene was familiar to them, and they knew that when the time came, they would be released. At last, Abdal carefully got to his feet, his eyes still locked on the deer now a hundred or so paces away. For a few seconds, the animal stopped in its tracks, its ears twitching as it picked up the sound of the human breathing, but it was too late, its fate was sealed.

Without uttering a word, Abdal snapped his hand down in a chopping motion and pointed towards the terrified animal. Instantly the dogs leapt forward and raced after their prey, their hearts racing in the thrill of the hunt.

Abdal climbed down and followed as fast as he could for though the dogs would have little chance of catching the deer in the vast maze of gulleys and ravines, the second part of the hunt had yet to be initiated.

Further along the wadi, the deer raced up a slope, desperate to escape the pursuing hounds. It already had a commanding lead, but the Saluki were relentless and followed as fast as they could. The deer stopped for a moment, its eyes wide with fear and its ears pricked at the sound of the running dogs. Again it turned, desperate to escape, but before it could resume, a sudden searing pain tore through its body, and it fell sideways into the dust, its head turning to snap at the thin wooden shaft embedded deep into its shoulder. Confused and desperate to flee, it staggered to its feet and stumbled further up the slope, but had gone no more than another dozen or so paces when another arrow found its target and again it fell to the ground, gasping in pain and fear. This time it only managed to get a few paces before collapsing as the pain of the two arrows swept through its body. Its tongue lolled from its gaping mouth, but it made no sound as the man responsible for its impending death emerged from his hiding place and notched another arrow into his bow.

'Your blood will warm my spirit, proud beast,' said the young man, 'your flesh will feed my people. Tonight, I will honour your life with prayers.' Without another word, he drew back the bowstring and sent a third arrow into his prey, though this time, it pierced the animal's heart, releasing it from its torment.

Within seconds the two dogs appeared over the crest of the hill and headed straight for the dead deer, excited by the chase and the smell of fresh blood.

'Steady, Hakim,' said the young man as the male Saluki started licking at the warm blood running from the killing wound, 'there will be time to eat later. You too, Sheba, away.' Immediately the two dogs dog retreated but sat just a few paces away, their bodies still shaking from the exhilaration of the chase.

'Where is your master?' said the man, looking back down the wadi. 'He will be impressed with the kill. It is a long time since we brought down such a prize.'

As if in answer to his question, a figure appeared in the distance and the young man stepped up on a rock to get his attention.

'Abdal Wahab,' he called, waving his bow in the air, 'over here. We will feast well tonight, my friend, and many nights hence.'

The approaching man climbed the hill surprisingly quickly for although he was over twice the younger man's age, he was hardened from his life as a hunter.

'Abdal,' said the younger man as he neared, 'look at my kill. Have you ever seen anything so great? The tribe will welcome us as saviours when we take this deer back to the camp.'

'Get down from that rock,' snapped the older hunter as he passed, 'these wadis are the haunts of killers and thieves, and each would gladly kill a man for fresh meat.'

'But it is a thing to celebrate, is it not?' said the younger man, jumping down to join the older hunter. 'Your plan worked, and the dogs drove it right into my arms. My hunting skills grow better by the day.'

'It took you three arrows,' said the older man, 'there are boys in the village who could have done it in one.' He dropped to his knees beside the deer and produced a knife before opening the main artery on the deer's throat, allowing the still-warm blood to pour out onto the rocky ground. 'Hakim,' he said, 'Sheba, come.' Both dogs pounced forward to begin lapping greedily at the growing pool of blood.

'Your aim needs to get better,' said Abdal, 'but that will come with time.'

'Why does it matter?' asked the younger man. 'Even if it were only wounded and managed to escape, the dogs would soon have caught it and brought it down.'

'This time, perhaps,' said Abdal, 'but you will not always have dogs and who knows, next time it may not even be a deer.' He looked down at the animal in the dust. 'If that had been a man and your strike was just a wound, then it could have cost you your life. You will continue to practise with your bow until you can hit a running hare at a hundred paces. Then and only then will we move on to the thousand other skills you must learn if you are to become a true Bedouin.'

'I am already a Bedouin,' said the young man, exasperated at the attitude of the more experienced hunter.

'Your mother was a Bedouin, as was your father,' said Abdal, 'but you, Hassan Malouf, are not. The years you spent with the Christians have softened your body and clouded your eyes. I would be better off teaching a babe in arms for his mind would be open, but with you, there is much to undo.' He turned to walk away as Hassan stared after him, not sure what to say. He had expected praise but had received only admonishment.

'Where are you going?' he shouted.

'To get the camels,' responded Abdal without looking back. 'You start butchering the deer.'

Chapter Two

Tiberias

March - AD 1185

King Baldwin lay in his bed, his pain temporarily soothed by the ever-increasing doses of poppy milk dispensed by the physicians. Incense lay heavy on the air, masking the smell of his sores, his breath, his affliction. At his side, as ever, sat William of Tyre, the prelate who had guided him since childhood as a teacher and advisor. A man hated by many but trusted by the king without question. A servant walked in and waited by the door for acknowledgement.

'What is it?' asked William, looking up from the medical book laying on his lap.

'My lord,' said the servant, 'you told me to advise you when the Lady Sibylla arrives.'

'Ah, good,' said William. 'Has she settled in?'

'No, my lord, she is weary from the road and has been shown to her quarters but said she would attend the king at his convenience.'

William looked towards the sleeping king. The poppy milk meant he spent much of each day in a state of unconsciousness, but the prelate knew Baldwin desperately needed to see his sister before death came on dark wings.

'Thank you,' said William. 'Tell the countess that the king is indisposed at the moment, but will receive her in the audience chamber, at the fourth bell this evening.'

'Of course, my lord,' said the servant. 'There is one more thing that perhaps you should be aware of.'

'And that is?'

'She is accompanied by her husband, the Count of Jaffa and Ascalon.'

'Guy of Lusignan is here?'

'He is, my lord.'

William frowned and glanced at the sleeping king before returning his attention back to the servant.

'So be it,' he said. 'Tell them I will give them time to rest, but I need to talk to them before the audience. I will be there at noon.'

'As you wish, my lord,' said the servant with a bow and walked backwards into the corridor, closing the doors behind him.

'Who was that?' murmured the awakening king. 'I heard someone talking.'

'Just a servant, my lord,' said William. 'He has brought news that your sister has arrived. She will come to see you this evening.'

'Sybil is here?' said Baldwin through cracked and swollen lips. 'Good. There is much to discuss.'

'And time enough to do it,' said William. 'But first, we will get you washed and dressed. It will do no good for you to hold any court in such a fashion. Are you hungry?'

'I will try something,' said Baldwin, pushing himself carefully up the pillows, 'though make it soft, and sweet.'

William glanced at one of the king's two personal servants standing at the far wall.

'See to it,' he said, and one of the servants nodded before walking quickly from the room.

'You,' said William to the second servant, 'bring warm water and fresh linen. The king will be getting dressed this day.'

'Of course, my lord,' said the servant and followed the first out of the door.

William stared at the king, his frown increasing at the milky blue glaze that had settled over the monarch's eyes. He lifted his hand and waved it slowly back and fore in front of Baldwin's face.

The young king tilted his head slightly.

'What was that?' he asked, still staring into space.

'Just testing your vision, my lord,' said William. 'Did you see my hand?'

'Alas not, nothing but a passing shadow. I fear my views of beautiful sunsets and pretty women must forthwith be experienced only from memory.'

'May God grant us a miracle,' said William with a thin-lipped smile.

For the next few minutes, the sickly king talked with the prelate. Subjects were random and far-ranging, but William was patient. These days, Baldwin seemed to take comfort from conversations devoid of the needs of kingship, and after being at his side for most of the king's life, the prelate was more than content to let him ramble now the end was near.

The next hour or so was taken up with feeding and dressing the sickly king. At only twenty-three years old, he should have been at the prime of his life, but the leprosy he had suffered since a child was now all-consuming and his rapidly failing health meant it was evident he would not last much longer. William stayed as long as he could and when the king was as comfortable as he could be, left the chamber to head towards Sibylla's chambers. Ten minutes later, he knocked on the countess' door and was allowed in by one of the servants who had accompanied her and her husband on her journey.

'Father William,' said a young man walking towards him, 'we have been expecting you.'

'My lord,' said the prelate with the slightest nod of his head, 'I trust you travelled well?'

'The journey was without incident,' said Guy of Lusignan, 'though my wife is currently resting. I hear you have been with the king. How is he?'

'Not good,' said William, 'but perhaps it would be better to talk with your wife.'

'I told you, she is sleeping,' started Guy, but was interrupted by someone coming from another room.

'It is fine,' said the woman tying a robe around her waist, 'I couldn't sleep anyway. Father William, it is good to see you again.' She walked forward to offer her hand, which William kissed gently. This time the bow was noticeably deeper, a subtle sign to the count, who it was that William considered more regal.

'My lady,' said William, 'you grow more beautiful by the day. Age is certainly an ally.'

'Thank you,' said Sibylla, 'but what of my brother? We received your letter telling us all is not well and came as soon as we could.'

'The king is frail, my lady, and that is why I wrote to you. I fear he will not see another month and he is keen to settle all matters of state before he dies.'

'Is it really that bad?'

'It is. He weakens by the day, but you know your brother, he is nothing if not a fighter.'

Sibylla turned to the handmaiden in the room.

'Lady Rose, could you arrange some food and wine for our guest, please.'

'I've eaten,' said William, 'but please, you go ahead.'

'I am rather hungry,' said Sibylla. 'Lady Rose, see what the kitchens can spare and find out if our staff have been looked after.'

'I'll send someone straight away,' said Rose and left the room.

'So,' said Sibylla, lowering herself into a cushioned chair and indicating the prelate should sit opposite her. 'Tell me about my brother.'

'Well,' said William, 'as I said, he is very sick and getting worse. Sometimes his mind wanders as his disease spreads, but on other days he is as sharp as ever. Today he is enjoying a better day, so it is timely that you arrived.'

'Do you know what he wants to discuss in particular?'

'I think the succession is on his mind. He knows full well that he is dying and wants to make the final arrangements for your son to be crowned at the Church of the Holy Sepulcher.'

'But our son has already been crowned as co-king,' said Guy, 'and stands ready to step up to the throne.'

'My lord,' said William, 'with the greatest respect, the title of co-king is ceremonial only and carries little authority. By doing this, the whole of Jerusalem will see that he is indeed the true king's heir and nobles will pledge their swords.'

'Why could this not have been done at Ascalon?' asked Guy. 'His home is there, not Jerusalem.'

'My lord,' said William, his tone more clipped. 'Please, I respect your place is alongside your wife, but do not forget, you had your chance to influence the succession when you were regent. If you had not gone about the business of antagonising Saladin at a time of treaty, then perhaps you would still hold that position. Now it is all we can do to keep the Saracens at bay, let alone argue amongst ourselves about where your son will be crowned king.'

'So, if all this has already been decided, why have we been summoned here?' asked Guy.

'Because Baldwin said so,' snapped William. 'Despite his afflictions, he is still king, and his word is law. It would be good if you were to remember that. Now, I suggest that if you are to accompany the Lady Sibylla to the king's audience, you keep your thoughts to yourself. Do not forget, you do not enjoy his favour, and he will suffer your attendance only out of respect to his sister.'

'And you would do well to curb your tone, priest,' said the count. 'When Baldwin is dead, you will be seeing me around a lot more, and I can assure you, there will be far less tolerance for those whose power exceeds their position.'

'We will deal with that day when it comes,' said William standing up. 'Until then, I am his voice and ears.' He turned to the countess. 'My lady, can I speak to you alone?'

'Anything you say to her you can say to me,' said Guy.

'My lord,' said Sibylla, turning to her husband, 'I am still tired from the road so really do not need the tension. Please grant me this favour.'

Guy stared at the prelate for a few moments before turning and striding from the room.

'Thank you, my lady,' said William, 'perhaps we can now talk freely.'

'Father William,' said Sibylla, 'when will you realise that Guy is my husband, and we share everything. I only asked him to leave because I am too tired to see you both argue like petulant children, but be aware, if I think that anything you say is relevant, then I will share it with him.'

'What you choose to do once I am gone is between you and God, my lady,' said William, 'and is none of my business.'

'So, say what it is that you came to say.'

'My lady, even in his weakness, the king still harbours great anger towards your husband. If he sees him at the audience, I feel that he may change his mind about your son and leave the choice of his successor to the whim of the Haute Cour.'

'That is ridiculous,' said Sibylla,' the royal lineage is clear on such matters, and the Council of Jerusalem has no rightful say.'

'That is what we all believe,' said William, 'but there is already talk amongst the nobles that if Baldwin was to renounce your son as heir, then the Haute Cour could possibly favour Isabella.'

'Over me? But she is only a child.'

'As is your son.'

'That will never happen,' said Sibylla, 'I have allies across the Outremer, and even if my son was withdrawn from favour, it is I that will be the Queen of Jerusalem.'

'My lady,' said William, 'do not think for a moment that you are short of support in such matters for my allegiance is to you and you alone. All I ask is that we avoid such conflicts by taking them from the mind of the king.'

'How?'

'By asking your husband to keep a low profile while he is here. Come to the audience, but I beg you, come alone.'

'He is my husband, William. How can I do that in good conscience?'

'Matters of relationships are beyond me,' said William. 'All I know is your brother still holds Guy responsible for the breakdown of the treaty between Jerusalem and Saladin.'

'It was Raynald of Chatillon who raided the Saracen caravans,' said Sibylla, 'not Guy.'

'But Guy was regent at the time,' said William, 'as well you know, and he turned a blind eye to Raynald's forays into Saladin's lands. When Raynald set out to plunder the caravan routes to Mecca, it was Guy who supplied the slaves to haul the ships overland to the shores of the Red Sea. With the greatest respect, my lady, your husband's hands are just as bloody as Raynald's. I beseech thee, just this once, come alone, and I will do everything in my power to ensure the succession goes ahead as planned. Another month or so, and all doubt will be gone, that's all I ask.'

Sibylla sighed and stared at the prelate.

'I will see what I can do,' she said. Across the room, a door opened, and Lady Rose entered followed by two serving girls carrying trays of meat and ale. 'Ah, the food is here. Are you sure you will not join me?'

'Thank you, but I have to go,' said William standing up. 'I will see you at the audience. Until then, if there is anything you should need, please send word to my chambers.'

'I will,' said Sibylla. 'And Father William, please do not judge my husband too harshly. He only has the interests of our son at heart.'

'Your son, my lady,' said William, not his.' Without another word, he turned and left the room, leaving the countess staring at his back.

Chapter Three

Karak Castle

March - AD 1185

The faintest of reds illuminated the distant mountains over the Negev, but already the lower bailey of the magnificent Karak Castle was alive with noise and movement. Slaves checked the loads of the pack horses over and over again, for to lose a load meant a severe beating or worse from their masters. Camels lay along the inner walls with their legs folded beneath them and chewing the cud as if they had not a care in the world. Each was loaded with stores, and young boys with buckets walked amongst them, making sure each was well watered before they left the security of the castle.

As the day lightened, the gates in the upper bailey creaked open, and all the handlers looked up the winding path, knowing their masters would be joining them imminently.

In the upper bailey, the squires had assembled the horses. Each was responsible for four including two destriers, the magnificent war horses needed for any self-respecting knight heading into battle. Most had been brought from Europe and were much valued by Christian and Muslim alike having been carefully trained in the art of warfare. The other two horses were smaller, but of hardier stock, local breeds well-used to the terrain and the heat of the desert. One was a packhorse carrying the knight's equipment, and of course, the other was the squire's own mount. His role was to provide everything his master needed while out on campaign and if it came to battle, to provide whatever back up the knight needed.

The toll of a bell rang out across the castle courtyards, focusing everyone's attention and as he watched, John William, a squire freshly arrived from England, watched in anticipation as the doors of the chapel swung slowly inward. A line of monks filed out and formed up either side of the doorway, forming a pathway to the courtyard. Next through the door came a priest and he walked slowly forward to stand at the end of the two lines of monks before turning to face the chapel door. In his hands, he held an incense burner, and as he swung it back and forth, the monks started a liturgy, its ethereal sound echoing off the high castle walls. Finally, the men they had all been waiting for emerged, each silent and focused as they walked between the monks and through the smoke to their horses. These men were tall and strong, their demeanour confident and authoritative.

Every man wore linen leggings and a chainmail hauberk over a linen undershirt. On top of the hauberk was a white tabard, emblazoned with a blood-red cross, and a heavy woollen cloak hung from the shoulders, again decorated with a bloody cross on a white background. These were the Templars, warrior monks sworn to defend the Holy-land from anyone who threatened the way of life for Christians across the Outremer.

John William stared in awe. He had been trained in the way of knighthood in England, and when his master, Sir Benjamin of Bristol, had taken the cross, he had gladly left the shores of his homeland to serve God and seek religious glory alongside the knight. The journey across Francia had been tough, so he was relieved when they had finally, reached Italia and boarded a ship in Venice, but before they had sight of the Holy-land, his master had fallen overboard in a storm and was lost beneath the angry waves. Luckily, another knight had taken him under his wing and after disembarking at the magnificent port of Acre, had brought him to Karak Castle to seek another master. Now, barely two weeks since he had arrived, he was about to head out on his first campaign led by a force of over fifty Templar knights, a fate he could only have ever dreamed of a few weeks earlier.

John William had seen the Templars around the castle, but never as they were now, sombre, threatening and ready for the campaign. Men who had offered brotherly advice only days earlier now ignored him and kept their silence, all focused on the task ahead. Each of the knights mounted their horses but waited for one last man to emerge from the chapel, the Templar who would lead them into battle.

Eventually, Karak's castellan emerged and strode to his own destrier in the centre of the courtyard. Again, John William stared in awe, for before him was one of the most famous of all knights, a Templar who was responsible for killing more Saracens than any other. He was brutal, ambitious and hated all Saracens with a passion. Although he was a Templar, and thus a man of God, he was one of the most feared men in Christendom. His name was Sir Raynald of Chatillon.

Raynald settled into his saddle and looked across at the seneschal waiting near the gate of the bailey. Gerard of Ridefort was an impressive man, and it was rumoured that he would be the next grandmaster of the order following the death of Arnold of Torroja in Verona a few months earlier. Gerard was also known as a fearsome fighter, but unlike Raynald, enjoyed the support and patronage of the holy father in Rome.

'Sir Gerard,' said Raynald, 'are we ready?'

'We are,' came the reply and after a moment's pause, Raynald of Chatillon urged his horse towards the castle gates. As the Templars passed, the rest of the patrol fell in behind them and headed out into the lands east of the Salt-sea.

Fifty leagues away, in the coastal city of Acre, another Templar stood on a dock watching as a team of slaves unloaded a ship into a waiting column of carts. His name was Jakelin De Mailly, a respected and pious knight whose prowess in battle was second to none. Alongside him stood one of his sergeants, Thomas Cronin, the man who had been at his side since the battle of Montgisard several years earlier.

'The sea air is a welcome relief from the heat of the desert,' said Cronin as they watched.

'Aye, it is said,' Jakelin, 'though I prefer my feet firmly on the ground than on the boards of a ship.'

'I take it you do not like sailing?'

'I do not. At least on land, my fate is in my own hands. Out there, you are at the whims of the weather. Many good men who set out to serve God in these lands have died without even seeing the coast.'

'Is not the fate of a man in God's hands?' asked Cronin with a glance at his comrade.

'Indeed, it is,' said Jakelin,' but he also gave us free will to do with as we like, and I prefer not to step foot on a ship if I can avoid it.'

Cronin grunted a reply and turned his attention back to the activity on the dock. To engage in any religious conversation with Jakelin De Mailly was a folly few men sought for he was steadfast in his devotion, and vocal in his argument, a trait he somehow balanced with his uncompromising ability to visit death upon anyone in the defence of Christianity.

Down below another ship berthed, and after signing the official papers from the dockmaster, the captain allowed the passengers to disembark before opening the hatches to offload his cargo. Within moments the dock became a melee of people as they waited near the officials collecting the necessary toll required to enter the city.

Cronin stared at the crowd before his eyes widened and he took half a step forward, recognising a face in the crowd.

'Brother Cronin,' said Jakelin, 'is there a problem?'

'Not at all,' said Cronin, 'in fact, quite the opposite.' Without another word, he strode down the hill and past the toll collectors into the crowd. The sea of new arrivals parted before him before he finally stopped before the person who had caught his eye, Sumeira of Greece.

'My lady,' he said, 'what are you doing here?'

The woman looked up and smiled in recognition.

'Thomas Cronin,' she said, 'hello again. I never expected to see you here, I thought you would be in Jerusalem.'

'I was there for a while,' said Cronin, 'but now serve elsewhere. I am here with some of my comrades to escort a caravan of provisions east of the Salt-sea, but what about you? The last I saw of you; you were on your way to Greece.'

'That was the intention,' said Sumeira, 'but I only went as far as Cyprus.'

'So why have you returned?'

'There is something I must do,' said Sumeira, 'a task to which I have sworn my future.'

Before Cronin could ask her to explain, a voice called out across the crowd.

'Thomas Cronin, by all that is holy, how is it you are here to greet us?

Cronin turned, recognising the voice.

'John Loxley?'

'Aye, he has come with me,' said Sumeira, 'as has Emani.'

'Your daughter is also here?'

'She is, though I suspect you may not recognise her, such is her growth.'

'How old is she now?'

'She will celebrate her fourteenth birthday this year.'

Cronin fell quiet for a moment and stared at Sumeira. They had been through much together ever since she had saved Hassan

Malouf's life several years earlier, but after the Templar's defeat at Jacob's Ford, she had left the Holy-land for the sake of her own, and her daughter's safety. For a few moments, their eyes met, lingering just a few seconds longer than would be expected.

'Cronin, my friend,' said Loxley walking up to the sergeant, 'how are you?'

'John Loxley,' replied Cronin with a grin, 'well met.' He turned to greet the physician who had been instrumental in saving his life in Chastellet and extended his arm, taking the man's wrist in friendship. 'You are looking well, my friend,' he said and turned to the young woman at the physician's side. 'And this must be Emani?'

'It is,' said, John Loxley. 'It has been a while since you saw her last.'

'Indeed, it has,' replied Cronin and turned to address the girl. 'You were just a child the last we met,' he said, 'but I see you are turning into a beautiful young woman.'

'Thank you, my lord,' said Emani with a slight bow of the head, 'I have heard much about you.'

'Now that worries me,' said Cronin with a laugh, 'unfortunately, my life is not one to be scrutinised too closely.'

'On the contrary,' said Emani, 'I have heard nought but good things from my mother and father alike.'

Cronin's smile softened, and his brows lowered in confusion as he looked back at John Loxley for an explanation.

'Emani,' said John Loxley before the sergeant could ask any questions, 'why do not you join your mother? We'll both join you in a moment.' He ushered the girl towards where Sumeira was waiting before turning back to face Cronin.

'Her father?' asked Cronin, 'I thought he was in Segor. What's going on?'

John Loxley took Cronin's arm and led him towards one side so they could not be overheard.

'Brother Cronin,' he said, glancing over to Sumeira and Emani, 'you are correct, he is indeed in Segor, or at least his remains are.'

'He is dead?'

'He is. We received a message a few months ago from one of Sumeira's friends in the city. Apparently, he was killed in a knife fight by a man who owed him money.'

'A fate well deserved,' said Cronin, 'but what did Emani mean when she said she has heard him speak of me?'

'She is referring to me, Cronin,' said John Loxley, 'she sees me as her father and has little recollection of her time here before she went to Cyprus.'

Cronin stared at the physician before asking the obvious question.

'So, you and Sumeira are married?'

'It's complicated,' said John Loxley. 'We live as man and wife, but our union has not yet been blessed in a church. I know you will see that as a sin, but when we arrived in Cyprus, the only way for them both to be accepted and safe was if they were part of a family. At first, it was just a ruse, but after a while, well, let us just say it became more permanent.'

'I am not here to judge, my friend,' said Cronin reaching out and grasping the physician's shoulder, 'as long as you are all safe and happy, then that is good enough for me.'

Before John could answer, Sumeira and Emani approached, cutting the conversation short.

'John, we should go,' said Sumeira, 'the line is getting shorter, and we need to pay the toll.'

'Before you go,' said Cronin, 'I have a surprise for you.' He pointed up the hill. 'Look up there, Sumeira, who do you see?'

Sumeira squinted her eyes and stared up at the Templar knight overseeing the activity on the docks.

'Is that who I think it is?' she asked eventually.

'Who is it?' asked Emani.

'Well, it looks like a man I thought long dead,' said Sumeira, 'but my eyes tell me differently.'

'Jakelin De Mailly,' gasped John Loxley, 'but he died at Marj Ayun. How could this be?'

'It is true that he fell at the battle of Marj Ayyun,' said Cronin, 'but he survived his wounds. He was taken captive and released in a prisoner exchange a few months later. He now serves Raynald of Chatillon with me as his sergeant.'

'This is wonderful news,' said Sumeira, 'and we all have a lot to talk about, but I see he is busy, so perhaps we can exchange stories once we have settled in the city.'

'Where are you staying?'

'We do not know yet,' said John. 'We were hoping to find rooms in a tavern before seeking something more permanent.'

'You will do no such thing,' said Cronin. 'You go and pay the toll and leave the rest to me. I will find you somewhere more comfortable.'

As John and Emani walked over to the trestle tables set up at the dock exit, Sumeira reached out and touched Cronin's arm. Again, the gaze was longer than would be expected, and the smile contained a palpable warmth.

'Thank you, brother Cronin,' she said, 'it is good to see you again.'

'And you, Sumeira,' said Cronin returning the smile, 'and I am glad you finally, found happiness.'

'He told you about us?' asked Sumeira, raising her eyebrows.

'Aye, he did.'

'And you are happy about the situation?'

'As long as you are happy, then so am I. Now you should go, for the gates are about to close. Meet us at the entrance of the Templar compound at dusk.'

'Thanks again, Cronin,' said Sumeira and watched as he strode up the hill to join Sir Jakelin and the cart-masters.

Chapter Four

Tiberias

March - AD 1185

It had been several days since Sibylla had arrived at Tiberias and though the initial audience with her brother had been uneventful, his mood had recently taken a turn for the worse, as had his health. Every evening she walked alongside her handmaiden to the king's personal bed-chamber and there talked with him well into the night, though sometimes she just sat in silence, listening to the incoherent rambles as the terrible disease ravaged his mind. Her husband did not accompany her on the visits, having finally agreed it would be disastrous to their family should Baldwin change his mind at the final hour and disinherit their son.

Tonight would be no different. Sibylla had bathed and donned her robes as befitted a countess and sipped on a glass of wine as she waited for Lady Rose to bring her cloak. As she waited, a commotion in the corridor brought her to her feet. The door burst open, and one of the king's messengers burst into her room, followed by one of her personal servants.

'My lady, forgive me,' gasped the servant, 'he just barged past me without explanation.'

'What is the meaning of this,' demanded Sibylla turning to the stranger,' I will have you flogged for this intrusion?'

'My Lady,' said the man, 'I have urgent news and could not risk delay.'

'What news?' demanded Sibylla.

'My lady, I have been sent by the prelate, Father William. He said to tell you that the king is at death's door and he is about to administer the last rights. He urges you to come forthwith to say your goodbyes.'

Sibylla swallowed hard, determined not to display any emotion in front of the stranger.

'Thank you,' she said, 'return immediately and inform the prelate that I am on my way.'

'Of course,' said the messenger and hurriedly left the room.

'My lady,' started the servant, 'please forgive me, I ...'

'Enough,' snapped Sibylla, 'where is Lady Rose with my cloak?'

'I know not, my lady,' said the servant, 'shall I go and find her?'

'No, there is no time. You will accompany me through the castle to the king's chambers.'

'Me?' said the servant, 'but I…'

'Stop blubbering, man,' said Sibylla, 'and follow me. All you have to do is make sure I am not attacked in the darkness. Can you do that?'

'Of course, my lady,' said the servant; 'I will protect you with my life.'

'I do not think it will come to that,' said Sibylla, 'but even so, I appreciate your pledge. Now come, there is little time.'

Ten minutes later, Sibylla strode into the king's bed-chamber, leaving the flustered servant outside. The room was heavy with incense and crowded with those closest to the king. At his bedside, two priests knelt on either side, saying prayers in unison.

'My lady,' said William as she pushed her way to the front, 'come, take my place.'

'Is he dead?' asked Sibylla, staring at her brother's grossly disfigured face.

'Not yet, but the angels wait to carry him to the gates of heaven. I think he only hangs on to say his goodbyes to you.'

The countess pushed past the prelate and sat on the bed alongside her brother, reaching out her hand to brush aside one of the few straggly wisps of hair he still had on his head.

'Your Grace,' she said softly, 'it is I, your sister, can you hear me?'

When the king did not reply, she glanced at Father William, receiving a nod of encouragement in return.

'King Baldwin,' she said, this time a little louder, 'it's Sibylla. I have come to pay my respects and to tell you I love you.'

This time the king's eyes fluttered open, and despite not being able to see her, he turned his head slightly towards the sound of her voice.

'Sibylla,' he whispered eventually, 'you came.'

'I have, Your Grace,' she said, 'wild horses would not have kept me away. It is time to say goodbye, dear brother. You have lived an honourable life, and I swear by all that is holy that your name shall be spoken in awe for generations to come.'

'Have you travelled far?' asked Baldwin.

Sibylla's brow frowned in confusion, and again she looked towards the prelate.

'His mind is failing, my lady,' said William. 'Just humour him.'

Sibylla turned back to her brother and smoothed his brow again.

'It has indeed been a long journey, brother,' she said. 'From the moment you were born, I knew you would one day be king. It was ordained by God himself. I just wish he would allow us a little more time to be the brother and sister we once were.'

'Sibylla,' said Baldwin, his voice even weaker. 'I am not afraid to die. I want to walk alongside our father once more and say, I did the best I could.'

'He will be proud of you, Baldwin,' she replied gently.

'Perhaps our lord will grant me the strength to walk tall once more.'

'I'm sure he will,' said Sibylla, wiping a tear from her eye, 'for there have been few so dedicated to his cause as you.'

'Sibylla,' said Baldwin, his voice now barely a whisper, 'promise me…'

'Promise what?' asked Sibylla, leaning forward.

Baldwin was fading fast, but with every last ounce of strength, he reached up and grabbed his sister by the hair, dragging her down until her face was next to his. His breath was fetid, and Sibylla gasped in pain but held up her hand to stop any intervention from the others.

'Promise me,' said Baldwin again, but the rest of the plea was lost to the gathered watchers as he whispered his last words into his sister's ear.

Sibylla felt the grip on her hair loosen, and as she raised her head, Baldwin fell back onto his pillow for the last time. One of the physicians approached to examine him, but the time had come and the man who had overcome seemingly insurmountable problems to become King of Jerusalem, finally died. The physician turned to the prelate and shook his head.

William of Tyre swallowed hard. He had been at Baldwin's side for many years, first as his teacher, then his mentor and finally, as his most trusted advisor. The journey had been intense as the young king had fought not only the enemies of Christendom, but also political corruption alongside a debilitating illness that would have killed many men far sooner. It was a heartbreaking loss, but not unexpected. Eventually, he looked up from Baldwin's corpse and turned to address the packed room.

'The king is dead,' he proclaimed, 'long live the king.'

An hour later, Sibylla talked to William of Tyre in an antechamber. Her eyes were red from tears, but she knew she had to stay strong. As mother of the new king, her position demanded it.

'Was he in any pain?' she asked, staring out of the window.

'I doubt he felt a thing at the end,' said William, 'the physicians made sure he was numbed with poppy milk.'

'He suffered so much over the years,' said Sibylla, 'why did God see fit to place him with such a burden?'

'It is not our place to question God,' said William, 'only to do his bidding.'

'It still seems so unfair,' said the countess, 'he did so many great things in his short lifetime, imagine what he could have done if he had enjoyed good health.'

'He did enough, my lady,' said William, 'more than most men, but now it is time for him to rest.'

'So, what now?' asked Sibylla, 'I suppose we should send for my son in Ascalon?'

'I have already taken the liberty of doing so, my lady,' said William. 'Messengers already race to the city to spread the news, and young Baldwin will be escorted back here under a strong military guard within days.'

'You sent for him without asking me?' asked Sibylla, an irritated look on her face.

'My lady, with respect, you were indisposed, and it was clear the king would not last the night. All I did was anticipate the outcome and saved us a few hours. Besides, he may be your son, but as the new King of Jerusalem, his safety is now the responsibility of the court and his regent until such time as he comes of age.'

'The boy is seven years old, Father William,' said Sibylla, 'and I am his mother. In future, any decisions regarding his welfare will be discussed with me first. Is that clear?'

'My lady,' said William, 'as you are aware, the succession was agreed on the condition that Count Raymond III of Tripoli would rule as regent until the boy is of age. You cannot change that arrangement without plunging the kingdom of Jerusalem into a crisis.'

'Do not fret, Father William,' said Sibylla,' I have no intention of creating a problem, only of being a mother.'

'Of course, my lady,' said William, 'but one more thing. What were the king's last words before he died?'

'I cannot share them with you, Father William,' said Sibylla, 'they will forever be between him and me. Now, I must go. Let me know when the funerary arrangements have been made.'

'Of course,' said the prelate with a nod of the head and watched her leave the room to return to her quarters.

At the same time, in the city of Acre, Sumeira, Emani and John Loxley sat across a trestle table from Jakelin De Mailly and Thomas Cronin, waiting for their evening meal to be served. To Sumeira's astonishment, Jakelin had spoken to the marshal and secured temporary lodgings within the Templar commandery itself in the south-eastern quarter of the city.

'Is there anything I can do to help?' asked Sumeira.

'No, you are our guests,' said Jakelin, 'and will be treated as such.'

Sumeira fell silent as an enormous, bearded knight brought a tray bearing four bowls of potage, a jug of watered wine and a loaf of bread from the kitchens. He placed them on the table before them before making the sign of the cross above the food. Everyone waited while the man retired, and Sumeira looked over at Cronin.

'This just doesn't seem right,' she said. 'Why are we being served by your fellow knights?'

'Actually, he's the under-marshal,' said Cronin with a smile. 'And it is his turn to serve this evening.'

'But is he not a man of power?'

'Indeed he is. In this city he is the second most powerful man at arms, only reporting to the marshal himself, but our way of life is simple. We eat only what we need, share the excess with those who are less fortunate, and while within the walls of the citadel, share all the work irrespective of rank.'

'The food smells delicious,' said Emani.

'It is humble, yet nutritious,' said Jakelin. 'Please, eat your fill, and if you wish for more, I will happily bring it from the kitchens.'

'I do not think that will be necessary,' said John. 'May we start?'

'One moment,' said Jakelin and closed his eyes to say a prayer of thanks before smiling at his guests. 'Please, proceed,' he said, and everyone picked up the wooden spoons to eat the food.

'So,' said Cronin, reaching across to break the bread into five equal pieces, 'tell us more of your adventure in Cyprus.'

'There's not much to tell,' said Sumeira, 'when we landed, there were no more ships due to sail to Greece for over a month, so we sought temporary lodgings. Of course, we had to pay our way so we immediately plied our trade in the markets, healing those who couldn't afford any medical help.'

'And you earned enough to support all three of you?' asked Jakelin.

'At first, it was difficult for often the sickest are also the poorest.'

'We asked them to pay whatever they could afford,' explained John. 'Sometimes there was the odd coin, but usually, it was with food or personal items. We never went hungry and managed to sell what we did not need to gain an income. Within weeks word spread and we were inundated by requests from rich and poor alike. Life started to get easier, so we decided to stay. That's it really.'

'So why did you come back here?' asked Cronin.

Sumeira glanced at John Loxley, receiving a nod of encouragement in return.

'Cronin, 'she said eventually, 'you are one of the most important people in my life. I would probably be dead now if it were not for you and Sir Jakelin. However, I have a confession to make. To my shame, from the day we first met, I have kept a secret from you.'

'A secret?' said Cronin.

'Something I was too ashamed to tell you, or indeed anyone. I committed a great sin and thought I could spend the rest of my life shielding it from those I love, but each day the burden gets heavier, and I have to make it right.'

'What could be so bad that it affects you so?' asked Cronin.

'Brother Cronin,' interrupted Jakelin, 'there is no need for our friend to share her secret. Perhaps she would prefer it remains hidden.'

'No,' said Sumeira. 'I have kept it concealed for too long, and if I am to make it right, I must open myself up to judgement.'

John Loxley reached across and squeezed her hand in support.

'The thing is,' continued Sumeira, 'when I lived in Segor, I was wed to a very jealous man. He would not let me out on my own, but one day a trade caravan arrived and amongst them were several westerners on their way to Egypt. One of them was from Greece and, when I heard him speak, I yearned to talk again in my mother tongue. That night I crept out and spent many hours in that man's company talking about my home country. Before I knew it, the night had almost gone, but before I could get back to the house, my husband found me and beat me for disobeying him. He also accused me of laying with the trader, but I swear, that did not happen. Anyway, a few weeks later, I found out I was with child, and despite my assurances, my husband always harboured a suspicion that I had lain with the trader. When my son was born, his skin was lighter than most other boys, and that only added fuel to my husband's suspicions. One night he came home and threatened that if I did not get rid of the boy, he would have him killed and fed to the dogs.'

'What did you do?' asked Cronin.

'What could I do? At first, I begged for him to change his mind, but it soon became obvious he would carry out his threat. So, as soon as the baby was weaned off the breast, I arranged for a local family to have him. It broke my heart, but if I had kept him, I knew his life would always be at risk.'

'Do you know where he is now?' asked Jakelin.

'I do not, but I still have contacts in Segor and intend to find out as soon as I can.' She looked across at Cronin. 'So now you know. My past is stained; I am not the person you think me to be.'

'On the contrary,' said Cronin eventually, 'I see a woman who took an opportunity to save her child and did so at immense personal cost. It is not for me to judge you, Sumeira, only God, but from what I can see, there is only goodness on offer.'

Sumeira smiled and wiped a small tear from her cheek before looking at Jakelin.

'And you, Sir Knight, do I see judgement in your eyes?'

'No judgement from me, my lady, only concern about that upon which you are about to embark.'

'What do you mean?'

'The Outremer is a far different place than when you left it. Even back then it was dangerous to stray far from any Christian enclave, but now it is far worse, and with the Salah ad-Din's forces in the ascendancy, the chances of you getting to Segor, finding your son and then returning safely to Acre are minimal at best.'

'I accept it will be difficult,' said Sumeira, 'but I have a plan.'

'Which is?'

'First I will travel to Al-Shabiya with the next available caravan. Once there, I will send a messenger to Segor, seeking information regarding my son's whereabouts before engaging a military escort to take me there. When I find him, we will return with all haste to Al-Shabiya before returning to Acre and back across the sea to Cyprus. Who knows, perhaps one day we will all be able to travel back to the place of my birth and live as a proper family.'

'And this military force. How will you find it?'

'There are mercenaries around every fortress are there not? I will engage enough to protect me upon the journey, and if we travel by night, I see no reason we cannot reach Segor undetected.'

'And you can pay for such men?'

'I will have more than enough funds soon enough.'

'What about Emani?'

'She will stay with me in Al-Shabiya,' said John Loxley. 'I know it seems strange for the man to stay behind while his wife treads the path of danger, but I do not know Segor, the people or the language. Sumeira is adamant she wants to do this, so the only part I can play is by being as close as I can while caring for our daughter.'

'Well,' said Cronin picking up his wine, 'it is a grand quest you have set upon yourself, Sumeira, and I can only hope God is watching over you.'

'I have to do this, Cronin,' she said, 'or I will spend every day for the rest of my life punishing myself for what I did. This way, I will find peace,' she paused before adding, 'one way or the other.'

'Let us drink to a favourable outcome,' said Jakelin lifting his glass, 'for until it fails, every mission is successful.' Everyone took a sip of the watered wine before Jakelin continued. 'And, of course, you are guaranteed success for at least the first part of that quest.'

'How so?' asked John Loxley.

'Because our work here is done and tomorrow morning, brother Cronin and I will be escorting a caravan of supplies to Karak castle above Al-Shabiya. I am sure there will be many cart-masters happy to give you passage for a small fee. However, if you wish to remain here for a while, I can arrange safe haven for as long as you want.

'No, your aid in getting us safely to Al-Shabiya will be greatly appreciated,' said Sumeira. 'The quicker we get there, the quicker I can be reunited with my son. You have my gratitude, Sir Jakelin.'

'It is the least we can do,' said Jakelin. 'Now drink up for there are stories to tell and plans to be made.'

Chapter Five

The Negev Desert

April - AD 1185

Hassan Malouf sat on a rock overlooking a herd of goats wandering through the sparsely vegetated wadi below. Since he had brought down the deer a few weeks earlier, he had been on several hunting trips with Abdal-Wahhab, with varying degrees of success. Sometimes they managed to bring back the occasional hare or even a brace of birds, but deer were becoming harder to find as they migrated across the barren desert. In between hunts he helped look after the tribe's flocks, a task he found strangely comforting and a far cry from the time he served alongside Thomas Cronin at the battle of Montgisard and the siege of Chastellet at Jacob's Ford.

Since then he had returned to his tribe and the girl who had nursed him back to health after a hazardous desert crossing. Day by day, he eased his way back into the Bedouin way of life, having lived in the city of Acre since he was a child and even being baptised as a Christian in the process. This new life was strange, yet subconsciously familiar and despite being still being conflicted between the teachings of Jesus and Allah, knew he had made the right choice.

'Hassan,' called a voice, and he looked around to see his young wife walking up the goat path towards him.

'Kareena,' he said with a smile, getting to his feet, 'what are you doing out here? You should be resting.'

'I am with child,' said Kareena, 'not ill. Besides, I have brought you some food, and as you are still so close to the goam, I thought we could share our midday meal.'

'There was no need to do that,' said Hassan, 'I brought plenty of food and water with me.'

'In that case,' she said with an exaggerated sigh, 'I'll just have to eat all this tender meat myself, and of course, as the cheese will spoil and there are far too many sweet dates for one, I suppose I will have to give it all to the goats.'

'You are a seductive devil, woman,' laughed Hassan, 'come, sit alongside me, and we will share the feast.'

'I thought you would change your mind,' said Kareena and sat down on the rock alongside her husband. She unwrapped the tied bundle and spread out the contents across the colourful linen cloth.

'A feast fit for a king,' said Hassan, looking at all the food, 'I will be as fat as Baten-Kaitos before the month is out.'

'We should enjoy it while we can,' said Kareena. 'The hungry months still outnumber those of plenty, and even if you do get as big as the seer, then there will be more of you to love.'

'Your words drip with honey, my love,' said Hassan, 'and they make me wonder what it is you want.'

'I want nothing except for you to be safe and happy,' said Kareena. 'The stories you tell of when you rode with the Christians, keep me awake with fear, and I am scared that one day, they will return to take you away from me.'

'I told you many times,' said Hassan, 'I will never return to that way of life. I am happy here with my own people and besides, how could I ever leave you again now we have a child to think about?'

'This is very true,' said Kareena, 'so perhaps it is time you rejected the Christian god and embraced the teachings of Allah.'

Hassan stared at her for a while before answering.

'I understand your concern, Kareena,' he said, 'and one day I will probably do what you ask, but for now, there are still some doubts in my mind.'

'The women say that the men are not happy that you have not embraced Islam yet, and they grow impatient.'

'I know,' said Hassan, 'as they have made it clear to me on many occasions, but my heart must be sure before I decide. Now, shall we eat? That meat is making my mouth water.'

'Eat your fill, husband,' said Kareena looking down at the shredded lamb. 'It is left over from last night's meal.'

Hassan picked up some of the meat and wrapped it in a flatbread along with some dried dates and took a bite.

'Will you be going far this time?' asked Kareena as he ate.

'I'll follow the wadi for a couple of days,' said Hassan, 'and then cross over to the far side of the red hills. The grazing is much better there.'

'How long will you be gone?'

'Ten days or so,' said Hassan,' perhaps more, but whatever happens, I promise I will be back before the full moon.'

'I will hate every minute you are away,' said Kareena.

'As will I,' said Hassan, 'but for now, let us enjoy being together and dream of what the future holds.' Both fell silent and ate quietly as they watched the goats wander amongst the boulders in the wadi below. Finally, Hassan stood up and helped Kareena to her feet. 'I have to go, my love,' he said, 'the goats are impatient for the sweeter grass higher up the wadi.'

'So already you bestow greater importance on the goats' happiness than that of your wife,' she said with a smile.

'Stop your teasing, wife,' said Hassan, taking her in his arms, 'you know that is not true.'

Kareena's smiles fell away.

'Be careful, Hassan Malouf,' she said, her hand reaching up to touch her young husband's face. 'I worry for you.'

'I will be fine,' said Hassan. 'Now go back to the goam. I will watch until you disappear from sight.'

Kareena smiled once more and turned away to head back to the Bedouin camp. As she walked, she wondered if she should have shared the warning given to her by Baten-Kaitos earlier that day. The seer had dreamed that a terrible fate awaited Hassan unless he denounced the Christian faith, but when pressed, was unable to give any more details. As Baten-Kaitos was one of those who had been pressurising Hassan to revert to Islam, Kareena had paid him little heed but had still decided to go out and find her husband before he had travelled too far with the herds.

'After all,' she thought, 'even if the seer had been right, the prophecy could still be years away.'

Unfortunately, the optimism was unfounded for though it would take a far different form than expected, the vision was about to become a brutal and terrifying reality.

Three days later, Hassan walked behind his herd of goats amongst a field of scrub on the side of a rocky hill. The sun had only been up an hour, and the goats sought the moist buds at the base of each branch, some still damp with the remains of the morning dew. Most of the herd focussed on their constant need to obtain food and moisture, but Hassan noticed a group had stopped and were staring nervously into a hollow near a lone palm tree. Thinking it may be a snake, or perhaps the lair of a bigger predator, Hassan approached carefully brandishing his shepherd's crook before him as a rudimentary weapon. He wasn't worried there may be any of the larger cats as they frequented the higher peaks, but there could always be a wild dog or even one of the smaller cats that lived in the wadis. Whatever it was, it had certainly spooked the goats, and he had to see the cause.

He reached the hollow and peered in nervously. At first, he could see nothing, but then a movement caught his eye, and he stared in surprise as a human leg was dragged slowly from view.

'Who is there?' asked Hassan, 'show yourself.' He lowered his staff and drew his knife. These hills were known for being the haunt of brigands, and he may have to defend himself. One thing was obvious though, the hiding place was not big enough for more than one man, so the danger was limited.

'Come into the open,' he said again, 'I mean you no harm.' When there was no response, Hassan made his way around to the far edge of the hollow to get a better view. Once there he could see a body of a man lying in the dust, his white thawb filthy with dirt and blood. Hassan climbed down and approached the wounded man.

'Hello,' he said again, 'can you hear me? My name is Hassan Malouf of the Nazar. You are hurt, brother. Let me approach and see if I can help.'

The man groaned, and Hassan took a few steps closer. Suddenly his eyes opened wide as he recognised the man's blood-stained face.

'Abdal-Wahhab,' he gasped, recognising the hunter, 'what happened to you?' Dropping the knife and crook, Hassan ran forward and lifted his friend's head out of the dirt. His face was swollen and bloody, and his nose broken from a severe beating, but what was more worrying was the broken arrow shaft sticking out of his side. 'Don't worry, my friend,' he said, as the wounded hunter opened his eyes, 'I will help you. Tell me what to do.'

'Hassan Malouf,' whispered Abdal, 'by what miracle are you here?'

'I just followed the normal goat trails,' said Hassan, 'but what of you? What brigand set about you?'

'It was no brigand, Hassan,' said Abdal, 'the arrow is from a bow borne by a Christian scout.

'The Franks did this,' asked Hassan, 'but why? What cause did they have?'

'Do you have any water?' asked Abdal, 'my thirst hurts more than the wound.'

Hassan untied the thong around his leather flask and poured it slowly into Abdal's mouth. Finally, the hunter turned his head away, coughing.

'Tell me what to do,' said Hassan again, 'can I withdraw the arrow?'

'There is no time,' said Abdal, 'you must get back to the goam and warn them.'

'Warn them of what,' asked Hassan, 'what happened here?'

Abdal gasped in pain as he adjusted his position.

'Listen,' he said, 'there was a Christian patrol on the road to Al-Shabiya. A few days ago, someone crept into their camp, killed one of their squires and stole a horse. The Franks found his trail and followed him inland. Unfortunately, I was also in the area, and they assumed I was his comrade. They caught the brigand and tortured him to death, but I escaped. For over a day, they followed me until one of their scouts managed to do this.' He looked down at the arrow. 'I hid amongst these rocks, and they soon gave up, but I overheard them saying they had managed to get their victim to talk before slitting his throat.'

'What do you mean, talk? What did he say?'

'It seems they made him say where he had come from and in an effort to save his life, he said a village three leagues north.'

'I know of no such village,' said Hassan.

'That's because there is none,' said Abdal. 'The only encampment anywhere near here is our goam.'

'But I know of no man in our village who would do such a thing?'

'Nor do I,' said Abdal, 'but a condemned man will say anything to save his own life, and I fear he has falsely labelled our goam as a haven for brigands.'

'But that means …'

'Hassan,' said Abdal. 'they are on their way there as we speak; you must get back to the goam to warn our people. These Christians are in a foul mood and intend taking retribution on our goam for a crime not of their making.'

'But there are families there, children. Kareena is there.'

'That's why you must make haste,' said Abdal. 'Allah himself has sent you to me, and it is only you who can stop this injustice.'

'How can I stop a Christian army? I am only one man.'

'By putting yourself between them and our people. You know their ways and how they think. Tell them who you are and the comrades you fought alongside in the service of their God. Once they are listening, explain that there has been a mistake. They will believe you, Hassan, they have to.'

'But what of you? I can't leave you here.'

'There is no other choice,' said Abdal. 'Leave me some water and get back to the camp as quickly as you can. When you get there, send the healer back to find me, but you must not hesitate.'

'I will never get back before the Franks,' said Hassan. 'They are too far in front.'

'My horse is hidden amongst the rocks further up the valley. Take him and ride like the wind. Use the goat paths wherever you can and with Allah's help, you may just get there in time, but you must go now before it is too late.'

Hassan stood up and retrieved his food bag from the floor a few paces away.

'This is all I have,' he said. 'The flask is half full, so should last a few days. I'll get someone to come back to help you as soon as I can.'

'Do what you can,' groaned Abdal, 'but you must go now.'

Hassan nodded and turned away.

'Hassan,' said Abdal, 'fly on the wings of an eagle, your people depend on it.'

Chapter Six

The Negev Desert

April - AD 1185

Raynald of Chatillon walked amongst his men. His mood was tense yet excited at the same time as the blood started to course through his veins. The familiar feelings were like a visit from an old friend, and his heartbeat increased as the anticipation of blooding his sword began to grow.

After discovering the dead squire the previous day, he, his Templar knights and a band of twenty mercenaries had left the main column camped near the southern road and had followed the brigand's trail inland. The signs were easy to follow, and by nightfall, they had managed to capture the culprit, though it irked him greatly that a second man had escaped. Still, he had exacted vengeance on the man responsible and had unexpectedly received some interesting information, the news that the brigand's camp was less than half a day's ride away. Now they were just a few minutes from the nest of vipers, and he needed his men to be focused on the task before them.

'You know what is expected of you,' he said as he walked,' these are the people who sold our women and children into slavery after they took Chastellet, sentencing them to brutal lives of hard labour or dying young in the whore houses of Damascus. These are the people who creep up and cut our throats in the darkness of the night, and men you once called brother now rot in their graves as a result. Make no mistake; whatever you may find on the far side of this hill, you must harden your heart and smite them from God's bountiful earth.'

The men looked to their equipment as he walked. Girth straps were tightened, gambesons donned, and scabbards loosened as they prepared for what was to come. Each was a battle-hardened veteran and knew what to expect. These smaller bands of Saracen brigands were relentless in their murder of Christian pilgrims, and no matter what the situation, there would be no quarter shown. Within minutes they were ready, and everyone mounted their horses.

'Our scouts tell me there are few warriors in the camp,' said Raynald riding his horse down the line, 'and I suspect their menfolk are out raiding. In a moment we will crest this hill and descend into the valley line-abreast. Upon the charge, do not hesitate. Drive into the camp with one purpose, kill everything that moves. Is that clear?'

'Aye, my lord,' responded the men.

'Then drink your last,' he commanded, 'and make ready.'

Some of the men drank deeply from their water flasks, knowing they may not have another chance for many hours.

'I do not need to remind you,' continued Raynald menacingly, 'that any man holding back from his duty will be dealt with by me, and the outcome will not be good. Do what you have to do, and at the end of this day, our chaplain will grant absolution to any man requesting it. Remember, this is God's work before us, and it is his will that we make these people pay for their sins.'

Everyone present knew what Raynald was capable of, and none wanted to be on the receiving end of his wrath. Whatever the task before them, each man was determined not to be found wanting.

'Are you ready?' called Raynald.

'Aye,' responded the men.

Raynald wheeled his horse around and led them up the hill. At the top, he stopped and waited as most of the men spread out either side. A dozen or so stayed fifty paces behind, ready to finish off any of the enemy who escaped the first charge.

Everyone stared down into the valley. Several dozen tents lay scattered between the two hills with two corrals at the far end, the first containing sheep and goats while the other held just over a dozen camels and horses. A few people walked around the camp while several more sat at campfires, preparing the tea to drink with their morning meal.

The man to the right of Raynald, Gerard of Ridefort, scanned the camp for a few seconds before turning to address the knight.

'That's a Bedouin camp,' he said, 'not Ayyubid.'

'Brigands come in many guises, my friend,' said Raynald, 'as you well know. Do not let your eyes be clouded by doubt.'

'But I see no sign of Saracen warriors.'

'They are probably already out roaming the roads looking for innocent pilgrims to rape and murder.'

'Or they could be out tending their herds,' replied Ridefort.

'You are too trusting, my friend,' said Raynald, 'that prisoner said he came from here, and that is good enough for me.'

'He said he came from around here,' said Gerard, 'this does not look like a place where brigands would gather.'

Raynald turned to stare at Gerard.

'You may have friends in high places, Ridefort,' he said, 'but out here I am the man responsible for keeping our people alive and safe. That means, what I say, goes, and if you do not like it, feel free to stay behind.'

'Brother Raynald...' started Gerard, but the knight was already standing up in his stirrups and addressing the line.

'When carrying out your duty,' he shouted, 'remember you are serving your king and you are serving God. Today we will revenge our many brothers and sisters who have suffered and died at the hands of these heathen. Make no mistake, I desire no slaves to feed, nor wounded to tend. Wipe them out, my comrades, we will show no quarter, there must be no survivors.' With a kick of his heels, he urged his horse down the hill, leaving Gerard of Ridefort waiting in his dust.

Down in the valley, Kareena emerged from her tent. The night had been uncomfortable, and she had hardly slept, worrying about the fate of Hassan. The seer had been vague with his premonition and though they often paid him little heed, this time he had been sombre in his delivery, urging Kareena to warn her husband to be careful. At the far end of the camp, women gathered around the fire while goats bleated from the paddocks, impatient to be taken out to pasture. The day was already warming and though she was with child, a full day of work lay ahead.

She headed towards the rest of the women by the main campfire but had only gone halfway when one of the dogs stopped running and stared at the hill behind her, the fur rising on his nape and a deep warning growl coming from his throat. Another dog started barking and ran past her towards the hill. She turned around and for a few seconds stared in confusion at the line of dust descending the slope just a few hundred paces away.

'Kareena,' called a voice as a young girl ran towards her, 'what's happening?'

Others left the fire and stared at the hill. Slowly, realisation dawned, and as a look of horror spread across Kareena's face, many started to scream.

Several leagues away, Hassan urged Abdal-Wahhab's horse as fast as he dared over the rocky ground. Stopping for neither rest nor water, he pushed the animal as hard as he could. Behind him, the hunter lay dying amongst the rocks, but Hassan had only thoughts of his wife and unborn child. The Bedouin were allies of the Christians and hated the Ayyubid just as much, but deep down inside he knew that despite the claims to piety, the Christian forces also contained men with hearts blacker than the devil's soul.

Back in the camp, Kareena turned to run from the oncoming riders. Many women tried to hide in their tents, but Kareena knew, if she was to have any chance of surviving, she had to make it to the rocks. She grabbed the hand of the girl at her side and dragged her towards the slopes at the far side of the valley. Panic broke out all around her, and the few men left in the tents emerged to see the line of bloodthirsty knights bearing down upon them. Some ran forward, desperate to try to calm the situation down and explain they were allies, but by now the horsemen were at full gallop, and the men were trampled underfoot.

A battle cry roared from every horseman's throat, and as the occupants of the goam ran for their lives, the Templars broke formation to cut down every man, woman and child.

Kareena reached the rocks and ducked out of sight, dragging the girl with her. Finding a small cleft in the rocky ground, she pushed the girl as far under an overhanging rock as she could before crawling in behind her and wrapping her up in her arms.

'Shhh,' she said, her voice shaking, 'you must stay quiet.'

The girl nodded, her eyes wide with fear. For almost an hour they listened as the encampment echoed with the noise of the Christians' attack. The valley echoed to the sound of screaming and the desperate pleas of the victims as they begged for mercy. Occasionally, steel clashed on steel as the few men still in the camp tried desperately to protect their families, but it was to no avail, and soon enough, the cries of the victims died away, only to be replaced with the cheering and celebrations of the attackers. Eventually, the noise died down, but Kareena stayed huddled where she was, hardly daring to breathe.

As she waited, she could hear the footsteps of soldiers searching the rocky slopes, seeking the many women and children that had ran that way.

Occasionally, a male laugh rang through the air accompanied by a scream of terror as one by one, the soldiers pulled the escapees from hiding and quickly dispatched them with a swipe of a knife across an unprotected throat.

Kareena swallowed hard, knowing there was no possibility of escape. The soldiers were getting closer, and the hiding place was only big enough for one of them. Finally, making a decision, she turned to the girl with tears in her eyes.

'Jahara, listen to me,' she whispered, 'whatever happens in the next few minutes, you must promise me you will stay silent and stay under this rock. Can you do that?'

The girl nodded, the fear evident on her face.

'I mean it, Jahara,' said Kareena, 'you must be as quiet as the moon and stay here until all the infidels have gone. Once you are sure, take some water and food and follow the setting sun until you find the southern road. You will see many carts passing each day and when you see any containing women, step out and ask for help. Do you understand?'

Again, the girl nodded, and Kareena leaned forward to kiss her on the cheek.

'Be brave, 'she said and crawled backwards out from beneath the rock. Staying low, she pushed as much dust and sand over the girl as she could, leaving just enough space for her to breathe. Finally, she covered the girl's face with a dead piece of brush until eventually, there was no sign anyone was there.

'Be safe, Jahara,' she said, 'and if you ever see my husband, tell him my last thoughts were of him and our baby.'

She looked over her shoulder. The searching soldiers were only a few dozen paces away, and she knew she had to act. Suddenly she got to her feet and started running. It took a few seconds before someone spotted her, but with a roar of glee, the nearest soldiers quickly run her down, cornering her against a vertical cliff of stone. She turned around, desperately pleading for her life.

'Shut your stinking mouth,' snapped one of the men and slapped her across the face, knocking her to the ground.

Kareena hit the floor hard, breaking her nose on a rock. At first, she just lay there, dazed at the impact. As the men laughed, she looked up, her eyes filled with hate. The men gathering around her did not wear the white coats of the Templars, but random clothing obtained from fallen enemies, and she knew she was dealing with mercenaries, brutal men devoid of mercy.

'Well, what have we got here?' asked one, pushing to the front. 'A little runner girl.'

'Pretty too,' said another man, looking over his shoulder, 'perhaps we should have some fun before we kill her.'

'If the whitecoats find out, we'll be in for a flogging,' said another. 'They look down on that sort of thing.'

'I'll take the risk,' said the first man undoing the sword belt around his waist. 'You keep an eye out for the whitecoats, the rest of you form a circle.'

Kareena whimpered, realising what was about to happen.

'No,' she pleaded in her own language, 'please, I am with child.'

The man dropped to his knees beside her and after rolling her onto her back, placed his hand over her mouth.

'Now you keep quiet, little running girl,' he said, 'and this will soon be over.'

'Quicker than she may think,' quipped one of the men and the rest burst into laughter.

'Shut your mouth,' snarled the man over his shoulder, 'or I swear I'll break your neck when I'm done.'

Kareena took advantage of the distraction and reaching out her hand, found a fist-sized rock. With all the strength she could muster, she smashed her attacker across his face, knocking a tooth from his mouth.

For a second, he was stunned, but turned back to glare at her, his face full of fury.

'Why you little bitch,' he spat, drawing his knife, 'I'll make you pay for that.'

Kareena screamed, but before her attacker could do any damage, a voice rang out across the rocks.

'You men, hold.'

'Shit,' murmured one of the men,' its Raynald himself.'

The group dispersed as the Templar knight rode his horse closer. He dismounted and walked through the rocks towards the attacker. The mercenary was now on his feet and rapidly adjusting his clothing. Raynald looked down at the young woman and then back at the mercenary.

'I warned you, Spaniard,' he said, 'we do not treat women this way.'

'Just some fun, my lord,' said the man nervously, 'no harm done. Besides, your arrival was timely. She is untouched.'

'Get out of here and assemble your men,' snarled Raynald de Chatillon, 'we are leaving.'

'Yes, my lord,' said the man and quickly followed his comrades back to the burning camp.

Raynald looked down at Kareena before reaching down to help her up. Kareena hesitated before taking his hand and getting to her feet.

'What's your name?' asked Raynald in Arabic.

'Kareena, my lord,' she replied nervously.

'Where are you from, Kareena,' said Raynald, 'you do not look like the people of this camp.'

'I was taken as a slave when I was a young girl,' said Kareena, 'so know not where I was born, but I have been part of this goam as long as I can remember.'

'So, you know what abominations these people are responsible for?'

'This is a Bedouin tribe, my lord, and we live only to herd and hunt. There is not one amongst us that have ever raised a hand against the Christians. Indeed, my husband fought alongside the Franks at Montgisard and Jacob's Ford. He served men such as yourself, men of Christ with white coats.'

'Your man served the Templars?'

'Yes, my lord.'

'His name?'

'Hassan Malouf. '

'I do not recognise the name. Why are you lying?'

'I am not lying, lord, he served as squire to someone called Cronin. Though he wore a black cloak.'

'A sergeant,' said Raynald, 'not a knight.'

'I do not know such things,' said Kareena, 'only that he is a Christian and has served you well. Please, I am with child, and I swear that if you let me go, I will not say who did this, only that it was brigands from the interior.'

Raynald de Chatillon stared at the beautiful young woman. He had not enjoyed female company since taking the oath many years earlier, and long-forgotten desires surged through his body.

'Turn around,' he said, his voice hoarse.

'My lord?'

'I said turn around.'

Kareena turned around slowly until she faced away from the knight. A few moments later, she felt his hand on her shoulder, and he leaned forward to smell her hair. Kareena closed her eyes, barely able to breathe. The hand seemed enormous, and she knew he could easily snap her neck if he so desired.

'You are very beautiful, Kareena,' said Raynald gently, 'your husband is a lucky man.' He breathed in the smell of her hair, clean and tinged with the smell of wildflowers.

Kareena swallowed hard, not sure what to do. Despite her fiery temper, she knew she would not be able to fight him off. The knight's hand reached around to caress her breasts, and Kareena closed her eyes in fear, deciding that if he decided to take her, she would not fight. Any more beatings could damage the baby, and she would not risk that.

'You say you are with child,' whispered the knight into her ear.

'I am, my lord,' said Kareena.

'In that case, I will pray for both of you,' he whispered, and as his one hand pulled her against his chest, the other dragged a knife across her throat.

Kareena's eyes widened with shock and pain, but as she struggled to breathe, Raynald de Chatillon wrapped his arms around her, embracing her as if a lover. His eyes closed and he whispered gently into her ear until finally, as the strength left her body, he lowered her down to die in the dirt. When he was sure she was dead, he made the sign of a cross before saying a silent prayer over her body. Finally, he got to his feet and after wiping his blade on her clothing, turned away, her name already forgotten.

'Ayyubid or Bedouin,' he said quietly, 'you are all Saracens to me.'

He strode away, not realizing that his every move had been witnessed by the young girl still hidden beneath a nearby rock.

Chapter Seven

The Southern Road

April - AD 1185

The supply caravan from Acre made its way slowly along the winding road towards Al-Shabiya. The town was an important stop for anyone headed south to the city of Segor or onward to join the silk routes that led east. As such, it was a melting pot of tribes and religions, each wary of each other, but respectful of the unwritten truce that allowed the busy trade market to exist.

High on the mountain to the rear, the magnificent sight of Karak Castle loomed over Al-Shabiya and the plains beyond, reminding everyone that any trouble would be struck down with immediate and overwhelming force. Karak also meant good custom for the traders, and every day, servants and officials from the castle scoured the market to make the deals that kept the garrison fed and watered.

'Mother, come and see,' said Emani, lifting the tail-curtain of the covered cart, 'I have never seen anything so magnificent.'

Sumeira climbed down and joined her daughter and husband walking amongst the carts. Every eye was on the castle for though the comfort of Al-Shabiya was less than a league away, the fortress dominated the landscape, both in size and design.

'Have you ever seen such a thing?' asked Emani in wonder.

'I have passed this way before,' said Sumeira, 'though have never set foot inside the castle.'

'Then this is your lucky day,' said Cronin, riding up behind them,' for by nightfall you will be safe within its walls.'

'We are going to the castle?' asked Emani, her eyes lighting up with excitement.

'Of course, you are,' said Cronin, 'how could we not let such a beautiful princess live within the walls of one of the most magnificent castles in Christendom.'

'You do not have to do that,' said Sumeira, 'we can find lodgings in Al-Shabiya.'

'I know you can,' said Cronin,' but I would not rest easy knowing you are staying in that den of thieves and beggars. I may not be able to get you quarters within the upper bailey, but I know the steward and can find you a place of safety within the lower courtyards, if, of course, that is acceptable to you.'

'Of course, it is acceptable,' said Sumeira, 'and once again, we are indebted to you.'

'The debt is owed in the opposite direction,' said Cronin, 'and besides, the offer is easily achieved.' They walked onward before reaching the gates of Al-Shabiya.

Many people who had bought passage with the Templar-guarded caravan offloaded their belongings and walked into the town before the caravan went on its way. The carts then turned off the southern road and headed up a long track towards the castle. The closer they got, the more impressive the fortress seemed with vast stone defensive walls shooting skyward atop severely sloping buttresses. The winding road led along the base of the fortress and past the infamous death pit, the stinking hole containing the remains of those thrown from the tower above. The constant stink and flurry of activity from crows and rats alike reminded any visitors of the awful fate that awaited them should they fall foul of the castellan.

Despite her disgust, Sumeira could not help but glance down into the pit, but quickly turned her head away at the sight of so much carnage and filth. Emani too gagged at the smell, and John Loxley hurried them forward, desperate to leave the stench behind as soon as possible.

'What sort of person does that to his fellow man?' he asked, further up the road.

'Sir Raynald of Chatillon is an uncompromising castellan,' said Jakelin from behind, 'his methods are severe, but his reputation goes before him like the strongest of armies. His enemies know that to cross him means certain death, and this way, he keeps that fear at the forefront of their minds. Do not forget, he suffered fifteen years as a prisoner of the Ayyubid and knows better than most what they are capable of.'

'It is an affront to God himself,' said John.

'Perhaps so, but it is better for everyone if you keep your thoughts to yourself, especially within the walls of Karak.'

The caravan rumbled onward and eventually, made its way through the heavily guarded outer gates into the lower bailey. The courtyard was huge and filled with people as they went about the castle's business. Travelling merchants sold their wares from folding tables or from trays hanging around their necks and many more gathered around as the carts finally came to a halt.

'Get these people back,' shouted a voice, 'before I have their hide stripped from their backs.'

Sumeira looked up, recognising the voice and was overjoyed to see yet another of the men who had shared the terrible siege at Chastellet.

'Is that Arturas?' she said, her face lighting up.

'Indeed, it is,' said Cronin, 'and a grumpier castle steward never walked these lands.'

'He is the steward of Karak?' laughed Sumeira. 'How did that happen?'

'He was wounded in a skirmish a year or so ago,' said Cronin, 'and is unable to ride again, at least, not with any great skill. The castellan gave him a role in the castle guard, and he quickly rose to take over the stewardship.'

'The last time I saw him, he led a band of mercenaries from battle to battle. I never thought I'd see the day when he was domesticated.'

'All men slow down,' said Cronin, 'and he is no different. However, I think he would take the saddle again in a heartbeat, given a chance.'

'I can't wait to catch up with him,' said Sumeira.

'There's no time like the present,' said Cronin. 'Come on, I'm sure he will be just as happy to see you.'

'Isn't he too busy?'

'On the contrary, he is the man who controls what rooms are available in the castle and more importantly, what is charged for them. I suspect now is the perfect time to broach the subject.'

An hour later, Sumeira, Emani and John Loxley entered one of the many store buildings in the lower bailey. To the rear, a door led through to a large room lit by a single window high in the wall. Behind them came Thomas Cronin and Arturas carrying the travellers' belongings. Sumeira had explained the nature of her visit, and Arturas had promised to help in any way he could.

'It's not big,' said Arturas, 'and it needs a clean, but it has a fireplace for when the weather gets colder.'

'It's perfect,' said Sumeira, 'thank you so much.'

'How much is this going to cost?' asked John Loxley, looking around.

'To you, my friends, there is no charge. All I ask is while you are here, perhaps we can call on your skills as physicians as and when needed.'

'Of course,' said John. 'That was always the plan anyway.'

'I can sleep in here,' said Emani, finding a modest storage cupboard in a side wall, 'it will be like having my own quarters.'

'I'm not sure about that,' laughed Sumeira, 'but we will see.' She turned back to the steward. 'Thank you so much, Arturas, it is good to see you again.'

'And you, my lady,' said the ex-mercenary. 'I just wish it were in more pleasant circumstances.'

'I must do what I have to do,' said Sumeira, 'but for now, I will make this room as clean as a palace.'

'I'm sure you will,' my lady,' said Arturas. 'I have to go and check the inventory of the supply caravan, but perhaps we could all catch up in the days ahead.'

'We look forward to it,' said Sumeira. Arturas left the room, and Sumeira turned to her husband. 'Well it's a start,' she said, 'and at least we will be able to sleep soundly at night. I do not think anyone will dare try to steal from us in this place; the punishment is just too severe.'

'This will do us fine for the moment, but we will see about finding something better after we've settled in. Perhaps the hospital will have something more suitable.'

'Karak will have its own physicians, John,' said Sumeira, 'be careful you do not push someone's nose out of joint before we've even settled in.'

'Trust me, my love,' he said. 'I have no intention of ending up in that pit.'

The next day, Sir Jakelin arranged a meeting between the two physicians and the under-marshal of Karak, Sir Richard of Sandford. Sandford was also a Templar and managed the defence of the citadel whenever Raynald of Chatillon was on campaign.

'So, you seek employment,' he said across the table where he was eating a bowl of watery soup.

'On the contrary,' said John Loxley, 'we request only permission to ply our trade within the castle.'

'I already have physicians,' said the under-marshal, breaking bread into his bowl. 'What makes you think I need more?'

'You can never have enough healers.' said Sumeira, 'especially in a place this big.'

'Rest assured; my men are well looked after.'

'I'm sure they are, but if you will allow us, we thought we could tend those who have little access to medicine. The poor and infirm. We could set up a small hospital in the lower bailey and make sure everyone has the chance to be healed.'

'Why would you do that?' asked Sandford. 'They cannot pay, and we will see little benefit from them even if they are healed.'

'Everyone deserves to be free from suffering,' said Sumeira, 'and if nothing else, at least there will be less chance for your men to catch diseases.'

'You can cure the pox?'

'In most cases,' said Sumeira, 'but there is so much more we can do. All we ask is a room where we can treat people and your permission to ply our trade.'

'And supplies?'

'We have brought some with us,' said John Loxley,' but we would seek a line of credit to purchase more from your stores.'

'At cost, of course,' interjected Sumeira quickly. 'As you said, income would be sparse, and we would last no time at all if what little we make went straight into Karak's treasury.'

'Ha,' snorted Sandford. 'You are a bold one, healer. First, you ask me to trade and then dictate the terms. I like that.'

He pushed the bowl away and wiped his bearded mouth with a cloth.

'This is what I will do,' he said. 'I will let you have your hospital, and you are free to treat the poor as you wish. Any supplies needed will be sold to you at cost plus five per cent. In lieu of rent, I want your commitment that should any of my men need treatment at any time; they can come to you with no charge being administered.'

'We turn nobody from our doors, my lord,' said John Loxley, 'and will treat your men like all others.'

'Hmmm,' grunted the under-marshal. 'I will speak to my steward and put things in hand. After three months, we will look at the situation again. Leave us, and I will be in touch as soon as the arrangements are made.'

John Loxley and Sumeira left the room, leaving Jakelin alone with the under-marshal.

'Is there anything else you require of me?' asked Jakelin.

'Actually, there is,' said Sandford. 'I am giving you a new posting.'

'To where?'

'To Nazareth. The castellan at Al-Fulah recently succumbed to an illness, and the castle needs a new commander. I want you to take the position.'

'I deserve no such position,' said Jakelin, 'I am happy to continue here under your command.'

'Your piety is only matched by your ability in battle,' said Sandford. 'Make no mistake, this is no reward for loyalty, there is a job that needs doing in Al-Fulah, and you are the man to do it.'

'What is this task?'

'The old castellan was a good man but lost his way amongst good living and cheap whores. The grandmaster was going to expel him from the order, but the illness saved him the trouble. Unfortunately, his lazy tendencies spread like a plague amongst the garrison there, and they need reminding of what is expected from knights of the realm. I want you to take fifty of our brother knights and restore some pride into those that are the first line of defence for the village where Gabriel visited Mary. Can you do that?'

'I can,' said Jakelin. 'When do I leave?'

'There is no time like the present,' said the under-marshal. 'Gather your things and select your men. You can leave in the morning.'

'Of course, my lord,' said Jakelin and turned to follow the two physicians out of the commandery.

With the meeting over, Sumeira and John Loxley returned to their temporary quarters in the lower bailey.

'That was straightforward enough,' said John Loxley. 'All we have to do now is make it work.'

'We have done it before,' said Sumeira, 'we can do it again. We have enough money for a few months, and by then, I should know more about Jamal's whereabouts.'

'Even if we are successful,' said John, 'we will have nowhere near enough to pay the bribes needed to find your son.'

'I know,' said Sumeira, 'and that is why I will be writing to my family in Greece.'

'To what end?' asked John.

'To ask them for twelve pounds of silver.'

John Loxley stopped in his tracks and stared at his wife.

'They have that sort of wealth?'

'They do, and much, much more.'

'Even so, what makes you think they would send it to you after all these years?'

'Because they are great believers in family and tradition. I am their only child which means that my son, Jamal, is their only grandson. Once they know of his existence, I'm sure they will do everything they can to bring him to safety.'

'I am not judging you,' said John Loxley, 'and will do whatever it takes to help, but even if they get the message and send the money, there is no guarantee it will arrive here intact. Twelve pounds of silver is a huge amount to be conveyed by messenger, and the road from Acre to Karak is filled with brigands.'

'Oh, it will not be coming here,' said Sumeira, 'it will not even be leaving Greece. The silver will be deposited at a Templar treasury in Athens and a simple promissory note conveyed by messenger to Karak under the seal of the order. Once here, the castellan is duty-bound to pay me its value in full upon demand. All I have to do is walk up to the treasury and deliver the note.'

Chapter Eight

The Negev Desert

April - AD 1185

Hassan reined in his horse and stared in despair at the terrible scene in the valley below. Every tent had been burned to the ground, and bodies lay everywhere, each surrounded by swarms of flies as they feasted on the blood shed by the Christian patrol's victims. He urged the horse down the slope and dismounted next to the buckets that still contained water for the now-missing goats. Despairingly, he started running through the devastated village, calling out the names of those he knew.

'Kareena,' he shouted, 'where are you? Baten-Kaitos, Najm al-Din, is anyone alive?'

Desperately he ran from tent to tent, hoping he would find a survivor amongst the smouldering remains. Bodies lay everywhere, each bearing the horrific wounds that had struck them down. Some had been run through with battle-worn lances while others had been hacked almost in half by giant swords borne by giant men. A few had been beheaded, their heads now staring accusingly towards Hassan as if he were the person responsible. Nobody had been spared, and the sorriest sight of all was where the children had been killed while still clinging to their mothers.

Hassan searched everywhere, calling out every few seconds, but nobody came. No voices answered, no dogs barked, and no goats bleated from the pens. The only sound was the caw of the crows and the buzz of the flies. Finally, he dropped to his knees and tilting back his head, let out a scream from the deepest recesses of his soul, a long, spine-chilling roar that echoed around the valley, lifting the crows from their blood-thirsty feast.

For almost an hour, Hassan stayed where he was, kneeling in the dust at the centre of the burnt-out village. His head was bowed, and tears came freely. He was devastated, both physically and mentally without the strength even to lift his head. All he could think about was the fate of Kareena and his unborn child.

Eventually, he heard a noise behind him and turned to see a girl standing a few paces away. Every inch of her was covered with soil, except for the tracks of the tears reaching down her cheeks to drip from her chin.

'Jahara,' he spluttered, wiping the moisture from his face with the back of his hands, 'you are alive?'

The girl nodded and wiped away her own tears.

'Are you hurt?'

The girl shook her head.

'Did you see what happened here?' asked Hassan gently, 'do you know who did this?'

This time the girl nodded, but still did not speak.

'Have you seen Kareena?' asked Hassan, hardly daring to breathe. Again, Jahara nodded, and Hassan paused before asking the one question he feared being answered.

'Jahara,' he said again, 'is she alive?'

This time it was the girl's turn to pause. Tears welled in her eyes, and as she shook her head, Hassan's life changed forever.

Night descended quickly over the Negev, and though he was exhausted, Hassan used the cooler hours to dig a grave near a lone fig tree in the valley. When it was done, he gently washed Kareena's body in warm water before wrapping it in three layers of linen. Finally, he placed her in the grave and covered her with leaves.

For a few moments, he stared down into the grave, not knowing what to do next. He became aware of Jahara and looked at her innocent face, now cleaned and with her hair covered with a scarf.

'You should say the Salat al-Janazah,' she said gently, the first words she had spoken since he had found her.

'I do not know how to,' said Hassan, his head dropping with shame.

The girl took his hand and turned to look in the grave. After a few moments, she started saying the funeral words usually spoken by the men at any burial.

'It is done,' she said a few moments later, 'now we can bury her.'

Hassan reached for the shovel and started to throw the spoil into the grave. Every time the earth landed on the body of his wife, his heart broke a little bit more until, by the time he finished, his body and mind were spent and he fell on top of the filled-in grave, exhausted.

The early rays of the sun found Hassan still sleeping on the grave of his wife. As he woke, the memories came flooding back, and the heavy weight of grief overwhelmed him like a desert storm. Eventually, he dragged himself to his feet and collected dozens of stones to cover the grave before walking back to the ruined camp. As he approached, three desert dogs ran from one of the corpses they had started to eat, sending the early crows skyward once again.

To his surprise, the girl was already there, kneeling next to a body in the centre of the camp. He walked over and squatted beside her. The body was loosely covered with a piece of scorched tent fabric. He lifted the end and saw the face of a woman, her hair still wet where Jahara had tried to wash her.

'Is she your mother?' asked Hassan gently.

The girl nodded.

'And your father?'

The girl turned and pointed to another covered body a few paces away.

'Oh, Jahara,' he sighed, 'I am so sorry.'

The girl stared into his eyes, her own seemingly devoid of emotion.

'We have to bury them,' she said, 'all of them.'

Hassan looked around. There were almost fifty bodies in total, far too many for one man to bury.

'Jahara,' he said, 'there are too many. It would take many, many days and the bodies are already starting to decompose.'

The girl got to her feet and held out her hand.

'Come,' she said, 'there is a place.'

Hassan stood and followed the girl towards a steep escarpment at the side of the valley. At the base, a dried-up pool had left a hollow a dozen paces wide and twice that in length, more than enough to hold the bodies.

'They must be laid on their sides,' said Jahara,' her voice flat, 'facing towards Mecca.' She pointed towards the south-east, emphasizing her message.

'Jahara,' he said, 'even if I can bring them here, how am I supposed to bury them?'

The girl did not answer. Instead, she turned her head to look up to the slopes above, and as Hassan followed her gaze, he suddenly understood.

For the rest of the day, Hassan used the horse and a length of rope to drag the bodies over to the makeshift grave. It was undignified, but by the time the sun started to set, every body in the camp was laying in the pit, three rows of slaughtered innocents. He collapsed against a rock and closed his eyes. His work was not yet finished, but the exhaustion was overwhelming.

Jahara walked over to give him a waterskin and he half-drained it in one go, pouring the rest over his head before looking up at the girl who was now staring at the only two bodies that were wrapped.

'You will see them again one day,' said Hassan, getting to his feet. 'They will be waiting for you in paradise.'

'I know,' said Jahara, 'but first there is retribution to be made.'

'Do not talk of revenge, little one,' said Hassan, 'they are the words of men, not girls.'

'One day, I will be a woman,' said Jahara coldly, 'and I will seek out those that did this to my people.'

'Jahara, these men were soldiers, and their trade is death. Put such things out of your mind. There is nothing you can do.'

'Do they not succumb to the poisons of the hidden desert plants,' said Jahara, 'or the sting of a scorpion placed in an empty boot? Does not their throat bleed when cut with a knife in the depths of the night or their skin scorch from the desert sun when their horses are stolen from beneath their noses?' She turned to Hassan. 'For that is what I will do, Hassan,' she said. 'I will grow, and I will get strong, and I will avenge my people. I vow this over the dead bodies of my mother and my father.'

'Jahara,' said Hassan. 'Your pledge does you credit, but we do not know who these men were. By the time you are old enough, they will be long gone.'

'Then I will follow them,' said Jahara, 'to the end of all lands if necessary, until either they or I lay dead. And you are wrong, Hassan, I may not know them all, but I know the two men who led them.'

'You do?'

'I saw them, Hassan, and heard them talk. One was rough and commanded others who were just as bad. They were not soldiers of the Christ God but were heavily armed. I believe they were paid men who fight for money.'

'Mercenaries?'

'Yes, that is the word. I could not understand them, but the first man who attacked your wife was called Spaniard. That much I know.'

'And you are sure of this?'

'I am, but there was a second man, a knight of Christ who wore a white cloak with a red cross.'

'A Templar knight,' said Hassan through gritted teeth.

'Yes, it was he who embraced your wife before slitting her throat.'

'And did you hear his name?' asked Hassan, his voice hoarse.

'I did not,' said Jahara, 'but I know him all the same.'

'How?'

'When I was younger, I would sneak from my tent at night and listen to the tales of the old men around the fires. I have heard many times that there is a Christian devil who lives in the castle above Al-Shabiya. His beard hangs down to his belly and is as red as the cactus flower. It was said that he is taller than all men and has killed more Muslims than there are stars in the sky. This was that man, Hassan; this was the man who killed your wife and baby.'

Hassan stared at Jahara. If she was right, not only were Templars responsible for the slaughter, but his wife had been killed by the most feared warrior in Christendom, Raynald of Chatillon.

'Come,' he said eventually, 'it is getting dark. We should get some sleep. In the morning you will say the Salat al-Janazah and I will do that which needs to be done.'

The girl nodded and followed Hassan back to the remains of the camp.

The following morning, they both stood at the top of the hill above the communal grave. The bodies were already covered with crows, and the smell made it difficult to breathe. For a few moments, the girl recited the funerary prayer before turning and nodding at Hassan.

'It is done,' she said, 'now we can bury them.'

Hasan walked towards a rock near the edge of the slope and leaning against it, tried to push it down the hill. Jahara tried to help but to no avail, so they tried another, this time a bit smaller. Jahara cleared some of the soil from in front of the boulder, and with two more heaves, Hassan sent it hurtling down the slope. As it rolled it dislodged other rocks and by the time it reached the bottom had caused a small landslide of stone and soil, covering half of the bodies. Three times they repeated the process with varying results until finally, Jahara walked up to the edge to peer down into the pit.

'It is enough,' she said, 'they are at peace.'

Hassan looked down the slope, gasping for breath. As the dust settled, he could see there was more than enough spoil covering the dead. His task was done.

Two days later, Hassan rode into a different Bedouin camp, ten leagues from where he had buried his wife. Jahara sat behind him on the exhausted horse, and they rode slowly to the centre of the camp. People came from their tents to see the strangers pass until one man walked out and stopped directly in their path.

'Greetings, stranger,' said the Bedouin, 'welcome to our goam.'

Hassan looked down at the man. His garb and demeanour singled him out as the chieftain of the village. For a moment, Hassan did not answer and just sat there in silence, totally drained, having ridden for two days and nights with no rest.

'Do you need help?' asked the man, concerned at the state of the riders and horse alike.

'Yes,' said Hassan weakly, 'we do.'

The man called out, and men and women came running to their aid.

Jahara was carefully helped from the horse first before being whisked away by a group of concerned women. Hassan slowly dismounted and handed the reins over to a boy.

'Take care of him,' said Hassan, 'he saved our lives.'

The boy led the horse away, and Hassan turned to the man who had first spoken.

'Are you the chieftain?' he asked

'I am,' said the man; 'my name is Youssef-bin-Khouri,'

'I am Hassan Malouf of the Nazar,' came the reply, 'and I seek your help, Youssef-bin-Khouri.'

'Our home is your home,' said Youssef, 'you are safe here.'

Chapter Nine

Acre

Seventeen months later

Sibylla walked along the torchlit corridors deep in the bowels of Acre castle. For the past month, she had walked the same route several times every day, once again, visiting a king clinging on to the last remnants of life. This time though, the monarch destined to become one of the shortest ever reigning kings of Jerusalem was none other than her own son, Baldwin V.

There were no tears in Sibylla's eyes for her son's death was expected and had been a long time coming. He always had been a sickly child, but over the past few months, he had grown considerably weaker, causing many in the court to whisper about the possibility that he was being poisoned.

Unaware of the rumours, Sibylla had gone about her business as normal, her heart already toughened to expect the worst. For the last six months, she had hardly seen him, having been tied up in the daily running of the court alongside the king's regent, Raymond III of Tripoli. Raymond and Sibylla had a strained relationship for though he had also been regent to the previous king, he also had a claim to the throne himself, if and when Baldwin V died.

Sibylla knew this, and though her motherly instincts were strong, they were dwarfed by her political ambition, and already there were plans afoot to move quickly when her son died. She walked into the bed-chamber to find William of Tyre and a physician next to the bed.

'How is he?' asked Sibylla sitting on the bed.

'Sleeping,' said William, 'and his fever has eased, but he gets weaker by the day.'

Sibylla took a cloth from a bowl at the side of the bed and bathed her son's brow.

'Have you bled him today?' she asked, looking at a silver pot on a table at the far side of the room.

'We have, my lady,' said William, 'though I feel at this stage, we should be focusing on prayer rather than leeches.'

'It seems it was never God's will that my boy would reach greatness,' said Sibylla. 'Perhaps he will be given such things in the kingdom of heaven.' For several minutes she just sat there, looking at her sick son. His body was stick-thin, and his skin, yellow. His hair was plastered to his head through sweat, and his breathing laboured. She knew he would soon be dead, but her crying was done, and all she could hope for now was a painless passing for the boy who would never see Jerusalem.

'I will be back in the morning,' said Sibylla eventually, getting to her feet. 'If anything changes in the night, call me straight away.'

'Of course,' said the physician with a bow.

Sibylla walked across the room and into the corridor, closely followed by the prelate.

'My lady,' he said as she strode away, 'can I speak to you?'

'Of course,' she said, 'what do you want to say?'

'Not here,' said the prelate, 'there are too many eyes and ears.'

'Come to my quarters after the evening meal,' she said, 'I will be alone, and you can speak freely.'

'Thank you, my lady,' said William and turned to return to the king's chamber.

Later that evening he stood near the fire in Sibylla's quarters, admiring an exquisitely embroidered tapestry hanging on the wall.

'It belonged to my father,' said Sibylla walking into the room. 'I had it brought from Jerusalem when we came here. It adds warmth to the room even on the coldest of nights.'

'Indeed, it does,' said the prelate.

'Wine?' asked Sibylla.

'Not for me,' said William, 'I want to talk of serious things with an unclouded mind.'

'It sounds serious,' said Sibylla, 'so I too will abstain.' She turned to the two servants in the room. 'You may leave us.'

'Yes, my lady,' said the two girls in unison and left the room, closing the door behind them.

'So,' said Sibylla, sitting in one of the many chairs, 'what is it that is so important, you fear being overheard would put you in danger?'

'I never mentioned any danger, my lady,' said William, walking over to stand behind the chair opposite her, 'at least not to me.'

'You intrigue me,' said Sibylla, 'are you saying there is a threat to my life?'

'Not at all, my lady, only to your position.'

'So, say what you came to say, Father William,' said Sibylla, 'I am listening.'

'My lady,' said the prelate, 'as sad as it is, you know as well as I that your son is not long for this world, and when he dies there will be confusion as to who will wear the crown of Jerusalem.'

'There is no confusion,' said Sibylla, 'my brother died childless, and my son, Baldwin V, grandson of the great King Amalric himself, lays on his own death bed only a few hundred paces away from this very room. When he dies, I am the only child left legitimately sired by Almaric. The throne is mine.'

'If only it were that easy,' said William, 'for there is also a counterclaim being considered by your half-sister.'

'Isabella is the daughter of a whore,' said Sibylla, 'and has no rightful claim.'

'It is unbecoming to call Maria Comnena a whore, my lady; she comes from the noblest of families.'

'She replaced my mother in my father's bed for nought more than station,' said Sibylla, 'in my eyes that makes her a whore.'

'Nevertheless,' said William, 'Isabella's claim is legitimate, and already her champions gather to press her credentials. I know for certain Raymond III of Tripoli and Balian of Ibelin speak on her behalf.'

'Neither of whom give me any concern,' said Sibylla.

'Well, they should for they are already drumming up support from the nobles in Nablus. I have heard rumours that Raymond may raise an army to oppose your claim and if we are not careful, we could soon have Christians killing Christians within sight of the walls of Jerusalem itself.'

'The Haute Cour would never allow it,' said Sibylla, 'besides, I have Raynald de Chatillon and the Templar grandmaster himself supporting my claim. Their armies will ensure my coronation will go ahead as planned.'

'But is that what you want, the throne of Jerusalem bathed in Christian blood? Even if you are victorious, which is not guaranteed, the Haute Cour will never accept you as queen, at least not while you are married to Guy of Lusignan.'

'Ah,' said Sibylla, 'so now we get to the real purpose of your visit, your hatred of my husband. Well, it will not work, William, I love him, and when I am queen, he will sit alongside me as king.'

'My lady,' said William, 'I have no wish to open old wounds. I only want to help the succession and return to Tyre to grow old as gracefully as I can.'

'So, why are you still here?' asked Sibylla. 'When my brother died, I did not ask you to stay.'

'You did not,' said William, 'but since your brother was a small boy, I advised him on many things from what fruits could be eaten in the desert to the best strategy to take a castle. In all this, he found strength and comfort, and when he died, I only stayed to make sure his successor was also schooled in such things. Alas, his heir is only days away from death, and my advice lays hanging on the breeze, without ears or mind to heed it.'

'I am not a child, Father William,' said Sibylla, 'and though I recognise what you did for my brother, I need no advisors to guide my path.'

'I know,' said William, 'and soon I will make my final journey to Tyre, but even though you desire no counsel, I ask you to hear me out with one last piece of advice.'

'And what advice would that be?'

'If you allow,' said William, 'I will tell you how you can, with guile and patience, get everything you want with the full support of the Haute Cour and without a single drop of blood being spilt. If I can get every noble in Jerusalem united on your side and all challengers sidelined under the law, would that be worth an hour of your time?'

'It would,' said Sibylla eventually. 'Sit down, Father William, and I will be the most attentive student you ever had.'

On the other side of the Salt-sea, Cronin watched from the castle walls as Raynald de Chatillon, and Gerard of Rideford rode from Karak accompanied by a hundred Templar knights and mercenaries. Their destination was Jerusalem for though they had received messages confirming the king was on his death bed in

Acre, they also knew that when he died, the funeral would take place in the Holy-city, as befit all kings of Jerusalem. The messages had also warned of political unrest and the potential need for military force in support of Sibylla's claim to the throne. Although welcomed, the letters were not signed by Sibylla, or even by any member of her court; they were signed by William of Tyre, a man who shared no respect or affection for Raynald.

'I fear there may be difficult days before us,' said Gerard of Ridefort as they rode. 'The succession has the potential to spark conflict.'

Raynald glanced over at the grandmaster. Gerard had been appointed to the highest rank of the Templar's order only months earlier but had remained at Karak due to the threat of attack from Saladin and the Ayyubid. The appointment had long been anticipated due to his popularity with the holy father in Rome, but it still seemed strange to Raynald that he now answered to a man he had commanded for so many years.

'Raymond will not raise an army against Sibylla, brother Gerard,' he said, 'he would not dare.'

'Raymond is a formidable man,' countered Gerard, 'and has oft made his own way against the wishes of the king.'

'I see no need for Raymond to declare war with Jerusalem,' said Raynald, 'and neither will he. Sensibility will hold sway against the petulance of courtly politics, of that, I have no doubt.'

'Perhaps,' said Gerard, 'but if God sees fit to pit brother against brother, we must ensure the conflict is brought to an end as soon as possible, both with blade and discourse.'

'Both are acceptable to me,' said Raynald without turning, 'Raymond of Tripoli tests my patience on a daily basis, and I will countenance it no longer.'

'What of your stepson?' asked Gerard. 'I hear you were once close.'

'We still are,' said Raynald. 'The fact that he is married to Isabella clouds the matter slightly, but Sir Humphrey is a good man and will do what he can to lessen the tension between all parties.'

'I hope you are right, brother,' said Gerard, 'for all our sakes.'

As the column rode out of sight, Arturas appeared on the castle walls alongside Cronin, staring out over the Holy-land

'I smell blood in the air,' he said eventually.

'We live in strange times,' said Cronin. 'Saladin grows his army by the day, yet still, we squabble like children amongst ourselves. I fear that unless we gain strong leadership in Jerusalem, we could suffer greatly at the hands of the Ayyubid.'

'Do you think Sibylla is the one to provide such leadership?' asked Arturas.

'I do not,' said Cronin, 'she is a woman and has never raised a blade in anger.'

'What about her husband, Guy of Lusignan? I hear he is a good leader?'

'In peacetime, yes, he commands great loyalty amongst his men, but again, he is untried in war. What we need is someone who has spilt enemy blood in the heat of battle.'

'You favour Raymond of Tripoli for the crown?'

'Why not? He may be an arsehole as a man, but his prowess as a fighter is well known. When Saladin attacks, as he inevitably will, I would rather have Raymond coordinating our armies than someone who's only knowledge of fighting is the political arguments in the corridors of Jerusalem.'

'A fair point,' said Arturas.

The two men looked towards Al-Shabiya in the distance. The village was growing month by month as its importance as a resting point on the southern road grew. People from every culture mingled there on a daily basis, and though Cronin had no doubt that it was infested with Saladin's spies, there was no way to find them without turning the whole town against the garrison. Occasionally, upon receiving accurate information, Raynald would send a patrol into the town to apprehend a known murderer or spy, but this was done more as a reminder of the castle's strength rather than any attempt to seriously impose law and order.

'Have you heard from Sumeira recently?' asked Cronin glancing at the steward.

'Aye, only yesterday she finally received the news she had been waiting for.'

'She must be relieved. It has been a long time.'

'It has, but she is now in possession of a promissory note to the value of twelve pounds of silver.'

'Then she is a rich woman,' said Cronin. 'A man could buy land and live a good life with such an amount.'

'Perhaps you should marry her and suggest such a thing,' said Arturas.

Cronin turned to him, and his brows lowered in confusion. 'What foolery is this?' he asked. 'There is no attraction between us, and besides, she is a happily married woman.'

'Her marriage has not been blessed,' said Arturas, 'as you well know, and nor is it likely to be. As for attraction, if you think that the way you both look at each other has gone unnoticed than you are more of a fool than I think you to be.'

'You think me a fool?'

'Only in matters of the heart,' said Arturas. 'The woman obviously likes you, but the longer you wait, the greater the chance that someone will step in and take your place.'

'Now who is the fool?' asked Cronin. 'First of all, the woman may not be married in the eyes of the church, but she is happy with John Loxley. He cares for her well, along with her daughter, and that makes me happy. Besides, even if that was not the case, and there was affection between us, which there is not, then my vows prevent me from engaging in any relationship with any woman, as well you know.'

'You mount a defence as great as these walls,' said Arturas, holding up his hands in mock surrender. 'Have I touched upon a wound perhaps?'

'You have not,' said Cronin, his heart aching at the lie, 'and I request we do not discuss the subject again. The company of women is forbidden to me until such time that I leave the order.'

'You have not signed up for life?'

'I have not.'

'When do you become a free man?'

'The order is not a prison, my friend,' said Cronin, 'but a choice, and I chose to serve for twenty years. I have five left.'

'And do you intend to leave?'

'I do not yet know. The thought of having a family is a strong lure, but my time within the order has brought structure to my life that I never had before. I do not know if I can live without it.'

'Well, if nothing else,' said Arturas, 'I strongly suggest you keep your head low. It would be a shame if you were to die with so little time left to serve.' His hand clapped down on

Cronin's shoulder. 'Stay safe, my friend, and think upon what I said.' He turned and left the battlements, leaving Cronin to ponder his words behind him

----

Chapter Ten

Jerusalem

September - AD 1186

Sibylla sat at the end of a long room deep in the heart of Jerusalem's citadel. Before her was the Haute Cour, the alliance of nobles, bishops and high-ranking vassals who voted on behalf of the people in matters of state. Over a hundred members stood in the room out of six hundred eligible participants, but nevertheless, it was the biggest assembly the court had seen for many years.

To the left stood those loyal to Sibylla, while on the right stood those supporting Isabella. Isabella and her main supporters, Raymond of Tripoli and Balian of Ibelin were still in Nablus but had sent powerful nobles to press her claim on her behalf. Arguments flew back and forth, and though there was never a risk of anyone coming to blows, the air was full of tension.

Sibylla looked around for Father William. After heeding his counsel in Acre, she had asked him to attend the meeting to support her in her claim as his opinion was well regarded across the Outremer. In his time, he had served as a personal advisor or teacher to the previous three kings, and there was nobody alive who knew their personalities as well as him. Earlier, he had already addressed the Haute Cour extolling Sibylla's virtues and suitability for office but was now nowhere to be seen.

She shifted uncomfortably in her seat. The arguments were not going well, and with Isabella having more supporters in the room than her, if it came to the vote, there was only one possible outcome. Finally, the noise died away, and the Bishop of Jerusalem approached Sibylla.

'Lady Sibylla,' he said with a bow, 'today we have heard presentations from both sides, each having merit in their argument, but as there is no clear preference, it has become clear that we need to go to a vote.'

'I need more time,' interrupted Sibylla, 'I have supporters who have not yet arrived, and the vote will not be fair.'

'My lady,' said the bishop, 'with respect, the honourable members of this court have duties to attend and have been away from their lands for far too long. Jerusalem needs a leader, and we can prevaricate no longer. We will go to the vote.'

He turned to face the chamber but stopped in his tracks when a voice called out from the doorway.

'Your Grace,' said Father William entering the room, 'I beg a few minutes more for there has been a significant development.' He walked through the room and knelt before the bishop making the sign of the cross before returning to his feet. 'Your Grace,' he said again, 'may I speak to the court?'

'Is this new information relevant?' asked the bishop.

'I believe it is'

'Then proceed,' said the bishop and walked to one side of the room.

'My lady,' said Cronin, turning to face Sibylla, 'can I ask you, in front of these good people, who will sit at your side as the King of Jerusalem?'

Sibylla stared at the prelate. William knew that Guy was unpopular amongst those in the room and reminding them of that fact would do her cause no good at all.

'I need you to answer, my lady,' he said.

'You know who it is,' said Sibylla, 'my husband, Guy of Lusignan.'

The crowd murmured amongst themselves, the tone dark and angry as William turned to the court.

'Guy of Lusignan,' he announced, 'come forth and make yourself known.'

The crowd parted as Sibylla's husband made his way to the front.

'My lord,' said William, 'in front of those present in this room, please state your allegiance to the one who should be Queen of Jerusalem.'

'You know my pledge,' growled Guy, 'what games are these?'

'I may know your pledge, my lord, but it is important such things are recorded before the Haute Cour.'

'I pledge my allegiance and my sword to Sibylla, Countess of Jaffa and Ascalon,' said Guy with a sigh.

'Thank you, my lord,' said William, 'you may retire.' He turned to the court. 'Who amongst you speaks on behalf of Isabella?'

'I do,' said another bishop stepping forward, 'I am the Bishop of Nablus, and represent her eyes, ears and mouth, by her proclamation and by the grace of God.'

'Thank you, Your Grace,' said William. 'I would ask you the same question. Who would rule alongside Lady Isabella, should she gain the throne of Jerusalem?'

'It will be her husband, Sir Humphrey of Toron.'

William nodded silently and turned to the room.

'Humphrey of Toron, come forth and make yourself known.'

'He is with his wife in Nablus,' said the bishop, 'as well you know.'

'On the contrary,' boomed a voice, 'I am here.'

A collective gasp echoed around the room as the knight walked through the door and down to the front of the court. He bowed to both bishops before turning to face William.

'Thank you for coming, my lord,' said the prelate. 'Are you aware that your wife has proclaimed that should she become Queen of Jerusalem; you would sit alongside her as king?'

'I am,' he replied.

'Then I would ask the same of you. In front of those present in this room, please pledge your allegiance the one who should be Queen of Jerusalem.

The room fell quiet as Humphrey looked around the expectant gathering.

'My allegiance,' he announced loudly, 'and my sword is pledged to Sibylla, Countess of Jaffa and Ascalon.'

The room erupted as the betrayal sunk in. Many just stared in shock, but Sibylla's supporters were overjoyed. No matter what happened now, there was no way that Isabella could become queen without the support of her husband, especially as half of those who had come to support her were loyal to Humphrey.

'My lord,' said the Bishop of Nablus, 'are you sure?'

'Certain,' replied Humphrey. 'This kingdom has had enough confusion and delay; what we need is a united Jerusalem to face Saladin in the coming months. For Jerusalem's sake and indeed, for the rest of the Holy-land, Sibylla is best placed to provide that unity.'

As the noise increased, the Bishop of Jerusalem struck his staff hard upon the floor, and the room fell silent.

'The matter is settled,' he announced loudly, 'the vote is cancelled. The lady Sibylla, Countess of Jaffa and Ascalon, will be crowned Queen of Jerusalem three days hence.'

'Wait,' said the Bishop of Nablus, 'there is one more issue to discuss.'

'Are you dismissing the will of the Haute Cour, Your Grace?' asked one of the knights in the room.

'Of course not, but queen or not, Jerusalem will be nothing without her allies.' He turned to face Sibylla. 'My lady, it pains me to remind you, but if we are to pledge allegiance, it will be to you and you alone. Guy of Lusignan is no king, and if you are to rule as a true monarch, he must not be at your side. Divorce him, and we will pledge our swords to Jerusalem. Stay with him, and the throne will carry as much power as if it were empty. The decision is yours.'

'That is an outrageous demand,' shouted William, 'who are you to lay terms upon the Queen of Jerusalem?'

'She is not queen yet,' said the bishop. 'In truth, it matters not who is queen, or indeed king, but if you want us to pledge fealty, then she must show that she too is willing to make sacrifices for the common good.' He looked around the room before turning back to the countess. 'My lady, there are barely a handful of men present who would answer a call from Guy of Lusignan should it come to war. Cut him loose, and we will rally to your banner; make him king and the Holy-land will be forever fragmented.'

Voices raised all around the chamber, and again there seemed little chance of agreement. Finally, Sibylla got to her feet and raised her hand. Almost immediately, everyone fell silent as they waited for her to speak.

'Men of the Haute Cour,' she said. 'I have sat here and listened to your arguments for the past few hours. Do not think for a heartbeat that I have not listened to your concerns, for I have taken them all in and judged them only on what is best for Jerusalem. The Bishop of Nablus is correct, and the protection of Jerusalem should be foremost in our minds. So, I ask you this. If I do as you ask, and divorce my husband, will you today pledge allegiance to me before God?'

Dozens of voices echoed around the room, each one promising their fealty.

Sibylla waited until the silence returned before turning back to face the bishop.

'Your Grace, I turn to you and ask this. If I do this thing for Jerusalem, does God expect me to rule alone?'

'No, my lady, for on the day of your coronation, there will be many nobles present who represent the best of Christendom, each from a respected family. When you are crowned queen, you will have a choice of suitors, each more than capable of serving at your side.'

'A marriage of convenience rather than of love,' said Sibylla.

'A necessary gesture, yet one that has been used to great effect for many years, including the marriage of your father to Maria Comnena, as you well know. If you agree to this one last thing, then there are no more obstacles in your path. You will be crowned Queen of Jerusalem within days.'

'And the final choice of husband will be mine?'

'It will.'

'In that case,' said Sibylla, 'I have made a decision.' She looked around in silence for a few moments before continuing. 'If you pledge your fealty to me today, in the sight of God, I swear that before I am crowned, I will divorce Guy of Lusignan.'

The men of the room let out a gasp of shock and broke into conversation. For several moments nobody moved until eventually, one of the Nablus knights walked forward.

'And this is your pledge?'

Sibylla looked over at her husband at the far wall, a tear in her eye as she saw the look of utter devastation on his face.

'As God is my witness,' she said.

'In that case,' said the knight, 'my sword is yours.' He dropped to his knee and bowed his head. The rest of the men followed suit until only three men remained standing, the two bishops and her husband, Guy of Lusignan. She looked over to him again.

'You would do this to me?' he asked simply.

'It is not a slight on you, my love,' she said, 'but it is necessary for Jerusalem and for God. I beseech thee, take the knee for though you are diminished in these men's eyes, you will never be in mine. Pledge your oath, my love, for the sake of Christendom.'

For a few seconds, he did not move until slowly he drew his sword and stared at his wife, his face devoid of emotion. The tension was palpable, and the Bishop of Jerusalem prepared to throw himself in front of Sibylla, should Guy try and attack her, but to his surprise, Guy placed the sword point down onto the slabs of the floor and dropped to his knee behind it.

'You always were my queen,' he said eventually, 'and in my eyes, nothing has changed. To you, Sibylla, Queen of Jerusalem, I pledge my sword, my fealty, my life.'

Chapter Eleven

Jerusalem

September - AD 1186

The following day, the annulment of Sibylla's marriage to Guy was carried out privately and swiftly by the Bishop of Jerusalem, witnessed by the Bishop of Nablus and three of the knights who had initially supported Isabella. Having achieved the best outcome they could have hoped for, most of the men who were loyal to Isabella set out for the journey home, politely refusing the invitations to attend the following day's coronation.

'Your Grace,' said Sibylla as the Bishop of Nablus climbed into his carriage, 'are you sure you will not stay and celebrate our newfound unity?'

'No, I have to get back and report to your sister,' said the Bishop. 'She will be upset, but the Haute Cour has spoken, and she will abide by the outcome.'

'Tell her that she is always welcome at my court and in time, I'm sure we will become powerful allies.'

'I will,' said the bishop, 'but for now, I will bid you farewell.'

'Travel safely, Your Grace,' said Sibylla as a servant closed the tailgate.

'Oh, one more thing,' said the Bishop as the cart-master climbed up onto his seat behind the horses, 'should things turn out not quite the way you expect, do not take it personally, it's just the way of the world.'

Sibylla's eyes narrowed as she considered the statement.

'What do you mean?' she asked.

'God works in mysterious ways, my lady,' shouted the bishop as the cart lurched forward, 'I wish you a long and fruitful reign.'

Sibylla watched him leave, still none the wiser about what he was talking about. Finally, she turned to walk back into the halls of the citadel. Whatever he meant, it was pointless worrying for by the time he reached Nablus, she would be Queen of Jerusalem, and there was nothing he or anybody else could do about it.

The following day, the nobles and priests of Jerusalem gathered in the Church of the Holy Sepulcher to witness Sibylla's coronation. The dome echoed to the sound of the hundred monks praying and chanting their incantations. Everyone in attendance saw the moment as a spiritual, yet unifying event as at last, after many years, they had a worthy and more importantly, healthy monarch to defend the Holy-land and lead the fight against the Saracens.

When the moment came, Sibylla knelt on a red velvet cushion as the Bishop of Jerusalem placed the gold crown upon her head, and everyone knelt in prayer. Finally, the prayers came to an end, and Sibylla walked up to the two waiting thrones. The larger of the two was empty, as she had the Diadem upon her head, but the second throne contained a crown, waiting for whomever she would proclaim king to sit beside her. She picked up the crown and turned to face the congregation. As she watched, a line of eligible nobles walked to the front, each one nominated by the Haute Cour as suitable candidates to be the new king.

'Two days ago,' announced Sibylla as the room waited in anticipation, 'I swore before God to divorce my husband for the good of Jerusalem. This I did, fulfilling my vow. Now, as Queen of Jerusalem, I fulfil the second part of my pledge and will select a king I believe will lead Jerusalem and rest of Christendom in God's service.' She looked along the line of candidates, each strong and noble knights from reputable families, and all with money and status. All were fair to the eye, and she considered for several minutes before taking a deep breath and addressing the congregation once again.

'My lords and ladies,' she said, 'my freedom of choice was given by the Bishop of Jerusalem in full sight of the Haute Cour and of God. Fealty was sworn by all present, accepting that the final choice was mine. Therefore, as it says in the bible, let not man put asunder, that which God hath coupled together, I hereby choose Sir Guy of Lusignan as my king.' She turned to her ex-husband. 'Sire, come forth and receive this crown, for I know no other man in Christendom more deserving.'

For a few moments, there was silence as Sibylla's choice sunk in, but as Guy stepped forward from his place at the back of the congregation, the air filled with challenge and argument.

'Shame on you,' called a voice. 'You have betrayed Jerusalem and God.'

'Treachery,' shouted another, 'how can we trust a word you say.'

More complaints followed, but as Guy continued his journey through the crowd, Raynald of Chatillon walked up to the bishop, speaking urgently into his ear. Finally, Guy climbed up onto the podium. Not once since he had left the back of the room did his eyes leave those of the woman he loved. He dropped to his knees on the same cushion that Sibylla had used only moments earlier, and as he waited, the bishop walked to the centre of the dais to address the angry crowd. He raised his staff, and the congregation fell quiet.

'People of Jerusalem,' he said. 'The choice of king was unexpected, but do not forget, two days ago, many in this room witnessed the pledge with their own eyes and agreed the final choice lay with the queen. Consequently, in the eyes of this church and in sight of the holy spirit, the decision is just.' He turned to Sibylla. 'Sibylla, he said, Queen of Jerusalem, you may crown your king.'

Sibylla looked down at Guy, and as more of the congregation voiced their outrage, she crowned her ex-husband, Guy of Lusignan, King of Jerusalem.

Twelve leagues away, Isabella sat at a table, her head in her hands. Opposite her sat her stepfather, Balian of Ibelin. At the far end of the room, Raymond of Tripoli paced the floor, his face red from rage.

'I knew it,' he said, 'I should have gone there myself. How could the bishop have allowed this to happen? Where is he anyway, he should be here answering for his actions?'

'He has retreated to the church for seven days of prayer,' said Isabella, looking up. 'The doors are locked, and he has left instructions that he is not to be disturbed.'

'We should break them down and drag him here by his heels,' snarled Raymond, 'the man is an imbecile.'

'We will do no such thing,' said Isabella with a sigh. 'He said that there was nothing he could do, William of Tyre expertly manipulated the Haute Cour in Sibylla's favour.'

'Helped by your husband pledging his support to Sibylla,' said Raymond, 'we should have him executed as soon as he returns.'

'What is the point?' asked Balian. 'What is done is done. All we can do now is plan our next move.'

'Our next move? Well, that is plainly obvious, we muster our armies and march on Jerusalem immediately. We will drag Sibylla from the citadel and proclaim Isabella as the true queen.'

'Listen to yourself,' shouted Balian, 'do you even know what you are suggesting? Do you really believe that we can lay siege to the Holy-city without every man in the Outremer rallying to her call?'

'Why not,' asked Raymond, 'the coronation was illegal, and if we act quickly, we can have men within the city before anyone realizes what is happening?'

'Raymond,' said Balian, 'there are over two hundred Templar knights in Jerusalem, another hundred Knights Hospitaller and heaven knows how many other men at arms, all loyal to Sibylla. If you do this, the streets will run with Christian blood, just at the time when we should be uniting against Saladin.'

'This whole affair is unjust and illegal,' said Raymond, 'and an affront to Isabella. I will not see it go un-rectified.'

'Enough,' said Isabella. 'There will be no attack on Jerusalem, and there will be no further counterclaim to the throne, at least not in my name. Let Sibylla have her moment of glory, and when the dust settles, I will pledge allegiance.'

'What?' gasped Raymond. 'Are you mad?'

'I have had my fill of plot and counterplot,' said Isabella, 'and will have nothing more to do with this situation. Sir Balian is right; it is time to move our focus onto the threat from Saladin. We have lost, Sir Raymond, our race has been run.'

The Count of Tripoli stared at her, hardly able to believe what he was hearing.

'No,' he said eventually, his voice heavy with menace. 'You may be giving up, but I will not. An imposter sits on the throne of Jerusalem, and as long as I have breath in my body, I will do whatever I can to make the situation right.'

'What are you going to do?' asked Balian.

'What I must,' said Raymond. 'Jerusalem may have been taken in by the woman's witchcraft, but Tiberias is populated by men of better sense. If you will not claim what is yours, Isabella, then I will. My grandfather was King Baldwin, the second of that name, so I have a worthy claim. Perhaps I should have pressed it sooner, but one thing is certain, I will die pursuing what is right rather than let that woman spend a day longer than necessary on the throne of Jerusalem. Fare ye well, Balian, good luck in serving Sibylla, I think you are going to need it.'

Without another word, he turned and left the room, slamming the door behind him.

'What is he going to do?' asked Isabella, 'surely he does not mean to declare war on Jerusalem?'

'His wife has ruled Tiberias for many years,' said Balian, 'and both are well thought of within the city. I suspect it would not take much to rally the occupants to his cause. I fear this is going to escalate, my lady, and when it does, we must be in a position to respond. I think our lives may depend on it.'

Chapter Twelve

Karak

October - AD 1186

Sumeira and John Loxley walked up the hill to the upper compound of Karak castle. The gates were open though guarded by two soldiers, each armed with lances and swords. Up above on the inner curtain-wall, another dozen soldiers looked down, watching the daily life that went on in the lower bailey.

'Hold there,' said one of the guards as they reached the drawbridge over the deep ditch surrounding the inner compound, 'state your purpose.'

'I have business with the Templars,' said Sumeira.

'What sort of business?'

'I wish to exchange a promissory note for money.'

'How much money?' asked the other guard.

'With respect,' said Sumeira, 'that is none of your business.'

'Oooh, a feisty one,' said his comrade. 'Watch your mouth, lady, you never know who may be wandering around the lower bailey in the darkest hours, and you wouldn't want to get hurt, would you?'

'Are you saying I am in danger?' asked Sumeira. 'Because if you are, I am sure the castle steward, who by the way, is a very good friend of mine, would be only too happy to ask you a few questions. Just to ensure my safety, you understand.'

'You know the steward?' asked the guard.

'Aye, I do. Arturas and I have been friends for many years. Now, are you going to let me through or not?'

The guard stepped aside, mumbling under his breath.

'The treasury is in the commandery,' said the second guard as they passed, 'over in that building.'

They followed the guard's directions before banging on a locked door, set deep into the wall. Eventually, they heard the sound of locks being drawn back and a servant peered around the door.

'We would like to speak to the treasurer,' said John Loxley.

'To what end?'

'We have a letter of credit,' said Sumeira, 'and wish to draw out funds.'

'Wait there,' said the servant and shut the door, locking it securely behind him. Ten minutes later he reappeared and this time, led them to a room at the end of a narrow passage. Inside, an aged Templar sat behind a trestle table, writing carefully into a giant ledger. The servant pointed to two chairs he had placed on the near side of the table. 'Wait,' he said, 'Brother Justin will attend you when he has finished his task.'

Sumeira and John Loxley watched with fascination as the knight created the perfectly formed words on the parchment with quill and ink, each carefully crafted and in a perfect line with its neighbour. Eventually, he finished writing and after blowing gently on the last of the wet ink, replaced the quill in the pot and carried it over to a niche in one of the walls. When he returned, he closed the book and placed it to one side on the pristine cloth covering the table, leaving only an ornate handled knife remaining before him.

'John Loxley,' he said eventually, looking up, 'and Sumeira of Greece. I hear you have a letter of credit and wish to draw down funds.'

'You know our names?' said Sumeira. 'How?'

'Of course, I know you,' said the knight. 'You are the physicians who run the hospital in the lower bailey, which, can I remind you, is currently earning no money for our order.'

'It is an agreement we have with the under-marshal,' said John Loxley.

'I know what it is,' said the knight, turning to stare at the man, 'I am just reminding you before we start that you are already in our debt. Now, what exactly is it that you want?'

'Brother Justin,' said Sumeira, 'my family deposited an amount of money in one of your treasuries in Greece and have sent me a letter of credit. I would now like to draw down the equivalent amount of funds.'

'And how much is this deposit?' asked the knight.

'Twelve pounds of silver,' said Sumeira, 'but we would prefer the weight in pennies rather than bars or artefacts.'

'Twelve pounds of silver pennies,' said the Templar, 'and what do you intend to do with such an amount?'

'Does it matter?' asked Sumeira. 'The money is legitimately mine, and surely I can spend it as I see fit?'

'You can,' said the knight, 'but twelve pounds of silver pennies is quite an amount, and certainly difficult to carry around without drawing the attention of those who would slit your throats to obtain it.'

'I know the risks,' said Sumeira producing the letter of credit, 'but would still like to draw the money down.' She slid the letter across the table.

Brother Justin stared at Sumeira for several moments before picking up the letter and sliding the blade behind the fold to cut the seal. He slowly read the letter before placing it back on the table and looking again at the physicians.

'The letter of credit is good,' he said, 'and I am happy to authorize six pounds of silver pennies, to be taken immediately.'

'Six pounds?' said Sumeira glancing at her husband, 'but we asked for twelve.'

'And twelve you will get,' said the Templar, 'six now and six when you produce a child before me called Jamal, along with evidence that he is indeed who you claim him to be.'

'I do not understand,' said Sumeira, 'how do you know my son's name?'

'Because it is written upon the letter of credit,' said the treasurer. 'Your family deposited twelve pounds of silver as requested, but on the condition that you were only issued the second half of the money upon delivery of your son. It is apparent from the letter that you intend to seek this child and use the funds to procure an armed escort to take you to Segor. This in itself is a risky business, and though I cannot stop you from trying, I strongly advise that you do not carry out this quest, not if you value your own lives.'

'Our lives are ours to live or lose,' said Sumeira. 'We do not answer to you or anyone else. Now give me my money.'

'Under our terms of service,' replied brother Justin calmly, 'I am bound by the letter's contents, and that clearly states, only six pounds of silver is to be paid upfront. With regards to answering to our authority, can I remind you that while you work and live within the walls of Karak, you are bound by our laws. Now, I cannot order you to stay or to go, but I am just saying that we already know Saladin is recruiting a vast army. In particular, we know he has warriors in Segor recruiting men to fight under his banner. If you were to go there, even with an armed escort, I suspect you would be either dead or enslaved within days, and the remaining six pounds of silver would forever remain unclaimed. So, what I would recommend is that you take some of your money to make your lives a little more comfortable but leave the rest with us for safekeeping. Before this year is out, we will know Saladin's intentions one way or another, and when we do, perhaps we can discuss the matter further.'

'Is there a higher authority to whom we can appeal?' asked John Loxley.

'You can wait until the castellan returns from Jerusalem,' said the knight, 'he may even be accompanied by the grandmaster himself, but I promise you the answer will be the same. Who would ever trust us again if it were revealed that we did not adhere to the contents of promissory notes?'

Sumeira stared at the knight, barely concealing her anger. Six pounds of silver was a princely amount, but she knew it was not enough. Despite her ire, she knew there was nothing she could do.

'I will take the half,' she said eventually, 'as per the letter, but will return to argue my case when the castellan returns.'

'As you wish,' said the knight and got to his feet. 'Remain here; I will get your money.'

Ten minutes later, he returned with a large bag of coins and a set of scales. Carefully he poured silver pennies into one of the trays until the scales were balanced. The servant took away the larger bag, and the knight poured the weighed coins into six smaller bags.

'You will sign a receipt,' he said, retrieving the journal he had been writing in earlier.

'Of course,' said John Loxley and waited as Sumeira signed her name.

'I have altered your letter of credit to reflect the withdrawal,' said brother Justin. 'If you decide to go ahead with this folly, and if by God's grace you are successful, just present it at any Templar treasury, along with your son, and you will receive the rest of your funds. Of course, if you present a child that does not look like you, or without proof that he is the correct child, we will confiscate the money, and you will be tried as a criminal.'

'What is to stop you doing that anyway?' asked Sumeira getting to her feet.

'My lady,' said the knight, 'we are a religious order, devoted to God's service. There is no need to lower ourselves to the standards of the devil. Now, is there anything else I can help you with?'

'No,' said Sumeira, 'we are done.'

'In that case, I wish you well,' said the knight and turned away as the servant stepped forward to show them out. As they walked through the door, the knight spoke up again.

'Oh,' he said, 'forgive me, but there is one more thing. Bearing in mind that you are now a wealthy woman, I no longer see the need to offer you premises for free. Henceforth you will pay rent on the hospital at the going rate. I will draw up the paperwork and have it sent down to you by tomorrow night. Thank you for your business.'

Sumeira scowled at the treasurer but said nothing. Instead, they just turned and walked down into the lower bailey.

Later that night, John Loxley and Sumeira sat at the small table in their room at the back of the stores. One thousand, four hundred and forty silver pennies lay in a small mound between them, the sum total of the six bags they had obtained from the Templar treasury.

'I suppose your family thought it was too much to risk the whole amount,' said John, 'and split it thus to ensure you had money to return to Greece.'

'That would be my mother,' said Sumeira, 'she was always the careful one. '

'So, what do we do now?'

'I'm not sure,' said Sumeira, 'how much does a good man cost to hire?'

'I have no idea.'

'Neither do I,' said Sumeira, 'but I know someone who has spent many years dealing with such situations.'

'I assume you speak of Arturas?'

'I do, he was a mercenary for many years so not only will he know where to find the sort of men we need, but also how much it is going to cost.'

'I'll go and find him,' said John and left Sumeira to pack away the money. Ten minutes later, the two men returned and sat at the table as Sumeira scooped three jacks of ale from a lidded barrel in the corner.'

'You wanted to see me,' said Arturas, after sipping his ale. 'If it is about the new rent for the hospital, I am sorry, but there is nothing I can do about it. The Templars own this castle and can charge whatever they want.'

'It's not about the rent,' said Sumeira, 'though I'm not happy they have changed their minds.'

'You must have angered them in some way,' said Arturas, 'what did you do?'

'Nothing really,' said Sumeira, 'they just found out we had come into some money and decided that we could afford to pay rent.'

'Ah, I see,' said Arturas. 'You have obviously received your money from Greece. How much are we talking about?'

'Over fourteen hundred silver pennies,' said Sumeira.

Arturas glanced between the two physicians.

'I am no moneyer,' he said eventually, 'but even I know that does not equate to twelve pounds of silver.'

'It is half,' said Sumeira, and went on to explain the situation.

'So,' said Arturas, 'what is it you want of me?' If it is to ride at your side, then regretfully I will have to decline as, in my current state, I would be a liability rather than an aid.'

'I realise that,' said Sumeira, 'and have only asked you here to ask for guidance.'

'In what way?'

'Our money is limited, and we have no idea how much anything costs. I can ask around the taverns, but that would mean drawing attention to our situation and suggest to many that we may have money to steal.'

'A sensible decision,' said Arturas. 'What do you want to know?'

'First of all,' said Sumeira, 'how much will experienced men at arms cost us?'

'That depends,' said Arturas, 'are we talking about knights or foot soldiers?'

'We will not be able to afford knights,' said John, 'but we do need mounted men.'

'Then we are talking about mercenaries,' said Arturas. 'One man, fully armed and with his own horse will cost you at least five pennies a day, perhaps more. Allow for his food and fodder for his horse, and you are looking at eight pennies a day. If the work is prolonged, he may reduce it a little, but you would want the best so allow the full amount.'

'So, if we allow fifteen days,' said Sumeira, 'five to get there, five days to find Jamal and another five to return, I currently have enough coins for twenty men.'

'It will not take ten days to get to Segor,' said Arturas, 'it is no more than twelve leagues away and can be done in two.'

'I know,' said Sumeira, 'but we will have to travel by night and take the lesser roads. I have been told the route is dangerous and Saladin has eyes everywhere.'

'Even so,' said Arturas, 'a body of men that large will be noticed. If you are determined to do this, I would recommend taking no more than two men, three at most. That way their passing may go unnoticed. I can recommend some men I know, hard men, but honest and well-used to the ways of the desert. They are not cheap, but they are the best around. I expect they would ride with you, but considering the risk, I would offer no less than ten pennies a day for a fixed term of twenty days, half upfront and half upon completion.'

'That could cost me half my purse,' said Sumeira.

'A price worth paying,' said Arturas, 'trust me, you do not want to trust your lives of lesser men, especially as you are going south.'

'Anything else?'

'You will need your own horse, and provisions of course. Allow another two hundred or so for those, but you will also need a good scout, preferably a Bedouin, to lead the way.'

'Do you know of any?'

'Not at the moment, but there is an alternative.'

'Which is?'

'The best scout I have ever ridden alongside.'

'And who is this man?'

'You already know him,' said Arturas,' I'm talking about Hunter.'

'Hunter is here?' gasped Sumeira, remembering one of the men who she had met in Segor years previously.

'He is not, but he is nearby. He owns a farm a few leagues from here, but I have heard his crops are failing and he is available for work. I'm sure if we ask him, he would be more than willing to help.'

'And the cost?'

'About the same as the others,' said Arturas, 'perhaps a little more.'

'That settles it,' said Sumeira, 'we'll engage Hunter as a scout, and along with two men of your choice, we'll start making plans as soon as we can.'

'Allowing another two hundred pennies for Hunter,' said John, 'leaves only a few hundred for bribes. It is not enough.'

'Leave that to me,' she said, 'I've had an idea.' She turned back to the steward. 'Arturas, thank you for your help. Could you now seek two suitable men on our behalf and contact Hunter? If he is agreeable, we will set out as soon as we are able. I will. Of course, pay you for your trouble.'

'There is no need for payment, my lady,' he said, 'consider it my contribution towards your quest.'

'Thank you,' said Sumeira.

'Are you sure about this?' asked Arturas. 'For the undertaking is fraught with danger and has little chance of success.'

'I've never been surer of anything in my life,' said Sumeira. 'You just find the men, leave the rest to me.'

The following morning, Sumeira once more sat at the table in the Templar treasury. A servant waited in silence near the door, waiting for brother Justin to arrive. Again, she looked around the room, impressed with the cleanliness, despite the sparsity of furniture.

'It is very clean in here,' she said, 'how is it kept so?'

'It is cleaned every day before final prayers,' said the servant, 'every inch scrubbed and washed with rose water, from floor to ceiling.'

'That must be hard work,' said Sumeira.

'I wouldn't know,' said the servant, 'for it is brother Justin who carries out the task, not I.'

'The treasurer cleans the room?' asked Sumeira, 'why?'

'You will have to ask him, my lady,' came the reply.

'Ask him what?' asked brother Justin entering the room.

'I was just commenting how clean this place is,' said Sumeira, 'and I understand it is your own hands that make it so.'

'Apart from prayer and meals, I spend my life in these rooms and have done so for many years. What message would I be sending if those who ask us to look after their money think we cannot even look after the room we work in?'

'Very noble of you,' said Sumeira.

'Can I get you some water?' asked brother Justin.

'I would like that very much,' said Sumeira, 'thank you.'

The treasurer walked over to a table and poured water from a pitcher into the most ornate glass Sumeira had ever seen.

'That's beautiful,' she gasped as he placed it before her. 'Where is it from?'

'I believe it was a gift from Saladin himself to a previous castellan,' said the knight. 'Unfortunately, when brother Raynald of Chatillon took over the position, he had every item of Saracen origin removed from sight.'

'Why?'

'I do not answer for the castellan,' said the knight, 'but there were twenty-four such glasses along with an exquisite glass pitcher. In a moment of weakness, I asked if I could have the set for my own quarters, but luckily for me, the castellan saw that it was the devil controlling my mind and smashed all except the glass in your hand. It was spared only to remind me of my weakness, and I will take it to my grave. So, what can I do for you today?'

'I am here to ask you for more money,' said Sumeira. 'Another six pounds of silver pennies.'

'I have already told you,' said the treasurer, 'the letter of credit forbids it.'

'I know, but I do not want that money, I am here to ask for a loan.'

'A loan?'

'Yes, for six pounds of silver pennies.'

'And what collateral do you have to secure such an amount?'

'The rest of the money from my mother,' said Sumeira.

The knight's eyes narrowed momentarily as he tried to decipher what was going on.

'I see you are confused, brother Justin,' said Sumeira, 'so let me explain. I have read the letter several times, and though it forbids me drawing down the remaining funds, it says nothing about using it as collateral against a loan.'

'It does not,' confirmed the knight.

'So,' continued Sumeira, 'I see no reason why I cannot take a loan, at the appropriate rate of interest, of course, using the remainder of the money as surety. If I am successful, I will repay the order when I draw down the balance, but if I default, you will have my signature to say you can use it to pay off the loan. I believe that is entirely ethical and fair, meeting all the requirements of the letter as well as maintaining the highest standards of the order.'

'Interesting,' said the treasurer, 'but matters of contractual alteration can only be agreed by the castellan himself, and he is in Jerusalem. I can agree in principle but cannot release the funds.'

'In any circumstance?'

'There is some leeway, but, in this case, I would prefer his countersignature.'

Sumeira thought quickly. The man before her had already admitted a fondness for finery, and there was one more thing she could try. It was risky, but she was desperate and had no other choice.

'Brother Justin,' she said eventually, 'yesterday, you gave us six bags of coins.'

'That is correct,' said the treasurer, 'exactly six pounds of silver. You saw me weigh it out.'

'I did, and I have no argument, the weighing was fair. If you agree to the loan and release the funds today, I will gladly sign for a similar amount,' she paused for a moment, gathering courage for what she was about to say.

'And?' asked the knight.

'But take only five bags,' she blurted out suddenly, her eyes screwed shut.

For a few moments, there was silence as the offer of a bribe sunk in. If the knight were honest, she could be arrested immediately and locked in a cell to be judged when the castellan returned, but it was her only chance of getting enough money, and now she had said it, there was no going back. As she waited, the images of the bodies rotting in the pit flooded into her mind, her probable fate if the knight before her was honest. Eventually, she opened her eyes and stared at the treasurer. He had neither spoken nor moved for over a minute.

'Well,' she said, swallowing hard, 'do we have a deal?'

Chapter Thirteen

Acre

November - AD 1186

Guy of Lusignan sat on an ornate chair in the council chamber in the Templar commandery in Acre. Around the central table sat the most important nobles in the Outremer, including the Templar grandmaster-Gerard of Ridefort, The Knights Hospitaller grandmaster-Roger De-Moulins, Balian of Ibelin and Reginald, Count of Sidon. Raynald of Chatillon, however, had returned to Karak to see to pressing business.

The meeting had been called by Guy ostensibly as an ascension council, but the men present were under no illusions, it was also meant as an opportunity to pay homage to Guy's new role as king. After Raymond of Tripoli had returned to his wife's fief of Galilee, Balian of Ibelin had reluctantly pledged his oath to Sibylla, despite still being a long-standing friend of Raymond.

For two days, nobles from across the Outremer came to pledge their allegiance, or at least to sign treaties of peace with Jerusalem, but the biggest, Raymond of Tripoli was conspicuous by his absence. When the formalities were over, most of those summoned headed off home, but Guy had requested that those now gathered in the chamber to stay to discuss the errant count's absence.

'Gentlemen,' said Guy when everyone had settled down. 'As you know, when I became king, I offered the hand of friendship to every noble across the Outremer, even those who did not support my wife in her claim to the throne.' He glanced at Balian before continuing. 'Most accepted,' he continued, 'but as we are all aware, Raymond has decided to snub Jerusalem and now hides behind his wife in Tiberias. Despite my messages, he continues to ignore me, and my spies tell me that he still has sights on the crown himself.

'They are the rantings of a disappointed man only,' said Balian. 'Give him some time, and he will see sense.'

'You would think so,' said Guy, 'and I was indeed leaning towards such thinking, except for two things. The first is that he has moved his army from his own fiefdom at Beirut and marched them into Tiberias. This in itself is a threat to Jerusalem as Tiberias is the main obstacle to Saladin if he decides to ride from Damascus in the north. If we cannot rely on the garrison at Tiberias to defend the northern roads, the Holy-city itself is at risk.'

'I cannot see that happening,' said Balian. 'Raymond may be stubborn, but he is no fool. He would never allow Saracens an open road to the heart of Christendom.'

'Oh, no?' asked Guy. 'Then perhaps you can explain this.' He threw a folded parchment across the table towards Balian. The Count of Ibelin stared at the king before opening the document and reading it silently to himself. Finally, he looked up, his face ashen.

'No,' he said, 'this cannot be true.'

'Whose signature lays at the bottom,' asked Guy.

'The Bishop of Nazareth,' said Balian quietly.

'Sorry,' said the king, 'please speak up.'

'The Bishop of Nazareth,' said Balian again.

'That is right, said Guy, the Bishop of Nazareth himself. Now, unless you know something that I do not, I am inclined to believe a man who holds such a high station in the service of the lord.'

'What does it say?' asked Gerard of Ridefort, growing impatient.

'Tell them,' said the king

Balian glanced down at the letter.

'It says,' he said eventually, 'that Raymond of Tripoli has requested a truce with Saladin, promising that if the Ayyubid attack Jerusalem, he will not intervene.'

'What?' gasped Gerard and the room broke into cries of anger and disgust as each took it in turn to read the letter.

Guy waited until the noise abated, the whole time his eyes never leaving those of Balian's. Finally, he held up his hand, and as the men fell silent, he turned to face them.

'This letter, if true,' he said, 'and I have no reason to believe it is not, means that not only do we have a man who covets the crown of Jerusalem sitting in one of our most important defensive cities at the head of a strong army, but that man will soon be an ally of our most feared enemy, Saladin. This situation is unprecedented and demands immediate action. That, my lords, is why I bade you remain. Now, the question is, what are we going to do about it?'

Raynald of Chatillon rode along the southern road to the east of the Salt-sea, glad to be away from the formalities and constraints of Acre. Two men rode before him, each with a banner atop a lance, one with the colours of Karak, the other showing the emblem of the Templars. Sir Jakelin de-Mailly rode beside him, and behind them, a double column of a hundred knights stretched out behind, each glad to see the back of the coastal city and its claustrophobic streets.

Out here Raynald felt he could breathe, unconstrained by the dense population, the formalities demanded by royal protocol and the complexities of political allegiances that followed everyone around like a bad smell.

The open plains of the Oultrejordain, by comparison, were places where a man could think and live with fresh air in his lungs and freedom in his heart. Every hour they rode, the terrain changed, from rocky hills and barren landscapes to lush green orchards of olive trees and carefully tended fields of crops. This was the place he loved the most, the beautiful lands east of the Salt-sea that he called home.

It had been a strange few weeks since Sibylla had been crowned Queen of Jerusalem. The anticipated uprising had not materialized, and the threat from Saladin's forces seemed to have diminished. Even the threat from the brigands that haunted the southern road seemed to have eased.

A movement caught Raynald's eye, and he looked over to see two riders galloping down the hill towards them, each clad in the black thawbs of the Bedouin scouts used by the garrison at Karak. He held up his arm, drawing the column to a halt and waited until the scouts rode up before stopping their own horses in a cloud of dust.

'My lord,' said one, 'there is a caravan less than half a league west of here heading north on the lesser road.'

'And?'

'I think it may be of interest to you, my lord, the people are Ayyubid and the caravan is protected by fifty horsemen.'

Raymond stared at the scouts. Ayyubid caravans were no stranger to the roads between Damascus and Egypt, but to be protected by what was a considerable force of horsemen, could mean one of two things. Either the goods on the caravan were extremely valuable, or it was carrying some very important passengers. Either way, his interest was piqued, and he knew he wanted to find out more.

'Are there any foot soldiers?' he asked.

'No, my lord. The horsemen ride either side of the caravan and are spread thinly with ten acting as an advance guard.'

'How many carts?'

'About fifty in total.'

'And the ground?'

'Open hills to the east, but a rocky hill on the western flank. A league to their front the slope becomes wooded with many trees, but it is sound underfoot and suitable for a mounted force to descend at speed.'

'Excellent,' said Raynald. 'Thank you, Mustafa. As usual, your information is both informative and concise.' He turned to Sir Jakelin. 'What do you think, my friend, shall we take a look?'

'I am yours to command,' said Jakelin, 'but would urge caution. Jerusalem still has a treaty of sorts with Saladin, and if we were to break it, it might give the sultan the excuse he needs to declare full war.'

'The treaty is nought but empty words on worthless parchment,' said Raynald. 'It is no secret that Saladin courts the tribes of the east to furnish him with men for his campaign against Jerusalem. Why would he do that if he meant to keep the peace?'

'His actions are cause for concern,' said Jakelin, 'but we should be careful not to add fuel to the fire. The alliance between the barons is fragile at the moment, and a united front may be difficult to achieve.'

'Your concerns are noted,' said Raymond, 'but nevertheless, I wish to see what sort of caravan demands fifty fully armed Saracens as an escort. Call the men to arms, brother, let us see what they are hiding.'

In the counsel room in Acre, the men had fallen quiet, shocked that one of their own had betrayed not only them but Christianity as a whole by promising not to fight the Saracens should they attack Jerusalem.

'I still find it hard to believe,' said Balian, 'I thought I knew the man. Never did I suspect he could do anything like this.'

'He should be stripped of all titles immediately,' said Gerard of Ridefort, 'and proclaimed a traitor.'

'That goes without saying,' said Guy, 'but titles are only words, and the removal is symbolic only.'

'Then confiscate his lands,' said Gerard. 'Without his income from Beirut, he will not be able to maintain his army for more than a few months.'

'Beirut is a fiefdom under the law,' said Balian, 'and has been so for generations.'

'Any fief is required to provide support to Jerusalem in time of crisis,' said Gerard, 'and as Raymond has already declared he will not meet that commitment, then he can no longer lay claim to the title.'

'So, what about Tiberias? asked Reginald, 'do we strip his wife of that fief?'

'His wife has committed no crime,' interjected Balian,' nor has she signed any treaty with Saladin. The treachery, if true, is his and his alone.'

'I suggest we brand him a traitor,' said Gerard, 'strip him of his fiefdom and march upon Tiberias as soon as we are able.'

'Wait,' said Roger De-Moulins, 'if you are suggesting waging war on fellow Christians, then I will have no part of it.'

'Then what do you suggest we do?' snapped his counterpart, 'let him get away with treachery?'

'We will negotiate,' said Sir Roger, 'point out the errors of his ways and demand he withdraws his men from Tiberias.'

'To where?' asked Gerard, 'if we are to take his fiefdom, he has nowhere to go.'

'Then he must disband his army and seek refuge in Tripoli. Whatever the answer, I will not raise a sword against a fellow Christian unless in self-defence.'

'Enough,' interrupted Guy, 'we argue like washerwomen. Sir Gerard is right, and we cannot let Raymond get away with this affront to Jerusalem, but Sir Roger also has a point, and we must exhaust every avenue before waging a war we cannot afford.' He paused and looked around the room. 'So, this is what we will do. Raymond of Tripoli is forthwith branded a traitor to Jerusalem and to the church. With immediate effect, he is forbidden to enter any place of worship outside the walls of Tiberias. Messengers will be sent throughout the Outremer telling them of this edict. Furthermore, he is immediately stripped of the fiefdom of Beirut, with that lordship to be awarded to a more deserving man as and when I see fit.' He turned to Balian. 'Sir Balian, you know

Raymond well. I charge you with the following task. You will ride to Tiberias and inform him of my decision. Tell him that he has until Easter to disband his army and leave Tiberias. Do that, and he will be allowed to travel to Tripoli without threat. However, if he misses the deadline, I will personally lead Jerusalem's army against Tiberias and if necessary, burn the city to the ground. Tell him that this is not open to negotiation. Is that clear?'

'It is, Your Grace,' said Balian.

'Good.' He turned to face the rest of the room. 'Gentlemen, I believe I am being overly fair in this decree, but if you have argument, state it now or forever hold your peace.' When nobody responded, he got to his feet. 'I thought as much,' he said 'so, in that case, our work here is over. Now, let us disperse for there is God's work to be done.'

Two hours after the scouts had first reported the caravan's position, Sir Jakelin and Raymond sat astride their horses hidden amongst a forest of olive trees. Behind them, their men spread out in line abreast waiting for the signal to advance. Through the trees, they saw the advance guards pass and a few minutes later, the first of the flanking horsemen. Raynald stared down as the caravan finally came into view. Consisting of over fifty carts and as many heavily laden camels and mules, it was obviously a trade caravan intended for Damascus, and though he knew all such travellers were protected by the treaty, his appetite was whetted. It could only have come from Egypt, and that meant there could be all sorts of riches being transported. He turned to face Jakelin.

'I have seen enough,' he said, 'prepare the men.'

Although doubting his commander's motives, Jakelin nodded his assent. His role was not to question his superiors but to provide his sword arm when required. This was such an occasion. He held his arm up into the air, his fist clenched. To either side, each man repeated the signal until everyone knew what was coming.

'Ready?' asked Raynald, still staring down at the caravan.

'Ready,' replied Jakelin.

'Advance,' said Raynald and urged his horse to a steady walk down through the trees.

Jakelin lowered his arm to point down the hill, his palm open and fingers extended. Either side of him, the rest of the

Templar knights urged their own horses into action, and the whole line started to ride down towards the caravan.

As the knights came into view, many of the wagons came to a halt and fear crept into the hearts of everyone in the caravan. They too knew that they were protected by a treaty, but Raynald's reputation preceded them, and they knew the southern road crossed through the heart of his territory.

Within moments, the Ayyubid outriders saw the threat and accompanied by shouts of warning and bravado, turned their horses to assemble into a defensive line between the Christians and the caravan. Raynald held up his arm and called out to the men either side of him.

'Close quarters, draw lances.'

Each of the knights closed into the centre and lifted their lances out of their holders in preparation for the attack. On either side of the Templars, another hundred riders appeared, the ever-present Turcopole cavalry who rode in support of the Christians.

Seeing the three strong units spread out across the hill, most of the defenders realised that resistance was pointless, and the anticipated charge never came. The Saracen commanding the line was furious, and his voice echoed up the hill, demanding his men attacked the Christians.

The line of mounted knights continued their advance down the hill, this time at a canter and as their speed increased, the Saracen escort broke ranks with many turning to ride away in a cloud of dust. Within moments the rest of the warriors followed suit and followed them down the hill to head for the barren foothills on the far side of the road. All that is, except one, the older warrior in charge of the escort.

The lone Saracen rider stared at the knights racing towards him, knowing his time on earth had finally come to an end. For the briefest of moments, he pictured his four wives and many children, but the thought passed quickly for though he had been abandoned by those he called brother, he knew he would soon enter the gates of paradise. He reached across and drew his scimitar from his belt.

'Allahu Akbar,' he roared and kicked the horse into a gallop, straight up the hill to meet the approaching Christians.

The Templars were now formed into a tight formation, a solid line of hardened men used to the furnace of battle. The classic line abreast formation was the preferred choice against any enemy force, and no man would break the line no matter how dense the enemy force. But with only a single man before them, Raynald shouted a fresh order along the line.

'Templars hold,' he roared, and the advance came to a shuddering halt.

'Sir Jakelin,' said Raynald, 'you will continue alone. Make an example of this simpleton.'

'Aye, my lord,' said Jakelin, and with a kick of his heels, continued his advance. Quickly his horse gathered speed, and as it broke into a gallop, Jakelin lowered his lance, tucking it tightly into the crook of his arm.

The Saracen kicked his own horse harder, and as the two men closed in on each other, everyone watching knew there could only ever be one victor. The two horses smashed together in a cloud of dust, and for a moment, nobody in the Christian ranks or the caravan could see the outcome, but as the dust settled, they could see only one man still sat upon his mount, Jakelin De Mailly, minus his lance.

As everyone watched, the Templar knight dismounted and walked over to the Saracen warrior, now on his knees with the lance sticking out of his back. He was still alive, but obviously mortally wounded.

As Jakelin approached the Saracen reached for the scimitar laying in the dust beside him. Jakelin kicked it away and stared down at his opponent. The man had been brave but foolhardy.

'You should have run with your comrades,' said Jakelin drawing his sword.

'I run from no infidel,' said the man through gritted teeth,

'You speak our language,' said Jakelin with surprise.

'The words foul my mouth,' gasped the man, obviously in great pain, 'but know this. By your acts today, you have sealed the fate of all the infidels. When the blood of thousands turns the desert red, know that it was your blade that consigned them to the grave.'

'Your words are nothing more than a dying man's curse,' said Jakelin, 'and I pay them no heed.'

'Perhaps not,' said the Saracen, 'but when you breathe your last, you will remember me, infidel. Now do what you must.'

Jakelin adjusted his feet, so they were shoulder-width apart.

'Say your last, Saracen,' said Jakelin, 'for your time is over.'

'Allahu Akbar,' whispered the Saracen and no sooner had the words left his lips than Jakelin's sword swept downward to cut clean through his enemy's neck.

Ten minutes later, every person in the caravan was lined up along the road, each on their knees with their hands behind their heads. The full force of Templar knights lined up before them, still astride their horses as a reminder that it was pointless trying to run. Many of the Turcopoles had dismounted to search the carts and had already uncovered many fine things from spices to the finest silks. Raynald and Jakelin walked slowly along the line of prisoners until finally, they came to a stop and stared down at a woman entirely covered head to foot with golden silk.

Raynald drew his knife and reaching down, lifted the veil with the tip of his blade, revealing the face of an extraordinarily beautiful young woman.

'Who are you?' he asked, using the local dialect.

'My name is Takisha,' she said quietly, 'the second cousin to Muzaffar ad-Din Gokbori.'

'Gokbori,' said Jakelin and turned to Raynald. 'My lord, Gokbori is…'

'I know who he is,' said Raynald, 'Blue-Wolf, the emir of Edessa and one of Saladin's most trusted generals. Our paths have crossed before.'

'My lord,' said a man next to the girl without lifting his eyes from the floor, 'if I may speak.'

'Continue,' said Raynald.

'My lords,' he said, looking up, 'my name is Fakhiri, and I am a simple cart-master. We seek no trouble and are only on our way to Damascus from Cairo to trade our wares. Our masters said there is a treaty in place to cross your lands, but if we have offended you, then I beg forgiveness.'

'If you are simply a trading caravan,' said Raynald, 'why did you have such a strong-armed escort?'

'The road is well known for its share of brigands,' said Fakhiri. 'They were for the protection of the caravan only and not for any military purpose.'

Raynald stared at the girl for a few more moments.

'And you,' he said eventually, 'why are you going to Damascus?'

'I am promised to a man there,' she said, her voice barely a whisper.

'And does this man have a name?'

'My lord,' interjected Fakhiri, 'the man's name is unimportant as is this girl. She is merely a gift from one man to another, nothing more.'

'So, tell me his name,' said Raynald again.

'My lord,' said Fakhiri, it is not important…,' but before he could say anymore, Raynald lunged forward and pressed his blade tight against the cart-master's throat.

'Now listen to me, Fakhiri,' he said. 'When a caravan travels with such a strong escort, that means one of two things. Either your goods are of such value that they far exceed the cost of the men guarding them, or there is someone important in the caravan who must be protected. Now I think it is the latter and this girl is the person in question. My guess is that she is promised to someone important, and I, my friend, want to know who he is. So, I will ask you once more before opening your throat. What is his name?'

'Let him go,' said the girl suddenly, 'and I will tell you his name.'

Raynald threw the man to the floor and turned to face the girl.

'Well,' he said, 'I'm waiting.'

'The man I am going to marry,' she said, 'is Al-Afdal ibn Salah ad-Din.'

Everyone fell silent as the information sunk in. Finally, Raynald turned away and strode back towards his horse. After a few moments, Sir Jakelin followed him.

'My lord,' he said, catching up with the Raynald, 'what are we to do?' Shall we release them?'

'You will not,' said Raynald mounting his horse, 'you will confiscate the goods and bring them to Karak.'

'What about the people?'

'Take them prisoner,' said Raynald. 'We will ransom the traders and sell the slaves.'

'And the girl?'

'Oh, she will be brought to me in Karak,' said Raynald.

'You risk Saladin's ire,' said Jakelin, 'it would send a better message if we were to let her go.'

'I grow tired of move and countermove,' said Raynald, 'and this charade needs to come to an end one way or another. The girl will be imprisoned in Karak and used as a pawn at my convenience. Now get the caravan moving, brother Jakelin. It needs to be behind the walls of Karak no later than noon tomorrow.' He urged his horse forward, his mind racing. It was a risky strategy, but one worth taking. God had delivered him an advantage, and he would be foolish to let it slip through his fingers. After all, it was not every day that he captured a woman promised to Saladin's son.

Sumeira sat at the table in her rooms in Karak. John Loxley sat opposite her, staring in disbelief at the five bags of coins in front of them.

'You actually bribed a Templar.' he said incredulously, 'are you mad, woman, have you finally lost your mind?'

'It was a risk,' said Sumeira, 'but it worked. I managed to get the rest of the silver.'

'Aye, you did, but at what cost?'

'John, stop worrying. We have the funds, and as soon as I return with my son, I can present the letter of credit to pay off the loan. All we need to do now is buy a horse and wait until Arturas provides the men. As soon as that is done, I can leave.'

'Yet worry I do,' said John, 'for every day this continues, brings closer the day that you ride through those gates, and it has to be said, that day could be the last I ever see of you.'

'We have discussed this,' said Sumeira, 'many times. Live or die, I have to do this for if I did not, I would go to my grave burdened with the knowledge that I abandoned my child.'

'And if you die, what about Emani?'

'I know you will look after her better than any father could,' said Sumeira. 'The hospital is beginning to make a profit and Emani has already displayed the virtues to be a fantastic physician. Together you will thrive in Karak, or indeed, anywhere you choose to go. I swear I will be careful and do everything I can to get back to you, but I have to try, John Loxley, or my life will not be worth living.'

'I understand,' said John with a sigh, 'but it worries me all the same.'

'God will look after me,' she said, reaching out to take his hand. A few moments later, a knock came on the door, and John swiftly moved the bags of coins out of sight. Sumeira slid back the small panel on the door and peered out.

'It's Arturas,' she said with relief and slid back the bolts to open the door.

'Arturas,' said John as he entered, 'welcome. Can I get you ale?'

'Thank you, but no,' said Arturas, 'I have only come to bring you news.'

'What news, has Hunter declined our offer?'

'He has not for I still haven't talked to him, but it is irrelevant as your quest cannot go ahead.'

'Why not,' asked Sumeira, 'I know the risks and am happy to proceed?'

'Because, my lady, the castle is about to lock down.'

'What do you mean, lock down?' asked John Loxley.

'There has been a call to arms from the castellan,' said Arturas. 'For some reason, he thinks we could be at imminent risk of attack, if not from Saladin's warriors then from his assassins. That means that with immediate effect, all the gates to the castle will be locked, and armed men will patrol every wall to ensure nobody goes in or out without us knowing.'

'But why,' gasped Sumeira, 'what caused this action?'

'I'm not sure,' said Arturas, 'but I have heard a rumour that Raynald has taken someone hostage, a woman believed to have close links to Saladin himself.'

'What?' gasped Sumeira. 'Has he gone mad?'

'It seems to be becoming a habit around here,' said John sarcastically.

Arturas looked at the physician, but Sumeira reached out and grabbed his arm.

'Listen to me,' she said, 'this makes no sense. Why would I be confined to the castle? I am a Christian and surely have the choice to risk my own life, should I choose.'

'You do, but this is not about you, it is about Karak. The Outremer is full of spies, Sumeira, and for all Raynald knows, you could be one yourself. Many Saracens spy for us and as hard as it is to believe, the same happens in the other direction.'

'There are Christians who spy for Saladin?' asked John.

'Every man has a price,' said Arturas, 'even Templars have been known to be corrupt.'

Sumeira glanced across at John who shook his head quickly, signalling she should not tell Arturas what she had done.

'The point is,' continued Arturas, 'you will now not be able to leave Karak, at least not without an armed guard sanctioned by Raynald himself.'

'For how long?' asked John.

'Who knows?' said Arturas, 'but I suspect there will be ransoms demanded. It will ease in a few months, these things always do, but in the meantime, you are stuck here, just like me.'

Chapter Fourteen

Karak

December - AD 1186

Sumeira stood at the fireplace at the back of her room, stirring a large pot of soup on the grid above the open flames. Despite the shutters being wide open, the smoke from the damp firewood still hung in the air, and she coughed as it forced its way down her lungs.

'What are you doing?' asked John Loxley walking through the door. 'Have you set the place alight?'

'It is the wood I bought from the caravan yesterday,' said Sumeira, 'I know not where he got it, but it is the devil's firewood, sure enough.'

'Leave it,' said John, 'and come and see. Something's happening in the courtyard.'

Sumeira lifted the pot from the grid and put it to one side before following her husband out of the door. They walked down the slope and joined a growing crowd gathered either side of the main gates. The people were held back by a double-line of foot soldiers leaving an open clearing at the centre of the courtyard.

'What's happening?' asked Sumeira, forcing her way to the front.

'There is to be a meeting,' said a man to her side, 'I heard a guard say there is a group of Saracens riding up the approach even as we speak.'

'I heard it's Saladin himself,' said another, 'and Raynald intends to kill him in front of us all.' Sumeira turned away, conscious that there was activity at the gates. As she watched, they swung open, and a group of six Saracen warriors rode through, seemingly oblivious to the vast crowd that had gathered to see them arrive. They rode into the centre of the courtyard and finally stopped as a man in a black cloak approached to meet them.

'Muzaffar ad-Din Gokbori,' said Cronin, stopping before the first rider, 'Emir of Edessa. Welcome to Karak Castle. Your message was received, and I bid you dismount. The castellan will be with you soon.'

'What is your name?' asked Gokbori, looking down at the sergeant.

'My name is Cronin,' came the reply.

'And you are a knight of the blood-cross?'

'I am a sergeant only,' said Cronin. 'My master will be with you shortly.'

'Perhaps he has forgotten who we are and scurries away to find a drinking vessel befitting an envoy of Salah ad-Din.'

'We are men of the one true God,' said Cronin, 'and take no pleasure in finery or displays of wealth. I'm sure water will be forthcoming as soon as my master returns.'

'Perhaps hospitality and respect mean something different to the Franks than it does to the Ayyubid.'

The Saracens stayed on their horses and looked around at the fascinated crowd before Gokbori turned back to face Cronin.

'Your master insults us with his lateness,' he said, 'are we nought, but curiosities to be gazed on by those who serve?'

'My apologies,' said Cronin, 'he should be here by now.'

'I will wait no longer,' said the Saracen. 'Tell your master I will be camped for one day two leagues west of here. If he wants to hear what I have to say, he must come to me.'

'And why would I do that?' asked a voice and everyone turned to see the giant figure of Raynald de Chatillon pushing his way through the crowd.

'Brother Raynald,' said Cronin, 'our guests were about to leave.'

'So it seems,' said Raynald. He stared at the Saracen, interested in seeing the man close up for the first time. Gokbori was a well-known emir and a favoured general of Saladin.

'Will you not take refreshment,' said one of the other Templars, stepping forward to offer the emir a flask of water.

Before the Saracen could respond, Raynald reached over and knocked the flask from his comrade's hands. The offering and acceptance of water secured hospitality and safety, and that was a guarantee he was unwilling to offer.

'So,' he said, turning to face the visitors. 'State your business, Saracen, for my day is full and my time important.'

'You know why I have come,' said Gokbori, struggling to control his anger, 'it is to secure the release of my cousin and demand reparations for the theft of the goods from a caravan you attacked on the southern road.'

'Attacked is a strong word,' said Raynald, 'for as I recall, only one man lost his life, a fool who had an urge to see paradise way before his allotted time.'

'That man was a brave and loyal servant of the sultan,' said Gokbori. 'His name will be remembered for many generations.'

'He was indeed brave,' said Raynald, 'but foolhardy, nonetheless. Anyway, back to the matter in hand. What makes you think I would pay anything to your master?'

'Because as you know, that caravan travelled under a treaty signed by King Baldwin himself. By attacking it, you risk war between us.'

'And which King Baldwin would that be?' asked Raynald with a laugh, 'for we have had two in as many years. One of them has lain rotting in his grave for over a year while the other was so weak he could hardly pick up a quill. Luckily for Jerusalem, the body of that king also fills a tomb and men of strength can once again command her armies.'

'The treaty was signed on behalf of the Kingdom of Jerusalem,' said Gokbori, 'and it matters not who wears the crown. If you do not return that which does not belong to you, then there will be consequences.'

Raynald took a step closer to the emir.

'You listen to me,' he said menacingly. 'That caravan was travelling through my lands, on my roads, and as it had a Saracen cavalry escort, I deemed it to have military intent. For all I know, those goods were intended to pay for more warriors for Saladin's army. So, as I have a duty to keep my people safe from the likes of you and your master, the confiscation of the goods was justified. There will be no reparations, Gokbori; you will leave this place empty-handed.'

'And the girl,' asked the emir, 'what of her?'

'What girl, there were many?'

'You know of whom I speak,' said Gokbori, 'my second cousin. Let me take her, and perhaps Saladin's anger may be appeased.'

'As I said,' replied Raynald, 'the contents of that caravan are mine, whether chattel or person.' He paused as the Saracen general returned his stare without flinching. 'There will be no negotiation, Gokbori,' he said eventually, 'so I suggest you and your men ride from here while you still have your lives. Your very presence offends me.'

'I will gladly leave,' said Gokbori, 'for there is no hospitality here, just the manner of devils. I should have expected no less from men who kill and steal in the name of a false God.'

'Careful, Blue Wolf,' said Raynald, 'you and your men are out on a limb, and I could have you hanging by your heels from the battlements in a few heartbeats.'

'You have a reputation as dark as a moonless sky,' growled Gokbori, 'and now I see why. We will meet again, Raynald of Chatillon, of that I am sure.'

'I look forward to it,' said Raynald and turned towards the guards at the gate. 'Escort these people out of here. I guarantee their safety only as far as Al Shabiya. After that, they are on their own.'

The Saracens turned their horses to leave the castle.

'Oh, Blue Wolf,' shouted Raynald as the group rode out through the gates, 'on the way down, cast a glance into the pit. You may learn something about me.'

A few minutes later, Gokbori and his men approached the stinking pit on the road at the base of the castle walls. The stench of death was overpowering, but their faces did not display the revulsion they felt. Gokbori held up his hand, calling his men to a halt. As they waited, the General dismounted and approached the pit to peer in. At first, he could see only decomposing bodies and clouds of black flies, but within moments his heart sunk as in the corner he spotted what the castellan had obviously wanted him to see: the rotting corpse of a young woman, draped in the finest of gold silks.

Back in the castle, the crowds were dispersing, excited about the drama they had just seen unfold with their own eyes. The lockdown had dragged on for weeks, and any break from the routine of castle life was always to be welcomed.

One person in particular though had more on her mind than the public humiliation they had just witnessed; her mind was firmly set on how she was going to escape the castle.

'John,' said Sumeira, 'we need to find Arturas.'

'For what reason?' answered her husband.

'Because I have to get out of here as soon as possible. I'm not quite sure what all that was about, but one thing is for sure, Saladin is involved, and he will not take this laying down.'

'Saladin is always a threat,' said John, 'I see no reason how that risk increases.'

'Did you not hear his words?' asked Sumeira coming to a halt. 'Did you see the anger upon his face? It was all he could do to keep his knife in his belt. No, whatever the intricacies, I suspect that when the news gets back to Saladin, things are going to get a lot more difficult around here.'

'So what do you intend to do?'

'I want Arturas to smuggle me out of the castle,' said Sumeira, 'I need to get to Segor before the roads are closed forever.'

Ten leagues away, Hassan Malouf sat cross-legged at the fire-place of the camp chieftain. Ever since the slaughter of his wife and fellow tribesmen over a year earlier, both he and Jahara had stayed at the camp to recover both mentally and physically.

For many months, Hassan had been filled with grief at the loss of his family, but as time passed, his heart hardened, and at last, his path had become clearer. Finally, he knew what he had to do and had asked Youssef-bin-Khouri for an audience. The two men sipped tea in silence as was the custom until eventually, the chieftain put down his glass and looked at Hassan.

'So, you have come to a decision?' He asked

'I have,' said Hassan, 'but with the greatest respect, I would rather not share it as it would offend you.'

'A man's choice is his own,' said Youssef, 'and not for me to judge.'

'Nevertheless, I would rather keep my thoughts to myself. It is enough to know that tomorrow I will leave this place and will probably never return.'

'It is a shame,' said the chieftain, 'for you have become like a son to me. Wherever your path leads, you have my blessing, Hassan Malouf, and there will always be a welcome within this goam. Are you sure I cannot change your mind?'

'I am sure, but what I do need is an assurance that you will look after Jahara. She is not of my blood, but she is important to me, and I need to know she will be safe.'

'You know as well as I that I cannot guarantee her safety,' said the chieftain, 'twice in the last few months she has fled the goam with the intention of finding those who attacked your people. She is headstrong, and I fear that one day soon, we will be unable to find her before she finds herself in a situation she cannot handle.'

'Have you had the women talk to her?'

'I have,' said Youssef. 'Her words are few, but when she does speak, it is only of revenge.'

'Is there anything you can do to stop trying to leave?'

'Our ties are of the heart; not the tether,' said Youssef.

Hassan shook his head with worry. He had wanted to move on for a long time, and it was only his concern for Jahara that had held him back.

'There is one thing we can do,' said Youssef eventually. 'It may not deflect from what her heart desires, but it may make her chances of survival a little better.'

'What do you suggest?'

'Perhaps we should not be denying her the road she seeks but providing her with the tools she will need whilst upon it.'

'What do you mean? There is no way any young girl can survive out there without the support of a family, whether of blood or association. Especially one who is seeking the death of another.'

'You are right,' said Youssef, 'unless, of course, you are Hashashin.'

Hassan stared at the chieftain with shock. The Hashashin were a secretive tribe feared across the Outremer by Christian and Muslim alike, not just for their reputation as assassins, but because of their religious fervour and unblinkered dedication to achieving their grisly tasks. For almost a hundred years they had expanded their reach, and now occupied many castles of the mountainous spine that reached across Persia and Syria, venturing out only to carry out their deadly missions as directed by their leader, Rashid ad-Din Sinan.

'I do not understand,' said Hassan. 'Hashashin are born, not made, and spend a lifetime learning their skills.'

'I know,' said Youssef, 'but perhaps we can train the girl in some of the ways that may keep her alive.'

'If you send her to Al-Khaf, she would be dead before even seeing the walls of the castle.'

'That is true,' said Youssef, 'so perhaps we can bring the training to her.'

'How?'

'In my cousin's village, thirty leagues from here, there is a man. He was once a Fedayeen, one of the most powerful and skilful of the Hashashin. Two years ago, I found him in the desert close to death. When I came upon him, his bones had been broken by his enemies, and he had been staked out to die in the sun. Despite his argument, I kept him alive and tended his wounds. I took him to my cousin's goam, and for many days he burned with fever. We set his bones, and though he is not the same man, he came back to health. Having failed in his mission, he was disgraced with his people and became an outcast. The woman who nursed him back to health won his heart, and as he could never go back to Al-Khaf, he decided to stay in the goam and now lives amongst us. This man can teach the girl some of the secrets of the Hashashin, should I ask.'

'It is not possible to learn their ways,' said Hassan, 'it would take a lifetime.'

'It would, but if she were to learn how to use a weapon and just enough skills to keep her safe upon the road, would that not go a long way to keeping her alive?'

'Perhaps,' said Hassan, 'but for how long?'

'Nobody can see tomorrow, Hassan Malouf,' said the chieftain, 'but what I do know is this. If we do nothing, her revenge will fester in her mind like a disease, and she will set out unprepared for what lays before her. If we do this, we will gain several years while she learns the skills needed. By then, her mood may have changed, but if not, at least she will have a chance to live.'

Hassan fell silent. It was not what he wished for Jahara but could see the sense.

'And you can do this?' he asked.

'I can try,' said Youssef.

'Then if Jahara agrees, she will have my blessing.'

'In that case, there is no more to say. Your horse is ready, and we will furnish you with whatever you need for your journey.'

'Thank you,' said Hassan.' I will never forget you, Youssef-bin-Khouri.'

'Nor I, you, Hassan Malouf. May your God go with you.'

The following morning, Hassan Malouf finished loading his horse with provisions before turning to see Jahara walking towards him.

'Hassan,' she said, 'I heard you are leaving.'

'I am,' said Hassan, 'there are things I must do. Have you talked with Youssef-bin-Khouri?'

'I have, and I accepted his proposition with all my heart. I leave to meet the Fedayeen tomorrow and will spend however long it takes under his tutorage.'

'That could be many years,' said Hassan.

'It will take as long as it takes,' said Jahara, 'but never will I forget what those men did to my people. And when I am ready, I will do what I have already vowed to do.'

'Despite the nature of your quest, Jahara,' said Hassan, 'I hope that one day you will find peace.'

'Thank you, Hassan,' she said and waited as he mounted his horse.

'Be safe, Jahara,' said Hassan looking down. 'I expect we shall never meet again.'

'Perhaps, 'said Jahara, 'but I would ask you one more thing. Where is it that you are going?'

Hassan looked into the distance.

'I am going to find my destiny, Jahara,' he said eventually, 'I'm going to find Salah ad-Din.' With that, he kicked his heels into his horse and rode westward out of the goam.

Chapter Fifteen

Tiberias

March - AD 1187

Balian of Ibelin waited in one of the outer chambers in the citadel of Tiberias. He had meant to arrive much sooner, but domestic matters in his fief of Nablus had held him up, especially as Saracen raiding parties were on the increase throughout the Outremer. Finally, he had found the time, and he had arrived in Tiberias just a few hours earlier. His men had been quartered in the barracks, and after eating some cold meat in the castle kitchens, he had been granted an audience with the man whose unwise acts were putting the whole of the Holy-land at risk, Raymond of Tripoli.

The sound of footsteps echoed down the corridor outside, and the door flung open as Raymond entered the room.

'Balian,' he announced, removing the gauntlets and casting them onto a nearby chair, 'I have been expecting you.' He walked past Balian and up to a table to pour himself a goblet of wine.'

'Drink?' he asked, holding the flask above a second goblet.

'Thank you, no,' said Balian. 'I have been adequately fed and watered.'

'Good,' said Raymond and turned to face the man who had once been his closest ally. 'So, I assume you have been sent by the imposters in Jerusalem to demand my immediate homage. Am I right?'

'Something like that,' said Balian.

'Well,' said Raymond, taking a sip of his wine, 'you have travelled far to say what you have to say, so let me hear it.'

'My friend,' said Balian, 'what has become of you? You are one of the proudest, and certainly the most fearless men I have ever known, yet your face is etched with lines of worry. This charade you find yourself upon must end soon or I fear it will be the downfall of us all.'

'You lecture the wrong person, Balian,' said Raymond, 'for it is those who lounge upon the thrones of Jerusalem who risk the faith. I only require what is best for the Holy-land and for Christendom, a leader who can defy the Saracens.'

'You talk of defiance yet have signed a treaty with Saladin himself,' said Balian. 'What message does that send anyone who may have some sympathy for your claim?'

'I need nobody's sympathy,' growled Raymond, 'and the message it sends clearly states that I play no games. If Jerusalem wants to have a war with Saladin, then so be it, but I will not risk my men to defend a kingdom who steals from those who have supported them faithfully for so many years.'

'Sibylla and Guy did not steal the throne, Raymond,' said Balian,' the Haute Cour voted, as is our way, and the outcome was just. I too was disappointed, but we have to forget the past and move forward.'

'Your opinion differs from mine,' said Raymond, 'but even so, answer me this. What sort of monarch strips one of his most loyal allies of his fiefdom and sentences him to exile in a land far from his own people?'

'I do not understand,' said Balian, 'how do you know about Beirut?

'Oh, come, my friend,' said Raymond, 'did you think such conditions could be kept secret for all these weeks? I too have spies, and these ultimatums were probably before me before you even left Acre. Now, let us waste no more time. Tell me exactly what they want, word for word.'

Balian sighed and walked over to pour himself a goblet of wine before draining it in one and filling it up again.

'Well, 'said Raymond, 'I am waiting?'

'The king demands that you stand down your army immediately,' said Balian. 'Those who want to return home will be given safe passage while those who still wish to serve will be absorbed into Jerusalem's ranks. Do this and you will be allowed to return to Tripoli with your family and chattels but will be forbidden to travel south of Tripoli's borders for as long as you may live.'

'And my wife?'

'The fiefdom of Tiberias will remain hers, and she can travel between it and Tripoli in safety for as long as she desires. This is your quarrel, not hers.'

'And if I refuse?'

'Guy will amass his army and ride on Tiberias within weeks. If he does, and the city resists, he will have no option but to assume that your wife has allied herself with you in this matter and she will share your guilt. You do not want to do this, my friend, Saladin's threat grows by the day, and we need every kingdom in the Holy-land united against him.'

'Saladin is not the man we think him to be,' said Raymond. 'His envoys were courteous and supportive. Since I signed the treaty, their raiding parties have steered clear of Tiberias. If he wants to attack Jerusalem, it is no business of mine.'

'Listen to yourself,' shouted Balian. 'You are talking about the deaths of thousands of fellow Christians. Are you really saying you could countenance such a thing for the sake of a piece of gold around your brow? Do you not have enough gold, enough land, enough power?'

'This is about none of those things,' roared Raymond, 'it is about the safety of the Holy-land. A woman and an imbecile sit on the throne of Jerusalem, and if that city falls, then you can be sure that the rest will quickly follow. So no, Balian of Ibelin, I will not disband my army, and I will not run to Tripoli like a scared dog. I will remain here and rule as a true leader must, with strength and strategic flexibility. Tell your new friends this, and if they decide to march on this city, I will meet them with a greater force than they can imagine.'

'You cannot match Jerusalem's strengths,' said Balian, 'even without her allies Sibylla can muster ten thousand men within days, many of them Templars and Hospitallers.'

'And how many men do you think Saladin can muster?' asked Raymond.

Balian fell silent and stared in horror at the man he once called friend.

'You have signed a treaty with Saladin,' he said, 'not an alliance.'

'I have the first and await the second,' said Raymond, 'though it is a formality only. Attack Tiberias, and you will find the same response from Saladin as if you attacked Damascus itself. Take that back to your king.'

'I do not know you anymore,' said Balian, 'the knight I once respected would have killed any man for even suggesting such a thing.'

'That knight has been betrayed time and time again,' said Raymond. 'Even the strongest trees can break in a storm. Now, you have your answer, so I suggest you leave.'

Balian drank the rest of his wine before throwing the wooden goblet across the room.

'I will relay your message, 'he said, 'but take no pleasure in doing so. Know this, Raymond of Tripoli, you have until Easter to fulfil the king's demands. Once the last of the celebrations are over, there will be no more negotiations, and Jerusalem's army will march. I expect I will be called upon to serve in that army, and if it comes to conflict, I will have no hesitation in drawing my sword against you.'

'So be it,' Balian, said Raymond, 'now get out of my city.'

Hassan Malouf rode towards a valley south of Damascus. His quest to find Salah ad-Din had not gone well, and he had wasted many days travelling south towards Egypt before someone had told him that the Ayyubid leader was actually in Damascus. Using the lesser roads, he had turned around and headed north, fully aware that what he was about to attempt would probably see him dead within the next few days. As he neared the city, his plans were thwarted again as no man was even willing to discuss Saladin, let alone say where he was, but Hassan knew that by simply asking the question, he would probably get what he wanted.

Sure enough, later in the day, a patrol of Saracens appeared on the horizon and after a few moments pause, rode down the hill to surround him on the road. Hassan stopped and waited until one of the men spoke.

'You,' he said, 'I hear you have been asking questions.'

'I have, my lord,' responded Hassan, 'I seek Salah ad-Din.'

'And what business would a stinking Bedouin have of the Sultan of Egypt and Syria?'

Hassan paused and stared around the patrol, knowing that once he stated the reason, there could be no going back.

'I want to offer my services,' he said eventually, 'I wish to join your forces and fight against the Christians.'

The leader of the Saracens returned the stare before bursting into laughter, as did his men. Hassan was confused. He had expected derision or anger, but not humour. Eventually, the laughter stopped, and the Saracen rode his horse a few paces closer.

'Tell me, Bedouin,' he said, 'what makes you think you are good enough even to breathe the same air as Salah ad-Din, let alone talk with him?'

'I know I am unworthy,' said Hassan, 'but I have information that he could use against the Christians.'

'What sort of information?'

'I have spent a lot of time amongst them and have knowledge of their castles, their habits, their strengths and their weaknesses.'

'And how were you amongst them, were you a scout?'

'I was,' lied Hassan, knowing that if he told them the truth, he would probably be dead within minutes.

'You are too young to be a scout of any merit,' said the Saracen.

'I was training alongside the great Abdal-Wahhab,' said Hassan, 'one of the greatest scouts amongst the tribes.'

'I have heard of this man,' said the Saracen; 'he rides with the Christians. Where is he now for I would gladly separate his head from his neck?'

'Abdal-Wahhab is dead,' said Hassan, 'struck down by those he served.'

'The Christians killed him?'

'They did.'

'Such a shame,' said the Saracen, 'for it takes that pleasure away from me. I hope he suffered.'

Hassan did not answer but waited for the warrior's next decision.

'I do not know whether to kill you now or wait until my master orders it,' said the Saracen eventually, 'perhaps you should choose. We accept no Bedouin into our armies so even if your information is good, your death is likely. So, the question is this. Do you want to die a quick death now, with little pain or die later with your death lasting many days?'

Hassan's heart sunk, but there was only one obvious choice.

'I will take my chances with your master,' he said.

'So be it,' said the Saracen, 'follow me.' He turned his horse and galloped up the slope with Hassan and his men close behind.

Within the hour, the patrol rode down another hill into a valley full of tents before dismounting and leaving the horses to the young boys who came running out to meet them.

'Come,' said the Saracen and headed into the centre of the camp.

Hassan looked around with incredulity. There were thousands of tents as far as the eye could see and though he had been on many campaigns with the Christians, never had he seen such a force. A few minutes later he was made to stand outside a much larger tent, guarded by six men swathed in black robes. Hassan knew them to be Mamluks, the feared warriors descended from slaves and heavily used by Saladin as bodyguards. The Saracen officer disappeared into the tent, and Hassan knew that one way or other, his life would either change dramatically in the next few minutes, or his body would be dragged to the outskirts of the camp to feed the scavengers of the night.

Finally, a servant emerged and beckoned him to enter. Hassan ducked through the tent opening and into the cool interior. Several more Mamluks stood around the wall, and the Saracen who had taken him prisoner stood talking to a second man in the centre of the tent. The second man was elegantly clothed in multi-coloured silks, but his demeanour was one of the warrior. Hassan stopped and stared, waiting to be acknowledged when from out of nowhere, one of the Mamluk's smashed him across the back of the head, sending him crashing to the floor. Before Hassan could move, the warrior's boot pushed his face into the plush carpet, making it difficult to breathe.

'Do not Bedouin dogs have manners?' growled the Mamluk. 'Prostrate yourself before our lord and master.'

Hassan gasped as the pressure eased and managed to turn his head slightly to see the two men still talking as if nothing had happened. Eventually, the conversation ended, and the man who had taken him prisoner left the tent, leaving the Saracen commander staring at Hassan on the floor.

'Get up,' snapped the Mamluk guard behind him and Hassan scrambled to his knees, though careful to keep his head down.

'What is your name?' asked the Saracen commander.

'Hassan Malouf,' replied Hassan, 'of the Nazir tribe.'

'I know of it,' said the warrior, 'a proud tribe scattered throughout the Negev. What brings you here, Hassan Malouf?'

'I wish an audience with your lord, Salah ad-Din.' said Hassan. 'I have an offer to make.'

'An offer,' said the warrior, 'it must be very valuable for you to think he may deign to speak to a rat such as you.'

'I hear he is a great man, in thought and deed,' said Hassan, 'and listens to pauper and king alike.'

'Perhaps so,' said the warrior, 'but to get anywhere near him, first you have to convince me. Stand up, Hassan Malouf, and say what you have to say.'

Hassan got to his feet and cautiously looked up, half expecting another blow from the Mamluk to his rear.

'Well,' said the Saracen, 'I am waiting.'

'With the greatest respect, my lord,' said Hassan, 'may I enquire to whom it is I am speaking?'

Within seconds he was struck to the floor again, and this time he felt the blade of a knife held against his throat.

'You ask nothing,' said the Mamluk guard, 'and only breathe because of the generosity of the man who stands before you. Now state your purpose, desert dog.'

'Let him up,' said the commander, 'his ignorance is that of youth, not disrespect.'

Hassan got to his feet again and looked up at the warrior, realising that his life was on the line and he was in no place to bargain.

'My lord,' he said, 'please forgive me, I meant no insult. I just thought it better to know what lord I was addressing.'

'I am Al-Afdal ibn Salah ad-Din,' said the warrior, 'now say what you came to say.'

Hassan could not believe his luck. He had always known he would probably never even see Salah ad-Din in person, so to be in the presence of the sultan's son was more than he ever could have hoped.

'My lord,' he said, 'I am Bedouin born, but for many years, have lived with the Christians all across the Outremer.'

'A Frankish term,' said Al-Afdal, 'and not one we use.'

'My apologies,' said Hassan, 'but the way I speak is from the many years I lived amongst the infidels. I do not mean to offend. He looked around before continuing. 'My lord, a few months ago, those I rode beside for many years, killed my wife and unborn child. They also slaughtered everyone in my village with only one survivor, a young girl who now lives elsewhere. I buried

119

them with my own hands and now seek revenge on those men and others of their kind. I finally saw their true nature, and if you will have me, I will share what I know about them.'

'We have many spies, Hassan Malouf,' said Al-Afdal, 'why would I trust someone like you? For all I know you could be a spy yourself, sent here by your Christian friends to gather information on their behalf.'

'I am no spy, my lord, and though you have eyes and ears everywhere, none will have the knowledge that I hold.'

'And why is that?' asked Al-Afdal. 'What is so special about you that you claim to be more important than any of my own men?'

Hassan paused. What he was about to say would either get him killed or pique the warrior's interest enough to grant him a few more minutes of life.

'Because, my lord,' he said eventually, 'the men I served were the Templars, and I have been in amongst the best of them. I have seen their castles, their commanderies, their tactics. I know when they pray, when they eat, their strengths and their weaknesses. I also know and have the trust of many who still serve.'

Al-Afdal stared at Hassan, his eyes cutting deep into the young man's soul.

'If I understand you correctly,' he said, 'you are saying that if I allow you to live, you will tell me everything you know about the knights of the blood-cross. What is to stop my men torturing you right now and getting the information I want anyway?'

'Nothing, my lord, and there is no need of torture for I will tell you everything I can and trust your judgement, but even if I talk until the new moon, there will be much unsaid for most is knowledge that cannot be conveyed.'

'Give me an example.'

'I know the hidden ways of Acre, every back street and alley. I know the traders who are loyal to the Christians and those who would shelter your men should they enter the city. I know what trails are preferred by the patrols and where they prefer to rest. All of this and more can be shown, but not taught. Let me live and fight alongside you and all this information will be yours.'

'And you will fight and die in the name of Allah?'

'I will,' said Hassan, 'all I desire is the chance to see the man who killed my family scream for mercy before I cut his throat.'

'And you know this man?'

'I do. He is the castellan of the castle they call Karak. His name is Raynald of Chatillon.'

The warrior's face hardened as he stared at Hassan.

'And you are sure it was this man who killed your woman?'

'I am, my lord, and one day, I will kill him or die trying.'

Again, Al-Afdal stared, and Hassan knew that his fate would be decided in the next few moments.

'Follow me, Hassan Malouf,' he said eventually, and left the tent, closely followed by the Mamluk bodyguards. Outside, he spoke to one of the other guards who turned away to run through the camp. The warrior turned to face Hassan.

'You are an interesting young man,' he said eventually, 'and have knowledge that I can use, but still, there is a risk you could be a spy or an assassin.'

'I am neither, my lord,' said Hassan. 'I am a man who now only has one aim in life, to kill those that killed my family.'

'We will see, Hassan Malouf, but first, you must prove yourself.'

'I am willing to fight anywhere you wish, my lord, put me amongst those who ride into battle first, and I will not let you down.'

'Killing in battle is easy,' said Al-Afdal. 'It is not so easy to kill a man face to face.' He turned to see the guard returning along with a bound and blindfolded prisoner. The guard threw the man at the warrior's feet.

Hassan looked down and recognised the brown tunic of a Templar chaplain.

'This is a Christian man of God,' said the Saracen. 'He was captured many months ago by my men when they ambushed a patrol who had attacked a village such as yours. All were killed except for this man who begged for his life and out of curiosity, we allowed him to live. I have since found out that despite his vows, he was amongst the many Christians who ravaged the women before putting them to the sword.' He looked up at Hassan. 'So, what do you think, Hassan Malouf, do you think we should let him live?'

'It makes no difference to me,' said Hassan coldly, 'do what you will.'

'Despite what your Christian friends told you,' said Al-Afdal, 'we do not kill for pleasure, only in defence of what is ours.' He looked down at the hooded prisoner. 'This man proclaims his innocence, and I find it difficult to decide his fate.' He looked back up at Hassan. 'This will be your test, Hassan Maklouf. In the next few minutes, he will either die or be set free. The decision is yours.'

'But how am I to decide?' asked Hassan. 'I know not the circumstances.'

'You may question him,' said Al-Afdal, 'and judge him accordingly. I care not whether he lives or dies; only the reasons why you make the choice. Kill him with good reason, and I will take you into our ranks, but kill him out of malice or in a misguided attempt to please me, then I will know, and you will share his fate. Similarly, if he is innocent as he claims, then you must let him go, but release him out of comradeship and you will take his place under the knife. Do you understand?'

'I do,' said Hassan, 'give me a blade.'

The warrior nodded to a guard who withdrew a blade from his belt and handed it to the Bedouin. Hassan stared at the knife before taking a step towards the whimpering prisoner.

'Wait,' said Al-Afdal. 'Any child can kill a nameless man. Remove his hood and look him in the eye. If he is proven guilty, let him know that it is you who are about to kill him. If he is allowed to live, then he needs to see what a true saviour looks like. Follow your heart, Hassan Malouf, and the right decision will follow.'

Hassan walked over to the kneeling prisoner. He reached down and removed the sacking from the man's head, casting it to one side.

The Templar chaplain looked up, his eyes squinting from the midday sun. A few seconds later, he realised he was looking at a Bedouin, most of whom were allies of the Christians. A look of recognition appeared in his eyes, and the faintest of hope flickered in his chest.

'I know you,' he gasped eventually, 'I recognise your face. I served with you in Chastellet. I saw you amongst the brothers.' He looked around desperately. 'Are they here, have they come to rescue me?'

'They have not,' said Hassan, 'and yes, your face is familiar to me. You looked after the spiritual needs of those I yearned to become.'

'But why are you here,' asked the chaplain, 'have you come to negotiate my release?'

'I have not,' said Hassan, 'I am here to be your judge, and if necessary, your executioner.'

The chaplain looked at the knife in Hassan's hand before looking back up into the Bedouin's eyes.

'But you are one of us,' he said, 'a member of the brotherhood. You can speak on my behalf, brother, you can beg them for my life.'

'I will do neither,' said Hassan, 'I will judge, and I will act accordingly.'

'I do not understand,' said the Chaplain, 'did I not treat you well? Have I ever offended you? Are we not brothers, you and I, united under the eyes of the Lord?'

'Perhaps once,' said Hassan, 'but no longer. I have had my eyes opened and now see you for what you are.'

'I am a man of God,' said the chaplain, 'nothing more, nothing less. I am certainly no murderer or ravager of women.'

'Were you there when the camp was attacked?' asked Hassan.

'I was, admittedly, but played no part.'

'Did the people your comrades killed beg for their lives?' asked Hassan.

'I do not know,' said the Chaplain, 'the memory is hazy, but I did not kill anyone, I swear.'

'Did you stop those who were slaughtering innocents?' asked Hassan, his voice cold. 'Did you even try?'

'You know I could not,' said the chaplain,' I serve the knights and do their bidding. They would not have listened even if I had. I am blameless.'

'If you are blameless,' said Hassan, 'answer me this. Did you give absolution to those who did the killing?'

'What?' gasped the chaplain, 'I do not understand.'

'You know perfectly well what I mean,' said Hassan, 'did you, in the name of your God, forgive every man who bloodied his blade that day?'

'Yes,' spluttered the chaplain, 'but that is what I do, I grant God's forgiveness on all who ask. He is all-seeing and all-powerful.'

'In that case, it was also your hand on every blade that drew blood. You and the cruel God who cuts down innocent children and women with babies still unborn, never to see the light of day. You are guilty, more than the men who did the killing.'

'No,' gasped the chaplain, 'wait.'

Hassan walked behind the chaplain, pulling his head back to expose his neck. The chaplain closed his eyes and started to pray, tears running down his cheeks.

'Know this, chaplain,' said Hassan, resting the blade upon his victim's throat, 'when you die, there will be no prayers, no service and no burial. Your body will rot in the desert, unknown and unremembered. And if there is indeed a God, I hope he sends you straight to hell.'

'No, wait,' gasped the chaplain again, but before he could say anything else, Hassan dragged the blade slowly across his throat, cutting deep into the flesh. Blood spurted out, and the chaplain's eyes opened wide with pain and horror. Hassan pressed the blade harder, pulling his victim's head until the gaping wound widened, and it fell backwards. Blood spurted upward from the severed artery, soaking Hassan as he sawed his knife back and fore to sever the spine. His eyes were cold, and dead, for though he was taking another man's life, all he could think about was his wife and unborn child laying in their grave. He had expected a feeling of relief, of satisfaction that someone had paid the ultimate price for their murder, but there was nothing, just an aching emptiness deep in his heart, a void that he somehow knew could never be filled. The chaplain's body fell to the ground though Hassan's fist still lay entangled in his victim's hair.

'You can let that go, Bedouin,' said Al-Afdal, and Hassan unclenched his fist to let his victim's head fall to the ground, the sightless eyes staring skyward as if yearning for the gates of heaven to appear.

'Your actions were not what I expected, Hassan Malouf,' said Al-Afdal, 'but your actions were justified.' He nodded towards a servant who brought a tray holding two empty glass goblets and a flask of scented rose water. Al-Afdal took the flask and filled both goblets before handing one to Hassan.

'Drink, Hassan Malouf,' he said, 'and be refreshed for in the next few days, we have much to discuss.'

Chapter Sixteen

Karak

April - AD 1187

Sumeira and John Loxley hid in the darkest of shadows near the main gates of Karak Castle, hoping that Arturas would make good his promise. The early hours were at their darkest, and they knew that if he did not show soon, they would have to return to their quarters to try another night.

'Where is he?' whispered Sumeira, 'he promised he would be here.'

'Be patient,' said John, 'he will turn up, I know it. I just hope he is careful because what he is about to do could earn him a place in Raynald's pit.'

'He will be fine,' said Sumeira, 'for we have been doubly careful with all arrangements. Only three people know what is about to happen, you, I and Arturas, and by the time anyone wonders where I have gone, I will be well on my way to Segor.'

John nodded for though the arrangements had taken far longer than anticipated, they had been thorough and secretive. What he did not know was that further into the shadows, another man was listening intently.

The time passed slowly, but as they were about to give up, the sound of careful footsteps came from the direction of the gate. They pushed themselves back against the wall, hardly daring to breathe as the man approached. If it were a guard, their plans would be dashed, and they could be reported to the castellan and tried as spies.

'Sumeira,' hissed a voice and both breathed a sigh of relief as Arturas appeared out of the gloom.

'Where have you been?' gasped Sumeira, walking towards him, 'it is almost dawn.'

'I could not get away,' said Arturas, 'I was held up in a briefing with the under-marshal.'

'It will be light soon,' said John, looking up. 'We will have to try again tomorrow.'

'We can't,' said Arturas, 'that's why I am late. From dawn, I will no longer be steward.'

'Why, what has happened?'

'It matters not, but if you want my help, you have to go now. I have dismissed the guards, but their replacements will be here soon. Tomorrow I will have no such authority. You have to go now or not at all.'

'Then let us make haste,' said Sumeira and turned to head for the gates.

'Wait,' said a voice and all three spun around to see the man who had remained hidden in the shadows.

'Who are you?' gasped John Loxley as Arturas stepped forward with his hand upon the hilt of his sword.

'Please, do not kill me,' said the man, 'my name is Fakhiri, and I was a cart-master in a caravan heading from Egypt to Damascus when we were captured. My mistress was used and murdered by your castellan, and I was placed to work as a slave. Every day I am starved and beaten, but still, my heart harbours hope that one day I will be free.'

'What do you want of us?' asked John Loxley. 'We cannot buy your freedom.'

'You cannot,' said Fakhiri, 'but I heard your plans and wish to come with you.'

'What?' gasped Sumeira. 'Why would we take you?'

'Because if you leave me here, I will tell them what I know and say you are spies working for Salah ad-Din.'

Arturas drew his knife and forced the slave back against the wall.

'Give me one good reason why I should not kill you right now,' he growled.

'Because it is almost dawn and you have no time to hide a body,' said Fakhiri. 'I know the lady is travelling alone as far as Al-Shabiya and though it is in the shadow of Karak, it is still a dangerous path. Let me go, and I swear in Allah's name I will protect her until she finds your comrades.'

Arturas stared for a moment before glancing over at John Loxley.

'It seems you have both been very talkative while you were waiting,' he said, 'what else does he know?'

'We have been here most of the night,' said John, 'I cannot recall everything we discussed.'

'I know that the lady is to meet two men on the outskirts of Al Shabiya tomorrow at dusk,' said Fakhiri, 'and from there she needs to head south to Segor. I know the road to Segor well, so perhaps I can help.'

'And how do I know you will not slit her throat as soon as you are out of the gates?'

'You do not, my lord, I can only swear that if you grant me this boon, I will forever be in your service.'

'Stay there,' growled Arturas, lowering his blade and walked over to Sumeira. 'What do you think,' he asked quietly, 'do we trust him?'

'I can't see that we have any other choice,' said Sumeira. 'If he tells the castellan what he knows, I will be back here before noon and branded a spy.'

'I could kill him and say he attacked me,' said Arturas.

'No, said Sumeira, I will not be responsible for anyone's death without justification.'

'Did you discuss the silver?' asked Arturas.

'No, why would we?'

'Because if you did and he heard you, then your life is in danger.'

'I'm sure we did not,' said Sumeira, 'and the silver is packed tightly in a purse hanging beneath my cloak. It will make no noise.'

'Then the decision is yours,' said Arturas, 'but I need it now.'

Sumeira hesitated and looked over at the frightened man. She could not see his features, but the tone of his voice suggested honesty.

'I will take him,' she said eventually.

'In that case,' said Arturas, 'you must go now. Head for Al Shabiya, but do not travel upon the road. A few paces east, you will find a goat path. Stay upon that and do not speak to anyone.'

'How do I find your men?' asked Sumeira.

'You do not, they will find you.' He turned to Fakhiri. 'If anything happens to this woman while she is in your care,' he growled, 'I swear I will find you, take you to Francia and make you live amongst the filth of the pigs. Do you understand?'

'I am a man of my word,' said Fakhiri, 'and will protect her with my life.'

'Make sure you do,' said Arturas, 'now follow me.' He headed towards the gates and after checking there was nobody around, opened a smaller side gate to let them through. Sumeira paused and turned to face her husband and handed him a folded parchment.

'If something happens to me,' she said, 'go to Greece and seek out my family. Their details are in here, and I have explained what has happened. They will take care of you and Emani.'

'I will not need it,' said John, 'for I have no doubt you will return to me. Be safe, Sumeira.'

Sumeira smiled and without another word, sidled through the part-opened gate, closely followed by Fakhiri. After many long months, her quest to find her son had finally begun.

John Loxley and Arturas walked back across the dark bailey and into the physician's quarters, closing the door behind them. John checked Emani was sleeping before pouring two mugs of ale and sitting at the table.

'So,' he said, 'what now?'

'Now we wait,' said Arturas. 'Hopefully, nobody will notice Sumeira's disappearance until it is too late, but then you will have to think of something to explain her absence.'

'I will tell them the truth,' said John, 'well, a version of it. I will not mention you or your part in this, but it is no secret she wanted to find her son.'

'And if they ask how she escaped the castle?'

'I'll feign ignorance and suggest she hid on one of the carts.'

'They could accuse her of being a spy,' said Arturas.

'What spy would leave her child behind?' asked John Loxley. 'Even the most suspicious mind would find that hard to reconcile. What worries me is that slave. His disappearance will be noticed quickly and might instigate a pursuit.'

'Nobody will pursue a slave,' said Arturas, 'and anyway, as soon as the alarm is raised, I will instigate a search of the castle. That will take a day, and by the time everyone realises he has gone, it will be too late.'

'So, who is waiting for Sumeira in Al Shabiya?'

'Two of my most trusted comrades,' said Arturas. 'They will serve her well, and if anyone can bring her back alive, it is them.'

'I hope you are right,' said John. 'It is just a shame that Hunter did not respond.'

'I sent him a message, said Arturas, but it is a difficult time out there, and a good scout is hard to find. I expect his services are well sought after by many men.' He picked up his mug of ale. 'Your wife is an extraordinary woman, John Loxley,' he said, 'let us hope God is looking over her.'

Outside the castle, Sumeira and Fakhiri had reached the bottom of the hill and now turned off the road to find the goat track Arturas had told them about. For the next hour or so they walked as fast as they dared, but the horizon was already light, and the day was about to dawn.

'We have to find somewhere to hide,' said Fakhiri.

'Why?' asked Sumeira, 'Al Shabiya is within reach. If we push on, we will get there by the time the sun clears the mountains.'

'We cannot risk it,' said Fakhiri. 'Even if our escape has not been noticed, this road will soon be full of traders and Christian patrols. If any of them see you, a western woman on foot with me, an Egyptian cart-master they will suspect foul play and ask questions. No, we should hide until dark and then continue the journey.'

'You are right,' said Sumeira. 'I am sure Arturas's men will wait for the pay is good and they would not want to miss out.'

'Do you have the purse about you?' asked Fakhiri.

Sumeira stared, realising she had spoken too freely.

'Why,' she asked, 'would that make a difference in your loyalty?'

'It matters not to me,' said Fakhiri, 'but you should be more careful with your words. If I were a man of lesser honour, that information could have cost you your life.'

'Then I hope you are a man of your word,' said Sumeira, 'now come, let us find that hiding place.'

The rest of the day was hot and uncomfortable for Sumeira and the cart-master. They had found a thicket to hide under, but the sun reached through the tangle of thorns, seemingly baking them alive. The one flask of water Sumeira had brought was quickly used up, and by the time darkness fell again, they were both desperately thirsty.

'This is not a good start,' said Sumeira, 'we are still in the shadows of Karak, and already we suffer.'

'It will only get better,' said Fakhiri. 'Come, we will be in the town soon enough, and we can drink our fill from one of the wells.' They headed out onto the path again and walked towards Al Shabiya in the distance. As they approached the town, two men appeared out of the gloom and stood either side of the path.

'Who are you,' asked Sumeira, 'are you the men arranged by Arturas?'

'You must be the physician,' said one.

Sumeira breathed a sigh of relief and walked forward to greet the men.

'Who is this,' asked the second man, looking at Fakhiri, 'we were told you would be alone?'

'This is Fakhiri,' she said, 'he helped me get here from the castle. He is a good man.'

'The only good Saracen is a dead Saracen,' growled the mercenary, his hand creeping to the knife within his belt.

'No,' said Sumeira, noticing the movement, 'I speak on his behalf and will not have him harmed.'

'He will betray us all,' said one of the men again, 'his kind always do. Better to kill him now rather than wait until it is too late.'

'There will be no killing,' said Sumeira, 'he is coming with me.'

'We were paid to protect one, not two. The price has gone up.'

'Why?' asked Sumeira, 'the road is no longer than it was yesterday, and I will pay for his food. When we reach Segor, he will take his own path into Egypt.'

'Nevertheless, I want another fifty silver pennies,' said the first man, 'business is business.'

Sumeira looked between the two men. Although she was frustrated, she had always known she would be dealing with mercenaries so they could hardly be judged on their morals.

'Fifty pennies,' she sighed and reached beneath her cloak to retrieve one of the purses.

'And we will take the rest of our payment upfront,' said the second mercenary, 'you know, just in case your friend there steals it on the road and disappears into the desert.'

Sumeira stared at the two men again but knew she had no other option. Slowly she retrieved the purse and reached in to grab a handful of coins.

One of the men walked closer and held out his hand as she counted out the price. Once done, she repeated the process with the second man before replacing the purse beneath her cloak. Both men counted their money again before walking to one side and talking quietly amongst themselves.

'I do not like this, my lady,' said Fakhiri quietly, 'I think they are plotting something.'

'Arturas assured me they were good men,' said Sumeira, 'let us wait and see.'

'Do you have a blade?' asked Fakhiri.

Sumeira turned to stare at the cart-master.

'Why?'

'Because if your friend is wrong, and we need something to defend ourselves, I would wager you do not know how to fight. Luckily, I do but have no weapon. So, do you have a knife?'

Sumeira hesitated before reaching to her own waste belt and retrieving a small ornamental dagger. She handed it over to Fakhiri.

'It is nought, but a child's plaything,' he said with disdain.

'It is all I have,' said Sumeira.

'Then let us hope I do not need it.'

Finally, one of the men returned while the other wandered over to two horses tied beneath a nearby tree.

'So,' said the first mercenary, 'it seems we have a problem. You see, when we agreed a price with our mutual friend Arturas, the southern road was far less dangerous. Now, with Saladin's warriors as thick as locusts from here to Egypt, the risks are far higher.'

'We have a deal,' said Sumeira, 'and you have been paid. I expect you to uphold your side of the bargain. Arturas spoke highly of you; he said you were the best he knew.'

'And we are,' said the man, 'but it has been a long time since Arturas earned his way with a sword. He has grown soft since living within the walls of Karak and has forgotten how hard it is to live out on the road.'

'So, what are you saying?'

'What I am saying,' said the mercenary, 'is that if you give me the rest of your purse, we will be on our way and leave you and your little Saracen friend here, unharmed.'

'What?' gasped Sumeira.

'You heard him,' said the second mercenary riding his horse over in the gloom, 'give us the money and we will not lay a finger on you. Refuse, and we will take the money anyway, but not before killing your friend here and having some fun with you first. It's been a long time since we have enjoyed the company of a woman as pretty as you.'

'You are no better than the brigands of the road,' spat Sumeira. 'Traitors to any man who calls themselves Christian.'

'We've never claimed to be pious,' said the first man, 'and are just looking out for ourselves, the same as most men out here in this God-forsaken hell-hole.'

'You won't get away with this,' said Sumeira.

'We already have,' said the mercenary placing his hand on the hilt of his sword, 'now hand over the purse.' Sumeira hesitated but knew there was nothing she could do. Frustrated, she reached beneath her cloak and retrieved the bag of silver. The man took it and threw it up to his comrade before turning to face Sumeira again.

'You are certainly one pretty woman,' he said, 'I think perhaps I should have some fun with you after all.'

'Leave her,' said the other mercenary, 'we have what we came for now let us be gone before someone comes along.'

'We have plenty of time,' said the first man. 'Nobody ventures out of the town after dark, and besides, we cannot let them live. They'll tell Arturas, and he'll hunt us down like wild dogs.'

'Then get on with it,' said the rider, 'I want to get away from here.'

Simon walked towards Sumeira, a sick leer spreading across his face.

'You bastard,' snarled Sumeira, 'you promised to let us go.'

'The world is a bad place, my lady,' said the mercenary, 'now, are we going to do this the hard way or the easy way.'

Before she could answer, Fakhiri let out an angry cry and ran the few paces between them to lunge at the man, knocking him to the ground.

'My lady, run,' he cried, producing the knife, 'head for the town.'

Sumeira needed no second warning and turned to run as fast as she could towards the walls surrounding Al Shabiya.

For a few seconds, the mounted mercenary was caught unawares and watched as Sumeira fled.

'Get after her,' roared the first man now getting to his feet. The horseman kicked in his heels and galloped after Sumeira as the first mercenary turned to face the cart-master. 'As for you, my little Saracen friend, let us see how brave you are without your head.' He drew his sword and as Fakhiri nervously fingered the ornamental knife, lunged forward to wreak his revenge.

Sumeira ran as fast as she could but knew she could never outrun the horse. Desperately she zigzagged across the open ground, her hair falling below her shoulders as it came loose from its ties, but try as she might, she could not lose the horseman. The ground underfoot was uneven, and just when she thought she might make it, she lost her footing and fell to the floor.

'Nice try,' lady growled the rider, dismounting from his horse. 'Sorry, but this is the way it must be.' He drew his own sword and placed it on Sumeira's neck, but before he could apply any pressure, another horseman galloped out of the darkness and smashed into him, sending him flying into the dust.

The mercenary was dazed, but unhurt. He got to his feet and looked around for his dropped sword, but it was lost in the darkness. He thought desperately, and though he was a seasoned fighter, he knew that without a weapon, he had little chance against an armed horseman. His horse was only a few paces away, but even if he could mount in time, he still had no weapon. His attacker was turning to race back, and the mercenary knew his only chance was to try and reach the safety of the town. He ran to his horse to grab the bag of silver before running hard into the few bushes between him and the town walls. As he passed Sumeira, he lashed out with his boot, catching her in the ribs and she fell gasping to the floor.

'Sumeira,' roared a voice and as her attacker disappeared into the night, the man who had ridden to her rescue quickly dismounted and ran over to help. 'Sumeira,' he said again dropping to his knees, 'are you alright? Who was that man?'

'Hunter,' she gasped, recognising the scout, 'you came.'

'I have,' he said, 'and by the look of it, just in time. Are you hurt?'

'Nothing broken,' she said, 'he just knocked the breath from my body.'

'Who was he,' asked Hunter, 'and how did you come to be out here with him?'

Sumeira's eyes widened as she remembered Fakhiri's predicament.

'Hunter,' she gasped, 'there is another one back there. The two of them attacked Fakhiri and me. You have to help him.'

'Who is Fakhiri?'

'I'll explain later, but you have to go and help him. He stands no chance against a mercenary.'

Hunter stood up and drew his sword.

'You stay here,' he said, 'I will be back as soon as I can.' He turned and ran into the darkness as Sumeira gingerly got to her feet. Nervously she looked around, worried in case her attacker returned, but the night was silent. She walked over to the horse and after calming it down with pats and gentle words, took the reins and followed hunter in the darkness. A few minutes later, she came upon a grisly scene, illuminated by the low hanging moon. Two men stood in the clearing, each with a blade in their hands. The third man lay dead on the ground, his clothing sodden with blood.

'You got here in time,' said Sumeira, turning to face Hunter, 'thank the Lord.'

'This was nothing to do with me,' said Hunter, 'he was already dead by the time I got here.'

She turned to Fakhiri, his hand still wrapped around the hilt of the ornamental knife.

'I do not understand,' she said, 'he had a sword. How did you manage to overcome an armed man so used to the ways of war?'

'He may have been used to the battlefield,' said Fakhiri, 'but there is no school as brutal as the back streets of Cairo.' He bent down to wipe the blood off the blade and onto the dead man's tunic before offering the knife back to Sumeira.

'Keep it,' she said, 'it is of no use to me.'

'What about him?' asked Fakhiri, looking down at the body.

'We should bury him,' said Sumeira.

'No,' said Hunter, 'we have little time, and there will be too many questions asked. He chose this fate, let him lie.'

'So, what do we do now?'

'We do what we came to do,' said Hunter. 'We have their horses so we can make good time.'

'You forget,' said Sumeira, 'I have no money to pay you. The other mercenary took it all.'

'I do this not for profit,' said Hunter, 'but from loyalty to a friend.'

'But what about money for bribes or to buy my son's freedom, what will we do for that?'

'My lady,' said Fakhiri quietly, 'if you will allow, I think I may be able to help.'

Sumeira and Hunter both stared at the slave with surprise.

'How,' asked Sumeira eventually, 'you have no coins?'

'I do not,' said Fakhiri, 'but if Allah is with me, I know where we can find something a thousand times more valuable than all the silver you once held in your hands.'

'Where,' asked Hunter, 'and what is it?'

'You will see soon enough,' said the cart-master, 'but first we have to head north.'

Chapter Seventeen

Jerusalem

April - AD 1187

Gerard of Ridefort, Roger De-Moulins and Balian of Ibelin waited in an antechamber for Guy to arrive. Now the Easter celebrations were over; they had been summoned to attend the king to address the situation regarding Raymond of Tripoli.

'Has there been any news?' asked Gerard.

'Not since I left him,' said Balian. 'He was adamant that he would not support Guy or Sibylla in any respect.'

'And you reminded him of the consequences?'

'I did, but the man was unmoved. I think he has backed himself into a corner and cannot see a way out.'

Behind them, a door opened, and King Guy strode in as all three dipped their heads in acknowledgement.

'Gentlemen,' he said, removing his riding gloves, 'we all know why we are here, that traitor Raymond continues to defy me, and I want him prized out of Tiberias.

'By force?' asked Roger De-Moulins.

'Yes, by force,' said Guy. 'He has had his chances and still ignores my demands. I want you to gather your men and put an end to his arrogance once and for all.'

'With respect, my king,' said Gerard, 'I do not think that is a good idea.'

'And why not?' asked Guy. 'Have we not allowed him enough chances to take the knee?'

'You have been more than generous,' said Gerard, 'but he is still a powerful lord and commands a strong army. Even with all our forces combined, the fighting will be fierce, and many will die. I just think that there is still room for negotiation.'

'If we wait any longer, we will look weak,' said Guy, 'I want him out, now.'

'Listen,' said Roger, 'what if we ride to Tiberias and give him one last chance to change his mind?'

'Balian has already done that,' said the king, 'and has returned belittled. Raymond does not want to know.'

'Yes, but if he tries again, this time with Gerard and me at his side, Raynald may be more inclined to see reason.'

Guy looked between them. The idea had merit for the men before him commanded three of the strongest fighting forces in the Outremer, the Templars, the Hospitallers and the army of Nablus. If all three turned up with the same message, then only an idiot would dare to ignore it.

'If I agree,' he asked, 'and you fail to get him to see sense, what action then?'

'Then, we will assemble our forces and lay siege to Tiberias,' said Gerard, 'but I think Roger De-Moulins is correct, it deserves one more attempt before we set Christian upon Christian.'

Again, the king paused before taking a deep breath and exhaling heavily.

'So be it,' he said, 'but if you are unsuccessful, I will hear no more argument and will bring the combined forces of Jerusalem down upon him. Agreed?'

'Agreed,' said the three men

'Get it done,' said Guy and without waiting for a response, left the room.

In Tiberias, Raymond of Tripoli paced the floor of the meeting chamber, nervous about the audience that was about to take place. The city was secured and his men in high spirits, but it was obvious that he could not maintain his stance much longer. Trade had dried up between Tiberias and Jerusalem, and without the taxes from Beirut, his treasuries were running low. His treaty with Saladin was holding well, but he knew he could not hold out much longer, and if he did not move against Guy and Sibylla soon, his case for the crown would weaken. Consequently, the meeting he was about to have with Saladin's envoys was crucial to his future, both in the short and the long term. A door opened at the far end of the room, and one of his knights entered.

'My lord,' said the knight, 'they are here.'

'Bring them in,' said Raymond and walked over to sit in a chair upon a raised dais at the end of the room. Although not high, it enabled his head to remain above those of his visitors while seated, a significant psychological advantage when negotiating with an enemy.

A few minutes later, the knight returned, this time followed by three Saracens. The first was elegantly dressed in swathes of ceremonial silks while the second was clad all in black, a Mamluk bodyguard for the emir who was about to negotiate on behalf of Saladin. The third was just a boy, a slave to the emir dressed as elegantly as his master.

The three Arabs walked across the room and came to a stop before the dais. The emir nodded his head slightly in acknowledgement, but the Mamluk remained stone still, his eyes fixed on the count. Four knights also entered the chamber and took their places either side of Raymond.

'Muzaffar ad-Din Gokbori,' said Raymond at last, acknowledging the emir, 'welcome to Tiberias. Your comfort and safety are my sole priority while you are here, please, take refreshment.'

One of Raymond's servants walked across the room and offered the emir a glass of crystal-clear water. Gokbori took only a sip in acknowledgement of the protection offered before handing back the glass.

'Count Raymond,' he said eventually. 'Your hospitality is both noted and welcomed. It is a shame others of your people do not also observe the rules of etiquette.'

'Alas, I cannot answer for my brethren,' said the count, 'but can assure you that while the treaty between Saladin and myself stands, there will always be a sanctuary behind these city walls for you and your people.'

'Indeed, said Gokbori, 'and I assure you, the sultan does not take your assurances lightly. It takes a great man to break with his fellows in the name of peace, and in recognition, he sends you this gift.' He snapped his fingers, and his servant ran forward to lay a wrapped package at the count's feet. As soon as he retired, one of Raymond's knights stepped forward to unwrap the gift, revealing a beautiful scimitar made from the finest silver inlaid with intricate patterns of gold.

'Your master is indeed generous,' said Raymond, 'and I will ensure the gesture is returned with the finest from my treasuries.'

'Salah ad-Din has no need of silver or gold,' said Gokbori, 'your friendship is enough. However, I requested this audience to discuss matters of far greater importance.'

'Feel free to speak your mind,' said Raymond, 'your words will stay within this room.'

'Count Raymond,' said Gokbori, 'the peace that our treaty brings is indeed welcomed by the sultan, but we find ourselves in a position that requires more.'

'Continue,' said Raymond.

'As you know,' said Gokbori, 'unlike our agreement, the treaty between the Ayyubid and Jerusalem has been continually broken by many Christians. Despite this, my master has withheld his armies in the hope of negotiated peace. Now, his resolve has finally broken, and he seeks retribution for a crime committed by the castellan of Karak, Raynald of Chatillon.'

'Raynald is a law unto himself,' said Raymond, 'he sees himself as untouchable by all parties, including the King of Jerusalem. What has he done so bad that threatens war?'

'A few months ago, a caravan travelled from Egypt to Damascus, safe in the knowledge that it would not be attacked. The entire contents of that caravan were to be the dowry of a woman destined to become the bride of one of Saladin's sons, a fortune the likes of which is seldom seen.'

'I heard about the attack,' said Raymond, 'a barbarous act though I did not know about the dowry. He is known as a greedy man, Gokbori, and I suspect that the chattels are already deep within the vaults of Karak castle. Even the King of Jerusalem will have little influence if you seek their return.'

'The valuables mean nothing,' said Gokbori, 'but the caravan also carried the bride, an Ayyubid princess who also happened to be my cousin.'

'So you want her back?'

'Alas, that is impossible,' said Gokbori, 'for the castellan had her murdered before casting her body into his stinking pit. Now, Salah ad-Din's son demands revenge and his father agrees that we will take no more insult.'

'So what do you want from me? I cannot wage war on Karak.'

'Nor do we expect you to,' said Gokbori. 'Salah ad-Din knows that to pursue Raynald of Chatillon is a path well-worn with little effect. Consequently, he wants to confront Jerusalem and demand they hand over the man responsible for this outrage.'

'Raynald of Chatillon is a high-ranking officer in the order of Templars,' said Raymond, 'and it is unlikely anyone will march against him.'

'Then Jerusalem will suffer the consequences.' said Gokbori. 'Either they hand him over, or we will cancel all treaties and march on the city.'

Raymond swallowed hard. The look in Gokbori's eyes said that this was no idle threat.

'And my part in this?'

'Of all the Franks, you are the only one to honour the treaties,' said Gokbori, 'and my master does not want you to suffer for the crimes of others. You have previously requested an alliance with the Ayyubid, and I am here to offer what you want, on one condition.'

'And that is?'

'To reach Jerusalem, we have to cross your territory, and though we could easily do so with strength, we would rather do so with your support. An alliance would enable that request.'

'It is true that I seek an alliance,' said Raymond, 'but I will not fight alongside Salah ad-Din against Christians, that is too much to ask.'

'Nor do we wish you to, but we have an offer that you will find difficult to resist.'

'Which is?'

'If you allow us to cross your lands with no opposition, we will ensure every man woman and child in Tiberias will remain unharmed in any war that follows. What is more, when Jerusalem falls, you will be crowned King of the Christians and allowed to rule the kingdom until the end of your days.'

'I do not understand,' said Raymond, 'why would you take Jerusalem only to hand it back?'

'There will be no handing back,' said Gokbori, 'the Holy-city belongs to all, Christian and Muslim alike. The gates will be open to all pilgrims irrespective of religion. You will be king, but of the Christians only, not the city.'

Raymond stared at the envoy. His mind was spinning. What he desired most was being handed to him on a plate, but at what cost? Deep in his heart, he knew that it was inevitable that one day Jerusalem would fall, but he had doubted that it would be in his lifetime. If he accepted Saladin's offer, Jerusalem would be taken by surprise, but the fighting could be minimal instead of a war that could last years and cost the lives of thousands.

'If I do this,' he said eventually, 'and you take Jerusalem, what will become of the Christian inhabitants?'

'We fight only our enemy's armies,' said Gokbori, 'not civilians. They will be allowed to stay or to leave, whichever is their preference. Those that stay will live alongside our own people as equal citizens of Jerusalem.'

'And when do you want my answer?'

'Our army has already assembled, Count Raymond, and I am leaving at dawn tomorrow so will need your decision by then. By the time I get back to Salah ad-Din and convey the results of this audience, I suspect we would move no later than the full moon. After that, there will be no further negotiation.'

Again Raymond thought furiously. Everything he ever wanted was laid out before him, power, riches and the Kingdom of Jerusalem, and all he had to do was turn a blind eye to the Saracen movements. If he refused, he would be plunged into a bloody battle for Tiberias, and the fight for Jerusalem would happen anyway. But if he accepted, his ambitions would be more than fulfilled with little bloodshed. The answer was obvious, and he got to his feet.

'Muzaffar ad-Din Gokbori,' he said, 'there is no need to delay. I give my word that I will not fall upon those that pass through my lands without provocation, but I bid you this. Do what you have to do, but the killing must be kept to a minimum. Jerusalem needs a strong king, yet I see no reason why it cannot be open to both of our peoples. Tell your master that I agree to his terms, and I do this in the name of Christians everywhere.'

Gokbori bowed his head in acceptance.

'In that case, Raymond of Tripoli,' he said, 'there is no more to say.' He nodded again before turning around and striding out of the door, closely followed by his bodyguard and servant.

'My lord,' said one of the knights at his side. 'Do you think that was wise?'

Raymond turned to stare at the knight.

'Wise or not, Sir Jameson,' he said, 'the deed is done. 'Now call the garrison to arms. Alliance or not, we will take no chances.' He left the room followed by two of the knights.

What did you think of that?' asked Sir Jameson when he had left.

'It makes me uncomfortable,' said the second knight. 'To ally with the Saracens against my brothers in arms leaves an unpleasant taste in my mouth.'

'As it does mine, we have to do something.'

'Like what?'

'Leave it to me,' said Sir Jameson. 'I will not stand by and see brother fight brother for no reason and besides, to reach Jerusalem, the Saracens will have to pass Nazareth, and I have family there.'

'What do you intend to do?'

'What I must,' said Sir Jameson, 'there is a Templar force garrisoned at the castle of Al-Fulah near Nazareth. I will warn the castellan there of the Saracen intentions.'

'If you are found out, you will be executed.'

'We have to do something,' said Sir Jameson, 'for to do nothing could mean that thousands of Christians will die needlessly.'

Several leagues to the south-east, Hunter and Sumeira followed Fakhiri as he rode north towards Damascus. Their pace was slow as the cart-master regularly scanned the horizon as if seeking a landmark.

'I think he is playing tricks upon us,' said, Hunter. 'We have been riding for hours without success. I think he is hoping a Saracen patrol may come by and take us prisoner.'

'We have to give him a chance,' said Sumeira, 'he saved my life back there so why would he betray us now?'

'I do not know,' said Hunter, 'but this does not feel right. What is he looking for?'

They both stared at the cart-master, who had stopped alongside a pile of rocks at the roadside. He turned around and smiled.

'This is it,' he said, 'the place where our caravan was captured.'

'And?' Asked Hunter.

'Come,' said Fakhiri, 'you will see.'

They dismounted and walked over to the rocks. Fakhiri bent down and removed several small stones before scraping in the dust beneath. Finally, he let out a cry of excitement and retrieved a small ornate chest before standing up and turning to face Sumeira and Hunter.

'What have you got there?' asked Hunter.

'What I told you about the caravan was the truth,' said Fakhiri, 'the girl the castellan killed was promised to the son of Salah ad-Din as a bride and the goods were part of her dowry.'

'Part of it?' asked Sumeira. 'You said all of it.'

'And I told the truth,' said Fakhiri, 'but what I did not say was the dowry also contained an item of jewellery more precious than any other in Syria. It was intended to be worn around Takisha's neck at her wedding, and she kept it close during the journey. As soon as I saw our horsemen flee the Christian soldiers, I knew there was a risk they would steal everything in the caravan. There was little I could do, but at least I could protect the necklace.' He held out the box for Hunter to hold before opening the lid. After a few second pause he reached in with both hands and withdrew the most beautiful thing Sumeira had ever seen. 'This is it, my lady, this is the Gehaz of Egypt.'

Hunter and Sumeira stared in silence. The heavy necklace glistened in the afternoon sun, but it was the hundreds of embedded jewels that caught everyone's eye, each one weaved onto an intricate web of gold and held in place by tiny golden clasps. The whole thing formed a beautiful, 'v-shaped' necklace of precious stones designed to reach down from the shoulders to finish in a point just below the navel.

'That is astonishing,' said Sumeira eventually, 'and is surely worth a king's ransom.'

'And more,' said Fakhiri. 'There is none other like it, and each jewel is worth ten times the amount of silver those dogs stole from you.' He stepped forward, holding the necklace towards Sumeira. 'Here,' he said, 'take it. It is yours to do with what you will.'

'What?' gasped Sumeira. 'No, I cannot. It is not yours to give or mine to take. It belongs to that girl.'

'Who now lies rotting in Raynald's stinking pit,' said Fakhiri. 'I knew the girl well, she was a good person, pure of heart and body. If she had known her fate, she would have wanted you to have it, I am sure.'

'But it is worth so much,' said Sumeira.

'Is it worth more than the life of your son?' asked Fakhiri.

'No of course not, but …'

'Then take it,' said Fakhiri. 'We can remove what jewels we need to pay our way and perhaps one day, once you have been reunited with your son, I can take what remains back to Egypt to be repaired.'

Sumeira looked across at Hunter.

'What do you think?'

'The decision is between you two,' he said, 'but from what I understand, we have little other option.'

She turned back to Fakhiri.

'If you are sure,' she said, 'then I will take you up on your incredible offer. I promise to use only as few as we need and will try to pay you back as soon as I am able.'

'There is no repayment needed,' said Fakhiri, 'you are a good person, my lady, and sometimes Allah rewards such people in mysterious ways. Think of this as his gift.'

Sumeira turned to give the necklace to Hunter.

'Will you carry this for us,' she said, 'I trust you with my life and know it is safer with you than anyone.'

'I am not so sure,' said Hunter with a laugh, 'it seems our little knife fighter from Cairo is a pretty safe wager.'

'I travel lightly,' said Fakhiri, 'you should carry the Gehaz.'

'In that case,' said Hunter, 'we need to head back to Al Shabiya.'

'Why?' asked Sumeira, 'can we not just pass it by?'

'Like it or not,' said Hunter, 'we will need silver coins for the journey. Once in Segor, we can sell more jewels, but we need silver now. Come, let us mount up. Once we have the coins, we can be on our way.'

Chapter Eighteen

The Road to Tiberias

April - AD 1187

Balian of Ibelin, Roger De-Moulins and Gerard of Ridefort rode three abreast along the road from Jerusalem to Tiberias. Behind them came a combined force of over five hundred men, not huge but enough to deter any attack by one of the many Saracen raiding parties that were known to be terrorising the lands around Jerusalem. The mood was sombre for they knew that if they could not persuade Raymond of Tripoli to swear loyalty to Guy, a war between the two cities would inevitably follow.

'We are wasting our time,' said Balian, 'I saw the mood of the man. He is not for turning.'

'So you keep saying,' said Ridefort, 'but we have to give it one last try.'

'I say that if he refuses, we attack him there and then,' said Roger De-Moulins.

'Honour forbids such an action,' said Balian, 'as you well know.'

'I have no treaty with him,' said the Hospitaller grandmaster, 'why would it besmirch my honour?'

'You know why,' said Balian, 'by entering his counsel chamber we are bound to the rules of negotiation, and besides, he is no fool, and I suspect he will be well guarded.'

'Who is that?' asked Gerard, staring at a group of four men riding hard down a slope to their front. 'It looks like they are in a hurry.' He raised his hand, bringing the column to a halt. The riders rode up to the column before reining in their lathered horses.

'My lords,' said the lead knight, glancing up at the Templar flag, 'to whom am I speaking?'

'My name is Roger De-Moulins, Hospitaller grandmaster,' replied Roger, 'this is Gerard of Ridefort, grandmaster of the order of Templars and this is Balian, Lord of Nablus. What is your business, Sir Knight, for your manner displays anxiety?'

'My lords,' said the knight, 'our meeting is fortunate. My name is Sir Jameson of Tripoli. I serve under Raymond, Count of Tripoli and current castellan of the citadel at Tiberias.'

'We know your master,' said Balian, 'and in fact, we are on our way to speak to him about his failure to acknowledge the new King and Queen of Jerusalem.'

'If you are going to try and change his mind,' said Jameson, 'I fear you are too late. There are things afoot that make your mission pointless and I urge you to turn back.'

'What things?' asked Balian.

'It shames me to say,' said the knight, 'but my master has agreed an accord with the devil himself. Just a few hours ago he agreed to allow Saladin free passage across his wife's lands to wage war upon Jerusalem. He promised not to fight the Saracens and in return would receive the crown.'

All three men stared at the knight in astonishment. Never had they heard of such treachery and their blood boiled.

'And you are sure of this?' asked Gerard.

'I was in the room when he made the alliance,' said Jameson. 'Even as we speak, the Ayyubid muster their armies and head towards the River Jordan. I could not countenance such treachery and left under cover of darkness to raise the alarm.'

'You did the right thing,' said Gerard. 'How long do you think we have before they reach Jerusalem?'

'I cannot be sure,' said Jameson, 'but I would guess a few days at the most.'

Gerard of Ridefort looked around at the column of men. They were all experienced fighters, but he knew that any army mustered by Saladin would be far, far larger.

'We cannot face them with just these men,' he said, 'we need reinforcements.'

'From where,' asked Roger, 'we are too far from Jerusalem or Acre to raise any significant force in time?'

'Then we must make do with what we have locally.' He turned to Balian. 'Sir Balian, you of all of us have a chance to get to your men in time. Can you ride to Nablus and bring them to Nazareth as fast as you can?'

'I can be back by dawn the day after tomorrow,' said Balian.

'That will have to do,' said Gerard. 'Ride like the wind, and in the meantime, we will send messages to the castles at Al-Fulah and Qaqan to mobilise their garrisons. We have Templars and Hospitallers in both, and what we may lack in numbers will be more than substituted with strength and ability.'

'We should also send messages to Jerusalem and Acre,' said Roger De-Moulins, 'and warn them of the Saracens' intent. If we should fall, then at least our comrades will be ready.'

'Where do we muster?' asked Balian.

'Meet at the Cresson springs,' said Gerard. 'Once everyone is there, we will march to meet the Saracens on the road.'

'So be it,' said Balian and turned to summon his men before galloping back the way they had come.

'Raymond has gone too far this time,' growled Gerard. 'Once this threat has been dealt with, God willing, I will ride to Tiberias myself and kill him myself.

'One thing at a time, brother,' said Roger, 'first we have Saracens to kill.'

On the eastern side of the Salt-sea, Hunter, Sumeira and Fakhiri had made good time and were now only a few leagues away from Segor. They had exchanged two of the jewels from the Gehaz for a purse full of silver coins in Al Shabiya and had ridden south for two days without any problems. Now, as they neared the town, the roads had become busier, and they resorted to travelling across country to avoid suspicious eyes.

'We are close,' said Fakhiri. 'Tonight we will sleep in the hills above Segor and tomorrow, I will walk into the markets to ask questions.'

'There is no need for you to get involved, Fakhiri,' said Sumeira, 'you have done more than enough.'

'I will not let you enter that place alone,' replied the cart-master, 'it is nought but a den of thieves who will slit your throat for a loaf of bread.'

'It is also filled with talented jewellers,' said Sumeira, 'artisans who can make the humblest of objects into items of beauty. I lived there for many years and saw these things for myself.'

'Perhaps so, but when it comes to money, all are as greedy as each other and would think nothing of relieving you of your coins, No, I will come with you and ensure you stay safe.'

Sumeira nodded, knowing that he made sense.

'Do you know where you are going exactly?' asked Hunter.

'When I fled Segor years ago,' replied Sumeira, 'I was hidden in a caravan by a sympathetic cart-master. I stayed with him for many months, and we became good friends. It turned out we lived not far from each other in Segor and knew some of the same people in the city. I aim to find him and seek his help.'

'So you do not know where your son is?'?'

'No, the person who told me Jamal's father had died also told me that the family who had taken him in had fallen on hard times and had moved to the poorer quarter of the city.'

'It is a big area,' said Hunter. 'I fear the chances of finding him are small.'

'If anyone can find out, Ahmed can,' said Sumeira. 'These people each know everybody else's business and hardly a word passes between anyone without their neighbour knowing.'

'So,' said Hunter, 'when do you go?'

Sumeira turned to the cart-master.

'Fakhiri, what do you think?'

'Midday tomorrow,' said Fakhiri. 'The markets will be busy, and we will not stand out so much, but first, you will need the clothing of an Arab woman and a veil to cover your head.'

'I agree,' said Sumeira, 'but have brought none with me.'

'Leave that to me,' said Fakhiri. 'I have an idea.'

The following morning, Sumeira woke up to see Fakhiri standing above her.

'Here,' he said, 'it is not pretty like the Frankish women wear, but it will make you invisible.'

Sumeira looked at the black thawb. Strangely, although she knew it would be hot beneath the heavy fabric, it somehow felt welcoming, having worn something similar for many years when she last lived in the city.

'Where did you get it?' she asked.

'Do not ask what you do not wish to hear,' said Fakhiri, 'but rest assured, I left a silver coin in its place. Now get dressed for the walk to Segor will take time.'

Several hours later, Fakhiri and Sumeira walked through the outskirts of Segor. Sumeira wore the black thawb with only her eyes visible beneath the veil upon her head. Nervously they walked through many alleyways towards the poorer quarter of the city, the place where she had earned a living as a physician for so many years. Men young and old sat on the doorsteps and hung around the street corners, sipping tea as they watched the strangers pass.

'I am not familiar with this place,' said Fakhiri, 'the people have daggers instead of eyes.'

'Ignore them,' said Sumeira, 'and walk with purpose in your step. If they think you are not from here, they will see you as prey and our days will be numbered. Look like you belong, and they will let you pass.'

'You seem very confident,' said Fakhiri.

'This was my home,' said Sumeira, 'and I had to fit in or die. Come, it is not much further.' They continued into the heart of Segor until finally, she stopped before a door set deep into a windowless wall. 'This is it,' she said, 'I just hope he is here.' She knocked on the door and waited but received no reply. She tried again, but when nobody answered, she turned to Fakhiri with a concerned look upon her face. Before she could say anything, an old woman opened the door opposite and stared at the strangers.

'Who is it you seek?'

'I'm looking for Ahmed the wagon-master,' said Sumeira. I know him from a few years ago. Is this his house?'

'It is but it has lain empty for many months.'

'Where is he?'

The woman shrugged her shoulders.

'Who knows?' she said. 'He is a busy man. What business do you have with him?'

'That is between the lady and the wagon-master,' said Fakhiri, 'and no concern of yours.'

'In that case, stay there and wait,' said the woman and turned to go inside.

'Wait,' said Sumeira, 'I am here to find my son, and I hoped Ahmed could help.'

'What is his name?' asked the woman.

'My son is called Jamal, but his father was known as Muthal. I have been told he is dead but have no proof.'

The woman stared at Sumeira for a few moments until she let out a small laugh.

'You are she,' she said eventually, 'the Greek woman who disappeared with his daughter.'

'You know of me?' asked Sumeira.

'Everyone knows about you,' said the woman, 'the westerner who played the trickster at his own game and left him looking a fool. Muthal offered a reward to anyone who could capture you and return his daughter to his family.'

'Do you know if any of his comrades still live?'

'Why would you want to speak to them? Muthal may be dead, but he still has family, and they would pay a pretty price for your head.'

'You mention his family,' said Fakhiri. 'Do you know where they live?'

'I may do,' said the woman, 'but these are my people, and this woman is a Frank. Why would I betray them to her?'

Sumeira glanced at Fakhiri before turning back to the old woman.

'What's your name?' she asked.

'Sada,' came the reply. 'What is yours?'

'Sumeira, and if you can tell me where Muthal's family lives, Sada, I can make you a very wealthy woman.'

Sada stared between Fakhiri and Sumeira for a moment before checking out the street to either side.

'Come in,' she said eventually, 'out here the walls have eyes.'

She stepped to one side, and Sumeira followed Fakhiri into a dark and narrow passage. Sada closed the door and led them into a courtyard at the centre of the building. Despite the limitations, the space was full of greenery, carefully cultivated to maximise the light. At the centre, crystal clear water magnified the azure mosaic tiles of a small pool and birds flitted between the lush foliage.

'This is beautiful,' gasped Sumeira, looking around. 'How do you keep it so green?'

'My home is very old,' said Sada, 'one of the oldest in the city and is built upon the remains of buildings from long ago. Many years ago, my husband was digging out here to plant a tree and found a mosaic floor. He thinks it was built in the days of our ancestors by men of Rome, but I do not know about such things. We cleaned away the soil and found steps leading down to a small cavern with its own spring. It was filled with statues to some ancient gods, but my husband sold them in the markets. That is the source of the water that now sustains me as I get old.'

'It is truly a sight to behold,' said Sumeira, 'you are very fortunate.'

'Where is your husband now?' asked Fakhiri.

'He is dead,' said Sada, 'killed for the price of a single coin in his pocket.'

'Does anyone else know of this spring?' asked Fakhiri.

'Not anymore,' said Sada. 'My family have all gone, and I allow nobody past my door.'

'Yet you allowed us access, strangers whom you have never met before.'

'There is a reason for that, Sumeira,' said Sada. 'Ahmed told me about you and said that a more trustworthy woman never walked under the sun. If he trusted you, then so can I.'

'Do you know him well?' asked Sumeira.

'I should do,' said Sada, 'I gave birth to him.'

Chapter Nineteen

Al Fulah Castle

April - AD 1187

Jakelin De Mailly marched from the commandery in Al Fulah castle to join his men in the bailey. In total, he had seventy knights at his disposal including fifty Templars and twenty Hospitallers. In addition, he had a hundred foot soldiers and another hundred Turcopole lancers. It wasn't a massive force but the best he could assemble at such short notice. He climbed up on a wall so he could be seen by everyone who had mustered to answer the call from Gerard of Ridefort.

'Fellow Christians,' he said loudly, 'trusted allies. As you know, yesterday we received a call to arms from our fellow countrymen. Saladin has mobilised his army and even as we speak, has sent advance forces to clear the way to Jerusalem. If we allow them passage, then his main army will follow, and the Holy-city itself will be at risk. I have no idea what lies before us, so look to your swords and harden your hearts. The future of the Holy-land is in our hands.'

He climbed down from the wall and mounted his horse before turning to face the gate towers.

'Open the gates,' he shouted, and as the giant timber gates swung inward, he kicked his horse and led the garrison out towards Nazareth.

Several leagues away a similar scene was happening in the castle of Qaqan where another hundred or so Templar and Hospitaller knights had mustered to answer the call to arms from Gerard of Ridefort. The threat from Saladin had been recognised, and the forces of Jerusalem were responding.

In the east, Raymond of Tripoli and his wife stood atop one of the outer gate towers in the city of Tiberias. All along the defensive walls, hundreds of men at arms stood shoulder to shoulder, each bedecked in their full armour and carrying their weapons. In the distance, a massive column of Ayyubid cavalry rode westward, bypassing Tiberias and heading towards Jerusalem. For the best part of an hour, the mounted army passed until eventually, they were nothing more than a dust cloud on the horizon.

'What now, my lord,' asked one of the sergeants at his side, 'shall I stand the men down?'

'No,' said Raymond, 'double the guard and send out patrols to keep an eye on them.

'Yes, my lord,' said the sergeant and turned away to his duties.

'Are you sure you have done the right thing?' asked Raymond's wife at his side.

'Absolutely,' said Raymond, though deep in his heart, there stirred the faintest flickering of doubt.

The following day, Jakelin De Mailly led his column of men towards the Cresson springs. On the way they had encountered another column of knights from Nazareth, members of the royal guard stationed there under the command of Reginald of Sidon and by the time the sun had started its downward journey, they saw the Christian encampment sprawled across the slopes of a hill above the springs that gave the place its name.

'It looks like we are in time,' said Jakelin, 'God be praised.'

They rode towards the camp, and after allowing the men to water their horses, Reginald and Jakelin walked towards the command tent pitched near the far side of the springs.

'Sir Jakelin,' said Gerard, emerging from the tent, 'well met. I was concerned our messenger may not have got through.'

'I came as quickly as I could,' said Jakelin. 'Is there any news?'

'Not yet. Our scouts are scouring the area, but as yet there is no sign. How many men have you brought?'

'Seventy knights,' said Jakelin, 'and about a hundred Turcopole horsemen. I also have a hundred foot soldiers, but they are a day or so behind me. I encountered Sir Reginald on the road, and he has fifty knights.'

'Excellent,' said Gerard, 'with those already here from Qaqan and the men we already have, we can field a force of over two hundred knights and almost a thousand lancers. That number could double when Balian gets here from Nablus.'

'If what your note said is correct,' said Jakelin, 'it will be nowhere near enough. Saladin has that many men in Damascus alone and that is without the combined strength of the Ayyubid tribes.'

'I realise that,' said Gerard, 'but we have also sent messages to Jerusalem and Acre. As soon as they understand what is happening, they will muster their armies, and the numbers will be better balanced. All we have to do is hold them until Guy arrives with the two armies. Have your men been seen to?'

'They are pitching camp at the northern end of the springs,' said Jakelin.

'Good, in that case, let me get you some refreshment. Tomorrow we ride out to meet those who threaten Jerusalem.'

A few leagues away, another two men slaked their thirsts, but these men did not enjoy the comfort of campaign tents, for they were hidden from sight deep within the rambling olive groves near to the Jordan River. Hidden across two valleys, another seven thousand men sat silently, their well-trained horses laying alongside them, waiting for the commands that would inevitably come.

Muzaffar ad-Din Gokbori replaced the stopper in the water gourd and handed it to the slave sitting behind him before turning back to face the man who was leading the push into Jerusalem. Before them was a wooden platter of goat meat and dates.

'The men are ready and awaiting your instruction, Al-Afdal ibn Salah ad-Din,' he said. 'Do you want me to send blades into their camp during the night?'

'No,' said Al-Afdal, 'the prize before us is indeed great, and this time I know Allah will help us wrest the Holy-city from the hands of the infidels, but we will do so with honour. Leave the night-time murders to the likes of the Hashashin; we will meet our enemy on the battlefield and defeat them with guile and honour.'

'Their number is small,' said Gokbori, 'our men will run over them like a desert storm.'

'It is not just about numbers,' said Al-Afdal, taking a slice of goat meat, 'for they have men of the blood-cross amongst them. Do not forget what happened to my father's army at Montgisard, where eighty of these knights led the Christians to victory against overwhelming odds.'

'They are men, nothing more, nothing less,' said Gokbori, 'and at Montgisard they took us by surprise.'

'This is my point exactly,' said Afdal. 'As a force, there is none finer in battle, but if we can thin their lines, their undoubted influence will be useless.'

'I assume you have a plan?' said Gokbori

'I do,' said Afdal, 'and tomorrow, my friend, you will have the chance to avenge the death of your cousin.'

Chapter Twenty

The Battle of Cresson

May 1st - AD 1187

The following morning, Jakelin De Mailly and Gerard of Ridefort walked along the line of Templar knights, checking their equipment and making sure they were ready. All through the Cresson valley, the other commanders were doing the same thing. The plans were made, and everyone knew that as soon as the scouts returned, they would be setting out towards Tiberias to try and find the Saracen force.

'We could do with more knights,' said Jakelin, 'perhaps we should wait until Balian gets here with his army.'

'He is still a day away,' said the grandmaster, 'I have had a message that he stopped off in Sebastea to celebrate a feast day.'

'The man is an imbecile,' snarled Jakelin, 'he knows the threat, we need him here.'

'Nevertheless, we can wait no longer. Every moment we wait is a moment nearer to Jerusalem for Saladin. As soon as the scouts report back, we will make our move.'

'My lord,' said one of the knights alongside them, 'they are here.'

Everyone looked up to see four horsemen riding down the path to meet them. Within seconds, Jakelin could see something was wrong as all four horses were tied tightly together... as were the men upon their backs.

'Oh, sweet Jesus,' whispered one of the knights, making the sign of the cross upon his chest, 'where are their heads?'

Everyone stared in horror as the horses came to a halt. Each horse was covered with blood from the corpses upon their backs, and though a few squires ran forward to take them under their control, it took several moments before they were calm enough for some of the soldiers to cut the bodies loose and lower them to the floor.

'When did they set out?' demanded Gerard

'At dawn,' said Jakelin, 'why?'

'Because they can't have ridden far in so little time which means the Saracens are almost upon us.' He turned to the lines of

Templars and Hospitallers. 'Mount up,' he roared, 'look to your weapons.'

'My lord,' said Jakelin, 'take a moment. This is not like Saladin; I suspect there is trickery involved.'

'Trickery or not,' said Gerard, 'I will not stand by while our men are slaughtered. Mobilise the men, Sir Jakelin, there is revenge to be sought.'

'My lord,' started Jakelin, but before he continue, another voice echoed through the morning air.

'Here they come!'

Jakelin looked up in horror as hundreds of Saracen warriors came galloping over the crest of the hill, each bearing one of the feared recurved bows. Almost immediately, the air filled with arrows and as the Christians raced to mount their horses, a rain of death fell amongst them.

'Shields,' roared Jakelin. The mounted knights were well-drilled and wheeled their mounts to launch an immediate counter-attack, and although some fell to the sudden Saracen assault, their heavy gambesons and chainmail hauberks ensured they suffered few casualties.

Although outnumbered by the Saracens, the force and aggression of the Templar counter-attack paid dividends, and the knights smashed into the front ranks of enemy horsemen. The Saracens were lightly armoured in cuirasses of studded leather, but the lesser weight meant their horses were more responsive and the fight quickly spread out across the valley. At first, the Saracens dominated the field, but the heavier armour and larger warhorses of the knights soon started to pay off, and they began to push the Saracens back up the hill.

Jakelin led from the front, his sword cleaving through leather and flesh alike. His prowess in battle was well known throughout the Outremer and those who had not yet seen him fight watched in awe as he despatched warrior after warrior. Despite losing ground the Saracens fought bravely, making the Christians fight for every step. Men died everywhere, but no quarter was asked or given. The sound of a horn rent the air, and Jakelin glanced over his shoulder to see another column of knights racing up from the springs, it was Roger De-Moulins and his force of Hospitaller knights.

The reinforcements ploughed into the swarming Saracens, and within moments the tide was turned. Another horn echoed through the valley, this time from the Saracens, and every Ayyubid warrior broke off from the fight to retreat up the hill. Those still engaged fought to the death, but within minutes it was clear the field belonged to the Christians. As an almighty cheer went up from the throats of every man, Roger De-Moulins rode up to Gerard of Ridefort.

'What happened?' he asked.

'They just appeared out of nowhere,' said the Templar grandmaster, 'it was all we could do to get to the horses in time.'

'Were you not warned by your scouts?'

'They were killed,' said Gerard looking around, 'and we were caught cold. The attack was well planned and executed. We have lost many men.'

'Yet the day is ours,' said Roger, 'I have lost few so will follow up the attack.'

'Is that wise?' asked Gerard, 'we should re-group.'

'We have them on the run,' said Roger De-Moulins, 'and have to maintain the advantage. You muster your men and follow us as soon as you can, we'll make sure they do not have enough time to reform.' Without waiting for a response, he wheeled his horse and galloped back to where his own men were regrouping. 'Form up,' he roared, 'we're going after them.' Within seconds the Hospitallers and another five hundred lancers raced up the valley to disappear over the crest.

Gerard of Ridefort watched them go, still in shock at the sudden attack. Behind him, Jakelin De Mailly strode over, his surcoat sodden with the blood of his victims. In his left hand, he carried the Templar standard.

'My lord,' he said, 'your standard-bearer took an arrow to his face.' He lifted the pole and drove it into the soft valley soil. 'I shall arrange somebody else to bear it.'

'No,' said Ridefort, 'I want you to carry it, Sir Jakelin, we are sorely wounded, and I want the men to see a true warrior carrying the standard.'

'As you wish, my lord,' said Jakelin and watched as the last of Roger De Moulin's men disappeared in pursuit of the Saracens. Moments later, the remaining foot soldiers and knights arrived from the camp and spread out to treat the wounded.

'My lord,' gasped a voice, 'a word.'

Ridefort turned around and recognised Sir Jameson, the knight from Tiberias who had first raised the alarm a few days previously.

'What is it,' asked Ridefort, 'and where is your horse?'

'Cut from beneath me, my lord, but there are more important things to discuss.'

'Speak your mind,' said Ridefort.

'My lord, I believe you should regroup immediately and form a defensive position.'

'Why, the Hospitallers have them on the run.'

'Look around you, my lord,' said the knight, 'I estimate you killed half of the attackers, but even the most cursory count will tell you there are no more than five hundred dead Saracens in this valley. Counting those that escaped, that means we were attacked by about a thousand warriors.'

'And?'

'If that is the case, where are the other six thousand?'

In the next valley, Roger De-Moulins galloped his horse at the head of his hastily mustered forces. More used to the familiar structure of a battlefield, his men were spread out with little ability to hear the commands of their grandmaster. Up ahead, the Saracens had stopped fleeing and were hastily reforming to face the pursuing Christians. He held up his hand and reined his horse to a halt, allowing the rest of his men to catch up.

'We have them cornered,' he shouted, 'Hospitallers to the fore.' As his knights formed up line abreast, the rest of the lancers closed in behind them, almost six hundred men at arms against barely three hundred exhausted Saracens.

'Prepare to advance,' he roared and withdrew his sword from its scabbard.

'My lord,' shouted a voice, 'look to the hills.'

The grandmaster looked up and stared in growing horror as hundreds more Saracen riders appeared over the ridgeline. 'There too,' shouted another voice, and De-Moulins turned to see a similar thing happening on the opposite hill. As he stared, hundreds more warriors appeared until the Christians were surrounded by almost three thousand mounted Saracen warriors.

With so many enemy all around them, Gerard knew he could not stand and fight, nor could he retreat the way he had come. The only way out was to head forward, through the reformed lines of the men they had been pursuing.

'It's a trap,' he roared, 'we have to get out of this valley. Follow me.'

He dug his heels into his horse and galloped further up the road, knowing that they needed more open ground if they were to have any chance of survival. The rest of his men followed, but as they raced towards the waiting Saracens, the rest of the enemy horsemen swarmed down from the flanking hills. Within moments the Christians neared the enemy lines at the end of the valley, but as they approached, hundreds of hidden archers rose from the undergrowth either side of the road. The air filled with arrows and at such close range, the effect was devastating. Iron tipped arrows tore through chainmail and men and horses fell all along the column. Behind the waiting Saracen lines, even more riders appeared, blocking off their escape route and De-Moulins knew they were trapped. He looked around, desperately seeking an escape route, but there was none. If any of his men were to survive, they would have to fight their way out. To the east, he saw a forest and immediately knew it was their only chance.

'My lord,' shouted one of his knights from beneath his shield, 'we are being slaughtered, what is your command?'

'Break lines,' roared the grandmaster, 'and head for the treeline.'

His signaller sounded the horn, and the column swung eastward beneath a deadly hail of Saracen arrows. Riding towards them head-on were hundreds of Saracen riders, and as the hail of arrows eased, De-Moulins knew that at last, they had a chance.

'For God and for Jerusalem,' he roared raising his sword, and as his men spread out around him, Roger De-Moulins smashed into the first rank of Saracen warriors.

In the next valley, Gerard of Ridefort took stock of the situation. Many of the lancers under his command had been killed or wounded but the Templars, equipped with heavier armour, had escaped relatively unscathed. The men gathered around the flag, waiting for orders from the grandmaster.

'I want any man unhorsed to stay here with the foot soldiers and see to the wounded,' he announced. 'Carry them back to the camp and see they are well cared for.'

'What about the dead, my lord,' asked one of the men.

'We will not have the opportunity to return them to their loved ones,' said Ridefort, 'so bury them where they fell. Use the prisoners to dig the graves.' He turned to Sir Jakelin. 'Are we ready?'

'We are, my lord, but I would urge you to take heed of Sir Jameson's warning. There are thousands of Saracens still out there and to leave the camp unguarded invites trouble.'

'We cannot let the Hospitallers have all the glory, brother Jakelin,' said Ridefort, 'how would that look in Jerusalem?'

'With respect, my lord,' said Jakelin, 'there is no glory in defeat. All I ask is that we wait until the Hospitallers return. If we ride to join them, we leave the camp ill-defended.'

'Your points are noted, Sir Jakelin,' said the grandmaster, 'but we have a task to do and will meet it head-on. Tell the men to mount up, we ride immediately.'

Before Jakelin could react, a voice shouted from the rear ranks.

'My lord, we are under attack!'

Everyone looked up to see thousands of Saracen warriors racing down from the hills to either side of the valley. Their battle cries filled the air, and for the briefest of moments, the Templars just stared in shock, knowing they would never reach their horses in time to mount.

'Don't just stand there,' roared Sir Jakelin, 'to arms.'

Every man ran to create a defensive wall, but within moments another cry filled the air.

'There are more behind us, my lord.'

Ridefort spun around. There were enemy horsemen in all directions, and in the distance, he could see another force sweeping down to attack the camp. The situation was desperate, but there was little he could do to help.

'Form a circle,' he roared, 'protect the banners.'

Every man on foot closed in to form a defensive shield, each one sworn to defend the Templar standard with their lives. Across the valley, the Turcopole cavalry raced across the open ground to engage the Saracens, but they were heavily outnumbered, and Ridefort knew that without Templars to the fore, there would be only one outcome.

'Ready,' he roared as the first wave of Saracen riders neared, 'remember, you are fighting for Jerusalem itself. Show these heathen what it means to be a Christian.'

The defenders roared their defiance, and as the Saracen cavalry smashed into the defensive wall, every Christian soldier knew that they were not just fighting for the Holy-land, they were also fighting for their lives.

Al-Afdal sat astride his horse on top of one of the hills, watching the battle unfold. The initial attack by his warriors had been successfully repelled, but with his overwhelming numbers, he knew it was only a matter of time before the Templar position was overrun. In the distance, he could already see his warriors wreaking carnage amongst the tents of the Christian camp, and he turned to one of the emirs at his side.

'Muzaffar ad-Din Gokbori,' he said, 'the day goes well. What news of the others?'

'Your plan has worked better than we could have imagined,' said Gokbori. 'The vanguard took the bait and followed our men into the trap. As we speak, the Christians have been routed with most of them dead or dying across the battlefield.'

'Most?'

'Some managed to get to the trees,' said Gokbori, 'but our men are hunting them down. They will not escape.'

'See to it that they don't,' said Afdal. 'I seek nothing but the total annihilation of these men. It is about time that Jerusalem knew we are serious.'

'As you wish,' said Gokbori,

Down in the valley, the Templars reorganised for the third time, each time their ranks a bit thinner. Despite their disadvantage, they had acquitted themselves well, and dead Saracens littered the field. The enemy forces had withdrawn to regroup, but De Mailly knew they would have only a few minutes respite.

'My lord,' he said, addressing Gerard of Ridefort, 'we can't just stay here, if they bring up their archers, we will be cut down without landing another blow. Someone needs to escape and warn Jerusalem.'

'I know,' said Sir Gerard. He looked over to where some of the horses were still tethered. 'If we make a break for the horses, some of us should get through, but we will need a rear guard.'

'We do not have enough men,' said Sir Jakelin, 'any reduction in numbers will see us overwhelmed. You and Sir Reginald should head for the hills, the rest of us will hold them back.'

'I will not leave you, Sir Jakelin,' said Gerard, 'my place is here alongside my brothers.'

'You are the grandmaster,' said Jakelin, 'your place is leading the order throughout Christendom, not to die pointlessly in a battle already lost. Jerusalem needs to be warned of what happened here, and Sidon needs to muster her army in support of King Guy. You have to leave, my lord, your death here will serve no purpose.'

The grandmaster glanced over to Reginald of Sidon. As much as his honour hurt at the thought of leaving the battle, he knew the survival of Jerusalem could rely on someone getting through to warn them. Finally, he nodded his head in agreement and looked up at the banner flying over their heads.

'I should take our banner,' he said, 'to deny it to the enemy.'

'It will be more useful here,' said Sir Jakelin, 'it provides a rallying point for our men.'

'In that case, serve it well, my friend, and if I survive, I will pray for you in Jerusalem.'

'Just make sure you tell them what happened here,' said Sir Jakelin, 'else it all will have been for nothing. Now, go while you still have a chance.' Without waiting for a response, he turned away to rally his men. 'Close on me,' he roared, 'line abreast, prepare to advance.' The weary men assembled alongside him, each one already covered with the blood of their enemies. Jakelin looked over his shoulder at the grandmaster and Reginald of Sidon.

'It has been an honour serving you, my lord,' he said, 'now be gone.' He turned to face the enemy again. 'Men of God,' he roared, 'advaaance!'

Up above on the hill, Al-Afdal and Gokbori watched with fascination before one of the men at their sides pointed to the far side of the battlefield.

'My lord, two of the infidels are using the distraction to escape. Do you want me to ride them down?'

Salah ad-Din's son stared at the two Christians who had now reached the horses.

'No,' he said eventually, 'let them tell the tale of what happened here today. Perhaps it will open the Christians' eyes.' His attention returned to the marching line of knights, fifty brave men marching towards certain death beneath a Templar flag.

'Gokbori,' he said, 'go down there and seek their surrender. 'The battle is won, there is no need for more men to die.'

'Are there terms?' asked Gokbori.

'Only one,' said Afdal, 'I want them to feel the pain of total defeat for the rest of their lives, and that means they must surrender their flag.'

When they were within a hundred paces of the enemy, Jakelin halted the advance, and his men fell silent, each of them staring at the enormous army to their front. As they watched, the Saracens surrounded them until there was an enormous circle of warriors surrounding the Templars. Jakelin and his men formed their own circle, facing outward with the flag in the centre. The noise fell away, and the Saracen ranks opened up to allow one of their commanders to walk through.

'Who speaks for you?' he asked, and Jakelin De Mailly stepped forward.

'I do,' he said, 'Jakelin De Mailly, and by the end of this day, my name will be burned into your worst nightmares.'

'I am Muzaffar ad-Din Gokbori,' replied the Saracen, 'and I have been watching you from the hill above. You are a brave man, Jakelin De Mailly, you all are, but your day is done.' He looked up at the hill before returning his gaze to Sir Jakelin. 'My master, in his mercy, has authorised me to accept your surrender. He gives his word that if you cede to him, you will all be taken to Damascus and ransomed back to Jerusalem at the earliest opportunity.'

'I have seen the inside of a Saracen jail,' said Jakelin, 'and will not do so again.'

'Do not be a fool, Jakelin De Mailly,' said Gokbori, 'you know you will all die here today, but you can save yourself and your men with one simple act. All you have to do is hand me your flag, and you all will live.'

'You want me to cede the Baucent?'

'A simple enough gesture,' said Gokbori, 'yet one my master insists upon.'

Jakelin looked up the hill to where several Saracen officers looked down from astride their horses under the Ayyubid flags.

'And who is your master?'

'Al-Afdal ibn Salah ad-Din,' replied Gokbori, the son of the sultan himself.'

'I am honoured,' said Jakelin, 'but tell your master that if he wants this standard, he will have to prize it from my cold dead hands.'

'I suspected as much,' said Gokbori, 'but what of your men? Are they not important enough to make their own decisions, or are you going to be their executioner?'

'Each has their own mind,' said Jakelin, 'and will make their own choice.' He raised his voice, so all the knights in the circle could hear him. 'If any of you men wish to go, then leave now. There is no need of us all to die here today and if life is the path you choose, then go with my blessing and God's forgiveness.'

For a moment, there was silence until one of the knights pushed his way to the fore. Sir Jakelin turned to look at the knight.

'Sir Edward,' he said, 'go in peace, my friend.'

'I am going nowhere,' said the knight, 'but beg permission to allow this scoundrel to live another day.' He turned and dragged a young boy from the circle, the last remaining squire alive.

'John William,' said Jakelin, recognising the squire, 'what say you?'

'I wish to remain, my lord,' gasped the boy through his tears, 'my place is to serve the order, and if God wills it that I die this day, then it will be in his service.'

Sir Jakelin stared at the squire. The boy's left hand clutched at a wound on his right arm and blood seeped through his fingers.

'You are wounded,' he said.

'It is a scratch only,' cried the boy with tears running down his face, 'and I can still hold a knife.'

Sir Jakelin turned to Gokbori.

'Do I have your word that this boy will live?'

'You do,' said the emir, 'any man who lowers the sword will keep his life but those that remain to defend your banner will be shown no mercy.'

Jakelin looked down at the boy again,

'My lord,' gasped John William, 'please, I beg you, let me stay and fight.'

'You are no use to me,' said Sir Jakelin, 'for you cannot even hold a blade, but your courage does you justice, and one day you will be a great knight.' He turned back to face Gokbori. 'The boy will go,' he said, 'as will Sir Edward.'

The knight's head spun around to stare at Sir Jakelin.

'My lord, what are you saying?'

'The boy will need a master,' said Jakelin, 'to make sure he does well in life. I charge you with his care, Sir Edward, take him to Jerusalem and there make him a knight of worth.'

'But my lord,' said the knight again, 'my place is here besides my brothers.'

'I am still your superior,' said Jakelin, 'and I command you to do as I say. Step from the line, Sir Edward, your path has been decided for you.'

For a few moments, nobody moved until finally, the knight grabbed the squire by the scruff of his jerkin and marched him forward towards the enemy lines. Immediately four Saracens walked forward to disarm them before leading them away.

'Anyone else?' asked Gokbori.

Nobody moved, and the emir turned to Sir Jakelin.

'I will ask you one more time, Sir Knight, cede the flag or die where you stand.'

'We will not cede the flag, Gokbori,' snarled Sir Jakelin, his fingers tightening around the hilt of his sword, 'so do your worst.'

'So be it,' said Gokbori and turned away to disappear into the Saracen horde.

The surrounding warriors closed ranks and faced the small group of Templars. Despite the number of men on the field, the place was silent, as if in reverence of the slaughter that was about to occur. Moments later, the sound of a Saracen horn echoed through the valley, and every warrior drew their swords.

Jakelin looked up at the black and white banner fluttering above his head. He lifted his hand to make the sign of the cross on his head and chest before drawing his own sword and raising it in the air.

'À moi, beau sire!' he roared, 'Beauséant à la rescousse!'

All around him, his fellow Templars echoed the battle cry, and as the Saracens advanced, they raced forward to embrace their fate.

Ten minutes later, the same horn echoed around the valley and the Saracen army retreated, leaving hundreds of dead surrounding the Templar flag. Many were Christian, but most were Saracens, victims of Templar ferocity. Amongst the carnage, one man remained on his feet. Jakelin De Mailly was severely wounded and covered with blood, both his own and that of countless enemies, but still he stood tall alongside the broken, but still standing banner. His breathing was strained, and he could hardly lift his sword, but he was determined to fight on.

Again silence fell, and every Saracen gazed in awe at the formidable Templar warrior who refused to die. Slowly, Sir Jakelin removed his helmet and cast it to one side. His head was battered, and blood flowed from the many places that had received a blow from a Saracen scimitar. He looked up and saw both Gokbori and Al-Afdal looking down from their vantage point on the hill above.

'What's the matter, Saracen,' he roared, using up the last of his strength, 'are you afraid of me? Does the strength of one mere mortal strike fear into those who do not believe? Your battle cries ring true, Muzaffar ad-Din Gokbori, God is indeed great, but it is not the god of Islam who looks down upon us, it is the father of our saviour, our Lord Jesus Christ. Hear his name and weep, Al-Afdal ibn Salah ad-Din, for one day you will be judged by the one true God.'

All eyes turned upward towards Saladin's son, waiting for the command. Al-Afdal sighed deeply for the man was truly a formidable warrior, but he had insulted Islam, and there was only one punishment. With the slightest movement of his hand, the lines of Saracen forces opened, and twenty black-clad warriors made their way to the front, each with swords drawn.

'Go to your god, Sir Knight,' said Al-Afdal quietly, 'sleep well.'

He dropped his hand in a chopping motion, and as the Mamluk warriors fell upon Sir Jakelin, Saladin's son turned away. His work at Cresson was done.

168

Chapter Twenty-One

Segor

May - AD 1187

Sumeira and Fakhiri sat on cushions in Sada's house, waiting for the woman to return. After explaining the situation, she had headed out into the town to see what she could find out.

'Do you think she can be trusted?' asked Sumeira.

'If she wanted to betray us,' said Fakhiri, 'she could have done so on the night we arrived. How many coins do we still have?'

'About a hundred,' said Sumeira. 'I also have six of the jewels we prized from the Gehaz. Hunter has the rest of the necklace and will protect it until we return.'

Fakhiri nodded and turned as the old woman entered the room.

'Sada,' said Sumeira standing up, 'you're back. Did you have any luck?'

'I did,' said Sada, 'but there is talk on the streets that Salah ad-Din's army has won a wonderful victory against the Christians in the north. Many of the people in Segor support the Sultan, and there will be a race to fight in his name. It is a dangerous time to be out on the street, and if you were to be caught, you would be killed without hesitation.'

'I walked these streets years ago,' said Sumeira, 'and though it was uncomfortable, there was never any serious threat to my life.'

'Things have changed in Segor, 'said Sada. 'Once we were an important trading hub and all were welcomed, but there is growing hate against the Christians. If Salah ad-Din attacks Jerusalem, the young men will flock to his cause in search of plunder and glory.'

'What about my son,' asked Sumeira, 'did you find him?'

'I think so,' said Sada. 'The family who looked after him fell on hard times so sold him in order to get food.'

'Sold him,' said Sumeira, 'to who?'

'To a slave-trader,' said Sada. 'He is intended for the salt mines of Damascus.'

Sumeira's heart fell. Cronin had told her of his time in a salt mine, and she knew it was nought more than a death sentence.

'The good news is,' continued Sada, 'he is still here for the caravan does not head north until two days from now.'

'Then we must free him,' said Sumeira, 'where is he being held?'

'On the other side of Segor, but the streets are dangerous and the slaves well-guarded.'

'Can you take us there?'

'I can, but if you are to do this, you must go tonight for by tomorrow, the city will be full of men, desperate to rip the hide from any Christians.'

'Thank you,' said Sumeira and turned to her comrade. 'Fakhiri, you have done enough for me already,' she said, 'and I cannot ask more. Take your leave and head back to Egypt with the Gehaz. I will take the jewels to the slave-trader and negotiate my son's release. You must go back to Hunter and take the rest of the Gehaz back to Egypt where it belongs.'

'You still have need of me, my lady,' replied Fakhiri. 'With respect, you are a woman, and in this city, your opinions matter little in such matters. I will stay and negotiate on your behalf, and once this matter is concluded, and if I still have your blessing, I will continue my journey home.'

'Thank you,' said Sumeira and turned to the old lady.

'Sada, you have done more than I can ever have expected.' She held out her hand containing one of the jewels. 'As promised, this is for you in payment for all you have done. Take it to a jeweller and exchange it for silver pennies. It is worth a fortune.'

Sada took the gem and stared at it for a long time before looking back up at Sumeira.

'Your generosity is appreciated, she said eventually, 'but I have no need for wealth. I have my home, my garden and my God, that is enough.' She handed the jewel back to Sumeira. 'Use it to buy your son's freedom, pretty lady; now we should go before the streets get too busy.'

Several hours later, Sumeira and Fakhri stood in the dark shadows of a storage building near the eastern edge of Segor. Sada had shown them where the slaves had been secured in an old stable before finally making her way back to her home.

For an hour or so, they watched the comings and goings around the stables, but it quickly became clear that there was no way of getting inside without being seen.

'I need to get closer,' said Fakhri, to see what we are up against.'

'Be careful,' said Sumeira and sunk back into the shadows as the Egyptian walked out onto the street. Less than an hour later, he was back and crouched down in the darkness.

'It is not good,' he whispered, 'I managed to get past one guard, but there are more within the stable. There is no way we can get anywhere near the slaves without being seen.'

'Then that settles it,' said Sumeira, 'we have to make a trade. Do you think you can find out who the slave-trader is? '

'I already know,' said Fakhri, 'for I overheard the guards talking. He is a man called Fawzi ab-Karim, and from what I can gather, he is not a man to be trifled with. If we approach him, we are taking our lives in our hands.'

'I see no other option,' said Sumeira, 'if we linger too long, then it will be too late.'

'I agree,' said Fakhri, 'what is it you want me to do?'

Early the following morning, the slave merchant, Fawzi ab-Karim, sat at a campfire outside the stable, waiting for one of the women to pour him a glass of tea. His dress suggested extreme wealth and his belly, a life of good food. To one side stood a giant of a man, clad in only leggings and a sleeveless jerkin, and two scimitars hanging from his belt. The scars on his face and arms suggested he was no stranger to violence.

Fawzi sipped at his tea and sighed. The following morning he was to leave Segor for the third time that year and head to Damascus. The rigours of the road were unpleasant, but he would trust no other to look after his business, and this time, the talk of a potential war had him already counting the profit in his mind. Wars were good for business, and though they seldom lasted long, Christians, in particular, were very lucrative goods.

A noise from the far end of the street made him look up, and he watched as two of his guards brought a small man towards him.

'My lord,' said one of the guards as they approached, 'this man was creeping around the stables. We were going to break his legs, but he asked to speak to you in return for great wealth.'

'I am always happy to hear anybody who promises such gifts,' said Fawzi, 'set him free.'

The guards threw Fakhri to the floor as Fawzi waved them away.

'Sit,' said Fawzi, indicating a cushion at the far side of the fire. 'Have some tea.' Fakhri looked at the slave-trader with surprise. His manner was gentle, and he had a friendly look upon his face.

'Thank you,' said Fakhri and made himself comfortable as the slave girl poured a second glass of tea.

'Thank you,' he said again, and the girl walked away, leaving the two men alone.

'You wish to speak to me?' said Fawzi eventually.

'I do, my lord,' said Fakhri, 'I am known as Fakhri, the cart-master, and I come on behalf of a third party who wishes to discuss a business transaction.'

'And why could this person not represent themselves?'

'Because they are Christian,' said Fakhri, 'and to be present in Segor at this time risks their lives.'

'Indeed it does,' said Fawzi. 'So they sent you to bargain on their behalf?'

'Yes, my lord.'

'And what is it they want?'

'My lord, they wish to purchase one of your slaves before you leave for the north and are willing to pay a healthy price.'

'Is it a male slave you seek?'

'It is, but not just any male, we are looking for a particular boy no more than nine years old. I have no more information than that except that his skin is probably fairer than you would expect for someone with desert origins.'

'We have a few boys available,' said Fawzi, 'and one in particular springs to mind. But these are young and strong, able to give many years work and to breed with other slaves when they are older. They are expensive, Fakhri the cart-master, and I'm not sure if your masters, whoever they may be, could afford him.'

He took another sip of tea, though his eyes never left those of the Egyptian, seeking any tell-tale signs of negotiating weakness.

'The cost is not important,' said Fakhri, 'the boy is.'

'Now you have me intrigued,' said the slave-trader, putting down his tea, 'what is so special about this boy that he commands such interest?'

'He is just a boy,' said Fakhri, 'whose mother is willing to pay well to set him free.'

Again Fawzi stared at the Egyptian, his mind racing at all the possibilities.

'Tell me,' he said, 'as you have so little information about this boy, how do you know I will provide you with the right one? I could supply any boy, and you would be none the wiser.'

'His mother will recognise him,' said Fakhri, 'and that is why she insists on seeing him first before paying the price.'

'Then bring her forward,' said Fawzi, 'she is free to inspect all my stock.'

'She cannot,' said Fakhri, 'for the reasons I have already stated. You have a great reputation, Fawzi ab-Karim, fierce but astute in the ways of business. This will probably be one of the best deals you will ever make, so I urge you to give it your best consideration.'

'That is quite a claim,' said Fawzi, even more intrigued, 'for I have sold beggars and nobles alike, many of whom made me a healthy profit.'

'I understand, said Fakhri, 'but this is different and to show willing, my mistress has sent you a gift.' He reached beneath his thawb, causing Fawzi's bodyguard to take a step forward. 'I carry no blade, my lord,' said Fakhri quickly, 'only this offering to prove we are speaking the truth.' He held out a purse and tipped one of the gems onto the slaver's outstretched hand. Fawzi stared, his face unreadable in the morning light. Slowly he held it up to the sky, watching the sunlight bounce off its multi-faceted surface.

'This is an advance payment,' said Fakhri, 'as a gesture of goodwill.'

'And there are more of these?' asked Fawzi.

'There are, and if you let the boy go, we will give you another five such stones, enough to purchase every slave you have ten times over. Six stones in all for the life of one worthless child.'

This time, Fawzi was impressed. Never in his life had he been offered so much money for just one prisoner. He placed the gem in a hidden pocket within his cloak and turned back to face Fakhri.

'I am interested in your proposal, Fakhri, the cart-master,' he said, 'but first, you should be aware of the conditions I trade under.' He looked up at his bodyguard. 'This is Dabae, the hyena. Not his real name of course but it suits his personality. Dabae has worked for me for as long as I can remember and has killed more men than I care to recall. One word from me, and he will gouge out one of your eyes and eat it while you watch. And that is just the start of what he would do if anyone should dare to double-cross me. I also have another dozen men with similar tastes. Do you understand?'

'I understand,' said Fakhri.

'Good. Make sure you do. Now, this is what will happen. Tomorrow, I will leave Segor at dawn along with a caravan of slaves heading for the markets of Damascus. Amongst them will be the boy you seek. As your master cannot come to Segor, we will go to her. Tell her to meet us on the road three leagues north to make the trade. If there is any trickery involved, I will cut the boy's throat before setting Dabae and his friends upon you both. Is that clear?'

'There will be no trickery,' said Fakhri, 'we just want the boy and will be on our way.'

'Good,' said Fawzi. 'In that case, we will meet again tomorrow. Now begone.'

Chapter Twenty-Two

Jerusalem

May - AD 1187

King Guy paced the room, his heart racing. Sir Gerard of Ridefort had just returned from Qaqa, the castle where he had run to after escaping the slaughter at Cresson and the tale he had to tell the king was one of fear and defeat.

'So you and Sir Reginald of Sidon managed to escape,' said Guy.

'We did due to the bravery of Sir Jakelin De Mailly and the rest of the squadron,' said Ridefort, 'they held back the Saracens, so we could live to warn Jerusalem.'

'And what happened to them?'

'I know not, Your Grace, I was at Qaqa for only a day and left as soon as could to bring you the news.'

'This is unacceptable,' said Guy, 'if it weren't for the traitor behind the walls of Tiberias, those men would all still be here. He has a price to pay, grandmaster, and I will personally see that it is a long and painful one.'

'Your Grace,' said Ridefort, 'I share your anger but now is not the time for revenge. We need to unite all the counties and face Saladin as soon as we can. By defeating our men at Cresson, Gokbori now has clear access to all the lands west of the Jordan. Without our intervention, he can rape and pillage to his heart's content, safe in the knowledge that we fight each other instead of pursuing him.'

'What do you suggest?' asked Guy.

'I think we should muster an army immediately,' said Ridefort, 'draw men from every garrison in the Outremer if necessary and hunt these Saracens down like the dogs they are. Once done, turn our attention onto Damascus and show Saladin that enough is enough and we will tolerate his people's claim to Jerusalem no longer.'

'You wish to attack Damascus?'

'Why not? Saladin already wants a war so let us give him one. Strike directly at the heart of the beast.'

'If we attack Damascus, it could rally everyone in the east against us.'

'It might, but if we strike quickly and take the city before winter sets in, he will have to wait until next year before retaliating, and by then we would have fortified the town against any attack. Without Damascus, he is powerless, and the tribes that follow his banner will see him weakened.'

'I do not have enough men to attack Damascus.'

'Then issue an Arrière-ban, Your Grace, mobilise the people against the threat of Saladin and the enemies of Jerusalem. All we need is one overwhelming victory and Jerusalem will be safe for a generation. Do nothing and these walls could be torn down within the year.'

'I don't know,' said Guy, 'it seems to me that whatever we choose, there will be only one chance to get it right and I'm not sure if an attack on Damascus is the right way to go.'

Before Gerard could respond, the door flung open, and Sibylla walked into the room followed by a knight, still dirty and exhausted from the rigours of the road.

'Sir Gerard,' said Sibylla, 'I'm glad you are here. I have news from Nazareth, and I think you should hear it.' She turned to face the knight. 'Tell them what you just told me.'

'Your Grace,' said the knight, 'I have just ridden from the castle at al-Fulah. Our patrols have reported that the battlefield at Cresson is littered with dead bodies. They counted over a thousand corpses including Templar and Hospitaller knights.'

'Is there nobody still alive?' asked Guy.

'A few,' said the knight, 'some made it to the safety of the treeline, but there are a dozen at most, all Hospitallers.'

'Is there any news of Roger De-Moulins?' asked Gerard

'Aye my lord,' said the knight turning to face the grandmaster, 'his men report him dead, killed by a Saracen spear through the chest.'

Gerard stared at the knight, hardly able to take it all in. If what he was hearing was true, it seemed the whole patrol had been wiped out.

'Is there any news of the Saracens?' asked Guy.

'No, Your Grace, they have disappeared, along with all their dead.' He turned back to face the Templar grandmaster. 'My lord, there is something else. In the valley where your men lost their lives, we found this.'

He handed over a tattered cloth and Gerard allowed it to unravel until it hung down to the floor. It was the Baucent, the war flag of the Templars.

'Where did you find it?' he asked quietly.

'In the centre of the field, my lord,' said the knight, 'clutched within the grasp of a dead Templar.'

'And was he alone?'

'He was surrounded by his brothers, my lord; it looks like they put up a fierce defence.'

'Thank you,' said Guy. 'Get yourself rested and report to me at last light to give a full report.'

'Yes, Your Grace,' said the knight and left the room.

'Jakelin De Mailly,' said Sir Gerard quietly when the knight had gone.

'What?' said the king.

Sir Gerard held up the flag.

'The man who protected this Baucent to the last, his name was Jakelin De Mailly, and a better knight never raised a sword. It was he who gave his life so I could escape. I will be forever in his debt.'

'There will be time to mourn, my friend,' said the king, 'but this is not it. Now we need to plan for one thing is certain, Saladin has his eyes on Jerusalem.

In the south, Sumeira and Fakhri had left the city and retrieved their horses before heading into the hills to find Hunter. Now, as dusk fell, they lit a small fire and boiled up a broth from a lamb they had bought from a shepherd.

'Do you think we can trust him?' asked Sumeira, referring to the slave-trader.

'I don't see that we have any other choice,' said Fakhri. 'He admitted he has your son and his eyes lit up at the sight of the gems. We will have to be careful, but he is a businessman, and the trade is too profitable to ignore.'

'So we go through with this?' asked Hunter at her side.

'We do,' said Sumeira, 'but there is no need for us all to be at risk.' She turned to Fakhiri. 'My friend,' she said, 'your help has truly been a gift from God, but it is time our paths diverged. Tomorrow, at first light, I want you to leave us and head back to Egypt with the Gehaz.'

'I am happy to stay,' said Fakhiri.

'I know,' said Sumeira, 'but there is no more you can do. Leave us the jewels we need and go home to your family. Your debt has been repaid tenfold.'

'Thank you, my lady,' said Fakhiri, 'my youngest brother has a farm not far from here so I will go there before heading back to Egypt. May Allah guide your steps.'

The following morning, Sumeira and Hunter made their way down from the hills to wait near the road. Fakhiri had gone, leaving them with twelve jewels to pay the trader. The morning dragged on, but eventually, they saw the caravan approaching from the south, a column of twenty carts followed by a line of over a hundred adults, each tethered to the next by a rope around their necks. Most of the wagons were covered or piled high with bales of cloth, but three held cages of iron and were packed with children of all ages. One of the carts was covered with layers of multicoloured cloth, an expensive luxury afforded only by men of status. Sumeira knew that it had to belong to the slave-trader and as it neared, stepped out from her hiding place to stand at the side of the road.

Almost immediately, one of the many guards raised the alarm, and the caravan rumbled to a halt. The guard grabbed Sumeira by the arm and pulled her to the cart before throwing her to the floor.

'Kamil,' chided a man from the cart, 'there is no need to be so rough, I believe this woman is here to do business.' He looked at Sumeira. 'Please, get to your feet, I promise he will not harm you.'

Sumeira stood and stared at the caravan-master.

'You must be Fawzi ab-Karim,' she said.

'I am,' said the trader, 'and you are?'

'My name is Sumeira,' she said, 'and I am here to purchase my son.'

'Ah yes,' said Fawzi, 'a mutually fruitful arrangement if I recall correctly. Do you have the agreed payment?'

'I do, said Sumeira, but first I want to see my son.'

Fawzi stared for a moment before letting out a laugh.

'You certainly are a feisty one,' he said, 'perhaps I should take you to the markets instead. A woman such as you would bring a pretty price.'

'Do so, and you will see none of the gems.'

'Your friend said you had them,' said Fawzi, his voice lowering with menace.

'I do, but they are hidden amongst the rocks. Once I have the boy, my comrade will bring them to you, but if anything happens to my son or me, you will never lay eyes upon them.'

'Sumeira,' said Fawzi with a smile, 'I am a businessman. I am not here to hurt you or rob you.' He got down from the cart and took her arm. 'Come, let us see if we can find your son.' He turned around to speak to one of the guards. 'Get the children down, and line them up at the side of the road.'

Several minutes later, a long line of tethered children stood alongside the caravan, each covered with filth and a look of fear in their eyes.

'They are not the best,' said Fawzi as he led Sumeira to the beginning of the line. 'Of course, they will be cleaned up before they reach the markets, but for now, you will have to excuse the stench.'

Sumeira walked along the line of terrified children. Most had been taken from encampments throughout the desert though some had been sold by their families to stave off hunger. She knew her son would be about nine years old by now, so immediately discounted the larger boys. Eventually, she reached the last cart and saw the line contained many around her son's age. A few had lighter skin, and though she thought she identified some features, she still could not be sure.

'Well,' said the trader, 'is he here?'

'I do not know,' said Sumeira, 'I thought I would recognise him, but now I'm not so sure.'

'You are wasting my time, lady,' said the trader, 'pick one and be done with it.'

'No,' gasped Sumeira, 'I do not want any boy, I want my own.'

'So how do we proceed?'

'There is one thing I could try,' she said, 'when my son went to his new family, I made them promise they would keep his name.'

'And you think they honoured that pledge?'

'I don't know, but they were good people, so perhaps they did.'

'What was his name?'

'Jamal,' said Sumeira.

The trader turned around and shouted along the line.

'Does any boy here have the name Jamal,' he shouted, 'speak now.'

Nobody stirred, but Sumeira suspected it was the trader's aggression that kept their mouths shut.

'I am looking for a boy called Jamal,' she called, starting to walk along the line. 'Please do not be afraid, I swear there is nothing to fear. If you bear that name, please step forward.' Again there was silence, and the trader took a deep sigh.

'It looks like the boy isn't here after all,' he said, 'but that does not mean I should not be compensated for my time.'

Before Sumeira could answer, a weak voice came from behind the line of children.

'My lady,' it said, 'my name is Jamal.'

Sumeira looked up in confusion for the voice came from one of the cages. Fawzi turned to one of his men.

'Are they all not here?'

'A few are too ill to stand,' said the guard with a shrug. 'I thought she would not be interested in the weak.'

'Bring him down,' said Fawzi, 'bring all of them down.'

A few moments later, another six boys were brought down from the carts. One collapsed into the dust, and not even a hefty kick from one of the guards encouraged him to sit up.

'Which of you spoke?' asked Fawzi and a skinny boy at the end raised his hand. Sumeira walked over and crouched down to look into his eyes. Immediately she could see the similarities between him and her dead husband, and she knew; this was the one.

'Jamal,' she said, 'is it really you?'

The boy stared back with no recognition. His eyes were empty, and the streaks of many tears cut valleys through the thick grime upon his face. He wore only threadbare leggings and the remains of a jerkin but even through his clothing, Sumeira could see his body was emaciated through lack of food. She held out her arms, and after a few moments, the scared boy walked into her embrace, though with his arms held firmly at his side.

'Are you happy with this one?' asked Fawzi, 'or would you like one who doesn't smell so bad?'

'This is Jamal,' said Sumeira, 'and I am taking him with me.'

'Your choice,' said Fawzi and turned to his men. 'Get these others back on the carts; we have wasted too much time already.'

Sumeira brushed the straggly hair from the boy's eyes and gave him a tearful smile.

'There is no need to be afraid anymore, Jamal,' she said, 'I am going to look after you.'

'Where's my mother?' he asked quietly. 'Are you taking me back to her?'

Sumeira paused, suddenly realising that the boy had only ever known one mother, the woman who had sold him into slavery.

'No, Jamal,' she said, 'I am taking you somewhere where you will be safe.'

'Come,' ordered Fawzi, 'there is business to conclude.'

Sumeira scooped Jamal up into her arms for though he was nine years old; he had the bodyweight of a boy half that age. She followed Fawzi back to the cart and placed Jamal back onto the floor.

'Well,' said Fawzi, 'where is my payment?'

Sumeira turned and waved towards the hill. Seconds later, Hunter appeared from behind some rocks and started walking towards the caravan. When he arrived, he looked at Jamal and Fakhal before retrieving a leather purse from beneath his jerkin.

'Give it to me,' snarled Fawzi and snatched the purse from Hunter's hand before pouring the gems into his own palm. For a few seconds, he was mesmerized, staring at the jewels as they sparkled in the desert sun.

'They are truly beautiful,' he said eventually, 'but it is not enough.'

'Why?' asked Sumeira, 'the price agreed was six gems.'

'Perhaps so, but the price was for one boy. Now I have one boy and two Christian adults, both of whom will bring a full purse in Damascus.' As he spoke, his guards closed in to surround them.

'Don't do this, Fawzi,' said Sumeira, 'you have a reputation that says you are firm but fair. It would be ruined if it were found out you are also a thief and a cheat.'

'Found out by who,' asked Fawzi, 'the Christians? The only dealings I have with the infidels is when I sell them in the slave markets. My reputation is safe, feisty lady, you just worry about getting me another twenty gems.'

'Twenty,' gasped Sumeira, 'that is impossible. You already have all that I had.'

'Don't think me a fool,' said Fawzi, 'I can see that these were prized from a necklace or something similar. Tell me where the rest of it is, and I will let you go.'

'It was a necklace,' said Sumeira, 'but it is no longer in my possession. Those gems were all that I had left.'

'Who took it,' asked Fawzi, 'the Egyptian?'

'Yes, but he has long gone. You will never find him.'

'We'll see about that,' said Fawzi and turned to his guards. 'Dabae, take three men and hunt the Egyptian down. I want that necklace.'

'As you wish, my lord,' said the guard.

Fawzi turned back to Sumeira.

'I am a man of my word,' said Fawzi, 'but the problem remains. The boy has been paid for, and he is free to go. However, your freedom and that of your comrade is a new transaction and needs to be resolved.'

'It is nothing less than treachery,' said Hunter, 'as well you know. Let her and the boy go and keep me. I am worth more than both of them combined.'

'Possibly not,' said Fawzi, 'for she is an attractive woman and such beauty is in great demand in the brothels of Damascus. Men will be lining up for hours to enjoy her charms.'

'You bastard,' said Sumeira, 'you never intended to let me go, did you?'

'I admit that when your little friend mentioned there was a western woman involved, my interest was piqued, and it has to be said, I am certainly not disappointed.' He paused for a few moments before coming to a decision.

'So, Sumeira,' he said, 'this is what I will do. Your son will be released immediately, as will your angry friend here. He can take the boy to freedom, but you will remain with me until my men return with the necklace. If it ends up in my possession, I swear you will be set free and escorted to the nearest Christian town or fortress. However, if the Egyptian cannot be found, and they come back empty-handed, then I will take you to Damascus and recoup my costs in the slave markets.'

'No,' shouted Hunter, 'take me in her place and let them go.'

'Even if I did,' said Fawzi, 'how long do you think a western woman and a child would stay alive out here?' No, my offer stands, but the final decision lies with the lady.'

'Don't accept,' shouted Hunter, 'it is an unjust offer.'

Throughout the conversation, Sumeira's eyes had never left those of the trader.

'Do you promise that both will be allowed to go in safety,' she asked quietly.

'You have my word,' said Fawzi, 'now what is it to be, freedom for the boy and your friend, or am I to sell all three of you in the slave markets?'

'I accept,' said Sumeira eventually. 'Let them go.'

'No,' shouted Hunter again, 'take me instead.'

Fawzi turned to the rest of his guards.

'Give them food and water,' he said, 'and let them both go. They are to come to no harm.' The guard nodded and turned away.

'So,' said Fawzi, 'our business is done. If I get the necklace, you will soon be reunited, but in the meantime, you may want to say goodbye to your son.'

Sumeira turned and looked at the scared boy standing just a few paces away. She dropped to her knees and held out her hand. Jamal walked over and took it gently.

'Listen to me,' she said, pointing up at Hunter, 'this nice man is a friend, and he is going to take you somewhere where you will be safe. I want you to go with him and very soon, I will join you and take you somewhere very special.'

'Where are we going?' asked Jamal.

'First to a huge castle,' she said, 'where you will meet a lovely man called John Loxley, and a very special girl called Emani. After that, we will be going on a ship to a beautiful country across the sea.'

'What is a sea?' asked Jamal, staring up into her eyes.

'A sea is vast like a desert,' said Sumeira, 'but it has water instead of sand.'

'Like an oasis?' asked Jamal.

'Something like that,' said Sumeira,' but far bigger than you could ever imagine. Once we cross it, we will go somewhere where you can grow up to be a healthy young man.'

'Is there food there?'

'There is,' said Sumeira, 'more than you could ever eat.'

'It sounds nice.'

'It certainly is,' said Sumeira, 'and one day we will make it our home. But first, you have to go with this man. His name is Hunter, and he is a very good friend. Will you do that?'

The boy nodded, and Sumeira looked up at the scout.

'Take good care of him,' she said, 'and if God wills it, I will see you in a few days.'

'I will find you and set you free, Sumeira,' said Hunter, 'I swear it.'

'Try it, and I will kill her immediately,' said Fawzı without turning around, 'before sending a Hashashin against the boy. Now there has been enough talking, take the child and leave before I change my mind.'

Sumeira picked up Jamal and after giving him a lingering kiss on his forehead, handed him over to Hunter.

'Do not try to free me, Hunter,' she said, 'or all this will have been for nought. Just take him to Karak and hand him over to my husband.'

'But what if they can't find Fakhiri,' he replied, 'what then?'

'At least my children will be safe,' she said, 'and no matter what happens to me, I will rest knowing that I did everything I could.'

'But…'

'There is no more to say, Hunter,' she said, 'just go while you still can, I'm begging you.'

Hunter eventually nodded in silence and without another word, turned away to walk back up the hill to the hidden horses.

'Take care of him, Hunter,' cried Sumeira, 'his life is worth more than all the jewels in the world.'

Hours later, Fawzi's caravan stopped for the night where the road widened and merged with a neighbouring plain. All the carts were secured alongside each other, and the many armed guards took it in turns to patrol the perimeter of the camp. Some oversaw a group of slaves as they scoured the plains for deadwood while others toiled in the last of the day's heat to dig a fire pit. Eventually, it was filled with wood, and as the flames of the fire reduced into layers of hot embers, they produced a large pot from one of the carts to make a communal soup.

Sumeira sat with her back against one of the cart's wheels. For the past few hours, she had travelled on the cart alongside Fawzi, but now he had lost interest, and she was tied to the wheel. Eventually, he returned and stood above her, chewing on a piece of meat taken from the pot.

'Are you hungry?' he asked.

Sumeira nodded silently.

'Cut her loose,' he said, 'and place her in a cage with the others.'

'So I am already classed as a slave,' said Sumeira, 'that didn't take long.'

'I prefer the word guest,' said Fawzi, 'at least until my payment has been received.'

'I think you will never see that necklace,' said Sumeira, 'there is more to Fakhiri than meets the eye.'

'For your sake, I hope I do,' said Fawzi, 'for it would be such a shame to spoil that very pretty face.' He paused to let the threat sink in before continuing. 'As you can see, the food is not yet done but rest assured, when it is ready, I will send some over.'

As he walked away, one of the guards cut her loose and took her to the back of a cart. He unlocked the gate and lifted her up into the cage before securing the lock and disappearing into the gloom.

The cage was full of both men and women, but one moved over to allow her a place to sit. Eventually, her eyes closed and though her mind was racing, she fell asleep, exhausted by the events of the day.

An hour or so later, someone brought a basket containing bread and fruit. They forced the food through the bars, and hands reached out in desperation. To the rear of the cart, the gate was unlocked, and another slave handed her a bowl of steaming soup, rich with vegetables and meat. Sumeira was shocked, and as the gate was refastened, she looked around at the rest of the prisoners, each staring at her in envy. Nobody tried to take the food from her, but Sumeira knew, there was no way she could eat it alone.

Slowly she lifted one spoonful to her mouth, enjoying the warmth and taste, but despite craving more, turned to the woman at her side.

'Here,' she said, offering the bowl, 'you take some.'

The woman stared in shock and took the bowl from Sumeira. Similarly, she ate one spoonful and passed it on before turning back to Sumeira with respect in her eyes.

'Thank you,' she said, before reaching beneath her ragged cloak and producing a half-hand of bread. 'Here,' she said, breaking it in half, 'for you.'

Sumeira took the small piece of the stale bread.

'What is your name?' she asked.

'Adela,' said the woman. 'I saw you with the cart-master. You said many words.'

'I did,' said Sumeira, 'he promised me many things, but I am not sure whether to trust him or not.'

'Do not,' said Adela, 'for he is not what he seems.'

Before Sumeira could answer, the woman pulled her cloak tighter and lay down on the cart floor, seeking whatever warmth she could find amongst the rest of the slaves, and as night finally fell, Sumeira did the same, not knowing what the following days may bring.

The following morning, Sumeira awoke just as the dawn was breaking across the eastern mountains. For a few seconds, she wondered where she was, but as soon as she smelled the stench in the cage, her memories came flooding back, and her heart sank.

The morning passed slowly, and the caravan continued on its way. By midday, the sun was at its hottest, and all the slaves were desperate for water. Eventually, the caravan stopped for the night, and some guards brought a bucket of water, allowing each captive one cup through the bars of the cage. Eventually, they reached Sumeira, and she drank thankfully. Someone shouted in the distance, and the guard turned to Sumeira.

'The master wants to talk to you,' he said. 'Stand back.'

He opened the gate and dragged her to where Fawzi was sitting on a stool. Behind him were the guards who had set out to find Fakhiri the previous day. She looked around, but there was no sign of the Egyptian.

'You didn't find him, did you?' she said. 'I told you he was a clever man.'

'Oh, we found him,' said Fawzi, 'but unfortunately for you, he did not have the necklace.'

'Where is he,' asked Sumeira, 'is he here?'

Fawzi nodded to one of the guards who walked forward and emptied a sack at Sumeira's feet. She gasped as Fakhiri's blood-soaked head rolled across the floor. For a moment, she felt sick before staring at Fawzi with renewed hatred.

'What sort of man are you?' she gasped, 'he did nothing to you.'

'He was complicit in denying me a perfectly fair business transaction,' replied Fawzi. 'Unfortunately, this means that you now belong to me to do with as I will.'

'I never believed you intended to let me go anyway,' said Sumeira, 'you are no better than a snake.'

'Think what you will,'' said Fawzi, but the reality is, you now have to pay the price.' He turned to Dabae. 'Take her away, and make sure she gets no food for two days. She needs to get used to the life that awaits her.'

Several hours later, Sumeira once again lay between several bodies, each as emaciated as the next. None had been fed that day, and the water ration had been halved. Despondent, she lay in the dark, unable to sleep. Not far away, she could hear the voices of the guards as they sat around the fire, each eating stew from the pot upon the fire. Eventually, she fell asleep but woke abruptly when she felt something tugging gently at her hair. She turned her head and saw Hunter outside the bars, his finger on his lips, indicating she should remain quiet.

'Hunter,' she whispered, 'what are you doing here?' I told you to go.'

'I know,' whispered Hunter, 'but couldn't leave without doing something.'

'Where is Jamal,' asked Sumeira, 'is he safe?

'He is safe,' said Hunter.' I came to try and free you, but it is impossible. I don't know which guard has the keys, and there are just too many of them.'

'Just go,' said Sumeira, 'before they see you.'

'I will,' said Hunter, 'but before I do, I wanted to give you this. It may help in the days ahead.' He put his hand through the bars and gave her one of the jewels from the necklace.

'Where did you get it?' she asked.

'Fakhiri gave it to me and said I was to give it to you when we reached safety. It was to be a gift to you and your family, but I thought you could make better use of it in the days ahead.'

'How? Fawzi wanted twenty more so would certainly not accept less.'

'He may not,' said Hunter looking around to see if any guards were approaching, 'but there will be others in Damascus who are not so greedy. Use it well and buy your freedom if you can. In the meantime, I swear your family will be well cared for.'

'Thank you,' said Sumeira, taking the tiny jewel. 'Now you should go before it is too late.'

'Be safe, my lady,' said Hunter, 'I will pray for you.' He stepped back, and as he disappeared into the night, Sumeira hid the jewel beneath her clothes. It was not much, but for the first time in two days, at least she had some hope.

Chapter Twenty-Three

Tiberias

May - AD 1187

Balian of Ibelin walked through the courtyard towards the citadel in the city of Tiberias. The last few days had been traumatic, for after arriving at the Cresson Springs a day too late, he had found nothing but death and destruction and for two days, he had put his army to burying the dead. Every Christian had their own grave, and though the locally hired Turcopole horsemen were the sons of converted Muslims, they shared a mass grave. The few Saracen bodies still on the field were thrown amongst the rocks for the scavengers.

Finally, after one of the priests had blessed the makeshift burial site, Balian had mustered his men and marched on to Tiberias. Now he strode purposefully to the citadel, in no mood for the attitude that Raymond of Tripoli had exhibited only weeks earlier. As he approached, the doors swung open, and he marched inside, removing his riding gloves and throwing them towards a servant standing at the door.

'Where is he?' he demanded.

'If you are referring to my Lord Raymond,' replied the servant, 'he is currently in counsel and will be with you shortly. Please wait here, and I'm sure he will send word when he is ready.'

'What I have to say will not wait,' said Balian, 'get out of my way.' He pushed past the servant and marched up the corridor to the audience chamber.

'My lord,' shouted the servant, 'you cannot do this.'

'Just watch me,' snarled Balian. He continued up the corridor but was stopped before the doors by two armed knights.

'Get out of my way,' he said.

'I can't do that,' said one of the knights, 'and I suggest you back away before you get hurt.'

Balian drew his sword, his face red with anger.

'If you do not stand down,' he snarled, 'I'll kill you both, now get out of my way.'

'Lord Balian,' said the second knight calmly, 'do not be a fool. Raymond will be finished soon enough, and your ire will be just as relevant in a few minutes. There is no need for blood to be drawn here today.'

Balian was still furious, but he knew the second knight talked sense. He put his sword back into his scabbard and stared back at the first knight.

'You and I may still have words later, my friend,' he said, 'for your manner offends me.' As he finished speaking the door opened, and three men walked out, each clutching at a pile of rolled parchments. Without waiting for permission, Balian pushed past them and into the audience chamber. At the far end, Raymond was standing at a table with another knight, each poring over an unfurled map.

'Raymond,' shouted Balian marching across the room, 'you and I need to talk.' Seeing his undoubted anger, the unarmed Count of Tripoli stepped back, but the knight alongside him stepped forward, placing himself between the two men.

'Hold there, my lord,' said the knight, 'and curb your anger. You are in the presence of Raymond of Tripoli, and this is his house. Show some respect.'

'Respect,' shouted Balian staring over the shoulder of the knight, 'why should I show respect to someone who has caused the death of over a thousand Christian soldiers? Where was their respect?'

'I have no idea what you are talking about,' said Raymond. 'If you are referring to the skirmish at Cresson Springs, then I assure you I had nothing to do with it.'

'Skirmish,' gasped Balian, 'is that what you call it? I feel the word slaughter is far more appropriate.'

'That is probably an exaggeration,' said Raymond, 'and even if it is true, I cannot be held responsible for the tactical ignorance of others.'

'Oh it is true,' Raymond,' said Balian, 'just go outside and check the blisters on the hands of my men, blisters that pay testament to the thousand graves we have spent the last few days digging. Graves that would not have been needed had you not signed a pact with the devil himself.'

Both men stared at each other before Raymond dismissed the knight.

'Sir Benedict, please leave us.'

'Are you sure, my lord?' replied the knight.

'I am sure. Lord Balian is upset, but we are allies of many years, and I am not at risk.'

'As you wish, my lord,' said the knight and left the chamber, closing the doors behind him.

'I wouldn't be so sure about that,' said Balian when they were alone.

'About what?'

'That you are not at risk. I should strike you down right now for what you have done. How does it feel, Raymond, to have the deaths of so many men on your conscience?'

'My conscience is clear, Balian,' said Raymond. 'I was nowhere near the battle and took no part in any conflict. How can I be held responsible?'

'Because you allowed them to ride through your land unchallenged,' shouted Balian. 'If you had had the courage to stand up to them, this would never have happened.'

'Yes it would,' roared Raymond, 'but with the added tragedy that first, they would have attacked Tiberias. What use would it have made to spill the blood of the people of this city when we could never have stood up to the Ayyubid anyway?' At least this way, the deaths were limited to soldiers and not civilians.'

'You could have hold them up,' said Balian, 'delayed them until we arrived with reinforcements. Even Saladin would have thought twice at the sight of Jerusalem's combined armies riding to the aid of Tiberias. By ignoring your sacred duty, you have personally caused the deaths of over a thousand good Christian men. You may as well have killed them yourself.'

Raymond snatched a knife from the table and strode across the room, his face red with anger. He placed the point of the blade against Balian's throat, but the Count of Ibelin did not flinch.

'Go ahead Raymond,' he said, 'what is one more death to you?'

For a few seconds, Raymond stared into Balian's eyes, the veins bulging on his neck. Finally, he turned away and flung the knife into a far corner.

'I had no idea what was about to happen,' he said as he walked away. 'All I thought was that they would burn a few farms and perhaps steal some stock. There was no way less than seven thousand Saracens could threaten Jerusalem.' He leaned on the table; his head bowed.

'How do you know how many there were?' asked Balian quietly.

'Because I had them counted as they passed,' said Raymond.

'And their outriders allowed you to do this?'

'Aye, they did.'

For a few moments, there was silence as the implications sunk in.

'Dear God,' said Balian eventually, 'you did it, didn't you? You actually made an alliance with Saladin allowing him to pass through Galilee without confrontation?'

'As I said, I had no idea of the consequences,' replied Raymond. 'He offered me peace, and I took it.'

'Is that all he offered,' asked Balian, 'was there not a whisper of the crown of Jerusalem?'

'Believe what you will,' said Raymond, the anger dissipating from his voice, 'the fact is that I made the decision in the best interests of Tiberias, and we must all live with the consequences, whatever they may be.'

'Well at least that is one thing we can agree on,' said Balian. 'But the question remains, what do we do now?'

'Why are you here, Balian,' said Raymond, turning around, 'is it to increase the burden upon my shoulders, for if that is your purpose, well done, you have succeeded.'

'I came here to help,' said Balian, 'and for one last time, to try and talk some sense into you. You have to stop this, Raymond, put an end to the animosity between you and Jerusalem. What is done is done, but now we must move forward and unite to face Saladin. If we continue to fight each other, we might as well all board the ships right now and retreat to Cyprus.'

'I cannot serve under Guy,' said Raymond, 'the man is an imbecile.'

'Then treat him as a figurehead only,' said Balian. 'He may decide the strategies, but he alone is not the only one making decisions. There are others that shape the way he thinks, Templars, Hospitallers, me, Reginald of Sidon and others. He holds counsels to discuss tactics, and your name is conspicuous by its absence. Be part of the solution, Raymond, not part of the problem.'

'It is too late,' sighed Raymond, 'my die is cast. I have sworn an oath to Saladin.

'Saladin is not a Christian,' said Balian, 'so the Bishop of Jerusalem can release you from your vow. Come back with me and pledge allegiance to Guy and Sibylla. Do that, and we can finally unite the armies against the Ayyubid.'

'They will have me cast in chains as soon as I walk through the gates,' said Raymond.

'No they won't,' said Balian, 'for I and the other barons will not allow it. We need your army, Raymond, and if we are to send Saladin back to Damascus, we need you.'

The following morning, Balian re-joined his army camped outside the gates of Tiberias. He had sent messages that they were returning to Jerusalem immediately, and most of his men were already mounted. His sergeants formed the men into columns and sent riders on ahead to make sure they did not ride into any ambushes, while squadrons of Turcopoles raced away to check the surrounding hills.

'My lord,' said one of the knights, riding up to him, 'the men are ready. Shall we advance?'

'Not yet,' said Balian, 'we are waiting for someone.'

'Who?'

The sound of several horns filled the air, and Balian turned to see a group of riders emerge through the gates of Tiberias. At their head was Raymond of Tripoli and behind him a standard-bearer with the flag of Galilee flying high above their heads. A few moments later, a column of horsemen followed, hundreds of men each fully equipped to fight a war.

'Him,' said Balian as they watched the count approach. 'The one man who may yet make a difference.'

'If I had my way,' spat the knight, 'he would be hanging from one of his own towers minus his entrails.'

'You just focus on the fighting,' said Balian, 'and leave the politics to others.' He kicked his heels into the flanks of his horse and rode up to meet Raymond.

'You changed your mind,' he said.

'You were right,' said Raymond, 'those men died because of me. My anger clouded my judgement, and one day I will be judged by God for my mistakes. Until then, I will do what I can to make amends.'

'And you will pledge allegiance to Guy and Sibylla?'

'It will leave a bitter taste in my mouth, but if that is what it takes to stop Saladin, then so be it. Rest assured, my friend, henceforth Jerusalem has my full support.

Balian smiled and nodded to the signaller. Moments later, another horn echoed through the air, and the combined forces of Nablus and Tiberias set out to join those of Jerusalem. The fightback had begun.

Chapter Twenty-Four

Karak Castle

May - AD 1187

In the chapel in the upper bailey of Karak Castle, the Templars knights prayed for the souls of the brothers who had fallen at Cresson. Each one was named by the chaplain in turn, and as each man in the room remembered his fallen brother, one of the sergeants walked down to light a candle at the front of the chapel. Once done, the chaplain recounted what had befallen the brothers, and in particular, the courage of the last man standing, Jakelin De Mailly. By fighting to the last man, each had honoured the tradition that no Templar would surrender as long as the Baucent remained standing. For three hours the service went on, filled with prayers and hymns, the chapel echoing to the chants of the Templars who still garrisoned Karak.

At the back of the chapel, Thomas Cronin sat without singing or chanting. Despite being a man of war and having seen many comrades die in the service of God, Jakelin De Mailly's death had affected him badly. As his sergeant, he had known the knight personally, and they had grown close as brothers in arms, despite the difference in status. Eventually, the service came to an end, and everyone filed out to return to their duties. Cronin walked over to the battlements and breathed in the cold evening air. A few moments later, the under-marshal appeared beside him, and they shared a moment of silence.

'He was a great man,' said Richard of Sandford eventually, 'both in battle and in contemplation.'

'He was,' said Cronin, 'and his passing leaves a great hole in the order.'

'It does,' said the under-marshal, 'but it can also be used as a rallying call to those who have doubts or fear.'

'What do you mean?'

'His name will be forged into the history books,' said Sandford, 'and hundreds of years from now, people will say his name in awe.'

'A fitting tribute,' said Cronin.

'So, what now for you?' asked Sandford.

'What do you mean?'

'You are without a knight to serve. Do you have any preference?'

'I will do whatever the grandmaster requires of me,' said Cronin, 'my commitment remains undiluted, now more than ever.'

'I take it that you wish to avenge Sir Jakelin's death?'

'I take on no burden of revenge,' said Cronin, 'only a desire to bring this holy war to an end.'

'Gerard of Ridefort lost many men at Cresson,' said Sandford, 'including his two sergeants. If you are happy to serve him, I will arrange for the posting to be made.'

'It would be an honour to serve the grandmaster,' said Cronin.

'Good. In that case, leave it to me.' He turned away and returned to the commandery while Cronin walked down into the lower bailey.

'Brother Cronin,' called a voice, and the sergeant turned to see Arturas walking towards him.

'Arturas,' said Cronin. 'I hear you have given up the role of steward?'

'Aye,' said Arturas, 'there was too much organisation involved, and I felt like a bird in a cage.'

The two men carried on walking down the slope.

'So what do you do now?' asked Cronin.

'Weapon training,' said Arturas. 'The money is poor, but I get to beat the shit out of boys wishing to be men.'

'It sounds good,' laughed Cronin, 'perhaps I may join you one day.'

'Always welcome,' said Arturas. They walked on a few more paces in silence. 'I heard about Cresson and the fate of so many of your fellows,' he said eventually, 'I also hear Jakelin died a hero's death.'

'If you call dying needlessly under a piece of tattered cloth a hero's death, then yes, he did.'

'You do not approve?'

'Dying in battle is one thing,' said Cronin, 'dying for a flag when the battle has already been lost is completely different. They would have been better off yielding and living to fight another day.'

'I would keep such thoughts to yourself,' said Arturas, 'I don't think many of your brothers would agree.'

'Any news of Sumeira?' asked Cronin eventually.

'Aye there is,' said Arturas. 'I would have come sooner but knew you would be engaged with your fellows in the commandery.'

'How is she, did she find her son?'

'Her son is here with John Loxley,' said Arturas, 'he was brought here by Hunter, but Sumeira was taken prisoner by a slave-trader on the southern road.'

'What?' gasped Cronin coming to a halt. 'How did that happen?' I thought you had furnished her with good men.'

'So did I but they betrayed me, and she only had Hunter and a slave for protection. One of them was killed and rest assured, the man who survived will feel my blade soon enough, but for now we need to focus on Sumeira.'

'Where is the caravan headed?'

'Damascus. She is to be sold in the flesh markets.'

'We can't let that happen, Arturas, she is a good woman and does not deserve such a fate.'

'I fear it is already too late,' said Arturas. 'Even if the castellan agreed to spare a rescue party, they would never catch up with the caravan.'

'What I don't understand,' said Cronin, 'is if Hunter was with her when she was taken by the slaver, why did he return without making any effort to flee her?'

'Trust me,' said Arturas, 'He was as upset as you, but she made him swear he would get her son to safety.'

'Where is Hunter now?'

'The moment he handed the boy over to John Loxley, he got a fresh horse and rode back out to find her. I offered to go with him, but his mind was set, and I would have been a hindrance.'

'You should have summoned me. I would have gone with him.'

'There was no time,' said Arturas, 'and besides, you were out on patrol, and as soon as you returned, we heard the news about Cresson.'

'That poor woman,' said Cronin. 'I have let her down, Arturas. I should never have let her go in the first place.'

'The decision was not yours,' said Arturas, 'she would have gone no matter what we said. All we can do now is hope that Hunter can reach her in time.'

Many leagues to the north, Fawzi's caravan had stopped for the night outside the walls of Damascus. The days had passed slowly for Sumeira, but the thought of her son with John Loxley and Emani made her smile. Whatever happened now, at least she knew he would be as safe as he could be. A sound came from outside the cart, and Sumeira turned to see the leering face of Fawzi.

'Well,' he said, 'here we are, at the gates of Damascus. This is where we part company, pretty woman.'

'As long as my boy is safe,' said Sumeira, 'that is all that is important.'

'You may not be as accepting in a few weeks,' said Fawzi, 'I have seen what becomes of women like you in Damascus and it is not pleasant. Why don't you simply tell me where you have hidden the rest of the gems, and as soon as I have retrieved them, I will let you go?'

'I have told you a dozen times,' sighed Sumeira, 'I do not know where they are. The last I saw of them; they were in the possession of Fakhiri.'

'Such a shame,' said Fawzi, 'I was beginning to like you.' He turned away and left Sumeira alone with her thoughts.

The day dragged on, and night-time fell. Sumeira slept fitfully but was woken in the night by the sound of men arguing in the distance. She strained to hear what was going on without success, but as the voices faded away, she settled down again, unsure of what she may face the following day.

The following morning the camp came alive. All the carts holding the goods from Segor made their way into the market, as did those holding the children, but the long line of adult slaves stayed where they were on the side of the road, each terrified at what was about to happen. One of the guards walked over and unlocked the cage, ordering the women to line up at the side of the road. All around them, mounted warriors rode everywhere, and carts were being loaded with all sorts of provisions. Herders ushered sheep and goats through the camp, oblivious to the lines of slaves, a common sight outside the walls of Damascus.

'Adela,' she said, to the woman she had befriended, 'what's happening? Are they taking us into the city?'

'No,' said the woman, 'there has been a change in fortune for the slave-trader. A man came to him in the night and offered a price for all the slaves. Fawzi was angry for he could get a better sum in the markets, but he had to accept.'

'Why?'

'Salah ad-Din is going to war, and he needs as many slaves as possible to service his army. We are waiting for the carts to take us away.'

'We are not going into Damascus?'

'No.'

'Then why do you look so worried? Is that not a good thing?'

'Why would it be good,' asked Adela. 'Wherever we go, we will still be slaves. The pretty women will be given to the warriors for pleasure while others will be used as beasts of burden and worked until they drop. In times of war, our men are used to attack the defences of the enemy before the masters commit their warriors. Whatever happens, you can be assured we will not get any better treatment in the hands of the Ayyubid.'

'Do you know where we are going?'

'I know we are heading west,' said Adela, 'but that is all.'

'Acre lies to the west,' said Sumeira. 'They must be intending to attack the city.'

'It matters not where we are heading,' said Adela, 'for we are unlikely to survive wherever we go. Keep your veil tight around your face, my lady, for as soon as anyone realises you are fair of skin, your days will be numbered.'

Sumeira pulled her clothing tighter around her body and lowered her head. A group of men approached, and she recognised Fawzi's voice amongst them. She looked up briefly, but her movement caught his eye, and a look of recognition crossed his face. Sumeira held her breath, wondering if he would point her out to her new owners. Instead, he just stopped and stared at the horizon, as if seeking something in the distance.

'It is strange how things work out, Sumeira,' he said quietly without looking down, 'but your fate is now out of my hands. Just so you know, I would never have sold you to the brothels and was considering keeping you for myself. Now that is no longer possible; I can only wish you well.'

'As long as it is away from you,' whispered Sumeira, 'then I will accept whatever lays before me.'

'As feisty as ever,' said Fawzi, 'a trait I fear is going to get you into serious trouble. Fare ye well, pretty lady for this is where we part.'

As he walked away, Sumeira allowed herself a small sigh of relief. Though she still did not know what was going to happen to her, at least she was alive and away from the dark streets of Damascus. And that had to be a good thing.

Chapter Twenty-Five

Acre

June - AD 1187

Guy of Lusignan sat at the head of a table in the main hall of the citadel. It had taken a few weeks, but he had finally managed to assemble all the important nobles from Jerusalem and the surrounding counties to discuss the increasing threat from Saladin. Amongst them was Balian of Ibelin, Raymond of Tripoli, Reginald of Sidon, Humphrey of Toron and Joscelyn of Edessa. The Templars were represented by Gerard of Ridefort, but as Roger De-Moulins had fallen at Cresson, there was no grandmaster of the Hospitallers present. Instead, his place was taken by Garnier of Nablus, the most senior Hospitaller knight available. King Guy stood and called the room to order.

'Gentlemen,' he said as the noise lessened, 'thank you for coming. It seems the recent devastating events at Cresson have finally focussed our minds to the threat from Saladin. Even as we speak, my spies report he has already mustered an army over twenty thousand strong in and around the city of Damascus. Make no mistake, the only reason he is amassing such a force is to launch an attack on Jerusalem. The only question is when?' He turned to look at a map hanging on the wall behind him. 'As you know, if he is to get a large army anywhere near Jerusalem, he has to pass the city of Tiberias.'

'It seems he had no problem doing so last time,' growled one of the other knights in the room.

Raymond winced but did not respond. He had already made peace with Guy and Sibylla, and although the relations were a little awkward, all had agreed to forget what had happened for the sake of the Holy-city.

'We respect your frustrations,' said the king, 'but we cannot undo what has been done. Sir Raymond has vowed allegiance to the crown and has pledged his army to Jerusalem's service. I have buried the past, and so should you.'

A murmur of quiet frustration rippled around the room, but nobody else spoke up.

'Anyway,' continued Guy, 'like it or not, Tiberias remains a strategic city in any forthcoming campaign. So much so, we believe that if Saladin hopes to have any chance of taking Jerusalem, first he has to take Tiberias. Its control over the western road and indeed the freshwater lake means he has to have control in order to maintain his supply lines. The question is this. Do we send all our resources to Tiberias and make our stand there or do we hold back and see what his intentions are first?'

For a few moments there was silence, but before anyone could respond, the door burst open and Raynald de Chatillon strode in.

'Your Grace,' said Raynald, 'I heard there was a council of war. I assume that the messenger you sent me got lost.'

'Sir Raynald,' said Guy, 'you are most welcome, but your order is represented by your grandmaster.

'With respect, Your Grace,' said Raynald, 'I look around this room and see few men who have confronted the Ayyubid as often as I. Some have even made treaties with them while I, and the men who serve in Karak, smite them on a daily basis. You need me at this council.'

'It is your continued harassment of Saladin that has brought us to this point,' said Reginald of Sidon. 'If you had just honoured the treaty, we would not be here today, and the men that died at Cresson would still be alive.'

'Cresson had nothing to do with me,' said Raynald, 'as you well know.' He looked over at the grandmaster. 'In fact, I would venture to say that had I been there, perhaps the outcome may have been different.'

'That's outrageous,' shouted Balian getting to his feet. 'Gerard of Ridefort 's actions were courageous, and he was lucky to escape with his life.'

'Yes,' said Raynald without taking his eyes of the grandmaster, 'he was.'

'This is not the time or place to argue such things,' said the king, 'and despite your undoubted prowess in battle, we do not need you here.'

'Let him stay,' said a voice, and everyone turned to stare at the Templar grandmaster. He got slowly to his feet and stared at the knight. 'Sir Raynald is right,' he said eventually. 'In hindsight, I could have handled it better, but God will be my judge, not you or any man here. In the circumstances, I believe we need a man of Sir Raynald's prowess, not just on the field of battle but amongst us here at the table. Let him speak, for he has my support.' He sat back down as the men in the room mumbled amongst themselves.

'Bring a chair for Sir Raynald,' said Guy eventually, and when the castellan of Karak was ready, the king turned back to the map.

'As I was saying,' he said, 'Tiberias is pivotal in any plan Saladin may have, and we need to know what to do about it.'

'Your Grace,' said Raymond of Tripoli, standing up, 'if I may.'

The king nodded and took his seat.

'Tiberias is a formidable city,' said Raymond looking around. 'Its outer walls are defended by towers and have never been breached. The citadel at the heart of the city is stronger again and more than capable of withstanding a lengthy siege. However, I have also talked to one of Saladin's envoys and know that this time, he is determined to succeed where before he has failed. He wants Jerusalem badly, and now he knows that I have reneged on the treaty we made, will have no hesitation in taking Tiberias.

'So you want us to reinforce your city, after what you did to us,' sneered one of the knights.

'On the contrary,' said Raymond turning to face him, 'I think we should do no such thing. If we commit any part of our army to defend Tiberias from within, there is a chance they will be trapped there and unable to fight. I suggest that we muster somewhere else, somewhere central where we can react to anything the Sultan does. By doing so, we can douse the fires of his advance before they become an inferno.'

'You would leave your city, undefended?' asked Balian.

'As I said, it is strong enough to withstand any attack for a few days. By that time, we can rally our men and rout the attackers from the outside.'

'Do you have a place in mind?' asked the king.

'Aye, I do,' said Raymond and walked up to indicate a mark on the map, 'here at Sephorie.'

Every man looked up at the map. Sephorie was a Christian stronghold on the main western road from Tiberias to the Mediterranean coast. The town itself was overlooked by a crusader castle, and the large springs would ensure there was plenty of water for any army based there. The King looked around the table.

'Well,' he said, 'does anyone have any comments.'

'I think it is a wise move,' said Raynald of Chatillon. 'Good access with clear views all around from the castle. Any garrison in the town would be well informed of any approaching army, yet central enough to respond to any incursion by Saladin, wherever that may be.'

'Grandmaster Gerard,' said the king, 'your thoughts?'

'I concur with Brother Raynald,' said Gerard. 'At Sephorie, we will not be constrained and will have room to manoeuvre. Unless others have a better plan, I believe this strategy will work.'

'Does anyone have any other comments?' asked the king.

When nobody spoke up, Guy turned to face Raymond of Tripoli.

'You have my gratitude,' he said, 'and it is noted that you are putting your own city at risk for the sake of Jerusalem. Take your seat, Lord Raymond, and welcome back to the council.'

The rest of the day was taken up agreeing on the detail, and by the time the meeting broke up, everyone knew their role and place in the forthcoming campaign. As they all left, Balian waked up to Raymond.

'That was quite a commitment back there,' he said, 'risking Tiberias for the sake of Jerusalem.'

'As I said,' replied Raymond, 'I have confidence in the city's defences and have no doubt that if the city is attacked, it will hold out until our armies arrive.'

'Well, you know better than any other,' said Balian, 'I just hope you are correct.'

Twenty-five leagues to the northeast, Hunter lay hidden amongst the rocks overlooking the road leading towards Damascus. He had ridden hard from Karak, but with so many patrols to avoid, the going had been slower than he would have liked. Now he waited less than a league away from the Ayyubid city, watching the road for the caravan he knew would be carrying the slave-trader.

Many came and went, but eventually, he saw the familiar colourful awning that covered the slave-trader's cart. Despite the recognition, his heart sunk for it was heading south, not north, heading back to Segor. Hunter crawled back into the shadows, despondent. He was too late, the trader must have already sold

Sumeira in Damascus. For the next hour or so, he waited, considering his options. He knew he could never get into the city without being seen, but he had a purse of silver in his cloak, and he was confident he could bribe someone to do so on his behalf. The only thing was, to do that, he had to know where Sumeira had been sent, and there was only one man who would know where that may be. Fawzi.

With his plan racing around his head, Hunter waited until dusk before following the slave-trader's caravan south. By the time it was dark, he had found it camped at the side of the road, the carts silhouetted by the light of the fires. He settled down to watch until eventually when the night was half gone, he crawled down from his hiding place and into the middle of the camp.

Inside his covered cart, Fawzi slept soundly. Business in Damascus had been good, despite not making as much as he had hoped from the slaves due to Saladin's envoys being tight with their silver. Now he was heading home for some well-earned rest before gathering the next lot of slaves from across the Negev.

The sound of his snoring joined others in the night, and though he was a light sleeper, the sound of a muted struggle outside the tailgate failed to rouse him. Moments later, a hand clamped over his mouth and a knife pressed against his throat, dragging him brutally from his money-filled dreams.

'Stay quiet,' hissed Hunter, 'and there is the slightest chance that I may let you live. Understand?'

Fawzi nodded, his eyes wide with fear.

'Good,' said Hunter, 'now I want you to answer some questions. Just nod or shake your head. Did you sell Sumeira in Damascus?'

The trader nodded in response.

'And do you know the man to whom you sold her?'

Again a nod

'Do you know where she is now?'

This time there was hesitation before the man nodded.

'Good. Now I want some information and am about to release my hand, but if you make the slightest sound, I'll cut your throat. Understood?'

Fawzi nodded, and Hunter lifted his hand from the trader's mouth.

'Right. What is the name of the man who bought her?'

'All the slaves were sold to Salah ad-Din,' said Fawzi. 'He sent envoys to buy all that they could.'

'Saladin,' said Hunter, 'why would he do that?'

'He is going to war with the Christians and will need as many slaves as he can get.'

'And Sumeira is with them?'

'She is.'

'Where are they headed?'

'I do not know.'

'Wrong answer,' hissed Hunter, pressing the blade harder against Fawzi's throat. 'Try again.'

'I think the city of Acre,' spurted the trader in fear, 'but cannot be sure. His army is vast and is spread out like sheep across the mountains.'

'Is she with any particular group or emir?'

'I am not aware of such things,' said Fawzi. 'The envoy came, gave me a low price and then went. He did not share any information.'

Hunter paused and stared at the slave-trader. The news wasn't good, but at least he knew Sumeira was alive and hadn't been sold in Damascus.

'One more question,' he said, 'give me one good reason why I shouldn't kill you right now?'

'Because I looked after her on the journey,' said Fawzi. 'She was not beaten or raped by my men. She was fed well, and her son has been released, which is what she wanted. Besides, does not your God preach forgiveness and mercy?'

Hunter grimaced. As much as he hated the man, he did not want to kill him in cold blood.

'Listen to me,' he said eventually. 'I am going to let you live, but I swear, if you raise the alarm before I am clear, I will make sure I kill you in the worst way I know how. Keep your mouth shut, and you will live to continue your barbaric trade. Understood?'

'Yes,' said Fawzi and watched as Hunter got to his knees to shuffle back to the tailgate.

Hunter turned around to climb down from the cart but stopped suddenly as he stared into the face of a man holding a knife. Before he could do anything, the man pulled back his arm and launched the knife towards him.

Hunter had no time to move, but the blade flew straight past his head, and he heard a gasp of pain behind him. He spun around to stare at Fawzi. The trader was now on his knees with a scimitar in his hands, and it was obvious that despite his pledge, he had intended to strike Hunter from behind. The fact that the blow had never come was mainly due to the stranger's knife now deeply embedded in his throat.

Fawzi clawed at the blade and tried to cry out, but the blood muffled any sound, and he dropped his scimitar before collapsing to the floor.

Hunter spun back around. The stranger who had just saved his life was just standing there, staring at him.

'What's happening,' he said, 'who are you?'

'His name is Basal,' said a voice in the darkness, 'and he is my brother.'

Hunter watched in astonishment as a familiar figure walked out of the darkness to join the man at the tailgate.

'Fakhiri,' gasped Hunter, 'what are you doing here?'

'That man,' said Fakhiri, nodding towards the dying slave-trader, 'killed one of my brothers thinking it was me. I came here to wreak my revenge.'

'I don't understand,' said Hunter, 'we need to talk, but first we need to get out of here before we alert the guards.'

'There is no need to rush,' said Fakhiri holding up a blood-soaked curved dagger, 'for there is nobody left to kill.'

Several hours later, Hunter and Fakhiri sat at a small fire in a wadi, far from the Damascus road, sharing what little food they had. Basal was keeping watch up on the Wadi edge.

'So you don't know where she is?' asked Fakhiri eventually.

'Only that she is somewhere between Damascus and Acre. Other than that, I have no idea.'

'There is much to think about,' said Fakhiri.

'What about you?' asked Hunter. 'How was your brother killed?'

'The slave trader sent men after me,' said Fakhiri. 'They were good trackers and found me soon enough, but I had already met up with my younger brother, Zosar. On the night they made their move, I was in a nearby village, and they mistook Zosar for me. He could not tell them what they needed to know, so they took his head. Others saw what happened, and when I returned, told me what had happened. It was obvious who was responsible, and I swore to avenge him but could not do it alone, so I sent for Basal and headed north.'

'Your arrival was timely,' said Hunter. 'I would now be dead if it were not for you.'

'Allah guided our footsteps,' said Fakhiri.

'How many brothers do you have?'

'There were five of us. The other two are in Egypt.'

'So what are your intentions now?'

'I need to speak to Basal,' said Fakhiri. 'He is the eldest of us all. He may want to head home, but I intend to stay here and see if I can find Sumeira.'

'Is that possible?'

'It may take time but can move amongst these people at will without raising suspicion. If she is alive, I will find her.'

'Is there anything I can do to help?'

'Not at the moment. If there comes a time that I need your help, I will seek you out or send a message.'

'You can always reach me by contacting a man called Arturas in Karak Castle.'

'He is the man who helped us escape,' said Fakhiri. 'He is trustworthy.'

'He is,' said Hunter. 'If there is anything you need, contact him, and if I am not available, he will help.'

'In that case, there is not much more to say,' said Fakhiri standing up. 'I will relieve Basal on watch. You get some sleep.'

'There is one more thing,' said Hunter, 'if you didn't get as far as Egypt, what did you do with the Gehaz?'

'It is safe,' said Fakhiri, 'and if we manage to rescue Sumeira, I will see to it that she and her family will live in comfort the rest of her days.'

The following morning, Hunter woke early but the two brothers had already gone. He packed his horse and headed back to Karak. Sumeira's fate was now out of his hands, there was no more he could do,

----

Several leagues away, Sumeira worked hard, preparing meat to send out to feed Saladin's army. Shepherds brought herds of sheep or goats to be slaughtered, and farmers sold their crops by the cartful. Overseers decided when and how many animals to kill and slaves butchered them into small chunks of flesh, ready to send out to the warrior camps.

Nothing was wasted; the bones were thrown into huge cooking pots dotted around the supply camp, along with any left-over vegetable matter. Each night at dusk, the slaves waited in line to receive a single bowl of food, before being chained up again in gangs of twelve. Although the women in each group often changed, Sumeira and Adela had formed a close friendship and did what they could to stay in the same gang.

Every night, the captives were counted, and again at first light. Nobody escaped, and those that tried were immediately beaten by the slave-traders. Occasionally, some were executed as an example, but slaves were worth money, and a severe whipping usually did the trick.

Darkness fell, and Sumeira waited patiently alongside Adela for their food. Tonight was special for there were several sacks of flattened bread alongside the pot and everyone was given half a loaf along with their soup.

The last few weeks had been hard for Sumeira, but the combination of luck and hard work had kept her alive and away from the eyes of the overseers who decided who would be sent to the warrior camps to pleasure the men. Each night, she and the rest of her group of slaves took their food and crawled into the back of a broken cart to sleep amongst the empty meat sacks piled up inside. The smell was awful, but they were warm and could remain hidden from sight until they were counted the next morning. Any conversation was carried out in whispers, but mainly they took the opportunity to sleep, exhausted by the day's endless labour.

Once the women had settled down, Sumeira sat back and gazed into her wooden bowl. It was half empty, hardly enough to keep anyone alive let alone strong enough to work for so many hours throughout the day.

'Do you have any meat in yours' asked Adela at her side.

'No,' sighed Sumeira, 'but we have the bread so I should be thankful for small mercies.'

'Here,' said Adela, fishing out a piece of mutton from her own bowl. 'I have two.'

'I cannot take your food, Adela,' smiled Sumeira, 'there is not enough as it is.'

'You shared yours with me many weeks ago,' said Adela. 'It is not much, but I want you to have it.'

Sumeira smiled and took the meat before placing it in her mouth and closing her eyes. She sucked on the mutton for as long as she could, savouring the taste until finally she swallowed and let out a sigh.

'That was as good as any meal I have ever eaten,' she said, 'thank you.' The two women ate the rest of their soup together before sitting back against a pile of sacks. Sumeira looked around the group of women, each as exhausted and as hungry as she.

'How long do you think this is going to go on?' she asked eventually.

'I listen to the talk of the overseers as much as I can,' said Adela. 'Much of the time, it is the boasting of idle men, but sometimes I hear things.'

'Like what?'

'Today, I heard that a second army is approaching Damascus. The tribes of the east have rallied to Salah ad-Din's call, and they are due any day. When they arrive, I think we will be on the move again.'

'Why?'

'Look around you,' said Adela, 'the amount of supplies needed to keep an army this size in camp is huge and can't be maintained for long. With another army to feed, Salah ad-Din will want to set out on campaign as soon as possible for if supplies run low, the tribesmen will leave. The Sultan's generals will send out foraging parties, but it will not be enough to feed the army, so the supply lines have to be maintained.'

'Adela,' said Sumeira, 'I have something to tell you, but you must keep it a secret.'

'I would never betray your trust,' said Adela.

Sumeira sidled up closer to Adela and whispered into her ear.

'I am going to try to escape,' she said.

'What,' gasped Adela, 'how?'

'Tomorrow, when we are unchained, I am going to sneak away when the camp is at its busiest.'

'You will be caught,' said Adela, 'and whipped. Don't do this.'

'It's too late,' said Sumeira, 'I have already bribed one of the guards.'

'What with? You had no coins.'

'I had a gem hidden about me,' said Sumeira, 'and used it to pay the gatekeeper. We have shared many smiles over the past few days, and I think he has become fond of me. Anyway, tomorrow, when we go for the water, I am going to hide near the well, and when the rest of the women return through the gate, he is going to miscount how many there are. If his word is good, then I will have several hours to make my escape.'

'It is too dangerous,' said Adela.

'I know it is a risk,' said Sumeira, 'but I cannot accept that my life ends here. I have to do this before it is too late.'

'Why are you telling me this?' asked Adela, looking around to make sure she could not be heard.

'Because I want you to come with me.'

Adela stared at Sumeira in shock.

'Why would you do this?'

'You have become like a sister to me,' said Sumeira, 'and I cannot leave you behind.'

'And the gate-keeper has agreed?'

'He has. I showed him the gem, so he knows it exists, but he will not get it until we are free. As we go through the gate, I will tell him where to find it.'

'But he could raise the alarm as soon as we have gone.'

'If he did that, I would tell the overseers he was involved, and they would punish him.'

'I don't know,' said Adela. 'it carries great risk.'

'Adela,' said Sumeira, 'we are going to die as slaves if we do not try something. Take this opportunity, I beg of you. Come with me.'

Adela stared at the western woman who had come to be a good friend in difficult circumstances. So far, she had been lucky, but Adela knew it was only a matter of time before she was discovered and suffered on behalf of all her countrymen.'

'I will do it,' she said eventually. 'Just tell me what to do.'

The following morning, all the women headed out of the compound to collect the day's water. As they passed through the gate, the overseer counted them out, tapping each on the shoulder with a cane. When it was Sumeira's turn, she glanced up, meeting his gaze. With a quick nod of the head, he confirmed the plan was to go ahead, and Sumeira dropped a stone at his feet with the gem's hidden location scraped upon its surface.

At the well, they took it in turns to hoist buckets of water. Sumeira waited nervously, knowing that the herdsmen would soon arrive to water their flock at the troughs, and that would be the only chance they would have.

Several minutes later, the moment she had been waiting for arrived as a herd of goats came running down one of the tracks to drink. They ran amongst the women, trying to get to the troughs and in the confusion, Sumeira and Adela ducked down behind a wall. For a few moments, they just sat there, waiting for someone to raise the alarm, but there was nothing except the noise of the goats and the chattering of the women. Eventually, the buckets were full, and the slaves started walking back to the compound. Sumeira looked up the goat path and knew this would be the most dangerous part of all. In the few minutes they would be exposed, and anyone would be able to challenge where they were going, but for days she had been watching the same path and knew that many other women had headed that way without being confronted.

Taking a deep breath, she got to her feet and hoisted the pole with her two buckets up onto her shoulders, hoping that a woman carrying water would be far less conspicuous than one with no burden. Adela did the same, and they walked as quickly as they dared, knowing that at any moment someone could order them to stop. Just a few minutes later, they crested the slope, and their spirits lifted. In front of them, at the bottom of the hill, was a tree-filled valley and for the first time in weeks, Sumeira thought they may actually have a chance.

Quickly they descended the slope, but just as they were about to enter the forest, a voice called out, demanding that they stop.

'It's just a shepherd,' hissed Sumeira, 'keep walking.'

'Stop,' shouted the man again, but though Sumeira had already reached the treeline, behind her, Adela had come to a halt.

'What are you doing?' gasped Sumeira from the trees. 'Come quickly.'

'I cannot,' said Adela. 'Freedom is a wonderful thought, but I have been a slave most of my life and would not know what to do. You go ahead, Sumeira, I will distract this man as long as I can to help you escape.'

'How?'

'We are women, Sumeira, we have our ways.'

'No, Adela,' said Sumeira, 'you are my friend. Please come with me.'

'It's too late,' said Adela with tears in her eyes. 'Now go while you still can.' Without waiting for an answer, she turned around and walked towards the approaching shepherd.

Sumeira's heart sank but knowing this would be her only chance, knew she had to keep going.

'Thank you, Adela,' she whispered and turned away to start running through the forest.

Chapter Twenty-Six

Sephorie

Late June - AD 1187

Raynald of Chatillon rode through the town gates at the head of a Templar column. On the hill above, men lined the ramparts of Sephorie castle, watching the horizon for any sign of Saracen activity. The town and the surrounding area were full of soldiers, over twenty thousand men and horses waiting for the inevitable battle to start. The call to arms had been well heeded, and the vast army included over twelve thousand knights from across the Outremer. More men were arriving daily, and confidence was growing that soon they would be able to match anything that Saladin could throw at them.

The column headed for the Templar camp on the eastern edge of the town while Raynald made his way up the hill towards the castle. Once inside, he handed his horse over to a squire and entered the main keep where the rest of the commanders maintained a war room.

Inside, a central table was covered with a map of the Outremer, and smaller maps lay on side tables, including one that had a rudimentary outline of the defensive walls of Tiberias. Several men stood talking on the far side of the room, and Raynald walked over to join them.

'Raynald,' said Gerard as he approached, 'you've arrived. How many men did you manage to muster?'

'Almost a hundred brother Templars,' said Raynald. 'There are a few more due from Gaza, but they have been delayed.'

'And who is this?' asked Ridefort, turning to face the sergeant at Raynald's side.

'This is brother Cronin,' said Raynald. 'He was Jakelin De Mailly's sergeant, and he comes highly recommended by the under-marshal at Karak. As your own sergeants were killed at Cresson, I recommend that you engage brother Cronin into your personal service.'

'Brother Cronin,' said the grandmaster, 'I have actually heard your name mentioned on several occasions, and always in a favourable manner. How long do you have left to serve?'

'A few years yet, my lord,' said Cronin.

'And what are your intentions when the time comes?'

'I don't know yet,' said Cronin. 'Perhaps go back to Ireland and start a farm.'

'It sounds idyllic,' said Ridefort, 'but I have to ask you a question that you must answer honestly.'

'If I am able to answer, I will be truthful,' said Cronin.

'You are aware, of course, of the circumstances in which Jakelin De Mailly died?'

'I am.'

'And you know that I left the battle to raise the alarm, knowing that the rest of the men were doomed to die?'

'I do.'

'So how does that make you feel, brother Cronin, that you may be serving the man who left your previous lord to die?'

'It is the way of war,' said Cronin, 'and I have no judgement other than that.'

'So tell me, if the same situation happened again, and it were you left to defend the flag, how would you respond?'

All the men in the room fell silent and stared at the sergeant. Cronin knew that what he said next could affect the rest of his time in the service of the Templars. But he had sworn to tell the truth, and he would honour that pledge.

'In truth,' he said eventually,' I don't think any man can guarantee how he will react in any given situation until he is in those actual circumstances. I have never run from a battle, my lord, and I have always honoured the Baucent. However, if the battle is lost and it meant saving the life of even one of my comrades, then I have to be honest and say the life of one of my brothers is more important than a flag. There can be honour in defeat, my lord, there is no honour in a pointless death.'

The grandmaster stared at the sergeant for a few moments as the unexpected answer sunk in. The room was silent, and everyone expected him to explode, for failure to defend the Baucent was a severe breach of tradition, in any circumstances.

'Brother Cronin,' he said eventually, 'if you had responded that way even a few months ago, I would have had you expelled from the order and whipped for cowardice. However, your reputation precedes you, and I know that you have served the order better than most. I have had many men serve me in the past, few of whom would have been so brutally honest, and I admire that in a man. So, knowing that it is I, and I alone that was responsible for Jakelin De Mailly's death, are you still happy to serve at my side?'

'It would be an honour, my lord.'

'Good. In that case, I charge you with only two things. Serve me as well as you did Sir Jakelin, and always tell me the truth, no matter how hard that truth is to bear. Is that understood?'

'It is, my lord,' said Cronin.

'Where are your horse and equipment?'

'In the stables in the town.'

'Then go and get them. You will be stationed here in the castle with me and will ride at my side on the forthcoming campaign.'

Cronin bowed his head in acknowledgement and left the keep as Ridefort turned to Sir Raynald.

'So,' he said, 'get yourself some water and come to the map. I will bring you up to date.

While one leader of men was being briefed in Sephorie, five leagues away on the Kafr-Sabt Plateau, another leader had called his own war council and sat on a cushion in his campaign tent surrounded by the men who would lead his army into war. Muzaffar ad-Din Gökböri and Salah ad-Din's son, Al-Afdal ibn Salah ad-Din had been given the honour of leading any attack while the Sultan's nephew, Al-Muzaffar Umar and the governor of Egypt, Al-Adil were tasked with supporting any attack with the remainder of the sultan's vast army. Other generals gathered around the main council, each impatient to take the battle to the Christians.

'Al-Adil,' said Saladin, 'please tell those present what you told me earlier.'

'My lord,' said Al-Adil, 'our scouts have covered every piece of ground between Tiberias and Acre. Some even went as far south as Jerusalem, and it seems that the only army that the Christians can call upon is the one encamped at Sephorie.'

'So there are no reinforcements on the way here?' asked Gokbori.

'No,' said Al-Adil, 'our spies tell us they have emptied every garrison from here to the sea.'

'How many men do they have?' asked Gokbori.

'From what we could see, perhaps twenty thousand.'

216

'We have the advantage,' said Saladin's son, 'and should attack immediately.'

'Let us not be too hasty,' said Saladin, 'first we should be in possession of all the facts.' He turned to Al-Adil. 'Please continue.'

'My lord,' said Al-Adil, 'though their numbers are lower than ours, there are at least ten thousand well-armed and well-trained heavy knights, including many Templars. The town has been well fortified, and it would take a siege of many weeks to break through to the castle. Even if we succeed, the fortress is atop a hill, and the fighting would be hard. I do not believe this is the place to face them.'

'I agree,' said Salah ad-Din. 'Their heavy knights are formidable but can be outmanoeuvred on open ground. Somehow we need to lure them out and face them on the plains.'

'How do we do that?' asked Al-Afdal.

Salah ad-Din turned back to Al-Adil.

'You say that most garrisons have been withdrawn from their castles.'

'They have, my lord.'

'Including Tiberias?'

'Raymond's army is with the rest of them at Sephorie. The city is lightly defended, and I can only assume that he thinks our treaty still stands.'

'The fact that he is with Guy's army means he has already broken the treaty,' said Salah ad-Din, 'and I have no problem with attacking Tiberias.'

'My lord,' said Gokbori, 'Tiberias is behind us. Surely, we should go forward, even if it means bypassing Sephorie and heading straight for Tyre or Acre?'

'We cannot leave them behind us,' said Salah ad-Din, 'for wherever we went, they would follow in pursuit. No, we should deal with them now for if we can break the back of their army once and for all, every city west of the Jordan becomes available, including Jerusalem.'

'So what will attacking Tiberias achieve?'

'I believe it will lure them away from Sephorie,' said Saladin, 'and they will ride to relieve the city. By doing so, they will have to pass the Horns of Hattin, and if we can lure them there, we will have every chance of meeting them in open battle.'

He turned to his nephew. 'Al-Muzaffar Umar, do we have any sappers available?'

'We do,' said Al-Muzaffar, 'a hundred miners and over a thousand slaves to do their bidding.'

'Excellent,' said Salah ad-Din. 'In that case, this is what we are going to do.'

For the next few hours, Saladin and his generals made their detailed plans, and by the time they rode back to their own commands, each knew exactly what was expected of them. The final battle for the Holy-land was about to start.

Chapter Twenty-Seven

Sephorie.

July 2nd - AD 1187

Guy of Lusignan was already out of his bed and at the map table in the war room when the news came. He lifted his head at the commotion and stood up straight when Raynald of Chatillon burst in, still covered with the dust of the road.

'Sir Raynald,' said Guy, 'you are your usual belligerent self, I see. What can I do for you?'

'Your Grace,' said Raynald walking straight over to the map table, 'this is no time for the niceties of court life, I have serious news.'

'Which is?'

'Saladin's army has surrounded Tiberias. The city is under siege.'

Guy stared at the Templar for a few moments allowing the news to sink in. The attack had not been unexpected, but now it had finally happened, it brought home the reality of the situation. Up until now it had all been talk and planning, but if the news was accurate, then he knew that he would be judged as a king by whatever happened in the next few days.

'Are you sure about this?' asked Guy.

'Reports are coming in from all our scouts. Last night, under cover of darkness, a Saracen army descended from the Kafr-Sabt plateau.'

Before Guy could answer, the door crashed open again, and Balian of Ibelin burst in.

'Your Grace,' he said, 'please forgive the intrusion but have you heard the news?'

'I was just being briefed by Sir Raynald,' said Guy. 'What have you heard?'

'There are riders down in the bailey,' said Balian, 'they have come directly from Tiberias. Their patrol was west of the city and got cut off by the Saracens. Only two men escaped with their lives. They say the city is already surrounded and there are more Saracens than they have ever seen before.'

The king turned to Raynald.

'Convene the council,' he said. 'We meet here in one hour.' He turned back to Balian.

'Sir Balian, call the men to arms. Double the guard on the city walls and send word to the Turcopoles, they are to assemble at the springs no later than dawn.'

'Aye, Your Grace,' said Balian and turned to leave the room.

'And find Sir Raymond,' shouted Guy, 'if it were not for him, we wouldn't be in this mess.'

In Tiberius, Raymond's wife, Eschiva of Bures, stood on the outer walls, staring out at the activity on the plain before her. At her side stood the Bishop of Nazareth. The gates of the city were closed and every man at arms she could muster lined the battlements, each heavily armed and ready to repel the Saracens. Below her, just out of range of the Christian crossbows, hundreds of Saracen warriors rode their horses around the city walls shouting challenges and showing off their riding skills. In the distance, thousands of foot soldiers marched into position as drums and horns filled the air. Eschiva knew the manoeuvres were more for effect than anything else, but it still made for an impressive sight.

'Have you sent a message to your husband?' asked the bishop.

'I have,' said Eschiva. 'We sent at least a dozen as soon as we knew the Saracens were coming so hopefully, some will get through.'

'Do you know where the king's army is camped?'

'The last I heard they were at Sephorie, but I see little to worry about. Saladin is a clever man, and even he will not want to besiege a fortress he has no chance of capturing.'

'What do you mean?'

'All this,' said Eschiva, waving her hand towards the Saracen riders, 'are mere theatrics to intimidate everyone inside the castle. Before this morning is out, their commanders will send envoys to discuss terms, and when they do, I will be ready.'

'Do you mean to surrender?'

'No, I mean to pay them,' said Eschiva. 'Come, there are things I need to prepare.'

A few hours later, they were both back on the wall. Most of the activity had died down, but in the distance, they could see many of the foot soldiers pitching tents. Both the bishop and Eschiva sat in chairs elevated on a raised platform so they could see over the wall without standing.

'My lady,' said one of the soldiers on the wall, pointing towards the camp, 'look.'

Escheva followed his gaze and saw four riders coming towards the city. The two outer riders carried flags, one the yellow of the Ayyubid and the other, all white, the symbol of surrender or peace. One of the men between the flags was dressed in colourful desert robes while the second was dressed all in black.

'I told you they would want to negotiate,' said Escheva getting to her feet to approach the wall, 'these people always do.' They watched as the riders approached and finally reined in their horses a few paces from the city walls. The man in the colourful robes looked up at the many faces peering down upon them.

'Lady Eschiva of Bures,' he called, 'my master sends you greetings and hopes you enjoy good health.'

'Hello Gokbori,' replied Eschiva, 'I am as well as can be expected. Tell your lord I thank him for his concern.'

Gokbori acknowledged with a nod and looked around.

'Lady Eschiva,' he said eventually, 'we have met many times, you and I, and I know you value straight talking, so I will be brief. Salah ad-Din, Sultan of Egypt and Syria, bids you open the gates and surrender the city you call Tiberias to him. If you do, there will be no need for a single drop of blood to be spilt here today, and when the franks have been driven from Jerusalem, as they will, he gives his word that he will place it back in your hands to rule as you wish.'

'That is a very generous offer,' said Escheva, 'but what if I decide to decline?'

'There is no room for negotiation on this,' said Gokbori, 'the choices are surrender the city or we will take it from under you. There is nothing else to discuss.'

'I think there is,' said Eschiva. 'and have prepared a counteroffer.' She turned to shout down into the bailey. 'Open the gates.'

The gates swung open and two men pulled a handcart through, leaving it a few paces away from the Saracens before hurrying back inside.

Gokbori rode up to the cart and stared down at the contents. It was filled with wooden chests and grain sacks.

'What is this?' he asked, looking up at Eschiva.

'The cart is filled with silver,' said Eschiva, 'along with rolls of the finest silk. There are another ten such carts waiting inside, along with one more which holds two hundred pounds of gold and jewel-encrusted treasures accumulated over many years by my predecessors. Tell your master that if he leaves us be, all the carts are his as a gift, and he has my word that we will not interfere in his affairs. If you want to attack Jerusalem, so be it. None of my men here will raise a sword against you.'

'And your husband?'

'He is with Guy of Jerusalem,' said Eschiva, 'not here. Tiberias is mine, and I will do whatever it takes to defend my city. My husband is his own man, Gokbori, and if he has decided to fight alongside the forces of Jerusalem, then he must face the consequences. Tell your master this. We may not be able to defeat such a magnificent army, but we will make you fight for every step until the streets of Tiberias are awash with Saracen blood and when the fighting is done, win or lose, you will still be no closer to Jerusalem.'

For a few moments, Gokbori stared up at Eschiva. Their relationship had always been one of mutual respect, and it hurt him now to do what he must.

'Lady Eschiva of Bures,' he said eventually, 'there is no need for me to convey your message, for my instructions are clear. If you do not cede the city, we will take it by force and dismantle it block by block if needs be. Your offer is noted, but respectfully declined so I will ask again, will you cede this city to the Sultan?'

'Should you not check with him?' shouted the bishop. 'There is a lot of silver and gold on those carts.'

'Lady Eschiva,' said Gokbori, ignoring the bishop. 'Look beyond me to the camp. Do you see a man upon a white horse?'

'I do,' said Eschiva.

'That,' said Gokbori, 'is Salah ad-Din himself. Rarely does he come so close to the battle but he is so determined to take your city, he will be leading the attack himself. Trust me when I say he has little interest in your trinkets, he just wants control of Tiberias. There is no need for anyone to get hurt but deny him, and death will fall upon the city like a swarm of locusts. So, for the last time, will you surrender Tiberias, or will you suffer Salah ad-Din's wrath?'

Eschiva stared at the emir. The fact that Saladin himself was there shocked her to the core, but deep inside, she knew she could never surrender Tiberias to the Saracens without a fight. Tiberias was a Christian city, and she knew that to hand it over, even temporarily would open the road to Jerusalem.

'Gokbori,' she said eventually, 'I have the utmost respect for you and your master. For many years we have enjoyed a cordial relationship, but today, you ask too much. You know as well as I that I cannot, and will not cede this city, no matter what the outcome. I turn down your master's offer and stand ready to repel your warriors. The decision is made; the answer is no.'

Gokbori took a deep sigh and stared up at Eschiva one last time.

'Then stand to your weapons, lady Escheva,' he said, 'for we will not stop until this city is ours.' Without another word, he wheeled his horse and galloped back towards the Saracen lines.

'Close the gates,' said Eschiva, 'and summon every man to the walls.'

Back in Sephorie, the war council gathered in the castle keep. Guy paced back and fore, listening to the views of his commanders. Each and every man present was experienced in warfare, and each was as strong-willed as the next. Tempers were frayed, and the room split roughly into those who wanted to stay in Sephorie to face Saladin when he advanced on Jerusalem and those who wanted to march immediately and relieve the siege of Tiberias. The arguments had raged for over an hour until finally, Guy slammed his fist down on the table, bringing the room to order.

'Enough,' he shouted, 'we are getting nowhere.' He paused and looked around the room. 'I have heard argument and counter-argument,' he continued lowering his voice, 'and yet we are still no closer to an agreement. Rarely has there ever been such a gathering of knights and lords more experienced than those that surround me now, yet we fail to agree on the most basic of tactics. So, I will ask each of you in turn for an answer, and the rest will remain silent while he gives an answer. Once I have heard everyone, I will make my decision. Agreed?'

'Aye,' came the collective reply and Guy turned to the nearest man to him.

'Sir Reginald,' he said, 'what says the Lord of Sidon?'

'Your Grace,' said Reginald, 'I will follow your lead whichever path is chosen, but if it were me in charge, I would leave Tiberias to Saladin and focus on defending Jerusalem. Anything else will be a waste of time.'

The king nodded and turned to the next man.

'Lord Jocelyn. How says Odessa?'

'I say we ride immediately,' said Jocelyn. 'Our men have fire in their bellies and will serve us well, but every day we delay will see that fire die a little bit more. Better to see them fight now while their blades are sharp than be on the defensive when the time comes.'

'Lord Garnier,' said the king, 'as the sole representative of the Knights Hospitaller, it falls to you to state the order's preference. Do we stay, or do we attack?'

'Your Grace,' said Garnier of Nablus, 'my men will not shy from the fight, but I strongly advise that you do not fall for this ploy. In my opinion, it is but a ruse to draw us from Sephorie and onto the plains of Hattin where we will be severely exposed.'

'Gerard of Ridefort,' said the king turning to the Templar grandmaster, 'what is the advice of the Templars?'

'We fight,' intervened Raynald de Chatillon before his superior could answer, 'and march with all haste. If Saladin is focused on breaching the walls of Tiberias, we can gain the advantage by attacking his rear lines.'

'It is likely that he still has men on the Kafr-Sabt plateau,' said Balian, 'and they could be a danger to our flanks.'

'All the more reason to move quickly,' interjected the grandmaster, glancing over at Raynald. If we attack now, we should catch the rest of the Saracen army unawares, and by the time they organise a counter-attack, we can be amongst those who besiege the city. Once there, it matters not how big Saladin's army is, the walls of Tiberius are stout, and with twenty-thousand Christian soldiers reinforcing their defences, the Saracens will dare not advance towards Jerusalem.'

Before he could continue, a voice spoke slowly at the end of the table.

'No,' said Raymond of Tripoli, 'no…no…no…no…NO!'

With every syllable, his voice raised until he was shouting, and his fists crashed down in anger.

'Listen to yourselves,' he shouted, staring around the room. 'Each of you acts as if he knows what is best for Tiberius yet you lose sight of what is really at risk here, Jerusalem. Yes, Tiberias is at risk, but we are fighting God's war, and we need to remember why we are here.'

'Lord Raymond,' said the king, 'are you saying that you are willing to sacrifice your city and all within its walls?'

'As I have said before,' said Raymond, 'Tiberias is more than capable of withstanding a siege, and even if the outer walls fall, the citadel at its heart is unbreachable.'

'The citadel will only hold so many,' said Balian, 'what about the common people of the city?'

'Some will die admittedly,' said Raymond, 'but many will live.'

'Slavery is not a life worth living for any Christian,' said Raynald, 'it is better to die than to take a knee to a Saracen.'

'The fact is,' continued Raymond, 'we have a secure position here in Sephorie, and after a few days wearing themselves out attacking Tiberias, many of Saladin's men will think about returning home.'

'Idiocy,' snapped Raynald, 'the Saracens are hell-bent on regaining Jerusalem, and even if you are correct and Tiberias can stand alone, there is no way that Saladin will allow his men to leave without as much as a sight of the Holy-city.'

'Saladin does not have an army,' countered Garnier of Nablus, 'he has a treaty between many tribes who fight for themselves as well as the Sultan. I agree with Lord Raymond. If they believe they are wasting time on the walls of Tiberias, it is possible they will grow disheartened and return to their families.'

'I do not agree,' snapped Raynald, 'I have fought the Saracens for years and know better than most the depth of their fanaticism.'

'And I have met Saladin himself in person,' shouted Raymond, 'so do not try to tell me what he will or will not do. If it was not for your continued disdain for hard-won treaties, then we would not be here in the first place.'

'I will not be talked down to by a traitor,' growled Raynald. 'It is one of your so-called treaties that allowed a Saracen army to slaughter over a thousand men at Cresson, so I suggest you keep your suggestions to yourself.'

'I had no idea that was their intent,' hissed Raymond.

'Nevertheless, my men died because of you,' responded Gerard of Ridefort, 'just because you were too cowardly to fight.'

'I am no coward,' roared Raymond and lunged towards the grandmaster, only to be restrained by Garnier of Nablus and Balian of Ibelin.

'Enough,' roared the king again as they pulled the two men apart, 'we should be fighting Saracens not each other.' The noise fell away again as the king stared around the room. 'I have made my decision,' he said, 'and tomorrow morning, under the shadow of the one true cross, I, Guy of Lusignan, King of Jerusalem, will lead the armies of God against those that assault Tiberias. Assemble your men, my lords, we are marching to war.'

Chapter Twenty-Eight

Tiberias

July 2nd - AD 1187

Escheva stared out of one of the higher windows in the keep at the heart of the citadel. From her position, she could see over the outer city walls and as far as the Saracen camp. It had only been a few hours since she had declined Saladin's offer, yet already the city was under brutal attack. Wave after wave of riders had ridden up to the walls, releasing volley after volley of flaming arrows high over the walls to land amongst the wooden settlements behind.

Already the flames had taken hold, and people rushed everywhere, desperate to douse the flames before they spread throughout the city. Black smoke filled the air, and those on the walls struggled to breathe or see.

'I have never seen such a thing,' gasped the Bishop of Nazareth at her side, 'their attack is overwhelming. How can we hope to hold them out?'

'We do not have to,' said Escheva, 'the walls are doing their job well. The fires do little damage and houses can be rebuilt, though I worry we are using too much water.' She turned to one of the servants in the room. 'Robert, take a message to the steward. Tell him to create a fire break two hundred paces from the outer walls. Tell him to pull down houses if he has to, but only use water to douse the flames this side of the break. The others can burn.'

'Won't the Saracens just keep sending their fire-arrows?' asked the bishop.

'As long as the walls hold, their arrows cannot reach that far,' said Escheva. 'In fact, I fail to see what they are hoping to achieve. Their archers have spent hours darkening the sky, but all we have lost is a few cattle and some buildings. What are they up to?'

She looked out at the walls again, watching the activity along the ramparts. All her men took refuge behind the stout castellations, with some peering out to release an arrow whenever one of the Saracens ventured too close. The door opened, and one of her commanders came in, his face dirty from the smoke and a trickle of blood running down his neck from a wound on the side of his head.

'Sir Richard,' she said, 'you are hurt?'

'A flesh wound only,' said the knight. 'The arrow deflected off my chainmail and fell somewhere in the city.'

'Do you need a physician?'

'I do not,' said the knight, 'and must return to the walls, but I have news, and it is not good.'

'Tell me.'

'The Saracens have been pounding the walls for hours,' said the knight, 'a folly I could not fathom. What is more, they built their own fires near the wall and poured pitch upon the flames to blacken the smoke and steal our breath. But when the wind picked up and blew away some of the smoke, their true purpose was revealed. Behind one of the fires, just out of arrow range, they have hundreds of men removing spoil from a shaft sunk into the ground.'

'Why would they do that?' asked the bishop.

'They are going to undermine the walls,' gasped Escheva and turned back to face the knight.

'Do you know what part of the wall they target?'

'We do not, my lady though it will be somewhere near the main gates.'

'Double the men in that area,' said Escheva, 'and arm a patrol to ride out against the tunnellers. We have to stop them.'

'We cannot,' said Sir Richard, 'most of my horsemen rode with your husband to Acre. I only have about fifty available, and there are over a thousand Saracen warriors guarding the shaft. If I send them out, they will be slaughtered.'

Escheva stared at the knight, her face creased with concern.

'Is there nothing we can do?'

'As you said, we can increase our men in that area, but if the walls fall, the Saracens will have the numerical advantage by far. All we can do is hold them back as long as we can while the rest of our men retreat to the citadel. They will find this place harder to breach than the outer walls.'

'We must gather provisions,' said the bishop, 'and stock the citadel while we still have a chance.'

'I have already given the order,' said the knight, 'and every corner is being filled as we speak. I think the citadel will be good for many days, but if they do decide to mine, then there is little we can do.'

'We must send riders to my husband,' said Escheva, 'and tell him what is happening here.'

'As soon as it is dark,' said the knight, 'I will send my best riders on the strongest horses. Now I must return to the walls and prepare what defences I can.'

'Thank you, Sir Richard,' said Escheva and watched him leave the room before turning to face the bishop.

'Your Grace,' she said, 'if the citadel falls, I am confident that Gokbori will spare my life, but not so sure that you enjoy the same protection. There are secret places within the citadel where we can hide you with enough provisions to last ten days or so. If Tiberias falls, I suggest you avail yourself of the hideaways and stay there until you know it is safe to come out.'

'If this citadel falls,' said the bishop, 'there will be no hiding from me. I will stay at your side with God's protection.'

'And if he is absent with that protection?'

'Then it will be because he has deemed it to be my time. I am not afraid, Lady Escheva, and will face God's will with courage and with grace.'

'Have you ever seen what Saracen warriors do to Christian men of God?' asked Escheva.

'I have not, but the tales have not passed me by.'

'Then you should know better than to take the risk. Death in any form is neither noble nor painless, and I have seen the strongest of men crumble with pain and fear. I strongly suggest that when they come, seek the safety I offer, and I will do everything I can to keep them away.'

On a hill outside the city, Salah ad-Din and Gokbori sat astride their horses, watching as their mounted warriors sent wave after wave against the city walls. The attack was relentless and no sooner had one attack eased than another would take its place, giving the defenders no time to rest or organise a counter-attack. Three mangonels hurled rocks at one of the walls, breaking chunks from the fortifications, but unlike the larger trebuchets, the wheeled catapults were too small to create any significant damage. Hundreds of men formed two lines into a sloping shaft heading underground towards the city walls and bucket after bucket of spoil passed through their hands to be emptied to the rear.

'It goes better than expected,' said Gokbori. The ground is soft, and at this rate, we can start the fires beneath the walls by the time it gets dark. By morning, the city will be in our hands, and we can think about capturing the citadel.'

'With Allah's grace, it will not come to that,' said Salah ad-Din.

Gokbori turned to stare at the Sultan.

'You think they will surrender?'

'I do not. But it was my intention to attack the citadel unless we really had to. This is about luring the Christian army from Sephorie.'

'Our scouts report that the Christians are still there,' said Gokbori. 'They may not be taking the bait.'

'Perhaps they do not know what is happening,' said Salah ad-Din.

'They know,' said Gokbori, 'for we found one of their patrols returning to the city. We allowed two to escape but followed them far enough to ensure they reached the Christian army and tell the tale.'

'Good,' said Salah ad-Din. 'I suspect those still inside the city will send more when the outer walls fall. Make sure enough get through our lines to raise the alarm. We need those Christians on the Hattin plains if we are to have any chance.'

'As you wish, my lord,' said Gokbori.

Five leagues away, Sumeira lay beneath a thicket deep in the heart of a forest. At first, she had made good time, and though she didn't know exactly where she was, she used the sun's location to head directly west, knowing that once she hit the River Jordan, she could follow it south to the Tiberias Sea. It had been three days since she had escaped the slave camp and although she had not eaten anything since, she was more worried about thirst having drunk the last of her water the previous night. Now she lay hidden, watching some local Arab women filling their gourds from a small stream winding its way through the forest.

When they finished, Sumeira crawled from her hiding place and ran towards the water. Falling to her knees, she scooped handfuls to her cracked lips before leaning forward to immerse her face into the pool. Once she had drunk her fill, she submerged her dry water-skin into the stream, allowing it to fill before splashing more water over her head to wash the sweat and grime from her skin. A twig snapped, and she spun around to see a teenage girl standing behind her with a basket.

Sumeira's heart raced. For a moment, the two just stared, each as surprised as the other. Sumeira knew that if she ran, the girl would probably tell someone about her, so somehow, she had to make a connection.

'Hello,' she said eventually, 'my name is Sumeira. I mean you no harm.'

The girl just stared back, unable to understand the southern dialect.

'Sumeira,' she said again, pointing at her own chest. 'You?'

The briefest of smiles flickered across the girl's face.

'Madi,' said the girl pointing to herself, 'Madi.'

'Hello, Madi,' said Sumeira and glanced at the basket. 'Do you have any food?' She pointed at her mouth before putting her hands together as if in prayer. 'Food?'

The girl understood immediately and produced an apple from the basket.

'Thank you,' said Sumeira and took a bite without taking her eyes off the girl. Madi watched and produced a second apple from the basket.

'Thank you, Madi,' said Sumeira again with a smile. She looked around, knowing she dared not stay any longer.

'Galilee,' she said, putting her hand above her eyes to mimic someone looking for something in the distance. 'Sumeira go to Galilee?'

The girl just stared back in confusion.

Having an idea, Sumeira knelt down and scooped up some water into her hands.

'Water,' she said, 'water.'

'Ma'an,' said the girl, 'Ma'an.'

'Yes,' gasped Sumeira, 'Ma'an. Where is the big water?' She threw her hands wide, 'where is the big Ma'an. Where is Galilee Ma'an?'

Suddenly the girl's eyes widened, realising what the strange woman was saying.

'Aljalil,' she said, using the local name, 'ma' kabi Aljalil.'

'Yes,' gasped Sumeira recognising the word Aljalil. 'Where is the big water?'

Madi pointed downstream.

'Ma' kabi Aljalil.'

Sumeira stared at the stream, realising it must be a tributary of the River Jordan. If so, all she had to do was follow it until it reached the river. She turned back to face the girl.

'Thank you, Madi,' she said, 'but if anyone asks, you didn't see me.' She pointed at the girl before covering her own eyes and pointing at herself. 'Madi not see Sumeira,' she said, repeating the gesture before putting her hand over her own mouth.

The girl mimicked Sumeira's gestures before pointing downstream.

'Adhhab,' she said, 'ma' kabi Aljalil.'

'Thank you, Madi,' said Sumeira, placing her hands in the prayer gesture again, and with the girl looking on, started walking backwards before turning away and running as fast as she could along the edge of the stream.

Back in Tiberias, Escheva and the Bishop of Nazareth were once more on the highest tower of the keep, gazing out to where a huge plume of black smoke soared skyward outside the city walls.

'That is the smoke from the tunnel,' said Escheva, 'Sir Richard sent word that they have lit the fires beneath the city walls. As soon as the supports have burnt away, the walls will collapse and create a breach.'

'And there is nothing we can do?'

'Our men will hold them for a while, but they are heavily outnumbered. They will be better off here, within the citadel.' She looked down to where people were still bringing food and water into the citadel. 'Soon I will have to close the gates,' she said. 'We cannot take everyone.'

'Thousands will perish,' said the bishop, 'we must take as many as we can.'

'And we will,' said Escheva, 'but even so, there will be far more in the city left to the whims of the Saracens.'

'I will pray for their souls,' said the bishop but before Escheva could answer, a loud rumble echoed across the city, and they both stared in horror as one of the main towers collapsed, sending curtains of flames and dust soaring into the evening sky.

'Oh sweet Jesus protect us,' said the bishop, forming the sign of the cross on his chest.

Escheva leaned over the battlements and shouted down to the guards in the bailey below. 'Close the gates, secure the citadel.'

'Aye, my lady,' shouted one of the men and what was left of the citadel guards started pushing the people back into the city streets. Within minutes the thud of a beam being dropped into place across the double gates indicated the task had been done.

'What of the men still on the outer walls,' asked the bishop, 'will we not let them in?'

'There are likely to be few that make it back,' said Escheva, 'and those that do will be hauled up on ropes. That gate remains closed until I say so. Come, I will show you where you can hide when the time comes.'

Chapter Twenty-Nine

Sephorie

July 3rd - AD 1187

By the time the first rays of sunlight cleared the Sephorie hills, most of the garrison was already on the road waiting to march to Tiberias. Over twenty-thousand armed men, including twelve thousand knights, stood in silence, each sworn to defend Jerusalem from the attentions of Saladin and his Ayyubid tribesmen. Many of the foot soldiers had answered the Arrière-ban, the general call to arms issued to every able-bodied man in the kingdom whenever the Holy-city was threatened, and though they were not full-time soldiers, they were duty-bound to fight in the king's name.

Of the twelve thousand knights, many were mercenaries, drawn to service on the promise of good pay and even better plunder, but the core of the army consisted of highly trained knights, and over a thousand Templars and Hospitallers.

Along the waiting column, each of the commanders sat astride their horses at the head of their own men, waiting for the king to descend from the castle. The morning was cold, but few complained knowing that within hours, the heat of the day would make the march unbearable.

A horn echoed above the town walls and as every man looked up, the gates of the castle opened, and the royal party emerged. At first, two lines of monks appeared, swinging pots of smoking incense and chanting verses in Latin. These were followed by the senior clergy who had also answered the king's call to action but behind them came the one thing that every Christian in the column was desperate to see.

'The true cross,' gasped one of the men in awe, 'I had heard rumours but never thought I would see it with my own eyes. Now I know we have nothing to fear.' He looked up at the man-made golden cross that was said to contain a sliver of wood from the actual cross upon which Christ died.

'Unless you are going to hide behind it,' said one of the Templar sergeants on a nearby horse, 'I suggest you rely on your wits and skill at arms to keep you alive.'

'But it contains part of the cross of Christ,' said the soldier. Surely God would never let any army under its shadow fail in its endeavours. Look what happened at Montgisard. Did not its appearance defeat the Saracens and send Saladin running for the hills?'

'I grant that it was there,' said the sergeant looking up as the cross descended from the castle, 'but I was there, and I suggest the victory was due more to the eighty-eight Templars who led the vanguard into battle. Now look to your equipment, we will be setting off in moments.' He rode off to join the contingent of Templars further down the line.

'Who was that?' asked the soldier.

'He is called Cronin,' said his comrade. 'His name is well known amongst the knights.'

'If anyone is going to die,' said the soldier, 'I expect it will be him. His words were blasphemous.'

'Perhaps so,' said his comrade, 'but he has fought many battles and still lives to tell the tale. We would do well to heed his words.'

A few moments later, King Guy and his entourage left the castle and rode down to take his place at the head of the enormous army. The men bearing the true cross slotted in behind him, and on either flank, the turcopole horsemen galloped forward to clear the way. All along the column, men prepared to march, some with anger in their hearts; some consumed with fear, but each knew that whatever lay before them, there was no turning back. The Holy-city was at risk, and this time, the threat of Saladin and his tribesmen had to be snuffed out once and for all.

A horn echoed through the air, and King Guy stood up in his stirrups, drawing his blade from its scabbard. He lifted it high in the air and wheeled his horse to face the army.

'For God,' he shouted, 'and for Jerusalem, advaaance!'

Up in the nearby hills, two men lay hidden deep in the undergrowth, watching every movement unfold. As soon as the column started moving, one of the Saracens crawled back into a hidden hollow and after stringing his bow, sent an arrow down into the valley on the far side of the hill. Several men were waiting for the signal, and as soon as the arrow thudded into the ground, they mounted their horses and dug in their heels. The Christians were on the move, and Salah ad-Din needed to know.

Several leagues away, Sumeira had made good ground and had reached the banks of a river. At first, her heart soared for she knew the rest of journey would be relatively easy, but she had no sooner nurtured the thought than she had to retreat into the undergrowth to hide from a Saracen patrol. She soon realised the area was swarming with Saracens and there was no way she could travel by day. Exhausted, she crawled further into the cover and lay down to wait for darkness, but despite her gnawing hunger, resisted eating the second apple the girl had given her the previous day. With access to the river, water was no longer an issue, and she allowed herself the luxury of drinking her fill from what was left in her water-skin.

The hours passed slowly, and Sumeira slipped in and out of sleep. The thicket offered some shade, but when the sun was at its highest, she risked crawling down to the water's edge, not just to fill her water-skin but to briefly immerse herself in the water to cool herself down. She lay there, hidden by a waterlogged branch for several minutes, allowing the water to reinvigorate her exhausted body. As she looked around, she realised that the bank above her hid her from the sight of anyone walking or riding along the river. The opposite side of the river had no such path, and she realised that if she stayed in the water and remained as close to the bank as possible, she could probably get quite far without being seen.

Knowing that if she hesitated, she would find too many reasons not to do it, she quickly removed her thawb and wrapped it around a stick. Once done, she placed her arms over the bundle and allowed the gentle current to carry her downstream. The going was slow, but every inch she floated took her closer to the sea and the safety of Tiberias.

For more than an hour, the water carried her south. Occasionally the river was too shallow, and she had to run across a ford to reach the deeper water on the other side, but luck was with her, and she managed to continue without being seen.

The current quickened, and though she tried to get purchase on the riverbed, she quickly found herself out of her depth and was swept downstream with little control.

Despite the speed of the water, she was at little risk. As a girl in Greece, her father had taught her to swim in the Mediterranean Sea, and over the past few years, she had swum many times in both the Tiberias sea and the Salt-sea. She also knew that the Jordan river was well known for its twists and turns and only in a few places was it deep enough to sweep someone off their feet. All she had to do was keep her head above water, and the riverbed would soon raise up to meet her once again.

Sure enough, a few minutes later, she felt soft mud beneath her feet and within moments, managed to stand up. As she gathered her breath, she looked further downstream. Ahead of her, the current grew faster, and she could see it grow angry as the flow encountered the many hidden rocks beneath the surface. She knew it would be far too dangerous to try to negotiate and decided that this was the place she would get out and rest. She reached up to grab a tree root but before she could move, heard the sound of approaching voices and tucked herself back against the riverbank as tightly as she could.

The voices got closer, and though she couldn't understand what they were saying, it was obvious the group consisted of women and children.

To her dismay, the women climbed down a shallower part of the bank and spread themselves out to wash baskets of clothes in the many pools at the water's edge. Despite her exhaustion and the fact that her inactivity meant she was getting colder by the minute, she knew she couldn't move from her hiding place or she would be seen instantly. The time crept on, and she knew that if they didn't move soon, she would have to take her chances, but just as she made the decision to take the risk, two cries carried through the air, one by a terrified mother, and the second by a small girl as she fell off a rock and into the swirling water.

The other women shouted in fear, and without hesitation, the girl's mother jumped in to try and reach her daughter. Immediately her heavy thawb got weighed down, and it was all she could do to keep her head above water. The shouts of fear turned to panic as the girl was swept into the faster central current and the women scrambled back up the bank to run along the path, leaving the mother clinging to a rock at the water's edge.

Sumeira was shocked. She knew that the chances of any of the women being able to swim were extremely low and even if they could, their thawbs would weigh them down, especially if the rapids emerged into deeper water further downstream. Without thinking of the consequences, she pushed herself away from the bank and into the central current.

In Tiberias, the screams were of a different nature. Overnight, the Saracens had attacked the breach in the outer walls, completely overwhelming the city's weakened garrison. Many were killed where they stood while others sought refuge in the sprawling streets and alleyways of the city. Despite the initial safety, the Saracen numbers were just too great and hundreds swarmed through the breach to burn Tiberias to the ground.

Up in the keep, Escheva and the officers who had made it to safety peered down onto the carnage below. Fires raged everywhere and screams echoed through the city, some with pain as they were put to the blade, others with fear as they were dragged away to see out their days as slaves to the Ayyubid. A few soldiers fought on in small enclaves, but the situation was hopeless. In less than a day, Saladin's warriors, aided by a hundred sappers and an army of slaves had breached the walls and now rampaged through the Tiberias unchecked.

'Did you manage to get messengers away?' asked Escheva, her voice quiet through fear and lack of sleep.

'Aye, I did,' said Sir Richard. 'Twenty men on fast horses. Hopefully, some will get through and tell the king what is happening here.'

'Do you think they will come?'

'Aye, I do,' said the knight, 'though whether they will be in time or not, I do not know.'

'What do you mean?' asked Escheva, 'we are safe enough in here.'

'Are we?' asked the knight, 'look there.' He pointed through the smoke to where hundreds of unarmed men were staring up at the citadel.

'Who are they?' asked the bishop at Escheva's side. 'They don't look like warriors to me.'

'They are not warriors,' said the knight, 'my guess is that those to the front are the sappers, while the rest are the slaves waiting to take away the spoil.'

'Are they going to dig another tunnel?' asked the bishop.

'Why not? It worked for them before, and in quick time. It seems this whole place is built on soft ground and if they work as well as they have been, the outer walls of the citadel could be down by this time tomorrow. After that, all they have to do is undermine the keep, and they will be amongst us. I reckon we have two days, three at most.'

'You have to surrender the city,' said the bishop turning to Escheva. 'Do it now while there is still a chance to negotiate.''

'They already have the city,' said Escheva. 'All we have left are the walls that surround us.'

'Then offer them the keep,' said the bishop, 'the jewels, the money. Offer them anything and everything; otherwise we will be killed.'

'We are already dead men,' said Sir Richard, 'and to cede now would only allow them to focus their efforts elsewhere.'

'What do you mean?'

'Tiberias means nothing to them, for their true target is Jerusalem, but they have to make sure the city is no threat to their rear. Even if we can keep them occupied for a few days, it gives my messengers a chance to reach the king and tell him what is happening here.'

'And if he doesn't get here in time?'

'At least we will have given them a chance to get ready for the fight. To cede now would allow the Saracens to immediately march on Sephorie or even Nazareth and the king's army may not be ready.'

'Then we are doomed,' said the bishop, turning his attention back towards the sappers. 'I suggest we all make our peace with God before it is too late.'

Despite the cold and her exhaustion, Sumeira struck out hard, swimming with the flow of the river. The centre was relatively clear of rocks, but she knew there were probably many beneath the surface. In front, she could see the girl as she struggled to stay afloat, he cries of terror loud over the sound of the rushing water. Within seconds, she passed the women on the bank who were hampered by their clothing and by the narrowness of the path.

Suddenly she smashed her head against a rock and for a few moments, got caught up in the swirl of the rapids. Her body tumbled over and over, and she lost all sense of direction, but seconds later her feet hit the river floor and she pushed up, gasping for air. She struck out again, and within seconds, the angry waters smoothed out as the river widened to form a deep pool. Sumeira looked around, but there was no sign of the girl. Desperately she took a breath and dived under the water, looking for any signs but to no avail. She resurfaced and took another breath before diving again to swim along the bottom of the murky river. Despite the low level of visibility, a sudden flash of red caught her eye, and she pulled herself to where a fallen tree-trunk lay wedged beneath the water. Grabbing another lungful of air, she pulled herself back under to where the girl's body lay trapped against the sunken tree. She grabbed the girl under her arms and summoning all her strength, pushed off the riverbed and back to the surface, carrying the girl with her.

On the riverbank, some of the women had reached the pool and waded in to drag them both to the side. One of them picked up the little girl and let out a cry of anguish when she saw there was no response. Sumeira thought back to when she had seen another child almost drown in Greece and knew she had only one option. Dragging herself to her feet, she staggered over and held out her arms.

'Give her to me,' she gasped, 'quickly.'

The woman hesitated but seeing the desperation in Sumeira's face, stepped forward and gave her the lifeless body.

Immediately Sumeira turned the girl around and allowing the child's body to fold forward, squeezed her torso to force out any water. Over and over again she pressed, and within seconds, the girl coughed forcing a flood of water to pour from her mouth.

The cries of fear were replaced with shouts of relief, and as the girl started crying, Sumeira handed her back. More women arrived along the path, and though many rushed to check the child was alright, others gathered around Sumeira, astonished at what she had just done. Everyone was talking at once, and Sumeira looked around desperately. Her thawb was nowhere to be seen, but she knew she had to leave as soon as she could before any of the patrols appeared.

'I have to go,' she gasped, trying to break through the circle of babbling women, 'please, let me through.'

Her heart raced, and her mind struggled to form a coherent thought. Faces swam in and out of vision, and as the noise became too overwhelming, Sumeira finally collapsed with exhaustion.

Chapter Thirty

The Road to Tiberias

July 3rd - AD 1187

The Christian column headed east, stretching back along the road as far as the eye could see. Foot soldiers laboured in the growing heat, and further forward, the Turcopole horsemen checked the route for any signs of an ambush, the lessons from Cresson having been painfully learned. Near the head of the column, Guy rode alongside Gerard of Ridefort followed immediately by Raymond of Tripoli and Raynald of Chatillon.

'You must have ridden this road hundreds of times,' said Gerard over his shoulder to Raymond.

'Aye, I have,' said Raymond, 'but never in a situation such as this.'

'How long do you think it will take?'

Raymond glanced back along the column.

'The pace is slow,' he said, 'so it is hard to judge. If the mounted men were to ride ahead, we could be there before nightfall, but the foot soldiers slow us down.'

'There will be no division of the men, interjected Raynald at his side, 'we will march and arrive as one army.'

'In that case, we probably won't get there until tomorrow.'

'What about water,' asked Gerard, 'in this heat the men will likely run out before dark? Can we resupply at the springs of Turan?'

'Have you ever been there?' asked Raymond.

'I have not, why?'

'They are nothing like those at Sephorie or Cresson, no more than a steady trickle flowing from the rocks halfway up the mountain. To fill every water-skin would take days. If we need to resupply, we will have to divert to the Springs of Kafr Hattin. There is more than enough water there for the whole army.'

Before anyone could respond, the sound of a warning horn echoed along the column, calling every man to arms.

'There,' said Gerard, pointing up the hill on their left flank.

As they watched, hundreds of Saracen riders appeared over the ridge to ride parallel to the Christian army.

'What are they doing?' asked Raymond.

'Looking to intimidate us,' said Raynald. 'Take no notice for as long as they are up there, they are of little risk. We just keep going as we are.'

'Should we not send horsemen against them?'

'No,' said Raynald, 'that's exactly what they want. As soon as we get anywhere near, they would just turn away and leave our men chasing shadows. Not only would that split the column, such tactics would quickly wear out our horses. We stick together.'

'Agreed,' said Guy from the front. 'Keep moving.'

In Tiberias, Lady Escheva pulled the blanket tighter around her shoulders against the cold of the morning. The night had been long, and the screams from the city had kept her from sleep, but eventually, she succumbed and had lain fully clothed upon her bed. Finally, the tiredness took over, but it had seemed only moments before someone was shaking her by the shoulder.

'My lady,' said a voice, 'wake up.'

She opened her eyes, instantly awake.

'Your Grace,' she said, seeing the bishop standing above her, 'what is it? Has the citadel been breached?'

'I don't think so,' he said, 'but Sir Richard wants us on the tower immediately. Something has happened.'

'What?'

'I don't know, the messenger only said we need to see for ourselves.'

Escheva jumped to her feet and grabbed a cloak before following the bishop out of her room and along a corridor to the tower stairway. Minutes later they emerged from the gloom into dazzling daylight as the morning sun climbed high above the hills to the east. She stopped and stared at the crowd already on the tower. Almost all of the guards were present, and they jostled for position, each keen to stare down into the surrounding city.

'Sir Richard,' she called, 'what's happening?'

'My lady,' said Sir Richard, turning to greet them, 'come, you need to see this.' He pushed some of the guards out of the way and waited as Escheva and the bishop walked to the parapet. 'Look, he said, what do you see?'

'The wall is still standing,' said the bishop eventually, 'they have failed in their task.'

'I wouldn't say failed,' said the knight, 'look again.'

For a few seconds there was silence before Escheva realised what he meant.

'Where is everyone?' she said. 'The streets are empty.'

'They are,' said Sir Richard. 'The Saracens have gone.'

'What?' she gasped.

'It's true,' said Richard. 'I have already sent out scouts, and they report the Saracen camp has long gone. They must have stripped it in the night.'

'But why?' asked Escheva. 'It makes no sense. They were only hours away from taking the citadel. '

'I can't be sure,' said Richard, 'but can only assume they have other things to concentrate on.'

'Like what?' asked the bishop.

'Like an approaching Christian army,' said Richard. 'I think that one or more of our messengers must have got through and Guy is marching to relieve Tiberias.'

'The Lord God has intervened,' gasped the bishop.

'We are not safe yet, Your Grace,' said Richard, 'but for now we can take care of our wounded and see about rebuilding our defences.'

'The bishop is right,' said Escheva, 'our prayers have been answered. All we can do now is pray that the army is victorious over Saladin.'

On the road to Tiberias, the Saracens started to send sporadic attacks against the Christian column. Small groups rode to within arrow-range before loosing as many arrows as they could and retreating before the defenders could respond. None of the attacks caused any major damage, but the constant harassment meant the column lost time, and the men were becoming frustrated. During another of the attacks, Sir Garnier of Nablus rode up the column to speak to the king.

'Your Grace,' he said, 'the men are suffering from thirst. We need to find water as soon as we can.'

'Tell those with two or more skins to share,' said the king.

'They already have,' said Garnier, 'but the heat and these constant stops are taking their toll. Unless we find water soon, I fear they will be in no condition to fight and may desert to find their own.'

Guy turned to Raymond.

'How far are the springs at Springs of Kafr Hattin?'

'About two leagues away,' said Raymond, 'no more than a few hours march.'

'And Tiberias?'

'There is no way we can get there before nightfall.'

'The men cannot wait that long,' said Garnier, 'we need water now.'

'The best we can do is to head for Kafr Hattin,' said the king. 'Sir Gerard, send messages to the outriders and tell them we are changing course. Tonight we will camp at the springs of Kafr Hattin and descend on Tiberias in the morning.'

'Aye, Your Grace,' said Gerard.

'Sir Garnier,' continued Guy, 'spread the word that within a few hours, there will be as much water as any man can drink. But tell them also that anyone found deserting will be cut down as if they were Saladin himself. Is that clear?'

'Aye, Your Grace,' said Garnier and turned his horse to return down the lines.

'Sir Raymond,' said Guy, 'you know this area better than any. Take us on the shortest route to the springs. '

'Aye, Your Grace,' said Raymond and broke the line to ride up to the vanguard with the new instructions. As he left, the king turned to the rest of the commanders.

'I know it breaks from the plan,' he said, 'but I have no other option. Besides, one more day will make no difference to the outcome. Our horses and men all need to be refreshed for the battle to come.' Without waiting for a reply, he turned to his signaller. 'Sound the advance,' he said, 'from here on in we follow Sir Raymond and the vanguard.'

For the next few hours, the Christian army followed a rougher road north, into the higher ground at the base of the extinct volcano known as the Horns of Hattin. The going was much harder, but the need for water forced them onward.

'How much further?' asked the king eventually.

'At the top of this hill is the village of village of Meskenah,' said Raynald. 'The plateau is barren, but the springs are less than a league from there in the foothills of Hattin. We will be there before nightfall.'

'I hope so,' said Gerard looking back over his shoulder to the stretched-out army, 'for the men are really struggling. Without water we are finished.'

They carried on toiling uphill, but though the slope was shallow, every step took its toll. The mid-afternoon sun seemed to get even hotter and beat down upon the arid ground like a fiery hammer, only to be reflected back up to bake the exhausted and demoralised army. Slowly they crept onward until eventually, they crested the hill and stepped onto the arid plateau. A welcome breeze played about their faces, and the pace quickened, everyone desperate to reach the springs. The front of the column was over halfway across when the king held up his hand, bringing them to a halt.

'Look,' he said and pointed forward to the base of the next series of hills. As they watched, Sir Raymond, who had ploughed ahead in the vanguard, raced back across the plateau to re-join the column.

'Your Grace,' he gasped as he reined his horse to a halt. 'We have a problem.'

'Spit it out, Raymond,' said the king, 'I grow impatient.'

Saladin must have guessed our intentions and has placed a vast army between us and the springs. Thousands of Saracens are marching this way, cutting us off from the water.

'How far are they?' demanded the king.

'Less than an hour,' said Raymond, 'We need to prepare for battle.'

Behind the king, Raynald of Chatillon looked up at the sky. The sun was nearing the horizon, and he knew it would soon be dark.

'Your Grace, Saladin will not attack in the dark, he would lose control of his men. I recommend setting up a perimeter here and making camp.'

'We need water, Raynald,' said the king, 'the men have used their last.'

'We can send patrols out during cover of darkness to try to get through,' said Raynald.

'Saladin knows what he is doing,' said Raymond, 'and will have the springs well-guarded. Even if any patrols get through, there would be enough for only a few dozen men.'

'So what do you suggest we do?'

'If we camp here, at least they will be rested. There is nothing we can do tonight, but as soon as there is enough light tomorrow, we can head for the Tiberias Sea. Most of the ground is downhill, and we can be there within the hour.'

'Does anyone else have any suggestions?' asked the king, looking around his commanders. When there was no reply, he turned back to Raynald. 'So be it,' he said. 'Split the army into three. Raymond, you and your men will form the first line of defence along with Joscelyn of Edessa. Balian and Bohemond will guard our rear with their armies while the knights of Jerusalem will form the centre body. '

'What about us, Your Grace?' asked Gerard.

'The Templars and Hospitallers will stay with me,' said Guy, 'but will form a quick reaction force to respond to any incursions from the Saracens. Keep the camps close together, so the perimeter is small. It will be easier to defend.'

Despite their frustrations, the commanders dispersed to their tasks. The hardest task of all was to keep their men's morale up for they had been promised water for hours and were about to be denied once again. For the next hour or so, half the men broke out the tents and made camp while the remainder formed a defensive perimeter. The enemy could now be seen, and hearts sank as they saw just how many they faced. As they watched, the Saracens closed in, surrounding the Christian army on all sides, taunting them with waterskins, freshly filled from the springs to their rear. Many poured water over their heads with disdain, adding to the anguish of those who had not drunk anything for many hours.

Suddenly a horse rode out from the Saracen lines and stopped midway between the forces.

'Here,' shouted the rider, throwing a full water-skin to within a hundred paces of the Christian lines, 'have this one, we have plenty.'

Although most of Raymond's men did not understand the warrior, the gesture was obvious, and several ran forward to claim the water.

'Hold the line,' roared Raymond but it was too late, and as the men neared the waterskin, they were cut down by a hail of Muslim arrows. The Saracen rider laughed out loud and rode back to the cheers of his men. Raymond took a few steps forward from the line and turned to face his own forces. 'The next man to do that will not have to worry about Saracen archers,' he raged, 'for I will have you cut down by one of our own. Hold this line, and I swear to you tomorrow, we will bathe in the Tiberias Sea. Now hold fast and place your faith in God.' He returned to the line, taunted and jeered by the massed ranks of Saracens just a few hundred paces away.

Darkness finally fell, and the Ayyubid army closed in until they were no more than an arrow flight away. Throughout the night, they denied the exhausted Christians any rest with constant chanting, beating of drums and praying. Before dawn, they added to their opponents' torment by setting fire to the dry grass on the plateau and pouring pitch into the flames. The breeze that had been so welcoming to Guy's army only hours earlier now turned treacherous and sent black, choking smoke amongst the camp. Arrows flew through the darkened sky, and though there was no full-on attack, by morning the Christian army had suffered hundreds of casualties. In the confusion, hundreds more deserted and by dawn, the army was severely depleted.

By the time the sun cleared the horizon, the arrow attacks had died down, but though the respite was welcomed, the torment continued as Saracen slaves led dozens of camels through the enemy lines, each carrying huge gourds of water upon their backs. As the Christians watched, Saladin's warriors quenched their thirst while jeering at their demoralised and exhausted enemy.

'Your Grace,' said Garnier of Nablus. 'Our men are dying of thirst. I'm getting reports that many men fled in the night, desperate to reach the springs. Our numbers are severely depleted.'

'How many?' asked the king.

'It's hard to say, but at least a few thousand.'

'Do you think they made it out?'

'Some perhaps but most were captured and killed. We heard the screams of many throughout the night some were burned alive before us this morning.'

'Your Grace,' shouted Gerard, appearing through the smoke alongside Raymond of Tripoli, 'we cannot continue like this. We have to attack or die where we stand without one drop of Saracen blood being spilt.'

'What do you suggest.' asked the king, 'we are surrounded?'

'Launch an immediate attack,' said Gerard, 'send Raymond and his army towards the Sea of Tiberias, and if they succeed in forging a path, the rest of us can follow. It will be costly, but if we remain any longer, we will all die here.'

The king turned to Raymond.

'Are your men up to such a task?'

'They would run through the gates of hell itself if it meant getting to the lake,' said Raymond. 'Just give the word and I will lead the attack.'

Guy turned to Gerard.

'And the Templars?'

'We will stay at your side,' said Gerard, 'and defend the royal person. We have to do this, Your Grace, there is no other option.'

'So be it,' said Guy. 'Spread the word, and at two blasts of the horn, the men of Tiberias will lead the charge down to the lake,'

Fifteen minutes later, the Christian army fell silent, knowing that in the next few minutes, many of them would die. Each prayed silently for protection, but all knew they had to prevail or die of thirst. Raymond's men knew that to them fell the greater risk, forging a path through an enemy position hundreds of men deep.

'Get ready,' shouted Raymond, drawing his sword. He licked his cracked lips, his swollen tongue filling his mouth. Seconds later, two blasts of the horn filled the air, and with an almighty roar, the men of Tiberias charged the massed ranks of Saracens. The Battle of Hattin had begun.

Chapter Thirty-One

The Battle of Hattin

July 4th - AD 1187

Raymond of Tripoli and the men from Tiberias swept down the hill and smashed into the front ranks of the Saracen army. Their momentum and pent up fury saw them instantly make headway, and though they were heavily outnumbered, the charge cut a swathe through the Ayyubid almost a hundred men wide. Steel smashed on steel and the air filled with the roar of battle as the two forces met in deadly and unforgiving combat. No quarter was given or asked and swords cleaved through flesh in all directions. The battle cries mingled with screams of pain as combatants fell on both sides, but it was Raymond's men who enjoyed the initial advantage. Their success took both sides by surprise, and Raymond's heart soared when he saw the mettle of his men.

'Keep going,' he roared, 'break through the lines.'

Those in earshot summoned up extra reserves of strength and redoubled their efforts, lashing out in uncontrolled fury at any man within range. Taken aback by the intensity of the attack, the Saracens gradually gave ground, temporarily stunned by the aggression of the rampant Christians.

Up on the edge of the plateau, King Guy and Gerard of Ridefort watched as the battle unfolded. Raymond and his men had made good ground, but from their higher position, they could see that the fight was far from being won, the depth of the Saracen lines were just too deep.

'They are forcing them back,' said the king, 'I think we should send the next wave to refresh the attack.'

'The enemy lines are just flexing,' said the knight in reply, 'as soon as the momentum eases, I fear the flanks will close in and cut them off.'

'All the more reason to keep up the pressure,' said the king, 'prepare your men, grandmaster, I think this is a perfect opportunity for a Templar charge.'

Before Gerard could reply, a roar erupted from the plateau behind them.

'My lords, the enemy are forming up to attack.'

The two men turned, and in the distance saw thousands of Saracens running into the centre of the plateau. From the slopes behind, thousands more joined those already in position, and within minutes, almost ten thousand men faced the Christian army across the barren plain.

'To arms,' shouted Gerard, 'shield wall.'

The cry was repeated throughout the army, and the Christians formed a defensive line across half of the plateau. The Turcopole horsemen raced into position on either flank and prepared to meet the Saracen cavalry with lances and swords.

'Sir Gerard,' said the king, 'what about the reinforcements for Sir Raymond?'

'There is nothing we can do for him,' said Gerard, 'the main threat lies in that direction.' He nodded towards the Saracen army facing them.

'What should we do?'

'What we will not do is stay here and hope for the best,' said Gerard. 'We will take the fight to them. Take to your horse, Your Grace, and gather your guards around you. I will lead my men into battle and cause a breach. You follow up with the main army and protect our flanks. If we break through, we will head for their commanders.' He pointed up the side of the mountain where a group of men sat astride their horses beneath the yellow banners of the Ayyubid.

'Do you think Saladin is there?' asked Guy.

'Oh he'll be there,' said Gerard, 'this opportunity too big for him not to be.'

'And you intend to reach him?'

'I doubt we will get anywhere near,' said Gerard, 'but if we can cause doubt in his mind, he may retreat, and once he does, the discipline of his men will fall apart. It happened at Montgisard; it can happen here at Hattin.'

'So be it,' said the king. 'You lead the vanguard, and we will follow you in. Good luck, Sir Gerard.'

'Luck plays no part in it,' said the grandmaster, 'it comes down to God's will and cold Templar steel.' He turned towards the group of Templars standing near their own horses. 'Mount up,' he roared, 'prepare to advance.'

Over a hundred Templars and three hundred Sergeants mounted their horses and urged them into position. The white-clad knights formed the first rank, lining up side by side, to create a formidable wall of battle-tested men upon well-trained war horses. Behind them, the sergeants formed up in two more lines upon their own steeds. Again, each man was well used to battle, and while the knights used shock and awe to drive a hole through the enemy ranks, their role was to immediately follow up and add fresh momentum to the charge.

Amongst them, just behind the grandmaster, Cronin unfastened the ties on his scabbard. He was a veteran of warfare and had fought under Henry in England before joining the Templars many years earlier. Beside him, a much younger man struggled to control his horse and glanced over at Cronin, the fear evident in his eyes. Cronin reached over and grabbed the harness, pulling the animal close to his own.

'You have to dominate your horse, my friend,' he said, 'or it will become a burden rather than an ally.'

'I know,' said the young man, 'I have never seen him like this.'

'They are clever beasts,' said Cronin, 'and know what is coming.' He looked into his fellow sergeant's eyes. 'How long have you been with the order?'

'Six months,' said the sergeant, 'but I only arrived in Acre two weeks ago.'

'So this is your first engagement?'

'It is,' said the young man.

Cronin looked over to where the Saracen army had already started advancing.

'Just remember,' he said, 'you earned that black cloak, the order would not have allowed you in if they thought you were not worthy. Remember your training, and whatever you do, do not hold back. If you hesitate for even a heartbeat, you will be dead before you see anything coming.'

The man swallowed hard and nodded.

'Now control your horse,' said Cronin, releasing the harness, 'and focus on what you have to do.' Both men turned to face the front as Gerard of Ridefort mounted his own horse and turned to face the Christian army. On both sides of the Templar line, thousands of men positioned themselves ready for the advance. Those already in the service of the king bore swords, axes or pikes, but many of the vassals who were only there due to the Arriere Ban possessed only farm implements for weapons.

To the left of the Templars, King Guy of Jerusalem and Balian of Ibelin sat astride their horses in front of half the army while on the right, Garnier of Nablus and Reginald of Sidon led the Hospitallers and the rest, a total of over ten thousand men. Ahead of them was a Saracen army equally as strong and every man knew that whatever the outcome of the battle, the fate of the Holy-land would be changed for a generation. Gerard of Ridefort waited until the army was ready before turning to face his own men.

'You know what we have to do,' he shouted, 'for we, like our predecessors, are God's sword arm. Strike deep into the heart of the enemy and show them what it is like to be on the receiving end of his wrath.' He eased his horse into the centre of the Templar line and turned to face the advancing enemy. 'Templars ready,' he roared.

A hundred knights flexed their fists around the lances sitting upright in the leather holders at the side of their saddles as the horses jostled for position. The grandmaster took a deep breath and stared at the thousands of Saracens across the plateau.

'These are the men who slaughtered our brothers at Cresson,' he shouted. 'Today, we do unto them what they have done unto us. Templars, advaaance!'

As one, the whole Templar line surged forward to confront the massed ranks of Saladin's warriors. Within moments the pace increased but nowhere along the white line did any man break rank.

'Present,' shouted the grandmaster a few moments later and every Templar lifted their lances from the holders and tucked them under their arms, pointing towards the enemy. With only a hundred paces between both sides, Gerard gave the final command.

'For the king,' he roared, 'for God, and for the Baucent, Templars *chaaarge*!'

With the sound of war horns echoing across the plateau, the Templar line broke into a gallop and seconds later, smashed into the Saracen army with a ferociousness born of frustration and hatred. The impact was like nothing the Saracens had ever experienced, and men fell in their hundreds before the unrelenting wave of white-clad knights. The front ranks stood no chance and were impaled on lances of iron-tipped oak while others were mown down beneath the deadly hooves of the well-trained horses.

As lances broke or become irretrievably lodged their victims' bodies, the Templars drew their heavy swords, each honed to a razor's edge yet strong enough to cleave through the thickest of leather armour. The impact was brutal and encouraged by their success, Guy gave the command for the rest of the army to follow. Horns rent the air again, and under the blaze of the mid-morning sun, ten thousand Christians raced into battle.

In response, the Saracen battle horns signalled the charge, and they surged forward to meet the Christians, two enormous waves of men crashing into each other in a sea of blood, flesh and bone. The scene was one of carnage, and men of both sides died in their hundreds. Within minutes, carefully maintained lines broke apart and the battle spread out across the plateau. In the centre, the Templar attack had driven a wedge deep into the central body of the Saracen army, but the impetus was weakening, and the grandmaster knew he needed more.

'Open order,' he roared, 'Sergeants to the fore.'

The knights spread out to open their ranks in a highly rehearsed manoeuvre, and the sergeants raced forward to fill the gaps. Reinforced, the attack gained fresh momentum and surged forward again, driving deep into Saladin's army.

Up on the hill, Salah ad-Din stood alongside Gokbori. From their position, they could see the whole of the plateau and their signallers communicated with their commanders using flags, horns and riders. The ferocity of the Christian attack had come as a surprise, but Salah ad-Din remained calm, knowing that although the knights of the blood-cross had a ferocious reputation, they were still mortal men and could be killed like any other.

'My lord,' said a warrior, running over to kneel before the sultan, 'I have news of your son, Al-Afdal.'

'Tell me,' said Salah ad-Din.

'He reports that the Christians who headed for the lake made initial headway but our men, with Allah's grace, have forced them back against the cliffs of Arbel.'

'Allah Akbar,' said Gokbori at Salah ad-Din's side.

'Do they still fight?' asked Salah ad-Din.

'Our men have withdrawn,' said the messenger, 'but only to await your command. The Christians are trapped, and your son asks do you want them for slaves, or do you want the hill to run with their blood?'

'This battle is not yet won,' said Salah ad-Din, 'and I need his army to reinforce us here at Hattin. Tell Al-Afdal, this is no time to take prisoners, and he must do what he has to do. Once the last of the Christians have drawn their last breath, he is to return here with all haste.'

'Yes, my lord,' said the messenger and turned away to return to his horse.

On the eastern slopes, Raymond's men had formed a shield wall at the base of a towering set of cliffs. Their initial charge down the slope had eventually lost impetus as many of his men had been distracted by the water flasks attached to the belts of any dead or wounded Saracens. Maddened by thirst, many had broken the line to retrieve the water, and in the confusion, the Saracens launched a counter-attack, driving deep into the flanks of Raymond's army. With his forces divided and at risk of being routed, Raymond rallied the remaining men and headed towards the cliffs, relying on their inaccessibility to protect his army's rear.

'Where is Guy?' shouted Jocelyn as the last of the men joined the defensive wall. 'He said he was going to send down reinforcements.'

'He must have problems of his own,' said Raymond. 'How many have we lost?'

'It's hard to say,' said Jocelyn, pulling back his chainmail coif and wiping the sweat from his brow, 'there are still pockets of men on the hill, but we can't get to them.'

Raymond looked at the Saracen army spread out across the slopes below their position.

'We can't stay here,' he said, 'if Guy doesn't send reinforcements soon, I fear we will be slaughtered.'

'I agree,' said Jocelyn looking at the exhausted soldiers in the defensive line, 'but the men are out on their feet. Without support from the main army, I can't see what more we can do.'

Up on the plateau, Raymond's predicament was far from the king's mind as he and thousands of his men fought for their lives against the swarming Saracens. The initial advance had paid dividends, but the sheer size of Saladin's army meant the Christians were countered at every move, and after almost two hours of fighting, neither side had made any ground. The sound of horns signalled the re-org and once again, Jerusalem's army retreated from the fray to catch their breath and treat their wounds.

'This is futile,' gasped the king, speaking to Sir Gerard and Raynald of Chatillon, 'we lose men in the hundreds yet still make no headway.'

'There is worse news, Your Grace,' said Balian, joining the commanders, 'our foot soldiers are deserting in droves and are spread out over the slopes of Hattin.'

'Traitors,' gasped the king, 'did you not warn them of the consequences?'

'They know full well the punishment,' said Balian, 'but they cannot fight on without water. Some were seen to approach the Saracen lines and beg to be put to death, such was their plight.'

'We have to do something,' said Gerard, 'to stay is to die. How far are the springs from here?'

'About a league,' said Balian, 'no more, but if we break for those, the Saracens will cut us down from the rear.'

'I don't see we have any choice,' said Gerard, 'Saladin is toying with us and knows we can't last much longer. If we stay, we all die, but if we break for the springs, some of us will get through and may just turn the tide.'

Before anyone could answer, Balian spoke up and pointed across the plateau.

'Your Grace, look.'

Several hundred paces away, fresh horsemen rode down from the Hattin heights to bolster Saladin's cavalry while the foot soldiers spread out to secure all routes off the plateau.

'If the cavalry attack, we are finished,' said Balian. 'We don't have enough horsemen to counter.'

Guy looked around the camp, knowing Balian was right. Given open ground, a massed charge against foot soldiers would be devastating, and he had to deny them the advantage.

'Pitch the tents,' he said suddenly.

'What?' asked Balian, turning to the king.

'You heard me,' said the king, 'pitch the tents. Put them as close together as you can, leaving only enough space to allow one man between them. If their cavalry wants to attack, let them first negotiate a forest of cloth and rope.'

'Will not their archer set fire to them?'

'Even better,' said Guy, 'for the wind blows in the direction of Saladin. The smoke will hide our intentions from him.'

Balian stared at the king, realising the tactic was actually very clever.

'Well,' he shouted, turning to face the men, 'you heard the king, pitch the tents.'

The weary men did as they were ordered, and within half an hour, hundreds of tents filled the battlefield. At the centre, stood the true cross, planted firmly in the Hattin soil. The king's tent stood next to it with the banner of Jerusalem flying high from its central pole. All around the temporary camp, those men who were left formed a shield wall, staring over the broken ground to the Saracen army who now had them completely surrounded.

'Your Grace,' said Raynald of Chatillon, walking over. 'Can I make a suggestion?'

'Speak your mind, brother,' said the king, 'we need all the help we can get, especially from the Templars.'

'As you know,' said Raynald, 'we lost half of our men in the first assault, but we are still able to fight. The Hospitallers also have men available, so I suggest the two orders combine forces and attack Saladin's position.'

'He is too well defended,' said Gerard, 'already his guards have repulsed three attacks.'

'That is true,' said Raynald, 'but now he has seen fit to surround our position, the Saracen lines at the base of the hill are not so strong, and I think a concentrated assault has a chance of breaking through.'

'I fear you may not get close to him,' said the king, 'and it is probable you will die in the attempt.'

'I have fought Saladin for many years,' said Raynald, 'and have sworn before God to kill him or die trying. Today it seems he has the upper hand, and if it is God's will that I fail, it will be with a blade in my hand, not running from him like a beaten slave. Just give the order, and we will renew the assault with everything we have.'

The king looked over at Gerard of Ridefort.

'What say you, Sir Gerard,' said the king. 'You are the grandmaster, is this a task worthy of your order?'

'Sir Raynald is the bravest of us all,' said Gerard, 'and if he says it can be done, then he has my full support.'

'In that case, do what you must do,' said the king. 'The army will follow you into the breach as soon as you carve a path.'

'Thank you, my lord,' said Raynald and turned away to find Garnier of Nablus to enlist the aid of the Hospitallers.

'Your Grace,' said Balian of Ibelin, 'even if we gain the advantage, there is just not enough room on the slopes for us to maintain a disciplined attack. Can I suggest I lead my men to the Hattin Springs to get as much water as we can?'

'Do you think you can break through?' asked the king, looking north towards the enemy lines.

'I think there is every chance,' said Balian, 'they will not be expecting any of us to break from the main army. Once free, we can get back here within the hour with as much water as we can carry.'

'I agree,' said the king. 'Take as many empty waterskins as you can carry and if you make it through, return here with all haste. There is still time to save this day, but without water, we are dead men.'

'I'll muster the men now,' said Balian and with God's grace, 'will be back within the hour.'

As Balian ran to gather his men, the king looked up at Saladin's position high on the slopes of the Hattin mountains. He took a deep sigh and turned to the Templar grandmaster.

'Sir Gerard,' he said, 'deploy a hundred of our best men to protect the true cross. If our plan falls short and we lose the day, instruct them to flee the field and return the cross to Jerusalem.'

'Can you not lead them yourself?' asked Gerard.

'I cannot,' said the king, 'too many men have fallen for this cause, and it is my place to see it through to the end.'

'Your Grace,' said Gerard, 'even if we were to break the Saracen lines, the hill is steep, and his archers will pick us off. If by some miracle we reach his position, his guards will probably take him to safety. You should take the chance to escape.'

'I know the risks,' said Guy, 'but I am the king, and my place is at the head of my army.'

Gerard took a breath and stared at Guy. The monarch was not known for his bravery, but on this occasion, his mettle was plain to see, and for the first time ever, the grandmaster saw steel in the king's eyes.

'If that is your will,' he said eventually, 'then we need to rally the men. There is probably one more push left in them, but after that, they are done. Come, Your Grace, it is time to show us the leadership that comes with the crown of Jerusalem.'

Half an hour later, the Christian army was formed up once again under the hammer of the afternoon sun. Every man who could wield a weapon stood in silence, each staring up at the flags of the Ayyubid. Many bore wounds, most were weak with exhaustion, and all had not touched a drop of water since the previous day. Despite this, each and every man was determined to sell his life dearly. The Templars lined up to the fore alongside the Hospitallers. At their head, Garnier of Nablus and Gerard of Ridefort sat astride their horses, ready to lead them into battle once again. Behind the forward lines, King Guy of Jerusalem sat astride his own horse alongside Reginald of Sidon, their two separate forces now combined into one. He looked to the far left where Balian waited with two hundred mounted men, ready to make a break for the Springs of Hattin.

'King Guy of Jerusalem,' roared a voice, 'we are ready.'

The king turned towards Gerard of Ridefort.

'You have the van, Sir Gerard,' shouted the king, 'lead us to glory.'

Sir Gerard turned his horse to face the Saracens. He drew his sword and held it high, standing up in his stirrups so every man in the army could see.

'For Jerusalem,' he roared, 'for the king and for God, *advaaance!*'

On the far left, Balian heard the battle horns echo across the plain and turned to his own men.

'You know what we have to do,' he shouted, 'we hit the lines at full gallop, slowing for no man, friend or foe. If you fall, you are on your own for we cannot afford to slow the pace. Remember, the rest of the army are depending on us. Succeed, and we may just save the day. Fail, and this plain will be awash with Christian blood. Knights of Nablus, 'are you ready?'

'Aye,' roared the men in response and as the king's army poured towards the Saracens at the centre, Balian's cavalry galloped straight for the nearest Saracen lines.

To the south, Raymond and the men of Tiberias were still trapped against the cliff face. Below them, the Saracen army was getting ready to attack their position, and Raymond knew that if he and his men stayed where they were, they would be slaughtered.

'Sir Jocelyn,' he asked over his shoulder, 'how many knights do we have left?'

'About three hundred,' said Jocelyn.

'And foot soldiers?'

'About another hundred.'

'Four hundred in all,' said Raymond, 'and we face an army five times that size.'

'It cannot be done,' said Jocelyn, 'we should surrender and take our chances.'

'I doubt they would accept,' said Raymond, 'and even if they did, we would spend the rest of our lives in slavery.'

'So what do you intend to do?'

Raymond looked around his men, knowing that what he was about to propose meant many would die, but many would escape.

'Rally the men,' he said, 'quickly, for there is little time.' A few minutes later, he climbed up upon a rock to face the few hundred survivors. 'Men of Tiberias,' he shouted, 'you know we face insurmountable odds and there have been suggestions of surrender. If we cede, the officers and I may eventually be ransomed, but men like you, despite your mettle, end up in the salt mines and usually die of thirst or are beaten to death by the guards. If anyone wishes to take their chances, you are free to leave, but there is another way.' He looked around his men, seeing glimmers of hope and utmost trust in their eyes. 'What I propose,' he continued, 'is that we do what the enemy least expects us to do, we charge them. Not with hopes of victory, but to break through their lines and escape to the shores of the Tiberias Sea.

'We have already tried,' that said one of the sergeants, 'and failed with almost twice as many men. What makes you think we can succeed this time?'

'Because this time, we will not pause to fight or retaliate, we will focus solely on the forward charge, keeping going without thought for any who fall at our side. Yes, some will die, but if we do nothing, then all of us will share that fate. At least this way, some will survive.'

'There are not enough horses,' said another man. 'Us foot soldiers will never make it.'

'On your own, no,' said Raymond, 'so some horses will carry two men. I know some will fall, but it is the best we can do, so, I say again. If you wish to surrender, there will be no judgement placed upon you by me or any other man here. Those who wish to take your chances with me, step forward now for there is little time.'

For a few seconds, there was a pause before most of the men stepped forward. Raymond looked at the remainder, seeing the despondency in their eyes.

'You men should feel no shame,' he said, 'for your decision is probably the bravest between the two. Once we have gone, raise a white flag as soon as you can and seek terms. If the rest of us get through, I swear I will send messages to Saladin and try to buy your freedom.' He turned back to those who wanted to go. 'The odds are against us,' he said, 'but with God's grace, some of us will live to see our families. Now gather the horses and form up. We started this together, and one way or the other, we will end it together.'

Minutes later, three hundred horses lined up at the top of the slope. In the distance, the men could see the glinting surface of the Tiberias sea, a teasing reminder of what lay before them.

'We will charge in a column of three,' shouted Raymond, riding along the line. 'Do not slow down or pause for anything, no matter what the reason. If you stop to grab a water-skin from an enemy, you will die. If you pause to help a comrade, you will die. Do not even exchange blows, just forge ahead with as much determination as you can. Do this, and I swear many of us will drink the sweet water of the lake before this day is done. Do you understand?'

'Aye, my lord,' shouted the men.

'In that case,' shouted Raymond, let us get this thing done.' He drew his sword and turned his horse to face the enemy lines at the base of the slope. Men of Tiberias, he roared, follow me.'

The column charged directly at the heart of the enemy. Saracen warriors launched themselves at their flanks, but Raymond and his men had momentum, and they crashed through the lines like a sword through human flesh. Ayyubid swordsmen hacked at the legs of the horses, and many fell, sending their riders crashing to the ground but still the column raced onward. Those who survived the fall tried to fight their way out but were mercilessly hacked to pieces by the swarming horde of Saracens.

'Keep going,' roared Raymond over his shoulder, 'do not stop.'

With renewed vigour, the remaining men urged the horses onward until minutes later, against all expectations, they broke through.

'Keep going,' shouted Raymond again as Saracen archers sent volleys of arrows after them, but though a few more fell, more than half of the column finally galloped out of range and onto the shallower slopes of the mountain.

'My lord,' shouted, 'Jocelyn from an adjacent horse, 'we did it. The column is through.'

'We are not safe yet,' countered Raymond, looking back up to the Saracen army behind them, 'they still have their cavalry. Tell the men to head for the lake and muster there. If we can last until dark, we have a chance.'

Up near the cliffs, Saladin's son sat upon his horse and watched the Christian column disappear.

'My lord,' said one of his men, 'shall I send our riders after them?'

'No,' said Af-Afdal, 'let them go. Their bravery deserves respect.'

'What about those that remain near the cliffs,' said the warrior. 'They fly a flag of truce and request clemency. Shall it be granted?'

'Not to them,' said Al-Afdal, 'unlike their comrades, their hearts are weak and deserve no mercy. Send them to their God.'

As the warrior left, Al-Afdal gazed at the disappearing column one last time.

'Enjoy the freedom while you can, Christian,' he said quietly, 'for your false kingdom is about to be destroyed by the fires of Islam.'

To the west, Balian and his men had broken through the Saracen lines, but at great cost. Half of his horsemen had been cut down in the fight, and as they neared the springs, they saw hundreds more warriors guarding the precious water source. With enemy to the front and no way to retreat, Balian had no other choice but to try and save what was left of his forces. He reined in his horse and turned to his men.

'Men of Nablus,' he shouted, 'we are done. Even if we fight on and reach the springs, we will not be able to get back to the king.'

'What are your orders, my lord?' asked one of the sergeants.

'All we can do now is save ourselves,' said Balian. 'Saracens lie at both ends of this track, but that way lies hope.' He looked down the steep slopes at the side of the path. The drop was severe but not vertical. 'Some of us may not make it,' he continued, 'but it's our only chance.'

The men hesitated, knowing that the chances of surviving were probably very low. In the distance, the noise of the pursuing Saracen cavalry grew louder, and the sergeant knew they had to act fast.

'Well,' he roared, 'you heard Lord Balian, what are you waiting for?'

Without waiting for any response, he urged his horse over the edge and down the slope, pulling a mini landslide of stones and dust behind him. For a few moments, the shocked men watched until he emerged from a cloud of dust at the bottom, seemingly unhurt.

'Come on' he roared, 'or die where you stand.'

Immediately, the rest of the men followed him over the edge and down the slope. Many horses stumbled and fell, throwing their riders into the landslide of bodies and dirt but by the time they reached the bottom, most managed to get to their feet unhurt.

'Mount up,' roared Balian, 'we need to get out of here,' and within moments, the men of Nablus were fleeing from Hattin as fast as their horses could carry them.

Up on the plateau, thousands of exhausted men fought for their lives. The massed Christian charge had been met with equal resolve and hordes of Ayyubid warriors raced forward to meet their foe in one last epic battle. Within minutes, tactics and formations were abandoned on both sides, and the fight spread out across the plains, each man fighting to the death. The heavier weapons of the trained knights cut Saracens down in their hundreds, but the enemy counter-attack was relentless, pounding the attackers like storm waves upon the shore. Time and time again, their lethal scimitars found exposed Christian flesh, striking their enemy down in equal number. Blood poured like water and the harsh landscape sucked it in, as thirsty as those being slaughtered under the desert sun.

Nearer the king, the thrust by the Templars and Hospitallers almost reached Saladin before being beaten back. Time and time again, they returned to the fray, each time getting closer but no matter how hard they pressed, the Saracen lines held. Behind them, Saladin's horsemen, unable to storm the camp, had dismounted and forced their way step by step towards the centre, intent on taking the Christian flag. The men defending the True Cross tried to escape, but it was of no use, the surrounding army was just too dense. Desperately they made the enemy pay for every step gained, but despite their bravery, the Saracens got closer and closer towards the king's tent.

Up on the hill, Saladin watched with increasing horror. The Christians were being slaughtered, but still they came. Just below his position, what remained of the Templars fought on foot, fighting with whatever they could to get nearer the Sultan. Many had been disarmed, but still, they came, lashing out with iron-clad fists and boots until they could claim a fallen weapon. Behind them, the last of the foot soldiers fought just as bravely, determined to sell their lives dearly. Saladin's officers shouted encouragement as the Christian army slowly disintegrated, but Saladin was silent, knowing that until the standard fell on the king's tent, the bloodshed would continue.

'Saladin,' roared a voice and he turned his gaze downward to where once again, the Templars were being forced back. In their midst was a tall knight and the Sultan immediately recognised him as Raynald of Chatillon, the man who had waged war on the Ayyubid for many years.'

'Saladin,' roared Raynald again from amongst the retreating army, 'this is not over. No matter how many you kill, God's army will keep on coming. Do you hear me, Saladin? No matter where you go or what you do, men like me, soldiers of Christ will seek you out and smite you down. This is not over, Saladin, it is just the start!'

The sultan did not answer and returned his gaze to the king's tent in the distance. The camp was fully ablaze, and the smoke swept towards his position, but above it all, he could see the banner of Jerusalem.

'My lord,' said a voice but Saladin held up his hand demanding silence, focussing on the king's flag. For a moment it seemed to sway unnaturally until finally, as all the Ayyubid chieftains watched, it fell into the flames. Saladin gasped and fell to his knees. Although there were still pockets of men fighting, he now knew the day was his.'

'Allah Akbar', he cried and prostrated himself face down on the ground in thanks to God. The banner of Jerusalem had fallen, the Battle of Hattin was over.

Chapter Thirty-Two

North of Tiberias

July 5th - AD 1187

Sumeira opened her eyes, not sure where she was. The air was warm, and the smell of burning wood filled the air. As her senses returned, she realised she was in one of the large tents used by the Arab tribes, and she sat up quickly to look around. To one side, two old women sat on cushions, mixing ingredients into a bowl to make the Harisa, a meal made from wheat, butter, meat and spices. The aroma was delicious, and Sumeira's stomach rumbled.

One of the women looked over and seeing Sumeira sitting up, brought her a bowl containing oranges and dates.

'Eat,' she said, giving Sumeira the bowl. 'There will be hot food later, but you must be hungry.'

'Thank you,' said Sumeira, and peeled one of the oranges as quickly as she could. 'You speak the language of the southern tribes, she said eventually, 'are you not of these people?'

'I lived south of the Salt-sea as a girl,' said the woman, 'but my husband is from Damascus, so I travelled here many years ago. I am now part of this tribe but remember the language of my father.'

'Where are we?' asked Sumeira. 'Is the Sea of Tiberias nearby?'

'The sea is far to the south,' said the woman, 'our village is on the banks of the Jordan just south of the Hulah lake.'

Sumeira was disappointed, but it was not the end of the world. It meant the river she had been following was definitely the Jordan and fed directly down to the Sea of Tiberias.

'How long have I been here?' she asked.

'One night and most of one day. You collapsed, so we made sure you were safe. Now you should eat and build your strength.'

'I have to go,' said Sumeira, 'I have to get to Tiberias as soon as I can.'

'You cannot travel south,' said the woman, 'not yet.'

'Why not?' asked Sumeira, popping a date into her mouth.

'Because there is a great battle being fought between the armies of Jerusalem and Salah ad-Din. It is said that more men have died than there are stars in the sky.'

'What?' gasped Sumeira, placing a second date back in the bowl. 'When did this happen.'

'All I know is what has been reported by some of the young men who returned to the village. Saladin attacked one of the Christian cities and then faced their king at the Horns of Hattin. Much blood was spilt, and many men died, but more than that, I do not know.'

'I have to go,' said Sumeira, 'I have to get back to my people before it is too late.'

'Strange lady,' said the woman, 'I do not know who you are or how you came to be here. All I know is that you saved one of our children, and for that, we are in your debt. I suspect you flee from someone who wishes you ill, but though we share allegiance to no Christian, we owe you a life so are willing to hide you until it is safe. If you leave now, you will be picked up by one of Salah ad-Din's patrols and taken back whence you came.'

'But I can't stay here,' said Sumeira. 'My children are waiting for me.'

'A few days will make no difference,' said the woman. 'Once it has quietened down, I will see you safely to the city, but for now, you have to stay hidden. Finish the fruit, and I will bring you some tea. Later we will share the Harisa and your strength will return.'

'Wait,' said Sumeira, 'what is your name?'

'My people call me Nadya,' said the woman.

'Thank you, Nadya, I am called Sumeira.'

'The thanks are to you for saving the child,' said Nadya. 'Now get some rest. I will wake you when the food is ready.'

Down at the edge of the Sea of Tiberias, Raymond and his men hid amongst the undergrowth, slowly recovering their strength. Their flight had been headlong, but with little sign of pursuit, they had finally reached the water's edge and plunged into the life-giving water without hesitation. Men and horses drank their fill side by side, staying in the cooling waters as long as they dared, but once done, retreated to the safety of a nearby wood and had spent the night in hiding, waiting for any signs of pursuit.

With the new dawn breaking, they started to emerge from cover and gathered together near the forest edge. They were in a sorry state, but they knew they were lucky to be alive. Raymond counted the survivors; just under three hundred men from the thousand that had left Tiberias just a few days earlier. Most carried wounds or injuries, and it was obvious they were in no state to fight.

'We made it,' said one of the men. 'By the grace of God, we are alive.'

'Alive but toothless,' said Raymond. 'It is all we can do to stand, let alone fight. We need food.'

'My lord,' said one of the soldiers, 'On the way here I saw a village further along the shore, perhaps we could barter for a sheep or two.'

'I also saw it,' said Raymond, 'and will lead a group of men to see what we can find. We should be back by noon but if we do not return, make your escape as soon as it gets dark. Until then, stay hidden and tend your wounds. Hobble the horses and let them forage but do not let them leave the forest.' He turned to Jocelyn. 'Post sentries further up the hill and if there is any sign of Saracens, do not wait for us, just do whatever it takes to get the men to safety.'

Hours later, all the surviving men gathered around a fire in the heart of the forest, waiting expectantly as the carcasses of four goats roasted amongst the flames. Their mouths watered at the smell, and the conversation was minimal. Since returning with the goats, Raymond and Jocelyn had kept away from the men, talking quietly about the disturbing news that Raymond had brought back with him.

'I knew the city had been attacked,' said Raymond, 'but did not expect the walls to have fallen so quickly. It seems that the streets swarmed with Saracens within a day.'

'And the citadel?'

'The shepherd knew no more, only that many people were killed before the Saracens left.'

Jocelyn looked over at the waiting men. Some had families in Tiberias and were already talking about returning as soon as they could.

'We have to tell them,' he said. 'They deserve to know.'

'I agree,' said Raymond, 'but first, let them eat. These past few days have been hard enough without the burden we are about to bestow upon them.'

An hour later, the men sat in a large circle, passing around the last of the bones from the goats. Each had managed to get some food, and the mood was lighter. Skins of fresh water passed from hand to hand with most men wishing that it were ale or wine. Finally, Raymond got to his feet and waited until the noise died down.

'Men of Tiberias,' he said, 'we have been through a lot together, these past few days. Many of our comrades did not make it, and when we get a chance, we will pray for their souls in a house of God. But now, I have terrible news that I must share. Today, when we bought the goats from the shepherd, he told me that the walls of Tiberias had already fallen before any of us had drawn a blade in anger. He said that two days ago, Saracens roamed the city killing men and women alike, with few escaping their attention. Any not killed were taken as prisoners and will have already been carted off to Damascus.'

'No,' said one of the men, 'I have a wife and child back there, please tell me this is not true.'

'It is true,' said Raymond. 'Some may have survived and hidden away, but there is no way of finding out.'

'We have to go there,' said another man, 'and find our families.'

'It is a pointless venture,' said Raymond. 'The city is probably still occupied, and there are countless Saracen patrols between us. We would get nowhere near and even if we did, are in no state to fight. What we have to do is accept God's will and do what we can to save ourselves.'

'Are you suggesting we leave our families there to die?' asked another soldier, getting to his feet.

'All I am saying is that it is pointless dying for a futile cause. By staying alive, you can honour their names, and if God is on our side, one day, your paths may cross again.'

'So what do you suggest?'

'I think that at first light tomorrow, we turn our heads north. Once we have passed the Hattin mountains, we turn west and head for Tyre. The journey will be tough, and we will have to avoid the Saracen patrols, but I think Saladin's thoughts will be upon Jerusalem, so we have a good chance.'

The men talked amongst themselves before the one who had stood turned back to face him.

'My lord,' he said, 'you know I have always been loyal without question, but I have to ask, is this a command, or is it an option?'

'We are fleeing for our lives,' said Raymond, 'and each man must take responsibility. To that end, on this occasion, each has a choice. You can ride north with me, or you can take your chances alone. Either is acceptable.' The men started talking amongst themselves again, arguing about the futility of riding to Tiberias. Finally, Raymond raised his hand and called for silence. 'I see it is a difficult choice,' he said, 'so I will leave it until dawn to hear your decision. At first light, I will ride north. Anyone who wishes to join me should meet me at the water's edge.' He turned and wandered into the forest, seeking the place where his horse was tied, and his saddle blanket lay on the ground.

'Get some rest, my lord,' said Jocelyn from the shadows, 'you have done all you can.'

Up on the plateau, just under a hundred Templar sergeants sat huddled together, closely guarded by two dozen Ayyubid horsemen. The battle had been hard-fought, but when the Christian banners fell, and the Saracens closed in for the kill, Jerusalem's king had finally seen the futility of carrying on and ordered the remainder of his army to lay down their arms. From more than twenty thousand men who had marched from Sephorie, only a few hundred were left. Most had been killed, thousands had deserted, while some, like the men of Tiberias, had fought their way out.

Any surviving foot soldiers had immediately been dragged away into slavery, but those men who were seen to be of value, like the Templar sergeants, had been detained and now awaited their fate at the hands of their Ayyubid captors.

Amongst their number was Thomas Cronin, the sergeant who had fought alongside the grandmaster during the battle. Like all the prisoners, he was weak from exhaustion, but apart from a raging thirst, his wounds were minor. Cronin looked around the group. Of those held captive, most carried wounds of some sort and many lay on the ground, already resigned to whatever fate awaited them, but there were also many who seemed untouched and still had an air of defiance. Knowing that their deaths were likely; Cronin knew they had to do something soon. Every moment they waited meant that death was getting closer, and it would be harder to escape.

Gradually the sun lowered towards the western mountains, and though the men had neither horses nor weapons, they gradually formulated a plan, and though it would cost many their lives, it was the best they could do.

'Why are we waiting?' whispered one of the men, crawling across to Cronin.

'Just a little while longer,' said Cronin.' We will have a better chance when it is dark. Half of the men will break south while the rest will head east. In the confusion, at least some of us should make it.'

The next half hour dragged slowly, but eventually, the sun disappeared and night fell. The Plateau was completely dark except for myriads of distant Saracen fires and the burning lanterns placed around the Templar prisoners. The Sergeants closed in for a final briefing.

'Listen to me,' whispered Cronin as loudly as he dared. 'There is no doubt that if we try to escape, some of us will die, but to remain here means that most of us see out our lives in slavery. Yes some of us may be ransomed, but we are mere men at arms, and as brutal as it may sound, we can be replaced easy enough by the order without them paying a single penny. Now, in a few minutes, we will rise as one and attack the guards in two areas. The south and the east.' He pointed into the darkness. 'Each direction is equally distant from the edge of the plateau, and we all have the same chance to escape. Reach the slopes, and they will not dare to follow on horseback, at least, not in the dark.'

'They will cut us down like barley,' said one of the men.

'Perhaps so, but which is better, to die like lambs or to fight to the end with everything we have? I know what I would rather do.'

'Aye,' said one of the men, 'me too.'

'There is no time to lose,' said Cronin, 'we may have no horses or weapons, but we have our courage, and we have God. One last charge to honour those that died and to support those who are destined to live. Who is with me?'

A murmur of support rippled around the prisoners.

'Then let us wait no longer,' he said, 'get to your feet.'

Every prisoner stood up, even the severely wounded for they knew that even though they had no chance to outrun any

Saracen, their deaths would give their brothers more time to escape.

'Even if I die in the next few minutes,' said Cronin, 'I will go to God knowing that I could not have served amongst greater men. Now, let us show these heathen that even in the midst of defeat, there is glory. Follow me, men of Christ, for the banner and for God.'

As one, every man turned to face south-east.

'Half of you go that way,' said Cronin pointing east,' the rest follow me.' Without another word, he started running, straight for the nearest Saracen guard. Instantly, the rest of the prisoners followed his lead, and within seconds, over a hundred Templar sergeants made a break for freedom.

Immediately the nearest guard sounded the alarm, but with over a hundred men spreading out in the dark, it was hard to organise a coordinated response. Saracen cavalry raced from the nearby camp and galloped amongst the fleeing prisoners, cutting them down without mercy. The night sky echoed with the cries of dying men, but for every one that fell, another took a few more steps closer to freedom.

Cronin pushed on as hard as he could, but a rider picked him out and galloped over to cut him down. The sergeant turned to face his attacker and at the last moment, threw himself to one side, just avoiding the thundering hooves of the horse. The rider galloped past before turning to resume the attack, but Cronin was already on his feet and racing directly for him.

By the time the horseman realised what was happening, it was too late, and Cronin hurled himself up to drag the man from his horse.

Both men landed amongst the rocks and dust. For a few heartbeats, both were dazed, but the warrior quickly recovered and reached for the knife in his waistband. With no weapon of his own, Cronin grabbed a rock and launched himself onto the warrior to smash it over and over again into his face. A fountain of blood spurted upward, but still, he hammered, the air reverberating with his primaeval screams. Every moment of thirst, pain and hardship he had ever suffered were taken out on his opponent's face, and within seconds, the Saracen's head was no more than a crumpled mess of blood, brain and bone.

Suddenly he stopped, coming back to his senses. He gasped at the state of the warrior but looked up quickly, knowing he had to keep going. A few paces away, the Saracen's horse stood waiting, its eyes wide and nostrils flaring at the smell of blood. Cronin picked up the Saracen's scimitar and ran over to climb up into the saddle. A few hundred paces away, more Ayyubid horsemen had seen the fight and kicked their horses into a gallop, determined to avenge their comrade's terrible death.

The Templar sergeant turned the horse towards the plateau's edge. Behind him, the air filled with the screams of men being hacked to death, but he knew he could do nothing to help. Despite the slaughter, some of his of the prisoners had already reached the edge and were disappearing out of view, seeking the safety of the rocky slopes below.

'Cronin,' shouted a voice, 'help me.'

He turned and saw a young sergeant limping desperately towards him. Cronin recognised him as the young man who had only arrived in the Holy-land a few weeks earlier, and though he knew that death was only seconds away, there was no way he could leave him there to die. He kicked in his heels and raced towards him.

'Get up,' he roared, 'quickly!'

The young sergeant threw himself upward, clinging on desperately as Cronin headed towards the plateau edge. More Saracen warriors closed in, their roars of anger echoing around the plateau.

'Come on,' roared Cronin, digging his heels into the horse's flanks, and moments later, with Saracen arrows flying through the air either side of him, Cronin launched the horse from the edge of the plateau and out into the darkness.

The following morning, near the Sea of Tiberias, Raymond walked out of the forest. To his surprise, all the men were already assembled and stood alongside their horses. He looked around, aware that every set of eyes was burning into his soul.

'So,' he said, 'have you made your choice?'

The man who had challenged his decision the night before stepped forward.

'Aye, my lord,' he said, 'we have.'

'And it is?'

'The thought of abandoning our loved ones burns like the fires of hell, but your words made sense, and it is pointless dying for no reason.'

'So we go north?' asked Raymond.

'We go wherever you tell us to go,' said the soldier.

'You have made the right decision,' said Raymond, 'and I swear by almighty God that I will do everything in my power to keep you alive. Now mount up, there is a long way to go.'

Chapter Thirty-Three

The Horns of Hattin

July 5th - AD 1187

Salah ad-Din sat on a pile of cushions outside his command tent on the slopes of what was left of the extinct volcano that gave the area its name. His army had left the battlefield the previous day and set up a new camp near the springs, allowing his men to take full advantage of its refreshing waters. As far as he could see, thousands of Ayyubid banners waved in the wind and the drums of victory filled the air. His men rejoiced with wild abandon, and though the noise was deafening, he allowed them to celebrate, knowing that they had just won the most important victory since the Franks had first invaded the Holy-land almost two hundred years earlier.

Before him, his servants had lain patterned blankets on the ground, each covered with ornate silver trays full of fruit, cold meat and flasks of chilled water. At the centre lay a barrel of crushed ice, a luxury carted from mountaintops hundreds of leagues to the east.

For half the day, the celebrations continued until finally, a horn sounded, and the mood of the camp changed. Thousands of men drew near, all anticipating what would come next.

As they watched, a double line of Mamluk warriors marched through the camp, escorting over two hundred Templar knights to face the Ayyubid Sultan. Each prisoner had their hands tied behind their backs, their faces bloody and broken from the beatings they had received at the hands of the Mamluks. The taunts of the Ayyubid warriors filled the air with their hatred for the warrior monks, but once the prisoners were in position, Salah ad-Din raised his hand, and the army fell silent.

As they waited in silence, the Mamluks brought a second group of prisoners to stand in front of those already in place, including all the barons and officers who had served so bravely in the battle. Salah ad-Din got to his feet and looked at the smaller group. Amongst them was Raynald of Chatillon and the King of Jerusalem, Guy of Lusignan.

'Bring the king and the butcher of Karak to me,' he said and waited as the guards separated the two men from the rest of the prisoners. Hardly able to stand, the king and Raynald staggered up the slope until they stood before the Sultan. Salah ad-Din stared at each man in turn, gazing deep into their eyes. The whole camp fell silent, every man straining to hear what came next.

'Raynald of Chatillon,' he said eventually, staring at the knight. 'You are a feared warrior, a beast to bring nightmares to the children of my people. Despite my many offerings of peace, you continued to seek war, breaking many treaties.'

'I do what God commands me to do,' said Raynald.

The sultan ignored him and turned to Guy.

'King Guy of Jerusalem,' he said, 'you are new to the throne and have a lot to learn about kingship. You led your men to defeat in a foolish cause, and there was only ever going to be one outcome.' He nodded towards a servant who poured a large goblet of water and brought it over to the Sultan. Salah ad-Din took it before offering it to Guy. 'Here, take it and quench your thirst.'

Guy took the goblet and drank half before turning and offering the rest to Raynald.

Instantly, the sultan's hand shot out and knocked the goblet to the floor, tipping the contents to the ground at Raynald's feet.

'I did not offer the water to him,' snarled Saladin, 'for I hold him responsible for the deaths of more people than I can count.' He turned to stare at Raynald. 'You no warrior,' he snarled, 'you are nothing more than a killer who hides his addiction behind a cloak of white. To you, I offer nothing but death.'

Before Raynald could move, two of the Mamluk guards grabbed him and forced him to his knees.

'This is for every tear shed, every drop of blood spilt and every soul taken in your name,' said Saladin, 'may you rot in hell for eternity.' He drew his Scimitar and with an almighty roar, swung it sideways across the knight's neck. Fountains of blood spurted skyward, and as Raynald's body fell to one side, his head rolled down the slope to land at the feet of the shocked Christian commanders. Guy stared in horror before lifting his gaze back up to face the sultan.

'Well,' he said, 'get on with it, but know this, I regret not one thing and will go to God with a clear conscience.'

Saladin stared back but instead of swinging his sword, gave an order to the general at his side.

'Muzaffar ad-Din Gokbori,' he said, 'get this man a fresh goblet of water. Kings do not kill kings.'

Minutes later, Salah ad-Din once more stood on the slope outside his tent, this time to address the rest of the prisoners. King Guy stood beside him.

'You men fought bravely,' said Salah ad-Din eventually, 'but it was Allah himself who dictated the outcome.'

'Allah Akbar,' roared the Muslim army behind the prisoners

'There is no shame in defeat,' continued Saladin, when the noise settled, 'for we have all felt its pain, and those who fought with honour deserve to be treated accordingly. Today, I give you life, and you will be treated fairly. If Allah sees fit to return you to your people, then always remember the mercy shown here today.'

A quiet gasp of relief rippled through the first group of prisoners, and they were led away into captivity. Once they had gone, Saladin turned his attention to the last group of prisoners, the two hundred knights kneeling in the dust.

'You men,' said Saladin, 'are the fiercest warriors I have ever seen. Your bravery and ability in war are undisputed, and the Christian king is lucky to have such men at his disposal. To be a warrior commands respect, but I know that if you were allowed to leave this place, my men would have to defeat you again and again until every last one is dead.' He paused and looked along the line. 'In respect of your undoubted prowess in battle,' he continued, 'I will not commit fellow warriors to the slow death of slavery. Instead, I will send you to be judged before your own God.' He nodded to the Mamluk commander, and before anyone could react, the Mamluk guards fell upon the prisoners, forcing them to their knees. Each prisoner had his arms stretched wide, leaving their upper bodies unprotected. Another line of Mamluks drew their scimitars, but as the army roared their approval, some of Salah ad-Din's officers and Holy-men begged for the honour of administering the killing blows. The Sultan nodded, and as Guy watched on in horror, each of the knights was beheaded in turn. Some cried out for mercy, some with fear but most closed their eyes and made their peace with God before the blades fell.

'No,' roared Guy at Saladin's side, 'what are you doing?'

'I am protecting my people,' said Saladin, 'as you protect yours.'

'You are truly are the devil,' gasped the king but there was nothing he could do, and as over two hundred knights died in the heat of the desert sun, the slopes ran red with rivers of Templar blood.

Two leagues away, Al-Afdal stood at the head of his army outside the gates of Tiberias. The breach in the walls had been repaired with a timber palisade, but only a few dozen knights manned the battlements. He knew it was for show only and waited patiently as a delegation approached from the city gates. The two horses, flanked by four knights drew closer, before stopping a few paces from the Saracen commander.

'Lady Escheva,' said Al-Afdal, 'I am honoured you have come to discuss terms in person.'

'It is only right,' said Escheva. 'I have heard the rumours from Hattin and would like to know the truth.'

'The truth is that my father secured a great and wonderful victory against the infidels,' said Al-Afdal. 'Their puny army was destroyed, and many thousands died needlessly in service to your false God. Many more have been taken prisoner and will see out their lives as slaves in the mines and in the quarries. Never has there been such a victory and the slopes of Hattin run red with Christian blood.'

'And what of the king?'

'He has been taken prisoner and will be sent to Damascus.'

'What about my husband, Raymond of Tripoli?'

'I had the honour of facing the men of Tiberias on the field of battle,' said Al-Afdal. 'Of course, they were defeated, but some managed to escape. The last I saw of them; they were fleeing for their lives towards the shores of Tiberias. I thought Raymond might already be hiding behind your skirts.'

'He has not come back here,' said Escheva.

'Nor should he come,' said Al-Afdal, 'for, by tomorrow night, Tiberias will be occupied by the forces of Salah ad-Din, Sultan of all Egypt and Syria.'

'So what are your terms?' asked Escheva.

'We demand the full surrender of the city by dawn tomorrow,' said Al-Afdal. 'You and all who wish to follow will be allowed to leave without harm.'

'That is not enough time,' said Escheva.

'It is all the time you have,' said Al-Afdal. 'Anyone still within the city walls when the sun clears the eastern mountains will have to stay and serve the Ayyubid.'

Escheva stared at the Saracen, knowing she had no choice. There was no way her depleted army could defend Tiberias.

'I accept,' she said eventually, 'and will leave the city as soon as it is light. You have won, Al-Afdal ibn Salah ad-Din, Tiberias is yours.'

Chapter Thirty-Four

Jerusalem

September 19, 1187

'My lord,' shouted the guard above the city gates, 'there's a group of men approaching. It looks like they are in trouble.'

The captain of the guard stared over the parapet. In the distance, he could see five men heading towards the city. Each was obviously exhausted, and one was being half-carried by two of his comrades. The state of their clothing and bedraggled hair suggested it had been a long time since they had seen civilisation and it was obvious, they needed help.

'Open the gates,' he said, 'and send for Lord Balian. This is something he may want to see.'

'Aye my lord,' said the guard and ran down the stone steps of the city walls. The commander followed him down and walked out to greet the five men. As he approached, four of the men stopped and collapsed to the ground while the fifth staggered towards him.

'Water,' he gasped through cracked and swollen lips. 'By the love of God, we need water.'

'Bring water,' roared the commander and grabbed the man before lowering him to the ground.

'Who are you?' he asked, 'and where have you come from?'

The man did not respond, as if he had already used all his strength. One of the guards ran over with a water-skin and poured a trickle onto the stranger's lips. The water seeped through to his mouth, and he grabbed desperately for the waterskin.

'Steady,' said the commander, 'there's plenty here.' The rest of the guards did the same with the remaining four men, and within minutes, each was sitting upright, drinking carefully from the skins.

'Come,' said the commander, 'we need to get you out of the sun.' eventually, they managed to stand and were helped through the gates into the city. Others came to help, and within minutes they were sat in the shade, each with pieces of peeled fruit in their laps brought by one of the traders.

'Commander,' shouted a voice, 'what's going on?'

The guard commander turned and saw Balian of Ibelin striding down from the citadel.

'My lord,' he said, 'we just recovered these men from outside the city walls. They were on their last legs, but I think they will survive.'

'Who are they?' asked Balian, looking at the bedraggled men, 'they look like they have been to hell and back.'

'I know not,' said the commander, 'but this one seems stronger than the others.' He pointed to the man who had initially begged him for water.

Balian walked over and crouched down before the bearded man, wincing at the sight of his burnt and blistered face.

'You are safe now,' he said, 'who are you and where have you come from?'

'My name,' said the man, his voice barely a croak, 'is Thomas Cronin, and we have come from Hattin.'

An hour later, Thomas Cronin and Balian sat across a trestle table in one of the ante-chambers in the citadel. The other four men were being taken care of by the physicians in the hospital, but Cronin had insisted he had to speak to the queen.

'I think I recognise you,' said Balian. 'Did you not serve Gerard of Ridefort as sergeant?'

'Aye, I did,' said Cronin, 'but we were both captured when the king surrendered. I have no idea if he lives.'

'He is alive,' said Balian, 'as is the king and many others. We have had word that they are prisoners in Damascus but as yet have not received any ransom demands.'

'What of my fellows,' asked Cronin, 'the Templar knights who fought at Hattin? Are they also alive?'

'Alas not,' said Balian. 'All were executed after the battle. As far as I know, only a handful of knights escaped Hattin with their lives.'

'What of you?' asked Cronin. 'The last I heard; you were attempting to get water for the army, but we never saw you again.'

'We tried,' said Balian, 'as God is my witness, but we were overwhelmed, and it was all we could do to escape with our lives. Eventually, we lost our pursuers and fled to Tyre. When I heard that Jerusalem was going to be attacked, I sent a message to Saladin and requested a truce so I could travel here and retrieve my family. He granted my request, but when I arrived, the queen begged me to take command. I have been here ever since. Anyway, Hattin was two months ago, where have you been?'

'We were prisoners,' said Cronin, 'but a few of us managed to escape. For days we were pursued by the Ayyubid but hid like snakes in the crevices and gulleys. Even then, most were found and killed but those who survived headed north, travelling away from the Saracen patrols. Day after day, we avoided capture and only managed to survive by stealing food and water from farms and villages. We kept moving and eventually, turned south desperate to reach a Christian city.'

'Where did you go?' asked Balian.

'Nowhere,' said Cronin quietly, 'for there is nowhere left to go.'

'What do you mean?'

'Everywhere we went, our strongholds, cities and towns had all been overrun. Every time we thought we reached safety; we found the Saracens had gotten there first. Even Acre is now in the hands of Saladin.'

'I knew about Acre,' said Balian, 'but not the rest. I had hoped that many had survived and I have sent requests for reinforcements.'

'There are no reinforcements,' said Cronin, 'and even if there were, they would never get through. The Saracens are everywhere. When we heard that Jerusalem was still standing, we decided to come here, but it is obvious that even here we will not be safe.

'Why not?'

'They are heading here, my lord,' said Cronin, 'Saladin is on his way.'

Balian stared in horror. Although he knew the Holy-city was always Saladin's ultimate target, the fact the attack was imminent shocked him to the core.

'You are sure about this?' he asked.

'I am,' said Cronin. 'We saw his army with our own eyes just a few days since. We came here as fast as we could, but I reckon they are only a day or so behind. That is why we have to warn the queen, the city needs to be called to arms.'

Balian stared at Cronin, his heart sinking.

'What's the matter,' asked Cronin, 'has anything happened to the queen?'

'The queen is fine,' said Balian, 'but in the absence of her husband, she has handed the responsibility of protecting Jerusalem to me.'

'Then you need to act,' said Cronin. 'The Ayyubid are only a day away, two at most. Call the garrison to arms.'

'That's the problem,' said Balian, 'there is no garrison to summon. Jerusalem's army went with the King to fight at Hattin.'

'That's ridiculous,' said Cronin. 'Nobody in their right mind would commit everything to one campaign and leave the Holy-city undefended. Surely there must be someone left?'

'I have fourteen knights,' said Balian, 'nowhere near enough to put up a fight.'

'What about the vassals,' said Cronin, 'there must be thousands of them. Call them to arms in the name of God.'

'Even if we do,' said Balian, 'how long do you think we would last against Saladin's battle-hardened warriors? And if what you say about the other cities is true, there is nobody left to send reinforcements. No, it looks like we are in this alone, Thomas Cronin, this time, Jerusalem must stand on her own.'

The following day, Jerusalem woke to see an enormous army camped outside the city walls. Within days, Saladin launched an enormous attack, but despite being massively outnumbered, the men of the city managed to keep the Saracens at bay. Day after day the assaults continued and even when the Ayyubid sappers managed to collapse one of the walls, the defenders fought on heroically, defending the breach with everything they had.

Cronin, despite his weakened state, took command of a portion of the walls and repelled every push that came with only a few hundred men at his command. Sixty were knighted by Balian, but within ten days, after Saladin had brought up a whole array of siege engines, the exhausted defenders knew that they could resist no longer.

On the eleventh day, Balian rode out to meet Saladin with Cronin at his side. The Sultan sat on a dais beneath a huge canopy, fanned by slaves on either side. As soon as they arrived, Saladin invited Balian and Cronin to partake of the refreshments, and they both immediately knew that they would be safe during the negotiations. Both sipped at the water and took a few dates, but they were keen to get started, and Saladin ordered the servants to take the trays away.

'So,' he said eventually, 'you have finally come to surrender the city.'

'We have,' said Balian, 'but with the greatest of respect, I need assurances.'

'Assurances?' said Saladin. 'And what do they consist of, considering we will take the city within days, even if you do not cede.'

'All I ask,' said Balian, 'is that any Christian within Jerusalem is allowed to leave peacefully.'

'And why should I do that?' asked Saladin. 'My people have been promised a great victory.'

'Because I know you are a just man,' said Balian. 'You have more than enough riches and slaves, surely you can just accept the glory of Jerusalem as your prize? The people I talk of are not soldiers; they are the poor and the sick. They will never be a threat to you and will only become a burden if forced to stay. Let them go, and we will leave the city within two days.'

'And if I refuse?'

'Then we will fight to the last man,' said Balian. 'Every Muslim prisoner will be put to death, and we will destroy every religious site in Jerusalem. Your victory will be celebrated amongst the rubble and rotting corpses.'

'You play a dangerous game, Balian of Ibelin,' said Saladin.' Be careful you do not chance your arm too far for I may just cut it off.'

'It is no game, my lord,' said Balian. 'I just seek to save as many lives as I can. You would do the same.'

Saladin pondered for a moment before holding up his goblet for a refill from one of his servants.

'I have promised my men great reward,' he said eventually, 'yet see the compassion in your request, so this is what I am prepared to do. Anyone who wishes to leave the city will pay a toll. Ten dinars for men, five for women and two for children. Anybody who can't pay the price will be enslaved.'

'The offer is generous,' said Balian, 'but there are at least twenty thousand who will not be able to pay the price. The poor should not be punished.'

Saladin took another drink of his water before replying.

'I will accept one hundred thousand dinars in return for all your poor. I suspect your clergy can easily find such a sum from amongst your holy places.'

'We have already spoken to them,' said Balian, 'and all we can raise is thirty thousand dinars.'

Saladin stared at Balian over the rim of his goblet, trying to judge if the man was lying.

'It is the best we can do,' said Balian. 'Let us both stop this unnecessary killing and do what we can to achieve peace.'

'I will allow seven thousand of your poorest to leave for thirty thousand dinars,' said Saladin finally, 'and that is my final offer. The decision is yours, Balian of Ibelin. The peace you speak of is now in your hands.'

Balian looked across at Cronin, receiving the briefest of nods in return. He turned back to Saladin.

'Then I accept the terms, Salah ad-Din,' he said, 'Jerusalem is yours; we will leave the city by dawn the day after tomorrow.

Two days later, as promised, tens of thousands of Christians left Jerusalem and headed north for foreign lands. After all tolls were paid, over seven thousand men women and children were taken into slavery, and on October 2, 1187, Jerusalem returned to Muslim hands for the first time in almost two hundred years.

Epilogue

The Jordan River

October 1187

Sumeira knelt at the edge of the river, pounding clothes against the rocks. She had been with Nadya and her people for over two months and had become accepted by all members of the village. Saracen patrols passed regularly but, on each occasion, the women hid her out of sight, knowing that if she were found, she would be taken back into slavery. In particular, Nadya had become a good friend, and it was with her that Sumeira spent most of her time.

'Has there been any more news?' asked Sumeira quietly.

'I have heard that Jerusalem has fallen,' said Nadya, 'as have many other Christian cities.'

'Have you heard anything about Karak?'

'Nothing,' said Nadya, 'but I believe it is a formidable fortress built on a rocky hill so perhaps the sultan has passed it by.'

'It is the greatest castle I have ever seen,' said Sumeira. 'Perhaps Saladin will negotiate with the castellan there and secure safe passage for all who dwell within. Do you think that is possible?'

'Salah ad-Din is a very wise man,' said Nadya, 'and has been known to show mercy when confronted with a repentant enemy. There is a very good chance that your family are still alive.'

'Then I must go there,' said Sumeira. 'I have to find out for myself.'

'You cannot go anywhere yet,' said Nadya, 'the country is still at war, and now all the Christian cities are in the hands of the Ayyubid, you would not be able to seek shelter on the way. Just stay here until it all dies down, and when there is peace, I will help you get to where you need to be, I swear.'

Sumeira sighed and turned her attention back to the washing. She knew that Nadya made sense, but the thought of her children being taken into slavery was almost too much to bear. Her mind wandered, imagining what life would be like if she ever got them back to Greece, but her daydream was abruptly cut short when a dozen Ayyubid horsemen appeared out of the trees and led their horses down to the river to drink. Sumeira looked around for somewhere to hide, but it was too late, they were all around her.

Desperate to hide her identity, she pulled the hood of her Thawb over her head and leaned further forward, as if totally focussed on washing the clothes. The men filled their waterskins and finally led their horses back onto the path, but just as she thought she would get away with the subterfuge, one of them walked over and pulled her to her feet.'

'You,' he snapped in a language she could not understand, 'bring me some food.'

When she did not move, the warrior got angry and pulled down her hood.

'Look at me when I am speaking to you,' he said, but stopped and stared in surprise when he saw the colour of her skin and hair.

'You are not of these people,' he said, 'who are you?'

Again, Sumeira was unable to answer, and the warrior pulled her up onto the path.

'Look what I have here,' he announced, 'I think it may be a westerner, perhaps escaped from the slave markets.'

The other men gathered around, staring at Sumeira with fascination.

'What should we do with her,' asked one, 'take her back to Damascus?'

'We could do whatever we like,' said another. 'Nobody knows she is here so she will not be missed. I have never had a western woman. We could take her into the forest and show her what real men are made of. After that, leave her body for the dogs.'

'We are not Christians,' spat the first man, 'and will not act like them.'

'Why not?' came the reply. 'They do worse with our women, so it is only just that theirs suffer the same fate.'

'We will do no such thing,' said a voice and every man looked up to see their leader riding over on his horse. Beside him rode a much younger man, dressed in the garb of a Bedouin.

'My lord,' said the first warrior, 'I was only jesting. What would you have me do with her?'

'Show me,' said the officer and the man yanked Sumeira's head back to expose her face.

'She is attractive,' he said, 'but her value belongs to the Sultan. Take her back to Damascus and sell her to the highest bidder. Bring the proceeds back to me, and I will see they get to the Sultan's treasury.'

'Wait,' said a voice and the Bedouin rode up to the side of the Saracen officer. 'I know this woman,' he said, 'and she has a greater value than any whore.'

Sumeira looked at the Bedouin and gasped with shock. It was Hassan Malouf, the boy whose life she had saved years earlier in Segor.

'Hassan,' she gasped, 'what are you doing here with them?'

Hassan didn't reply but turned back to the officer.

'My lord,' he said, 'many years ago, this woman saved my life when I was all but dead. Her skills as a physician are renown far and wide. If you sell her to the brothels, you will make some coin, but I believe she has a far greater value, treating the wounds of our men in the battles to come.'

'We already have physicians,' said the warrior.

'I know, but this one is trained in both Christian and Muslim ways. Let us take her to our destination, and I swear she will not escape.'

'Why should I trust you?' asked the Saracen. 'If she saved your life, you may be tempted to set her free.'

'Her kind has done far too much damage for me to ever do that,' said Hassan. 'By allowing her to live, I repay my debt, but that payment does not include freedom. If she escapes, then I will forfeit my life.'

'So be it,' said the Saracen. 'Tie her on a horse and watch her like a hawk.'

Two men bundled Sumeira up onto a horse and led it over to Hassan. He took the reins and tied them to his saddle.

'Hassan,' she hissed when the men were out of earshot. 'What are you doing? Do they know you are a Christian?'

Hassan turned to stare at Sumeira. His eyes were cold, and she saw no friendship in his gaze.

'I am not a Christian,' he said. 'I know now that I never was, nor ever could be.'

'I don't understand,' said Sumeira, 'what caused you to change your mind?'

'The blood of my wife and unborn child,' said Hassan, 'spilt by the blades of a Christian army. Two innocents amongst many who were slaughtered for just being different. I saw the true nature of Christians that day and will never forgive them as long as I live.'

'We are not all like that,' said Sumeira, 'you know that. Do not judge us all by one bad act.'

'You waste your time,' said Hassan. 'I only spoke up because you once saved my life. Now we are even so if you cause any problems and they want to kill you, I will not stop them.'

'What are you saying?' gasped Sumeira, 'we were friends, Hassan, please don't be like this.'

'Save your breath, Christian,' he said, 'for there is a long way to go.'

'Why?' asked Sumeira, 'where are you taking me?'

'We are headed west,' said Hassan, 'to the city of Acre. There you will be held prisoner until such time that your services are needed.'

'My services, what do you mean?'

'Saladin took the city a few weeks ago,' said Hassan, 'but we expect a counter-attack from the Christians. When they do, there will be casualties. You will treat the wounds of our men and get them back on the walls.'

'No,' gasped Sumeira, 'I will not do it.'

'Then you will die,' said Hassan. 'Either way, you are never going to see your family or friends again. Now I have repaid my debt, you are nothing more to me than any other Christian prisoner.'

'I don't believe you,' said Sumeira. 'Inside that skin is still the young man who became my friend. That will never change.'

'If that is what you believe,' said Hassan, 'perhaps this will help to convince you otherwise. Without warning, he raised his hand and slapped her hard across the face making her cry out with pain.

Before she could respond, he kicked his horse and followed the rest of the patrol along the river path, pulling Sumeira's horse behind him.

Despite the pain and shock, deep inside Sumeira still nursed the faintest of hope. At the first chance she got, she would try and escape, even if it meant another beating, for the thought of being a prisoner in the city of Acre filled her with dread.

Little did she know that she faced two long years incarcerated in the coastal city as a slave of the Muslims, but even those would fade into insignificance when compared with the horror that was to follow, the carnage that was the siege of Acre.

The End

Continue the Story

Guy was eventually, released from captivity and in AD 1189, launched a significant counter-offensive against Saladin, by attacking the city of Acre. The siege that was to last over two years became one of the most pivotal actions in the struggle for the Holy-land. It also involved the most famous crusader of them all: **Richard the Lionheart**.

Find out what happened next in Templar Fury, the exciting fourth book in the series.

Pre-order your copy now

The Brotherhood Book IV

TEMPLAR FURY

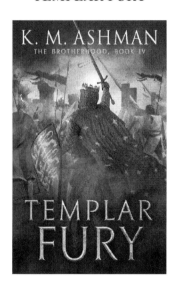

Author's Notes

As usual in these sorts of books, historical facts have been intertwined with fiction, enabling a much easier read around the reality of the battles and the events leading up to pivotal points in history. Wherever possible, I have stuck to the facts, but allowance must be made for artistic license. In the notes below, I have tried to highlight the more important information, separating fact from fiction.

Terminology

The term 'Saracen,' was a general derogatory name often used for any Arab person at the time. It did not refer to any one tribe or religion and was considered offensive by many of the indigenous cultures.

Similarly, the term 'Crusader' was never used in the twelfth century as a reference to the Christian forces. They were usually referred to as the 'Franks or Kafirs' by the Saracens.

The 'Outremer,' was a generic name used for the Crusader states, especially the County of Edessa, the Principality of Antioch, the County of Tripoli, and the Kingdom of Jerusalem.

The Knights Templar

The order of the poor fellow-soldiers of Christ and of the Temple of Solomon was formed in or around AD 1119 in Jerusalem by a French knight, Hugues de Payens. They were granted a headquarters in a captured Mosque on the Temple Mount in Jerusalem by King Baldwin II.

At first, they were impoverished, focusing only on protecting the weak on the road to Jerusalem, but after being supported by a powerful French Abbot, Bernard of Clairvaux, the order was officially recognised by the church at the Council of Troyes in AD 1129. From there they went from strength to strength and soon became the main monastic order of knights in the Holy-land. Their influence grew across the known world, not just for their deeds of bravery, but because of their business acumen and the order went on to become very wealthy and very powerful.

The Emblems of the Templars

The Templar seal was a picture of two men riding a single horse. This is thought to depict the order's initial poverty when it was first formed though conversely, one of the rules of the order was that two knights could not ride one horse. Another explanation talks about the representation of 'true' brotherhood, wherein one knight rescues the other knight whose horse is probably injured. Intriguingly enough, there is a plausible commentary regarding two soldiers on a single horse, written by Saladin's chronicler Bahaed-Din Ibn Shaddad (referenced from Knight Templar 1120 – 1312 By Helen Nicholson)

On June 7, 1192, the Crusader army marched to attack the Holy-city, (then occupied by Saladin). Richard's spies reported a long-awaited supply train coming from Egypt to relieve Saladin's army...when Richard received information that the caravan was close at hand...a thousand horsemen set out, each of whom took a foot soldier (on his horse) in front of him...At daybreak, he took the caravan unawares. Islam had suffered a serious disaster...The spoils were three thousand camels, three thousand horses, five hundred prisoners and a mountain of military supplies. Never was Saladin more grieved, or more anxious.

When travelling or going to war, they rode under a white flag emblazoned with a red cross. Some historians believe it was in honour of St George, who's spirit many soldiers believed was seen at the battle of Antioch in AD 1098 during the first crusade.

The image of the cross was also used on other items of clothing and equipment by the Templars, and indeed other orders of warrior monks (though not in red.) However, research shows that the red cross was not officially adopted until it was awarded by Pope Eugene III in AD 1147. Before this time, the knights wore only a plain white coat.

Templar Ranks Used in This Book

The grandmaster was head of the Templars and was in charge of the entire order, worldwide.

During times of war, the seneschal organised the movement of the men, the pack trains, the food procurement, and other issues involved in moving an army.

The marshal, on the other hand, was very much a military man, and the master would usually consult with him, as well as the seneschal before making any final decisions on tactics.

King Baldwin IV

Baldwin IV ruled the kingdom of Jerusalem at the time, and though others claimed otherwise, he was also the king of the Oultrejordain, the lands to the east of the River Jordan and the Dead-sea. He suffered terribly from leprosy and though was often debilitated by the disease, often led his forces into battle, even if it meant being carried on a stretcher. Despite his young age, he was considered a strong and capable leader.

When he died in 1185, his nephew, also called Baldwin, ascended the throne with Raymond of Tripoli as his regent. However, when Baldwin V died the following year, his mother, Sibylla, through political agility managed to claim the throne, though not before promising to divorce her unpopular husband, Guy of Lusignan. In return, the Haute Cour (High Court) of Jerusalem allowed her to choose anyone she wanted to reign beside her as king. To their surprise, when she was crowned, she chose the man she had just divorced, Guy of Lusignan.

William of Tyre

William is reputed to have been the king's teacher when Baldwin was a boy and went on to become his advisor and chronicler. Whether he had the level of influence he enjoys in our story is unknown, but there is no doubt that his chronicles have become the best record about life in Jerusalem at that time.

Raynald of Châtillon

Raynald was the son of a French noble who joined the third crusade in AD 1146. He served as a mercenary in Jerusalem before marrying the princess of Antioch, Constance of Hauteville in AD 1153. This made him the Prince of Antioch, and he soon became known for his brutality and warlike tendencies. Always in need of funds, his reign was cut short in AD 1161 when he was captured by the Muslim governor of Aleppo after a raid in the Euphrates valley against the local peasants. He spent the next fifteen years in jail before finally, being ransomed and set free.

King Baldwin made him 'Regent of the kingdom and the armies,' in AD 1177 and he was one of the leaders at the famous battle of Montgisard.

In 1182, Raynald and his men manhandled a small fleet of ships overland to the Red Sea. Once there he attacked Muslim ships and cities up and down the eastern coast, as well as Egyptian ports and sea caravans to the west. Eventually, Saladin's brother, along with an Armenian Admiral called Lu'lu raised a Muslim fleet and sailed down the Red Sea to catch the Frankish ships at anchor. Raynald and his men abandoned their ships and fled into the Arabian desert, receiving help from some local Bedouin. Eventually, most of Raynald's men were captured and executed, but Raynald himself escaped and returned to Karak.

In 1187, Raynald broke a truce and attacked a caravan on its way between Egypt and Damascus, confiscating its goods and holding many of the people prisoner. When Saladin sent envoys to negotiate their release, Raynald treated them with disdain and refused to negotiate. Saladin was incensed and swore that should he ever capture Raynald, he would be executed.

At the battle of Hattin, Raynald was indeed captured, and Saladin was true to his word, beheading Raynald after first refusing him water.

Jakelin De Mailly

Jakelin De Mailly was a real French Templar Knight who became renowned for his ability in warfare. During the bloody battle of Cresson, he fought bravely until finally, he was the last Christian standing. The enemy gathered around and fell quiet as he continued to fight alone. Men lay slaughtered all around him, and eventually he was overwhelmed by the numbers. A few years later, an unknown chronicler of the time recorded the following account.

"He was not afraid to die for Christ. At long last, crushed rather than conquered by spears, stones and lances, he sank to the ground and joyfully passed to heaven with the martyr's crown, triumphant. It was indeed a gentle death with no place for sorrow, when one man's sword had constructed such a great crown for himself from the crowd laid all around him. Death is sweet when the victor lies encircled by the impious people, he has slain with his victorious right hand . . . The place where he fought was covered with the stubble which the reapers had left standing when

they had cut the grain shortly before. Such a great number of Turks had rushed in to attack, and this one man had fought for so long against so many battalions, that the field in which they stood was completely reduced to dust and there was not a trace of the crop to be seen. It is said that there were some who sprinkled the body of the dead man with dust and placed dust on their heads, believing that they would draw courage from the contact. In fact, rumour has it that one person was moved with more fervour than the rest. He cut off the man's genitals and kept them safe for begetting children so that even when dead the man's members – if such a thing were possible – would produce an heir with courage as great as his."

Raymond III of Tripoli

Raymond III of Tripoli was also lord of Galilee due to his marriage to Eschiva of Bures. When Baldwin IV died, he was lured away from Jerusalem, leaving Baldwin's sister to claim the throne unchallenged. Raymond was incensed and vowed to claim the throne for himself. Consequently, he garrisoned his army in Tiberias and even made a pact with Saladin, promising not to intervene if the Sultan attacked other states in the Outremer. After the battle of Cresson, he repented his ways and swore allegiance to Jerusalem, fighting at the battle of Hattin two months later.

The Battle of Cresson

In early 1187, Raymond allowed Muzaffar ad-Din Gokbori and over seven thousand warriors, safe passage through Galilee. The Templar grandmaster, Gerard of Ridefort and the Hospitaller grandmaster, Roger De-Moulins quickly gathered their forces and faced Gokbori at Cresson. Men from Al Fulah castle and Aqaq castle joined them, but the battle resulted in a total defeat for the Christians, with only a few knights escaping with their lives. Gerard of Ridefort managed to escape, but Roger De-Moulins was killed in the battle.

The Siege of Tiberias

On July 2, 1187, Saladin laid siege to the city of Tiberias. Within a day, his sappers managed to undermine the outer city wall allowing his army to break through the following day. The citadel still held, so his sappers started digging again but after hearing that the Christian army had left Sephorie and was on their way to lift the siege, left Tiberias to face them in battle. After the battle of Hattin, The Saracen army returned to Tiberias and Eschiva of Bures handed over the city. She was allowed to leave for Tripoli with all her belongings and supporters.

The Battle of Hattin

The Christian army mustered at Sephorie, around twenty thousand men at arms. After hearing that Tiberias was under attack, the king called a war council to discuss options. The Hospitallers and Raymond of Tripoli advised against reacting against Saladin, but Gerard of Ridefort advised that they attack immediately. Guy took Ridefort's advice and set out to relieve Tiberias on the morning of July 3, 1187.

When it became clear they would not reach Tiberias by nightfall, the army changed course for the Springs of Kafr Hattin. Unfortunately, the Muslim army cut them off, and the Christians were forced to pitch camp overnight on the arid plateau near the village of Meskenah. Throughout the night, the Saracens surrounded the king and his army, preventing their access to water and setting light to the surrounding grasslands.

The crusaders were going crazy with thirst and on the morning of July 4, came under attack from Muslim mounted archers

Raymond of Tripoli made two attempts to reach Lake Tiberias and eventually succeeded before escaping towards the city of Tyre. Other crusaders tried breaking out towards the Hattin springs but were cut off by the Saracen army. Many of the infantry deserted and were either taken prisoner or cut down on the slopes of Hattin.

Records claim that at least five knights deserted to the Saracens and begged to be put to death. To avoid a charge by the Saracen horsemen, Guy had the tents re-erected before re-engaging the Saracens. Despite getting close to Saladin's position, they were driven back on at least three occasions until finally, when the king's tent fell, Guy admitted defeat and surrendered to Saladin. An eyewitness account of this is given by Saladin's 17-year-old son, al-Afdal. It is quoted by Muslim chronicler Ibn al-Athir.

"When the king of the Franks [Guy] was on the hill with that band, they made a formidable charge against the Muslims facing them, so that they drove them back to my father [Saladin]. I looked

towards him, and he was overcome by grief and his complexion
pale. He took hold of his beard and advanced, crying out "Give the
lie to the Devil!"
The Muslims rallied, returned to the fight and climbed the hill.
When I saw that the Franks withdrew, pursued by the Muslims, I
shouted for joy, "We have beaten them!" But the Franks rallied
and charged again like the first time and drove the Muslims back
to my father.
He acted as he had done on the first occasion, and the Muslims
turned upon the Franks and drove them back to the hill. I again
shouted, "We have beaten them!" but my father rounded on me and
said, "Be quiet! We have not beaten them until that tent [Guy's]
falls." As he was speaking to me, the tent fell. The sultan
dismounted, prostrated himself in thanks to God Almighty and
wept for joy."

After the battle, Saladin had more than 200 knights
beheaded but took most of the barons into captivity. Eventually, a
ransom was paid, and they were released. King Guy and Raynald
of Chatillon were taken before the Sultan where Guy was offered
water which he accepted. This was a tradition that meant his safety
was guaranteed, but when Raynald reached out to take a drink,
Saladin slapped his hand away, accusing him of breaking the
treaty. He subsequently had Raynald beheaded, some say by his
own hand while others say it was done by the royal guards. King
Guy expected a similar fate, but Saladin allayed his fears by
stating, 'Kings do not kill kings.'

Within months, Saladin went on to capture fifty-two cities
or fortresses, including Acre, Nablus, Jaffa, and Toron. Jerusalem
held out until October when Balian of Ibelin, who had escaped the
Battle of Hattin with his life, finally surrendered it to Saladin in
return for the guaranteed safety of thousands of civilians.

The Brotherhood Book IV

Find out what happened next in **Templar Fury**, the exciting fourth book in the series.

Pre-order your copy

The Brotherhood Book IV

TEMPLAR FURY

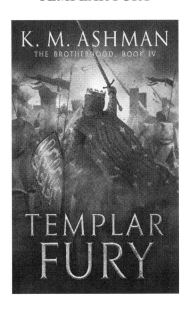

More books by K M Ashman

The India Summers Mysteries
The Vestal Conspiracy
The Treasures of Suleiman
The Mummies of the Reich
The Tomb Builders

The Roman Chronicles
The Fall of Britannia
The Rise of Caratacus
The Wrath of Boudicca

The Medieval Sagas
Blood of the Cross
In Shadows of Kings
Sword of Liberty
Ring of Steel

The Blood of Kings
A Land Divided
A Wounded Realm
Rebellion's Forge
Warrior Princess
The Blade Bearer

The Brotherhood
Templar Steel – The Battle of Montgisard
Templar Stone – The Siege of Jacob's Ford
Templar Blood – The Battle of Hattin

(Coming Soon)
Templar Fury – The Siege of Acre
Templar Glory – The Road to Jerusalem

Standalone Novels
Savage Eden
The Last Citadel
Vampire
The Legacy Protocol

Audio Books
Blood of the Cross
The Last Citadel
A Land Divided
A Wounded Realm
Rebellion's Forge
The Warrior Princess
The Vestal Conspiracies
The Tomb Builders
The Mummies of the Reich

Contact Kevin at:

Website -   **KMAshman.com**
Facebook - **https://www.facebook.com/KMAshman**
Email –   **Silverbackbooks1@gmail.com**

Printed in Great Britain
by Amazon